Skinny Dip

Skinny Dip

Carl Hiaasen

ALFRED A. KNOPF   NEW YORK   2004

THIS IS A BORZOI BOOK
PUBLISHED BY ALFRED A. KNOPF

Published in the United States by Alfred A. Knopf, a division
of Random House, Inc., New York, and in Canada by Random
House of Canada Limited, Toronto
Distributed by Random House, Inc., New York

www.aaknopf.com

Knopf, Borzoi Books, and the colophon are registered
trademarks of Random House, Inc.

A portion previously appeared in *Men's Health Best Life*.

Library of Congress Cataloging-in-Publication Data
Hiaasen, Carl.
Skinny dip : a novel / by Carl Hiaasen.— 1st ed.
p. cm.
ISBN 0-375-41108-9
1. Agricultural industries—Fiction. 2. Ex-police officers—
Fiction. 3. Marine scientists—Fiction. 4. Everglades (Fla.)—
Fiction. 5. Hazardous wastes—Fiction. 6. Attempted
murder—Fiction. 7. Married people—Fiction. I. Title.
PS3558.I217S575 2004
813'.54—dc22   2004044106

Manufactured in the United States of America

First Edition

In memory of Warren Zevon

Acknowledgments

I am most grateful for the advice, enthusiasm and talents of Esther Newberg, Liz Donovan of the *Miami Herald*, Bob Roe of *Sports Illustrated*, Burl George, Nathaniel Reed, Sean Savage, Capt. Mike Collins, the mysterious Sonny Mehta, my tenacious sister Barb, my spectacular wife, Fenia, and Dr. Jerry Lorenz, one of the many unsung heroes of the Everglades.

Skinny Dip

One

At the stroke of eleven on a cool April night, a woman named Joey Perrone went overboard from a luxury deck of the cruise liner M.V. *Sun Duchess*. Plunging toward the dark Atlantic, Joey was too dumbfounded to panic.

I married an asshole, she thought, knifing headfirst into the waves.

The impact tore off her silk skirt, blouse, panties, wristwatch and sandals, but Joey remained conscious and alert. Of course she did. She had been co-captain of her college swim team, a biographical nugget that her husband obviously had forgotten.

Bobbing in its fizzy wake, Joey watched the gaily lit *Sun Duchess* continue steaming away at twenty nautical miles per hour. Evidently only one of the other 2,049 passengers was aware of what had happened, and he wasn't telling anybody.

Bastard, Joey thought.

She noticed that her bra was down around her waist, and she wriggled free of it. To the west, under a canopy of soft amber light, the coast of Florida was visible. Joey began to swim.

The water of the Gulf Stream was slightly warmer than the air, but a brisk northeasterly wind had kicked up a messy and uncomfortable chop. Joey paced herself. To keep her mind off sharks, she replayed the noteworthy events of the week-long cruise, which had begun almost as unpromisingly as it had ended.

The *Sun Duchess* had departed Port Everglades three hours late because a raccoon had turned up berserk in the pastry kitchen. One of the chefs had wrestled the frothing critter into a sixty-gallon tin of guava custard before it had shredded the man's jowls and humped snarling to the depths of the ship. A capture team from Broward Animal Control had arrived, along with health inspectors and paramedics. Evacuated passengers were appeased with rum drinks and canapés.

Later, while reboarding, Joey had passed the Animal Control officers trudging empty-handed down the gangplank.

"I bet they couldn't catch it," she'd whispered to her husband. Despite the inconvenience caused by the raccoon, she'd found herself rooting for the addled little varmint.

"Rabies," her husband had said knowingly. "Damn thing lays a claw on me, I'll own this frigging cruise line."

"Oh, please, Chaz."

"From then on, you can call me Onassis. Think I'm kidding?"

The *Sun Duchess* was 855 feet long and weighed a shade more than seventy thousand tons. Joey had learned this from a brochure she'd found in their stateroom. The itinerary included Puerto Rico, Nassau and a private Bahamian island that the cruise lines had purchased (rumor had it) from the widow of a dismembered heroin trafficker. The last port of call before the ship returned to Fort Lauderdale was to be Key West.

Chaz had selected the cruise himself, claiming it was a present for their wedding anniversary. The first evening he'd spent on the fantail, slicing golf balls into the ocean. Initially Joey had been annoyed that the *Sun Duchess* would offer a driving range, much less a fake rock-climbing wall and squash courts. She and Chaz could have stayed in Boca and done all that.

No less preposterous was the ship's tanning parlor, which received heavy traffic whenever the skies turned overcast. The cruise company wanted every passenger to return home with either a bronze glow or a crimson burn, proof of their seven days in the tropics.

As it turned out, Joey wound up scaling the rock wall and taking full advantage of the other amenities, even the two-lane bowling alley. The alternative was to eat and drink herself sick, gluttony being the principal recreation aboard cruise liners. The *Sun Duchess* was renowned for its twenty-four-hour surf-and-turf buffets, and that's how Joey's husband had spent the hours between ports.

Pig, she thought, submerging to shed a clot of seaweed that had wrapped around her neck like a sodden Yule garland.

Each day's sunrise had brought a glistening new harbor, yet the towns and straw markets were drearily similar, as if designed and operated by a franchise. Joey had earnestly tried to be charmed by the native wares, though many appeared to have been crafted in Singapore or South Korea. And what would one do with a helmet conch clumsily retouched with nail polish? Or a coconut husk bearing a hand-painted likeness of Prince Harry?

So grinding was the role of tourist that Joey had found herself looking forward to visiting the ship's "unspoiled private island," as it had been touted in the brochure. Yet that, too, proved dispiriting. The cruise line had mendaciously renamed the place Rapture Key while making only a minimal effort at restoration. Roosters, goats and feral hogs were the predominant fauna, having outlasted the smuggler who had been raising them for banquet fare. The island's sugar-dough flats were pocked with hulks of sunken drug planes, and the only shells to be found along the tree-shorn beach were of the .45-caliber variety.

"I'm gonna rent a Jet Ski," Chaz had cheerily decreed.

"I'll try to find some shade," Joey had said, "and finish my book."

The distance between them remained wide and unexplored. By the time the *Sun Duchess* had reached Key West, Joey and Chaz were spending only about one waking hour a day together, an interval usually devoted to either sex or an argument. It was pretty much the same schedule they kept at home.

So much for the romantic latitudes, Joey had thought, wishing she felt sadder than she did.

When her husband had scampered off to "check out the action" at Mallory Square, she briefly considered seducing one of the cabin attendants, a fine Peruvian brute named Tico. Ultimately Joey had lost the urge, dismissing the crestfallen young fellow with a peck on the chin and a fifty-dollar tip. She didn't feel strongly enough about Chaz to cheat on him even out of spite, although she suspected he'd cheated on her often (and quite possibly during the cruise).

Upon returning to the *Sun Duchess*, Chaz had been as chatty as a cockatoo on PCP.

"See all those clouds? It's about to rain," he'd proclaimed with a peculiar note of elation.

"I guess that means no golf tonight," Joey had said.

"Hey, I counted twenty-six T-shirt shops on Duval Street. No wonder Hemingway blew his brains out."

"That wasn't here," Joey had informed him. "That was in Idaho."

"How about some chow? I could eat a whale."

At dinner Chaz had kept refilling Joey's wineglass, over her pro-
tests. Now she understood why.

She felt it, too, that dehydrated alcohol fatigue. She'd been kicking
hard up the crests of the waves and then breast-stroking down the
troughs, but now she was losing both her rhythm and stamina. This
wasn't the heated Olympic pool at UCLA; it was the goddamn Atlantic
Ocean. Joey scrunched her eyelids to dull the saltwater burn.

I had a feeling he didn't love me anymore, she thought, but this is
ridiculous.

Chaz Perrone listened for a splash but heard nothing except the deep
lulling rumble of the ship's engines. Head cocked slightly, he stood at
the rail as solitary and motionless as a heron.

He hadn't planned to toss her here. He had hoped to do it earlier
in the voyage, somewhere between Nassau and San Juan, with the
expectation that the currents would carry her body into Cuban waters,
safely out of U.S. jurisdiction.

If the bull sharks didn't find her first.

Unfortunately, the weather had been splendid during that early
leg of the cruise, and every night the outside decks were crowded
with moony-eyed couples. Chaz's scheme required seclusion and he'd
nearly abandoned hope, when the rain arrived, three hours after leaving Key West. It was only a drizzle, but Chaz knew it would drive the
tourists indoors, stampeding for the lobster salad and electronic poker
machines.

The second crucial element of his plot was surprise, Joey being a
physically well-tuned woman and Chaz himself being somewhat softer
and out of shape. Before luring her toward the stern of the *Sun Duchess*
under the ruse of a starlit stroll, he'd made certain that his wife had
consumed plenty of red wine; four and a half glasses, by his count. Two
was usually enough to make her drowsy.

"Chaz, it's sprinkling," she had observed as they approached the
rail.

Naturally she'd been puzzled, knowing how her husband despised
getting wet. The man owned no fewer than seven umbrellas.

Pretending not to hear her, he had guided Joey forward by the
elbow. "My stomach's a disaster. I think it's time they retired that
seviche, don't you?"

"Let's go back inside," Joey had suggested.

From a pocket of his blue blazer Chaz had surreptitiously removed the key to their stateroom and let it fall to the polished planks at his feet. "Oops."

"Chaz, it's getting chilly out here."

"I think I dropped our key," he'd said, stooping to find it. Or so Joey had assumed.

He could only guess what had shot through his wife's mind when she'd felt him grab her ankles. He's gotta be kidding, is what she'd probably thought.

The act itself was a rudimentary exercise in leverage, really, flipping her backward over the rail. It had happened so fast, she hadn't made a peep.

As for the splash, Chaz would have preferred to hear it; a soft punctuation to the marriage and the crime. Then again, it was a long way down to the water.

He allowed himself a brief glance, but saw only whitecaps and foam in the roiling reflection of the ship's lights. The *Sun Duchess* kept moving, which was a relief. No Klaxons sounded.

Chaz picked up the key and hurried to the stateroom, bolting the door behind him. After hanging up his blazer, he opened another bottle of wine, poured some into two glasses and drank half of each.

Joey's suitcase lay open for re-packing, and Chaz moved it from the bed to the floor. He splayed his own travel bag and went foraging for an antacid. Beneath a stack of neatly folded boxers—Joey was a champion packer, he had to admit—Chaz came upon a box wrapped in tartan-style gift paper with green ribbon.

Inside the box was a gorgeous set of leather golf-club covers that were embossed with his initials, C.R.P. There was also a card: "Happy 2nd Anniversary! Love always, Joey."

Admiring the silken calfskin sheaths, Chaz felt a knot of remorse in his gut. It passed momentarily, like acid reflux.

His wife had class, no doubt about it. If only she hadn't been so damn . . . observant.

In exactly six hours he would report her missing.

Chaz stripped to his underwear and lobbed his clothes in a corner. Packed inside his carry-on was a paperback edition of *Madame Bovary*, which he opened randomly and placed for effect on the nightstand by Joey's side of the bed.

Then Charles Regis Perrone set his alarm clock, laid his head on the pillow and went to sleep.

The Gulf Stream carried Joey northward at almost four knots. She knew she'd have to swim harder if she didn't want to end up bloated and rotting on some sandbar in North Carolina.

But, Lord, she was tired.

Had to be the wine. Chaz knew she wasn't much of a drinker, and obviously he'd planned it all in advance. Probably hoped that the fall from the ship would break her legs or knock her unconscious, and if it didn't, so what? She'd be miles from land in a pitching black ocean, and scared shitless. Nobody would find her even if they went looking, and she'd drown from exhaustion before daylight.

That's what Chaz probably figured.

He hadn't forgotten about her glory days at UCLA, either, Joey realized. He knew she would start swimming, if she somehow survived the fall. In fact, he was counting on her to swim; betting that his stubborn and prideful wife would wear herself out when she should have tucked into a floating position and conserved her strength until sunrise. At least then she'd have a speck of a chance to be seen by a passing ship.

Sometimes I wonder about myself, Joey thought.

Once a tanker passed so close that it blocked out the moon. The ship's silhouette was squat and dark and squared at both ends, like a high-rise condo tipped on its side. Joey had hollered and waved, but there was no chance of being heard above the clatter of the engines. The tanker pushed by, a russet wall of noise and fumes, and Joey resumed swimming.

Soon her legs started going numb, a spidery tingle that began in her toes and crept upward. Muscle cramps wouldn't have surprised her, but the slow deadening did. She found herself laboring to keep her face above the waves, and eventually she sensed that she'd stopped kicking altogether. Toward the end she switched to the breaststroke, her legs trailing like pale broken cables.

We've only been married two years, she was thinking. What did I do to deserve *this*?

To take her mind off dying, Joey composed a mental list of the things that Chaz didn't like about her:

1. She tended to overcook fowl, particularly chicken, due to a lifelong fear of salmonella.
2. The facial moisturizing cream that she applied at night smelled vaguely like insecticide.
3. Sometimes she dozed off during hockey games, even the play-offs.
4. She refused to go down on him while he was driving on Interstate 95, the Sunshine State Parkway or any surface road where the posted speed limit exceeded fifty miles per hour.
5. She could whip him at tennis whenever she felt like it.
6. She occasionally "misplaced" his favorite George Thorogood CDs.
7. She declined to entertain the possibility of inviting his hairstylist over for a threesome.
8. She belonged to a weekly book group.
9. She had more money than he did.
10. She brushed with baking soda instead of toothpaste. . . .

Come on, Joey thought.

A guy doesn't suddenly decide to murder his wife just because she serves a chewy Cornish hen.

Maybe it's another woman, Joey thought. But then why not just ask me for a divorce?

She didn't have the energy to sort it all out. She'd married a worthless horndog and now he'd heaved her overboard on their anniversary cruise and very soon she would drown and be devoured by sharks. Out here you had the big boys: blacktips, lemons, hammerheads, tigers, makos and bulls. . . .

Please, God, don't let them eat me, Joey thought, until after I've died.

The same warm tingle was starting in her fingertips and soon, she knew, both arms would be as spent and useless as her legs. Her lips had gone raw from the salt, her tongue was swollen like a kielbasa and her eyelids were puffy and crusted. Still, the lights of Florida beckoned like stardust whenever she reached the top of a wave.

So Joey struggled on, believing she still had a slender chance of survival. If she made it across the Gulf Stream, she'd finally be able to rest; ball up and float until the sun came up.

She had momentarily forgotten about the sharks, when something heavy and rough-skinned butted against her left breast. Thrashing and grunting, she beat at the thing with both fists until the last of her strength was gone.

Cavitating into unconsciousness, she was subjected to a flash vision of Chaz in their stateroom aboard the *Sun Duchess*, screwing a blond croupier before heading aft for one final bucket of balls.

Prick, Joey thought.

Then the screen in her head went blank.

Two

At heart Chaz Perrone was irrefutably a cheat and a maggot, but he had always shunned violence as dutifully as a Quaker elder. Nobody who knew him, including his few friends, would have imagined him capable of homicide. Chaz himself was somewhat amazed that he'd gone through with it.

When the alarm clock went off, he awoke with the notion that he'd imagined the whole scene. Then he rolled over and saw that Joey's side of the bed was empty. Through the porthole he spied the jetties that marked the entrance of Port Everglades, and he knew he wasn't dreaming. He had definitely killed his wife.

Chaz was dazzled by his own composure. He reached for the phone, made the call he'd been practicing and prepared himself for what was to come. He gargled lightly but otherwise made no attempt at personal grooming, dishevelment being expected of a frantic husband.

Soon after the *Sun Duchess* docked, the interviews commenced. First to arrive was the ship's solicitous security chief, then a pair of baby-faced Coast Guard officers and finally a dyspeptic Broward County Sheriff's detective. Meanwhile, the *Sun Duchess* was being combed from bow to stern, presumably to rule out the embarrassing possibility that Mrs. Perrone was shacking up with another passenger or, worse, a crew member.

"Exactly what time did your wife leave the stateroom?" the detective asked.

"Three-thirty in the morning," Chaz said.

The specificity of the lie was important to ensure that the rescue operation would focus on the wrong swatch of ocean. The ship's location at 3:30 a.m. would have been approximately seventy miles north of the spot where he'd tumbled his wife overboard.

"And you say she was going to 'scope out' the moon?" the detective asked.

"That's what she told me." Chaz had been rubbing his eyes to keep them red and bleary, as befitting a hungover, anxiety-stricken spouse. "I must've nodded off. When I woke up, the sun was rising and the ship was pulling into port and Joey still wasn't back. That's when I phoned for help."

The detective, a pale and icy Scandinavian type, jotted a single sentence in his notebook. He pointed at the two wineglasses next to the bed. "She didn't finish hers."

"No." Chaz sighed heavily.

"Or take it with her. Wonder why."

"We'd already had a whole bottle at dinner."

"Yes, but still," the detective said, "you're going out to look at the moon, most women would bring their wine. Some might even bring their husbands."

Chaz cautiously measured his response. He hadn't expected to get his balls busted so early in the game.

"Joey asked me to meet her on the Commodore Deck and I told her I'd bring our wineglasses," Chaz said. "But I fell asleep instead— okay, make that passed out. We'd had quite a lot to drink, actually."

"More than one bottle, then."

"Oh yeah."

"Would you say your wife was intoxicated?"

Chaz shrugged gloomily.

"Did you two have an argument last night?" the detective asked.

"Absolutely not." It was the only true piece of Chaz's story.

"Then why didn't you go outside together?"

"Because I was sittin' on the can, okay? Taking care of some personal business." Chaz tried to make himself blush. "The seviche they fed us last night, let me just say, tasted like something the cat yakked up. So I told Joey, 'Go ahead without me, I'll be along in a few minutes.' "

"Bringing the wineglasses with you."

"That's right. But instead I must've laid down and passed out," Chaz said. "So, yeah, it's basically all my fault."

"What's your fault?" the detective asked mildly.

Chaz experienced a momentary tightness in his chest. "If anything bad happened to Joey, I mean. Who else is there to blame but myself?"

"Why?"

"Because I shouldn't have let her go out so late by herself. You think I don't know that? You think I don't feel a hundred percent responsible?"

The detective closed his notebook and got up. "Maybe nothing happened to your wife, Mr. Perrone. Maybe she'll turn up safe and sound."

"God, I hope so."

The detective smiled emptily. "It's a big ship."

And even a bigger ocean, thought Chaz.

"One more question. Has Mrs. Perrone been acting depressed lately?"

Chaz gave a brittle laugh and raised both his palms. "Don't even start with that! Joey definitely was *not* suicidal. No way. Ask anybody who knew her—"

"*Knows* her," the detective interjected.

"Right. She's the most positive person you'll ever meet." The emphatic response was meant to strengthen Chaz's position with the authorities. He knew from his amateur research that relatives of suicide victims commonly deny seeing prior symptoms of depression.

The detective said, "Sometimes, when people drink—"

"Yeah, but not Joey," Chaz broke in. "Drinking gave her—*gives* her—the giggles."

Chaz realized he'd been gnawing on his lower lip, which actually turned out to be a fine touch. It made him appear truly worried about his missing wife.

The detective picked up the copy of *Madame Bovary*. "Yours or hers?"

"Hers." Chaz was pleased that the bait had been taken.

"No giggles here," the detective remarked, glancing at the open pages.

"I haven't read it," Chaz said, which was true. He had asked the clerk at the Barnes & Noble for something romantic but tragic.

"It's about a lady who gets misunderstood by just about everybody, including herself," the detective said. "Then she swallows arsenic."

Perfect, Chaz thought. "Look, Joey was happy last night," he said, not quite as insistently. "Why else would she dash out at three-thirty in the morning to go dancing on the deck?"

"In the moonlight."

"Correct."

"The captain said he ran into some rain."

"Yes, but that was earlier," Chaz said. "About eleven or so. By the time Joey went out, it was beautiful."

Before the *Sun Duchess* had departed Key West, Chaz had checked the weather radar on TV at a famous bar called Sloppy Joe's. He had known that the skies would be clear by 3:30 a.m., the fabricated time of his wife's disappearance.

"The moon was full last night," Chaz added, to give the false impression that he'd seen it himself.

"I believe that's right," the detective said.

He stood there as if he were expecting Chaz to say more.

So Chaz did. "I just remembered something else. There was a raccoon, a rabid raccoon, running loose on the ship."

"Yes."

"I'm serious. Ask the captain. We were held up for hours leaving Lauderdale last Sunday while they looked for it."

"Go on."

"Well, don't you see? What if Joey got attacked when she went out on the deck? What if that deranged little monster went chasing after her and she accidentally fell overboard or something?"

The detective said, "That's quite a theory."

"You ever seen an animal with rabies? They get totally whacked."

"I already know about the raccoon," said the detective. "They trapped it in the crew's laundry and removed it from the ship at San Juan, according to the captain's log."

"Oh," Chaz said. "Well, it's good you checked that out."

"We try to be thorough." This was spoken in a barbed tone that Chaz felt was inappropriate for use on a distraught husband. He was glad when the detective finally departed, and further relieved to learn that he was free to start packing. The stateroom had to be vacated soon, as the *Sun Duchess* was being prepared for its next cruise.

Later, as Chaz Perrone followed the porter down the gangway, he saw two blaze-orange helicopters rising from a pad at the Coast Guard station on the other side of the port. The choppers banked and sped off toward the Atlantic, where a cutter and two smaller rescue vessels were already hunting in grids for Joey. The Coasties would also be sending up a Falcon out of Opa-locka, or so Chaz had been assured.

He glanced at his watch and thought: Thirteen hours in the drink, she's history.

They can search all they want.

Hank and Lana Wheeler lived in Elko, Nevada, where they owned a prosperous casino resort that featured a Russian dancing-bear act. The bears were raised and trained by a semi-retired dominatrix who billed herself as Ursa Major.

Over time the Wheelers had become fond of Ursa and treated her as kin. When one of her star performers, a 425-pound neutered Asiatic named Boris, developed an impacted bicuspid, the Wheelers generously chartered a Gulfstream jet to transport the animal to a renowned periodontic veterinarian at Lake Tahoe. Hank and Lana went along for moral support, and also to sneak in some spring skiing.

On the return flight something went sour and the plane nosedived into the Cortez Mountains. Federal investigators later determined that, for reasons unknown, the convalescing bear had been seated in the co-pilot's position at the time of the crash. Film recovered from a 35-mm camera owned by the Wheelers revealed several snapshots of Boris squeezed upright behind the steering yoke. In one frame, Ursa Major was curled laughingly on the beast's lap, tipping a bottle of Bailey's Irish Cream to its unfurled lips. In a subsequent photo, Boris had been posed in headphones and tinted aviator glasses.

Taped communications between the Gulfstream and control towers en route confirmed a highly festive, and possibly distracting, atmosphere aboard the Wheelers' jet. Why it had suddenly gone down remained a mystery, though Ursa's assistant surmised that the bear's sunny humor had evaporated dramatically once the Xylocaine wore off. During the aircraft's fatal corkscrew plummet, controllers attempting to radio the cockpit received only bestial snorts and grunts in reply.

The Wheelers were worth a pile of money, which after probate was divided evenly between their two young children. Joey Wheeler, who had been named after the singer-actress Joey Heatherton, was only four years old when her parents died. Her brother, named after the comedian Corbett Monica, was six. Each of the kids came immediately into approximately $4 million, plus a guaranteed cut of the weekly keno handle at their late parents' casino.

Joey and Corbett were raised in Southern California by Lana Wheeler's twin sister, who conspired zealously but without success to loot the trust fund in which the children's inheritance had been placed. Consequently, both orphaned Wheelers reached adulthood with their fortunes intact but their innocence abraded.

Corbett lit out for New Zealand, while Joey headed to Florida. There she informed no one of her wealth, including the stockbroker who would become her first husband. She and Benjamin Middenbock dated for five years and were married for four more, until fate intervened in the form of a sky diver who fell on Benny one sunny afternoon as he practiced fly casting in the backyard. The sky diver's parachute had failed to open and he had descended silently, though like a sack of cement, upon Joey's husband, who had been breaking in a new Loomis 9-weight. The tragedy left Joey alone, stupefied and richer than ever, thanks to a seven-figure settlement check from the skydiving company's insurance carrier.

It was the second time in her young life that she had unwillingly profited from the death of loved ones, and she could scarcely bring herself to think about the money, much less put a dent in it. Misplaced guilt led her into charity work and a modest lifestyle, though she had retained a weakness for Italian shoes. Joey Wheeler hoped someday to establish a regular life among regular people, or at least to find out if such an existence was possible.

She met Chaz Perrone one January afternoon in a parking lot outside the Animal Kingdom attraction at Walt Disney World, where she'd just made a flying tackle on a teenager who had swiped the purse of a Belgian tourist. The culprit, who belonged to a group of youths being chaperoned by Joey, supposedly had been diagnosed with chronic attention deficit disorder. Oddly, the young man's capacity for concentration was not so diminished that he'd failed to focus on a genuine Prada handbag amid the heaving throngs of tourists. Nor had his focus wavered even slightly as he stalked his elderly victim from the Giant Anteater exhibit all the way to DinoLand, where he'd made the snatch.

Joey had chased the pimpled creep through the ticket turnstiles and brought him down hard on the hot pavement outside the park.

While holding him for Disney security officers, she'd shaken from his pockets a Gucci key chain and a Tiffany cigarette lighter, casting further doubt on the nature of his disability.

Chaz Perrone, having watched the takedown from a departing tram, had hopped off to compliment Joey on her pluck. She'd found him impossibly handsome, and had done nothing to discourage the flirtation. Chaz had proudly informed her that he was a biologist, and that he was attending a convention of distinguished scientists working to save the Everglades. He'd further confided that he was supposed to be taking a VIP safari tour of the Animal Kingdom but was instead sneaking out to play Bay Hill, the favorite hometown golf course of none other than Tiger Woods.

Joey had been attracted to Chaz not only by his good looks, but by his involvement in such a lofty mission as rescuing Florida's imperiled wilderness from greedy polluters. At the time he'd seemed like a fine catch, though in retrospect Joey realized that her judgment had been skewed by previous disappointments. Before meeting Chaz, she had been dumped in chilly succession by a tennis pro, a lifeguard and a defrocked pharmacist, a grim streak that destabilized her self-esteem as well as her standards.

So she'd been eager, if not reckless, for steady companionship. The courtship had been a whirlwind campaign of roses, love letters, candle-lit dinners, whispered endearments—Chaz had been relentlessly smooth, and Joey had melted with minimal resistance. Her most distinct memories of their first twelve months of marriage were scenes of reliably torrid sex, which turned out to be Chaz's singular shining talent. It was also his obsession. During their more revelatory second year together, Joey came to realize that she'd mistaken her husband's indefatigable urge to rut for ardor, when, in truth, for him it was no more personal than isometrics. She also became acutely aware that Chaz did not regard matrimony as an exclusive carnal arrangement.

Other wives might have bailed out, but Joey was too proud and competitive. She resolved to immerse herself avidly in all aspects of her husband's world, and to become what the self-help books called "a true life partner." Her plan was to make Chaz need her so fervidly that he'd knock off the bullshit and clean up his act.

The anniversary cruise seemed like a good opportunity to put her plan into action, so Joey had accepted the invitation with high hopes. She had looked forward to "re-connecting" with her husband, as the relationship experts advised. The biggest challenge would be engaging Chaz in at least one intimate conversation that did not concern the peerless durability of his erection.

Once at sea, unfortunately, the breakthrough moment had never presented itself. Or perhaps it had and Joey had found herself not sufficiently motivated. Except for the sex, Chaz simply wasn't a very compelling fellow. The more Joey had listened to him—*really* listened—the emptier she'd felt. For a scientist, Chaz seemed dishearteningly blithe, self-centered and materialistic. He rarely spoke of his work in the Everglades, and he seemed largely unfazed by the rape of the planet. He displayed no anger about the push for oil drilling in an Alaskan wildlife refuge, yet he bitched for a solid hour, spewing half-masticated shreds of clam, upon hearing from another cruise passenger that Titleist was raising the price of its golf balls.

It had struck Joey that she could spend the rest of her life faking enthusiasm for her husband's interests, and that he wouldn't care one way or the other. So, why in the world had he married her? Joey had intended to pose that very question during their late-night stroll on the *Sun Duchess*, but then she'd changed her mind. The slate clouds and the drizzling rain had depressed her, and all she'd wanted to do was go back to the room and crash.

She'd been staring off toward Africa, thinking of God knows what, when Chaz bent down to pick up something he'd dropped on the deck; a key, he'd said. Joey had been perturbed to feel his moist hands closing around her ankles—she'd figured he was about to spread her legs so he could slip her a fast one, Chaz being keen on outdoor quickies. The last thing she had expected him to do was throw her overboard.

The worthless shithead, Joey thought.

Because here I am, parched and delirious and half-blind, clinging to the same fucking shark that tried to eat me.

Which is absolutely ludicrous, so I must either be dead or getting damn close. . . .

He knew he couldn't get his hands on the money, even if something happened to me. He knew from day one that my inheritance was untouchable. So why did he do this?

It made no sense to Joey Perrone. Nothing did.

Not Chaz; not the lazy, sweet-smelling, rough-skinned shark; not the seagulls piping excitedly overhead—can't a person even die in peace?

Not the low *chug-a-chug* of an outboard engine, growing louder; not the *slappety-slap* of the waves against . . . what, the hull of a boat? Don't believe your ears, Joey told herself. What would a boat be doing all the way out here?

Didn't make sense. Neither did the faraway voice calling to her, a man's voice urging her to hang on, honey, just hang on for another minute.

Then the same voice saying it's okay, I've got you now, so let go, come on, let it go!

Something lifted her as if she were as light and free as a bubble. Glassy droplets streamed down her bare legs as she rose from the water, her toes brushing the foamy tips of the waves.

Then came a huddled warmth, the smell of dry linen and a sleep nearly as deep as death.

Three

"Don't move," the man said.

"Where am I?"

"Safe. Try to lie still."

"What about the shark? Did I get bit?"

"What shark?"

"The one I was hanging on to when you found me."

The man laughed softly. "That was a bale of grass."

"Don't tell me," Joey said.

"Sixty pounds of Jamaica's finest."

"Terrific." In her delirium she had mistaken the burlap wrapping for shark hide. "Where am I?" she asked again. "I can't see a damn thing. What's wrong with my eyes?"

"They're swollen shut."

"From the salt? Please tell me that's all—"

"And jellyfish stings," the man said.

Joey reached up and gingerly touched her burning eyelids. A Portuguese man o'war must have brushed against her face while she was drifting.

"You'll be okay in a day or so," the man told her.

Joey groped under the covers. She was wearing what felt like a fleece pullover and light cotton sweatpants.

"Thanks for the clothes," she said. "Or I should say, thank your wife."

"Actually, they belonged to a friend."

"Is she here now?"

"Hasn't been for ages."

So they were alone in this place, Joey and the stranger who had rescued her. "I can still hear the ocean in my head," she said.

"It's right outside your window. You're on an island."

Joey was too worn-out to be afraid. She liked the man's voice. He didn't sound like a psychopath or a sex criminal. Then again, she had a history of getting first impressions wrong.

"Sit up," she heard him say. She smelled lemon and tasted strong hot tea when he held the cup to her lips. She drank every drop. Next there was vegetable soup and she finished that, too.

"I wish I could see what you look like," she told him, "since you've seen all of me."

The man said, "Sorry, but that's how I found you."

Stark naked on a bale of pot, Joey thought ruefully. She shivered from the flooding warmth of the soup, and for a moment she feared she might throw up. The man took the cup and lowered her head to the pillow.

"Back to sleep," he said.

"I swear I smell a wet dog."

"You do. He's a pain in the ass, but he almost never bites women."

It hurt when Joey smiled, her skin was so taut and raw. "What kind is he?" she managed to say.

The man whistled and Joey heard the brisk click of canine toenails on a wooden floor. A clammy nose poked against her neck. She patted the animal's head before the man whistled it back to its unseen corner.

"He feels like a bruiser," she remarked.

"Doberman. Can't swim for shit," the man said. "Joey, are you feeling well enough to tell me what happened?"

"How'd you know my name?"

"It's engraved on the inside of your wedding ring. I took it off before I put you in the bathtub."

"You gave me a bath?"

"No offense, but you stunk like a bong."

Joey checked her left hand—the platinum band was still there. The man easily could have stolen it, but he hadn't. He could have made her believe that she'd lost it in the ocean, but instead he'd returned it to her finger. By now she was ready to believe he was a decent guy. The early signs were promising.

"I was thrown off a boat," she told him.

"What kind of boat?"

"One of those giant cruise ships. The *Sun Duchess.*"

The man sounded doubtful. "You'd need fifteen-foot seas to get pitched off a cruise liner. It wasn't nearly that rough last night."

Joey said, "I didn't get thrown off by a wave. I got thrown off by my husband."

"Oh."

"You don't believe me?"

There was an unreadable silence in the room. Joey raised her head and turned toward where she thought the man was sitting. "I didn't just fall overboard, okay? The bastard pushed me."

"That's a shitty move," the man said.

Joey told him exactly how Chaz had done it.

"But why?" the man asked.

"I don't know. I swear to God I don't."

She heard him rise and slide his chair away from the bed. She asked where he was going.

"There's no phone in the house. I've been charging my cell off the boat's battery," he said.

"Wait a minute. Who're you going to call?"

"First the Coast Guard and then the cops."

"Please don't," Joey said.

"Why not?"

"Tell me your name."

"It's Mick."

"Mick, please," she said, "don't call anybody. Not yet, okay? I need to sort this out in my head."

"Let me help. What your husband did is called attempted murder, and I'm pretty sure it's still against the law."

"Please wait."

The man said, "Fine. Whatever you say."

His voice came from farther away, and Joey knew he was standing in the doorway. She figured that he was humoring her. "You're gonna call anyway, aren't you? Soon as I'm asleep, you're gonna sneak out to your boat and phone the cops."

"No, I won't. That's a promise."

"Then where you going, Mick, huh?"

"To take a leak. That okay with you?"

She sagged back on the sheets and laughed to herself, thinking: Sometimes I'm such a pill, I swear to God.

The Coast Guard expanded the search to almost three thousand square miles, though most of its effort focused on a trapezoidal sector off the northern Miami-Dade coastline that corresponded to the false information provided by Chaz Perrone. He remained confident that the searchers wouldn't find Joey, but he held a secret fear that if the sharks were negligent, her body might wash ashore somewhere down in the Keys. That would poke a gaping hole in his fictional chronology, and serve to energize the annoying Broward detective.

Only an hour after leaving the *Sun Duchess*, Chaz got a scare. He was watching television in his room at the Harbor Beach Marriott when there was a teaser for the evening news: A charter boat out of Ocean Reef had snagged a dead body while trolling for billfish—stay tuned for details!

Breathlessly, Chaz shot out of the bathroom, where he had been masturbating fruitlessly over a stack of Danish pornography. Through three minutes of laxative commercials he trembled in dread, waiting to hear if it was his wife who'd been reeled in by the startled anglers.

The newscast began with shaky helicopter footage of the charter boat at anchor, followed by a zoom-in shot of the corpse—cloaked in a bright yellow tarp—being hoisted on a stretcher to a Coast Guard cutter. Interviewed later at dockside, a sun-bleached young mate on the charter boat said of the gruesome catch: "We knew right away it wasn't no sailfish because it didn't jump."

Eventually, the grave-spoken newscaster revealed that the victim was a tourist from Newport News who had vanished three days earlier after crashing his rented Wave Runner into a pair of copulating loggerhead turtles. Chaz fell back on the bed with a hoot of relief—his wife remained safely lost at sea.

Chaz had chosen to stay at the Marriott because of its proximity to Port Everglades and the Coast Guard station. His house was only thirty minutes away on the interstate, but he felt that staying closer and readily available to the authorities would fortify his credibility. It was important to appear to be keeping a vigil.

He was surprised when a reporter from the *Sun-Sentinel* tracked him down, but he didn't lose his cool. The reporter explained that she had been checking the daily police logs when she'd come across the missing-person report, which listed the Marriott as a contact point for the subject's husband.

"Have you heard anything yet?" Chaz asked the reporter, who said she hadn't.

"When was the last time you saw your wife, Mr. Perrone?"

"It's *Dr.* Perrone."

"Oh? What's your specialty?"

"Wetlands ecology," Chaz said.

"So you're not an M.D."

"No, I'm a biologist." Chaz hoped that the woman on the other end of the line couldn't hear the grinding of his molars. It annoyed him when people got snooty about addressing him as "Dr."

The reporter asked, "So when'd you last see Mrs. Perrone?"

Chaz gave an abbreviated version of the same account that he'd given the detective. The reporter didn't exactly sound riveted, which was fine with Chaz. A big splash in the media was the last thing he wanted.

"Do you have any theories about what might have happened?" the reporter asked.

"I can't imagine. You ever heard of anything like this?"

"Sure. People disappear off these cruise ships every now and then, but usually it turns out to be . . ."

"Turns out to be what?" Chaz asked, though he well knew the answer: drunken accidents or suicides. Oh, he'd done his homework.

"They're not telling me very much. It sure is frustrating," he added.

"I'll call you if I hear anything," the reporter said. "How long will you be at this number?"

"Until they find her," Chaz replied stoically.

Afterward he hurried down to the lobby and phoned Ricca from a pay booth.

"Something terrible's happened," he told her. "Joey fell off the ship."

"Fell off? How?"

"Least that's what they think. They can't find her anywhere."

"Oh my God," said Ricca.

"It's just unbelievable."

"You think maybe she jumped?"

"Why would she do a thing like that!"

"Maybe she found out about us."

"Absolutely not."

"Well, that's good," said Ricca.

There was a pause on the other end that Chaz deciphered immediately.

Ricca said, "Maybe she found out about something else."

"Please don't start with that shit. Not now," Chaz pleaded. Ricca didn't trust him as far as she could spit.

"Maybe *someone* else. Like another girlfriend."

"Don't be asinine. You're the only one."

"As if."

"Ricca, I don't have time for your Glenn Close impersonation right now. Half the U.S. Coast Guard is out hunting for my wife—boats, jets, helicopters, it's unbelievable."

"You don't have any other girlfriends? Really, Chaz?"

"Yes, *really*. Look, I'd better sign off—"

"I could come by tonight," she suggested, "take your mind off all this depressing stuff."

He was tempted to say yes, but Ricca was a noisy one. On no less than three occasions, her orgasmic caterwauling had brought hotel security officers thundering to the door, certain that an ice-pick murder was in progress. No such tumult could be risked tonight—it would be poor form for a husband to be caught bonking a mistress less than twenty-four hours after his wife had perished.

"Call you tomorrow," Chaz said to Ricca.

"Baby, I'm awful sorry about Joey."

"Me, too. Good-bye, Ricca."

"Wait. Who's Glenn Close?"

Chaz stopped at the hotel bar and ordered a martini. Rolvaag, the Broward detective, found him there.

"You want a drink?" Chaz asked.

"Let's go for a walk," the detective said.

Chaz poured his drink into a go cup and followed Rolvaag outside. The sun was setting and the weather was mild and breezy, just like the night before. A wedding was taking place at the hotel, the bride posing for photographs in front of a lush bougainvillea hedge in the courtyard. She was a voluptuous young Cuban woman, maybe nineteen or twenty, and Chaz found himself devising impure fantasies about the honeymoon arrangements.

"No luck yet," Rolvaag said.

"What?"

"Finding your wife."

"Oh."

"They'll probably knock off tomorrow," Rolvaag said.

"You've gotta be kidding! I thought they had to search for at least a week."

"I don't know what the standard procedure is. You'd have to ask the Coast Guard."

"But they can't give up already!" Chaz said, thinking: This is too good to be true. He had been dismayed when the search was extended to the south, knowing it would put spotter aircraft in the vicinity of his crime.

"I've got a few more questions," the detective said. "Routine stuff, but not particularly pleasant."

"Can't we do this some other time?"

"Won't take long."

"Jesus Christ, then, let's get it over with." Chaz hoped he sounded appropriately exasperated.

"Have you taken out any life-insurance policies on your wife?" Rolvaag asked.

"No, sir."

"Did she take out any coverage on herself?"

"At my suggestion, you mean?"

"At anybody's suggestion."

"Not that I know of," Chaz said.

"It's easy enough to check, Mr. Perrone."

"And you will, I'm sure. By the way, it's *Dr.*"

The detective shot him the most curious look before plodding on: "Do you have a business partnership with your wife? Joint investments, trading accounts, real-estate holdings—"

Chaz cut in: "Let me save you some time. Joey has her own dough. Lots of it." Inwardly he congratulated himself for sticking to the present tense. "And if she dies, I don't get a cent. The money goes into an irrevocable trust."

"Who's the beneficiary?"

"The World Wildlife Mission. Ever heard of 'em?"

"Nope," Rolvaag said.

"They go around crusading for endangered penguins and panda bears. Stuff like that."

"Doesn't that bother you, Mr. Perrone?"

"Of course not. I'm a biologist, remember? I'm all about saving wildlife."

"No, I meant the fact that you won't be getting any of your wife's money."

"Hey, it's not mine," Chaz countered mildly. "It's a family inheritance. She can do whatever she wants with it."

"Not all husbands would take that attitude."

Chaz smiled. "Hey, if she suddenly changed her mind and decided to leave it all to me, I definitely wouldn't rip up the check. But that's not what she wants."

"Was this a source of friction between the two of you?"

"Definitely not. She laid the whole thing out before we even got engaged. Her folks died in a plane crash and left her a bundle—what was I supposed to say? 'Cut me in for half, would you, darling?' "

The detective asked how much Joey was worth. Chaz said he didn't know precisely, which was true.

"Would you guess several million dollars?" Rolvaag asked.

"That's my impression, yes. The pre-nup didn't put an exact number on it," Chaz said.

He failed to add that he'd signed the pre-nuptial agreement fully anticipating it would be scrapped at a later date. In his unshakable vanity Chaz thought that he would eventually charm his new bride into sharing her vast inheritance. He had pictured the intimate ceremony taking place in the bedroom, of course, after a night of athletic lovemaking—Joey, still aglow, unfolding the pre-nup and holding it to the flame of a lilac-scented candle. It had never happened, though, and after nearly two years of waiting Chaz had given up hope. Joey wasn't hoarding the family fortune so much as ignoring it, which Chaz regarded as a crime against nature. What was the point, he'd asked himself, of staying wed to a wealthy woman who refused to act like one? The answer: There *was* no point.

"And after you were married," Rolvaag was saying, "what was the financial understanding between you and Mrs. Perrone?"

"Simple. Separate checkbooks, separate bank accounts," Chaz said. "We split the bills down the middle."

"I see."

"How come you're not writing this down?"

"Not necessary," said the detective. "Do you have a lawyer, Mr. Perrone?"

"Do I need one?" Chaz asked.

Up until then, the conversation had gone exactly as he'd imagined it would. "I mean, is there something you're not telling me? Did they find any evidence that points to, you know, a crime?"

"No, sir," Rolvaag said. "Earlier I noticed you using the pay phone in the hotel lobby. I'm curious why you weren't calling from your room—you know, for the privacy and all."

"Well—"

"And then it occurred to me that you might be speaking with your lawyer," the detective said, "because that's the sort of thing some lawyers would do—have their clients phone from a pay booth."

"Why?"

"Because that way the hotel won't have any record of the outgoing call," said Rolvaag. "Some of these guys, they see too many bad movies."

Chaz said, "I don't even know any lawyers."

"All right."

"I was calling our cleaning lady. I had to give her the alarm code to the house, since I won't be there when she comes Monday. I forgot all about it until I was in the elevator on my way down to the bar."

"Well, you've had a lot on your mind," Rolvaag said.

"Her name is Ricca, you want to check it out."

"Not necessary."

"Ricca . . . now what the heck is her last name?" Chaz mumbled, as if to himself.

By now the two men were on the beach, trudging through the soft sand in the direction of the jetties. Chaz was satisfied with the way he'd covered himself on the phone call; the detective seemed totally suckered.

Abruptly Rolvaag stopped and placed a hand heavily on Chaz's shoulder. "Look out there, Mr. Perrone."

For a long chilling moment Chaz was afraid to raise his eyes. Obviously the stroll was not so casual—the detective had set him up in the cruelest way. Chaz's knees began to wobble as if they were coming unhinged.

But it turned out that Rolvaag wasn't pointing at Joey's bloated corpse in the surf, as Chaz had dreaded. He was pointing at the twinkling outline of a cruise liner off the coast. The ship's prow was aimed out to sea.

"That's the *Sun Duchess*," the detective said. "They kept her in port two extra hours to finish the search."

Chaz took a slow breath and tried to conceal his giddy relief. "And there was no sign of my wife anywhere on board? Nothing?"

"Afraid not."

"So she's definitely in the water," Chaz said.

"That would be a reasonable assumption."

"Joey's a swimmer—I mean, like, a champion swimmer. They can't give up searching after only a day or two. They *can't*."

Rolvaag said, "I understand how you feel."

"So what'm I supposed to do?" Chaz's voice cracked convincingly, the result of many private rehearsals. "What the hell do I do now?"

They turned back toward the hotel, the detective saying, "Is there a clergyman you could call, Mr. Perrone? Someone close to the family?"

"Let me think," Chaz said.

Inside he was laughing like a jackal.

Four

Mick Stranahan tied a white bucktail on his line and began casting from the dock, therapy that as a bonus would provide fresh snapper for dinner. It had been awhile since a woman had been on the island, and Stranahan wasn't sure what ought to be done about Joey Perrone.

He had no reason to doubt her story, or to believe it. Certainly he had no good cause to get involved, as that surely would bring aggravation—more time on the mainland, for one thing, and to Stranahan every minute spent in a city was misery. The headaches he brought back were no more painful than a railroad spike in the crown of his skull.

These days he traveled to Miami only to restock provisions and to cash his disability check, a dubious annuity for shooting a corrupt judge who had shot him first while being arrested. Mick Stranahan was in no way disabled, but the State Attorney's Office had needed a plausible reason to retire him at the doddering old age of thirty-nine. A gunshot wound was a better excuse than most.

Stranahan hadn't wanted to give up his job, but it had been discreetly explained that for political reasons the state attorney could not keep on staff an investigator (even a productive one) who had killed a duly elected judge (even a crooked one). So Stranahan had accepted the ludicrous buyout and purchased himself an old wooden stilt house in Biscayne Bay, where he had lived mostly unmolested for years until Hurricane Andrew smashed the place to splinters.

That night Stranahan had been staying in Coconut Grove with his sister, whose useless husband was too busy whoring it up at a lawyers' convention in Boston to fly home and install the shutters. Two days later, in a smotheringly hot calm, Stranahan had launched his skiff and made his way through the floating debris back to Stiltsville. There he had found, where his home once stood, eight bare pilings. He'd circled them once and then pointed the boat south.

Eventually he had stopped at an island that was more of a coral knob, scarcely broad enough for the modest L-shaped house that occupied it. The concrete structure had weathered the hurricane admirably, though the tidal surge had punched out the windows and swept away the contents of both floors, including the caretaker. Mick Stranahan had been pleased to accept the job.

The owner was a well-reviewed Mexican novelist whose complex personal life sometimes impelled him to seek haven in foreign jurisdictions. In eight years he'd come to the island only four times, never staying more than a few days. During the last visit Stranahan had noticed in the writer's face a mealy pallor and etched haggardness. When Stranahan asked if he was ill, the man laughed and offered to arm-wrestle for a million pesos.

Nonetheless, Stranahan foresaw a day when a ranger's boat would arrive with a notice saying that the old writer had died and that the island was being sold to the National Park Service. In the meantime, it was Stranahan's intention to remain in the concrete house until he was officially evicted.

His only permanent companion was a Doberman pinscher that had been slung ashore during a tropical storm two Octobers ago. Stranahan assumed that the half-drowned animal had toppled off somebody's boat, but no one came looking. The dog proved to be as dumb and stubborn as a mud fence, so Stranahan had named him Strom. Ultimately he managed to master the two tasks for which Dobermans are genetically programmed—barking and frothing—and might have made a passable watchdog if it weren't for his poor vision and clumsiness. Stranahan often kept Strom tethered to a coconut palm; otherwise the knucklehead was apt to go skidding off the seawall at the mere glimpse of a passing boat.

Stranahan glanced sympathetically at the dog, which was dozing in a patch of shade under the palm tree. Three fat mangrove snappers flapped noisily in the bucket, but the Doberman didn't stir. He showed a commendable lack of interest in most of Stranahan's endeavors, including fishing and the occasional romance. Female visitors were greeted with a perfunctory sniff and then largely ignored. It was as if

Strom knew they were destined to be short-timers, and thus saw no point in bonding.

The dog's opinion notwithstanding, Mick Stranahan didn't consider himself an eccentric or a hermit, even though at age fifty-three he lived alone on an island at the edge of the Atlantic with no landline, satellite dish or personal computer. It was sadly true, however, that the women who came to stay rarely lasted more than a few months, until the unrelenting peace and tranquillity drove them over the edge. Stranahan was sorry to let them go but it was kinder than marrying them, which had been a habit when he'd lived on the mainland.

Without knowing anything about Joey Perrone, Stranahan was impressed by her strength and composure. Many swimmers would have been either catatonic or yammering incoherently after a blind night at sea, but Joey was perfectly cogent and sharp. Stranahan was inclined to give her some downtime, as she had requested. He knew what it was like to survive a murder attempt, if that's what really had happened to her.

Part of him instinctively wanted to know more, to ask nosy questions and dig around like in the old days. A wiser inner voice told him to drop it—Mrs. Perrone and her marital crisis would be departing soon, and then the cops could sort out her story.

After all, I'm retired, Stranahan reminded himself as he unhooked another fish.

Retired.

After all these years, it still sounded absurd.

"What were you doing out there, anyway?" Joey asked.

"Out where?"

"The ocean. In that little boat of yours."

Stranahan dipped the fillets one by one in egg batter. "First of all, it wasn't exactly the ocean," he said. "It was only about a half mile off Elliott Key. And I was looking for tarpon."

"In other words, what you're telling me, I would've floated ashore anyway."

"Yeah, one way or another."

"So, technically, could we even call that a rescue?" she said. "Even though I was sort of digging the idea of being rescued."

"Be careful of the stove," said Stranahan.

Each slice of fish went first into a bowl of bread crumbs, then the frying pan. Joey heard the sizzle when the fillets landed in the hot oil; she counted eight and wondered if that would be enough for both of them. Never had she felt so famished.

"Tell me about yourself, Mick. I promise your darkest secrets are safe with me," she said.

"How are you feeling? Your eyes better?"

"I won't know until you take off this damn blindfold."

"It's not a blindfold," he said, "and you can take it off whenever you want."

He had cut a strip from a towel, soaked it in cool freshwater and aloe, then knotted it gently around Joey's brow. An hour earlier, stubbornly trying to get around the house by herself, she'd tripped over a sack of dog food and nearly busted an ankle.

"I don't even know your last name," she said.

"Stranahan."

"And exactly what do you do, Mr. S., besides plucking damsels from the deep blue sea?"

"Actually, it wasn't so deep. Maybe twenty feet where I found you."

"Okay, that's enough. You're determined to spoil this whole adventure for me," Joey said. "It's bad enough that I apparently owe my life to some Rastafarian pot smuggler. Now you tell me I was, like, five minutes from the beach at the time of my so-called rescue."

"Would it help if I said I saw a fifteen-foot hammerhead in that very same place last week?"

"You're kidding."

Stranahan shook his head. "Seriously. It was eating a stingray for lunch."

"No shit!"

"You want limes or tartar sauce?" he asked.

"Both." Joey jumped slightly when he took his hand in hers.

"It's okay," he said, and led her outside to a picnic table on the wooden deck. She flinched at the sudden wash of sunlight, so he told her to leave her eyes covered. With no assistance she was able to find the food, wolfing down four pieces of snapper and two helpings of black beans and rice. Afterward Stranahan brought her a piece of Key lime pie and a cold beer.

"Best meal I ever had," she declared, groping for another napkin.

"I'd say you're going to be just fine."

"What's that sound—a helicopter?"

"Yep. Coast Guard," Stranahan said, watching a distant orangish speck streak across the bay.

Joey said, "Wonder if they're searching for me."

"Could be."

She shifted restlessly. "You want to go back inside?"

"Why?" said Stranahan.

"Is the sun going down? I can tell because it's getting cooler. Is it pretty tonight—the sunset?"

"I've never seen a bad one."

Joey said, "Tomorrow the towel comes off and I finally get to find out what you look like. I'm guessing a middle-aged Clint Eastwood."

"Then you're in for a major disappointment."

"But you're tall, right?" she said. "Late forties?"

"Early fifties."

"Gray around the temples?"

"You want another beer?"

"Not just yet," Joey said. "Give me your hands again."

Stranahan laughed. "I don't think so. They're awful fishy."

"You eat with your fingers! I like that."

"My table manners aren't what they used to be," he said. "Comes from living alone, I guess."

Joey said, "How many times have you been married? I know it's incredibly rude to ask but, well, I've got a hunch."

"Six," Stranahan said. "Six times." He stood up and began gathering the plates off the table.

"Jesus. I was going to guess three."

"See, I'm full of surprises."

"What happened?" Joey asked, but all she got in reply was the bang of the screen door. Moments later she heard a running tap and the clink of dishes in the sink. When Stranahan came back outside, she apologized.

"What for?" he said.

"Being so nosy. I figured you must be pissed, since you slammed that door."

"Naw, the hinges are rusted to hell is all." He placed a cool bottle in her hand. "But it's true, six ex-wives is nothing to brag about."

"At least none of them tried to murder you," Joey said.

"One came pretty close."

"Really? She go to jail?"

"Nope. Died."

Joey's breath seemed to catch in her throat. She took a long unsteady slug of beer.

Stranahan said, "Relax, honey. I didn't kill her."

"Who was she?"

"When I met her? A waitress, just like the rest of 'em."

Joey couldn't help but giggle. "You married *six* waitresses?"

"Actually, it was five. The last one was a TV producer."

"Oh, Mick—"

"And they were all fairly wonderful at the start. Whatever went wrong was usually my fault."

"But what in the world were you thinking? I mean, honestly, by the time you got to number six—"

"Oh, I wasn't thinking," Stranahan said. "Love isn't about thinking. You should know that."

Joey Perrone leaned back and turned her draped face toward the fading light. "The sky out there, I bet it's all pink and gold. God, I must look like a horror with this blindfold."

"Is Chaz your first husband?"

"Second. The first one died." She added quickly: "In an accident."

"That sucks."

"He was a stockbroker. Chaz is a biologist."

Stranahan said, "The no-see-ums are chewing you up. Let's go back inside."

"Funny, the only time my eyes really hurt is when I cry," she said. "If only I could stop."

"Come on, take my hand."

"No, I like it out here. The bugs don't bother me." Joey gave a defiant sniffle. "And, listen, it's not that sonofabitch Chaz Perrone that I'm bawling about. I'm ninety-nine percent sure I didn't even love him anymore."

Stranahan said nothing. He was an expert on dying relationships, the grinding hollowness that sets in until someone makes a move.

"But what Chaz did out there," she went on, pointing at the water, "it just hacks me off royally. You've got no idea."

Yeah, I do, Stranahan thought. The question was hanging there, so he went ahead and asked: "Then what's making you cry?"

"Oh, I suppose it's realizing that my whole life adds up to this one

moment and this one place and this one"—she swept an arm angrily—
"stinking, lousy situation. No offense, Mick, but half-blind on an
island with some stranger isn't really where I expected to be at this
point in time. This isn't the shape I expected to find myself in at age
thirty whatever."

"Listen, you're going to be okay."

"Oh right. After my fucking husband, pardon my French, threw
me fucking overboard on our fucking anniversary cruise! How exactly
does a woman put something like that behind her, huh? How does one
'get past' that sort of personal setback?"

Stranahan said, "Seeing him hauled off in handcuffs might help the
healing. Why don't you let me call the police?"

Joey shook her head so vehemently that he thought the towel
might fly off. "The trial, Mick, it's going to be a nightmare—my word
against his. He'll probably say I got trashed and fell over the rail.
That's what he's already told the Coast Guard, I'm sure. Four years ago
I got a dumb DUI up in Daytona, which Chaz's lawyers will dig up in
two seconds flat. 'Kindly get up on the witness stand, Mrs. Perrone,
and tell the court how your tennis-pro boyfriend dumped you for a
swimsuit model, so you drank a whole bottle of cabernet and parked
your car in the middle of A1A and went to sleep—' "

"Okay, calm down."

"But I'm right, aren't I? My word against his."

Stranahan allowed that things could get ugly in court. "It's none of
my business, Joey, but is there money involved? Would Chaz have gotten rich if you'd died?"

"Nope."

"Not even life insurance?"

"None that I know of," Joey said. "Now you see why I'm so . . . I
don't know, dazed. Him trying to kill me doesn't make sense. He
wanted a divorce, all he had to do was say so."

She asked Stranahan what he would do in her place.

"Take off the wedding ring, for starters," he said.

Joey sheepishly tugged the platinum band off her finger and
palmed it. "Then what?"

"I'd go straight to the cops," Stranahan said, wondering what other
options she might be contemplating. He decided not to ask, as a breeze
kicked up and seemed to carry away Joey's anger.

"You're smiling. That's good," he said.

"Because it's wet and it tickles."

"What tickles?"

"Mick, please tell me it's the dog."

Stranahan peeked under the table. "Strom, you're a very bad boy," he said, reaching for the Doberman's collar.

"Guess he likes me," Joey said with an acid chuckle. "But they all act that way, at first."

Detective Karl Rolvaag belonged in the Midwest. This he knew in his heart, and he was reminded of it every day when he went to work.

Practically anywhere in the upper Midwest would have been fine; Michigan, Wisconsin, Minnesota or even the Dakotas. There the crimes were typically forthright and obvious, ignited by common greed, lust or alcohol. Florida was more complicated and extreme, and nothing could be assumed. Every scheming shitwad in America turned up here sooner or later, such were the opportunities for predation.

"I don't care much for Mr. Perrone," Rolvaag remarked to his captain.

"Already?"

The captain's name was Gallo. He was fond of Rolvaag because Rolvaag made him look good by closing many difficult cases, though socially the detective wasn't exactly a barrel of laughs.

"You think he pushed her?" Gallo asked. "Not like we could ever prove it if he did."

Rolvaag shrugged. "I just don't care for him is all."

They were having coffee at a truck-stop diner on Road 84. It was nearly midnight and Rolvaag was in a hurry to go deal with the rats that might or might not be scampering loose inside his car.

"The dead wife," Gallo said, "tell me again how much she's worth?"

"Thirteen million, give or take. The trust officers are working up some numbers."

"But hubby's not in line for a penny, right? Not even life insurance?" asked Gallo.

"Not that I can find, but it's still early in the game."

"Be awful dumb for him to lie about something like that."

"I agree." Rolvaag snuck a glance at his wristwatch. It had been six hours since he'd left the pet store. He hoped the rats hadn't nibbled a hole in the shoe box.

"What's the next of kin say about young Chaz?" Gallo asked.

"Mrs. Perrone's parents are deceased and her only brother lives on a sheep farm in New Zealand."

Gallo frowned. "Christ, that's an expensive phone call. Try to keep it short and sweet."

"You betcha." Rolvaag sometimes lapsed into *Fargo*-speak when Gallo nagged him about something stupid. The detective had moved to Fort Lauderdale from St. Paul because his wife had inexplicably yearned to experience humidity. A decade later she was back in the Twin Cities and Rolvaag was still in Florida, divorced and sweating like a hog for eleven and a half months of the year.

However, tucked in his briefcase was salvation in the form of a letter from the police chief in Edina, Minnesota, a pleasantly civilized suburb of Minneapolis. The police chief had offered Rolvaag a job working major crimes, of which there were few. Rolvaag intended to give his notice to Captain Gallo as soon as an opening in the conversation presented itself.

"And I suppose nobody on the cruise ship saw or heard a damn thing," Gallo was saying. "Pretty girl goes over the side and everybody's snoozin'."

Without a trace of sarcasm Rolvaag explained that he hadn't had time to interview all 2,048 other passengers, or the crew. "But nobody's come forward, either," he added.

Gallo twirled a set of car keys on the pinkie finger of his right hand. "And the Coast Guard, they're done?"

"As of tomorrow noon, yeah. They'll keep one chopper up until sunset, but that's mainly for show," Rolvaag said.

"Is hubby real upset or what?"

"He says all the right things, but it's like he memorized a script."

Gallo smiled crookedly. "Karl, even if she floats up somewhere—"

"Yeah, I know."

"—unless her neck's been wrung or he capped her in the noodle—"

"Right. We can't prove a thing."

"He got a babe stashed somewhere?"

"I'm checking on that."

"But let's say he does—"

"I know. It doesn't automatically mean he killed the wife." Rolvaag was aware that Gallo, having several girlfriends himself, could be somewhat defensive on the subject of adulterers.

"But you don't believe Perrone, I can tell," Gallo said.

"I don't believe we're getting the whole story about his marriage, no."

Gallo laughed. "Karl, you ain't *never* gonna get that. Not from any husband, including yours truly."

"But your wife isn't missing at sea."

"This one's buggin' you, isn't it? I know 'cause you got that Norwegian prince-of-gloom look on your face."

Rolvaag forced a smile. "It's just another case," he said, which was not really how he felt about it.

"You still got all those giant snakes?" the captain asked.

"Just the two, yeah. They're only seven-footers."

"And you still feed 'em those fucking rats?"

"They won't eat stir-fry, unfortunately."

"I can't believe the condo commandos haven't evicted you yet."

"They keep trying," Rolvaag said.

Most of his neighbors in the building owned small dogs and were terrified at the possibility of Rolvaag's pythons escaping. His legal costs already had surpassed six thousand dollars.

"Christ, Karl, they're fucking reptiles. Why don't you just get rid of the damn things?"

"I like them."

"More important, do they like *you*?"

"We get along fine. In return for food and shelter, they give me unconditional indifference."

Gallo said he knew a topless dancer in Oakland Park who would be thrilled to have the snakes for her stage act. "She'd give 'em a good home, too. The kind we all dream about."

"Thanks anyway." Rolvaag stood up. "I'd better get going before those damn rodents hot-wire my car."

"You're one bent penny," Gallo said, not unkindly. "Let's wrap up Mrs. Perrone by Friday, okay?"

"Friday?"

"Hey, they can't all be winners, Karl. Some cases, there's only so much you can do."

Especially in six days, Rolvaag thought irritably. He said, "One thing her husband told me, she was a star swimmer back in college."

"Yeah, well, I seriously doubt she practiced diving off ocean liners or swimming with sharks. Give it till Friday, Karl. You can keep the file open, but let's slide it to the bottom of the pile."

"You betcha."

Later, driving home with the box of rats, Rolvaag remembered the letter in his briefcase. He was miffed at himself for not mentioning it to Gallo, so that the captain could begin processing the paperwork for Rolvaag's resignation.

First thing Monday, the detective vowed. He was looking forward to getting out of this steaming sump and moving back to Minnesota. He truly was.

Five

Charles Regis Perrone was a biologist by default.

Medical school had been his first goal—specifically, a leisurely career in radiology. The promise of wealth had attracted him to health care, but as a devoted hypochondriac he was repelled by the idea of interacting with actual sick people. Perusing X rays in the relatively hygienic seclusion of a laboratory had seemed an appealing option, one that would leave plenty of time for recreation.

Chaz's master plan was derailed by his own lubricious appetites. During those pre-med years he spent more time in condoms than he did in the stacks, and consequently meandered through the University of Florida with a less than dazzling 2.1 GPA. Not many medical schools avidly pursue C students, but Chaz wasn't crushed. He'd already decided that being a doctor would cut too onerously into his social schedule, and that he would devise another way to get rich.

In the meantime he sailed forth into the world armed with his Ken-doll good looks, his priapic affability and a bachelor's degree in a subject he loathed—biology. Three months after graduation he reluctantly moved back home with his mother, whose new husband, an addled ex–RAF pilot named Roger, delighted in tormenting Chaz with odd pranks. Whenever he snuck into a bathroom to whack off, which was several times a day, Roger would turn up the Irish Rovers full blast, rap on the doorjamb and chant, "Bad monkey! Bad monkey!" in an eerie falsetto.

Chaz suffered under his mother's roof, but without a job there seemed no escape. Only one prospective employer had displayed a glint of interest in his college credentials—the Bay County Humane

Society, which was looking for just the right person to hose down the kennels twice a day.

It dawned on Chaz that he was doomed to minimum-wage hell unless he obtained a master's degree, so he purchased one from a popular diploma mill in Colorado. The eight-week mail-order course guaranteed graduation (with honors) for a fee of $999, which Chaz remorselessly conned from his mother. Any topic vaguely related to biology was acceptable for a thesis paper, double-spacing being the only academic requirement. Chaz's opus, researched one afternoon in the produce section of the local supermarket, was titled "A Comparative Analysis of Late-Season Oranges, Ruby Grapefruits and Tangelos."

Ten days after mailing off the finished manuscript—a cashier's check clipped to the cover page, as required—he received a certified letter stating that the school had been shut down, stripped of its accreditation and evicted from the strip mall where its "campus" had been headquartered.

Grudgingly, Chaz accepted the fact that he might have to physically attend classes in order to secure an advanced degree. His mother, having stumbled upon the more unsavory elements of his porn collection, expedited his departure by imposing on a cousin who taught at the University of Miami's Rosenstiel School of Marine and Atmospheric Science. Although Chaz's GRE scores were nearly as forgettable as his grades, the politesse of nepotism prevailed and he was admitted to the master's program.

It was a buoyant and eager postgraduate who arrived at the Rosenstiel campus on Virginia Key, for he had grandly envisioned himself sailing the lazy tropics on a schooner, tracking pods of playful bottlenosed dolphins. In this fantasy, Chaz held binoculars in one hand and a frosty margarita in the other.

Had he bothered to scan the curriculum in advance, he would not have been so poleaxed by the tedious reality of field biology. His first assignment was assisting a doctoral candidate in a study of coastal sea lice, an experience that reignited Chaz's antipathy toward the great outdoors and all denizens great and small.

Among his chores was collecting gobs of algal weed that harbored the tiny granular organisms, which were not true lice but rather the larvae of *Linuche unguiculata*, the thimble jellyfish. Chaz's initial aversion to his subject was justified on the second day, when the pests somehow burrowed beneath his wet suit and colonized his upper torso with an itchy pustular rash—a painful condition spectacularly exacerbated by an ill-advised choice of colognes. Before the first semester was half over, Chaz looked like he'd been dragged from a burning oil rig. He stiffly informed his faculty supervisor that the only sensible purpose for studying sea lice was to isolate a toxin that would wipe them off the face of the earth.

Clearly, Chaz had neither the hide nor the perspective required for scientific inquiry. Worse, he had no interest whatsoever in the lesser species. As an undergraduate he had muddled through classroom biology by memorizing just enough to pass the exams. In the field he couldn't fake it so easily. The work was sweltering, repetitive and just plain *hard*. Every time Chaz asked if he could go play with dolphins, he was told to fetch another tub of kelp.

His family connection spared Chaz the ignominy of flunking out. Instead, he was steered along a path of study that minimized his exposure to nature—the breeding cycle of captive mosquito fish. After two years of sullenly tending aquariums, he emerged with a marginal M.A. in marine biology. At graduation the entire Rosenstiel faculty rose as one to cheer Chaz as he crossed the stage, so elated were they to see the last of him.

To his own surprise, he had no sooner laminated his diploma than he was offered a job. The company was a famous cosmetics manufacturer that conveniently had no use for the oceanic sciences and no concern about Chaz's lackluster grades. The firm merely needed a presentable face on staff—what serious biologists scornfully refer to as a "biostitute"—who would dutifully attest that its perfume products contained only negligible levels of toxins, acetones and carcinogens. Recruiters for the cosmetics company were impressed by Chaz's fastidious grooming and handsome features, which they felt would enhance his effectiveness as an expert witness, especially among female jurors.

He was assigned to the company's Jacksonville plant, where he was given an office, a small laboratory and a starter batch of one hundred white mice. These he occasionally swabbed with Blue Passion, Shiver or whatever new fragrance was being test-marketed at the time. Every now and then a mouse would manifest a tumor the size of a kumquat, causing Chaz to snatch up the wretched critter with barbecue tongs and heave it into a culvert behind the building. The idea of scientifically documenting such malignancies was never contemplated—

Charles Regis Perrone would not be laying his immaculate fingertips on diseased vermin, not for a lousy thirty-eight grand a year.

Then one morning, while shredding newspapers for the rodent cages, he spotted a headline that would change his destiny: CONGRESS MULLS $8 BILLION PLAN FOR EVERGLADES RESTORATION.

Fortune appeared to Chaz in a mystical burst of green light. With a zeal that would have flabbergasted his former college professors, he embarked upon an ambitious research project that ultimately connected him with a person named Samuel Johnson Hammernut, known as "Red" to both friends and enemies. Hammernut's name had become familiar to Chaz through archived newspaper articles that alleged recurring atrocities against his fellowmen—specifically, immigrant farmworkers—as well as the planet itself.

At first, Red Hammernut had been wary of Chaz's audacious proposition, but soon he'd come around. It was he who was now phoning Chaz at three in the morning at the Marriott.

"What's this I heard?" Red Hammernut barked from what sounded like a NASA wind tunnel.

Chaz peered at the digital clock. "Where are you?" he asked.

"Africa, 'member?"

Red Hammernut, in quest of a world-record tarpon, was calling from a satellite phone aboard a mother ship somewhere off the coast of Gabon.

"So what's this about Joey?" he said. "Is it true?"

Chaz sat up in bed, suddenly alert. "I'm afraid so, Red. We went on a cruise and she . . . well, she must've fallen off the ship. They can't find her anywhere."

"Damn."

"How'd you know about it?"

"It was in the Fort Lauderdale papers. Lisbeth faxed me the story," Red Hammernut said.

"But how'd you figure out where I was?"

"I called up that girl reporter and told her I was your uncle. Ha!"

"Oh."

Chaz understood that this was not a sympathy call, such sentiment being alien to Red Hammernut's character. The man wanted information, and he also wanted to remind Chaz of his larger responsibilities.

"I don't know what happened," Chaz said carefully, in case Detective Rolvaag was tapping the hotel line. "Joey went up on deck in the middle of the night and she didn't come back. Nobody saw her go overboard, but that's the assumption."

"Why, sure. What the hell else could it be?" Red Hammernut's voice whorled in the static. "What a tur'ble fucking thing, just tur'ble. Tell me, son, they still out searchin' for her? The Coast Guard boys, I mean."

"Until tomorrow at noon. Then they call it quits."

"Well, I'll be damned."

Chaz could picture the stumpy little Cracker lounging in the cabin of the yacht, lapping at a tumbler of Jack Daniel's. His freckled bowling-pin legs would be sunburned to a bright pink, and the sea breeze would have made a comedy of his sparse coppery comb over. The round white circles around Red's squinty eyes—caused by his absurdly over-sized Polaroids—would present the visage of an irradiated lemur.

"You need anything, Chaz, anything at all," Red Hammernut said. "I can have six private choppers in the air at dawn, that's what you want. We'll do our own goddamn search and rescue!"

Anxiously, Chaz wondered how many drinks Red had guzzled. "That's very generous," he told him, "but they've been up and down the coast a dozen times. They'd have found her by now, don't you think? The water's full of sharks."

"Oh man," Red Hammernut said. "You hear all that noise?"

"Sure do," Chaz said.

"Rough as a cob out here. It's gotta be blowin' thirty knots."

"You be careful."

"Hell, son, ain't you even gonna ask about the fishin'?"

"Right. How's it going?" Chaz sensed it was time to wrap up the chat, before Red abandoned all pretense of genuine concern.

"Sucks doggie schlongs, that's how it's goin'. Four days and we haven't jumped one tarpon over a hundred pounds," Red Hammernut complained. "You're the ace marine scientist, what's the goddamn deal? Where's my fish?"

Chaz had no idea. "Maybe they're spawning," he said lamely.

When Red Hammernut laughed, he sounded like a constipated mule. "Spawning, my ass! Don't tell me you needed a Ph.D. to come up with *that* one? A Ph.D. that *I* fuckin' paid for?"

"Well, that wasn't my field of study." Chaz strained to conceal his annoyance.

"What's not your field?"

"Migratory game fish."

Red Hammernut guffawed. "That's too bad, 'cause I could use some honest-to-God expertise right now. This little operation's costin' me about three grand a day."

Then maybe you should've started with something small and dumb, Chaz felt like saying, like perch. Red Hammernut had taken up sportfishing only three months earlier.

"Maybe your luck'll change tomorrow," Chaz offered, but the crusty bastard couldn't lay off.

"I trust you know more 'bout sharks than you do 'bout tarpon," he said, "if you catch my drift."

The guy's unbelievable, Chaz thought, joking about what happened to Joey.

"I think we're losing the signal!" Chaz shouted into the mouthpiece. "You take care of yourself, and we'll talk when you get back."

"For sure," Red Hammernut said. "Hey, I'm real sorry about the missus. A damn shame is what it is."

The little shitkicker was trying to sound sincere, but Chaz wasn't fooled. The man had the heart of a scorpion.

"You be careful," Red added in an unmistakable tone of warning. "You hear me? Be real damn careful. Am I comin' through?"

"I hear you fine, Red."

Joey Perrone awoke before sunrise and unwrapped the strip of towel from her head. Although her eyelids remained tender from the man o'war stings, her vision seemed clear. Quietly she made her way to the bathroom, where she tried to ignore the blotched and bleary woman in the mirror.

She had slept in an oversized Stanford jersey and a pair of white jogging shorts that had belonged to one of Mick Stranahan's ex-wives, the television producer. When Joey had inquired how long that particular marriage had lasted, he'd said, "Depends who you ask."

Gingerly she washed her face, then managed to gargle without making a peep. Afterward she hunted through the vanity and found a rubber band for her hair.

Stranahan was asleep, sprawled on a sofa in the living room. Joey tiptoed up to him and leaned as close as she dared. In the half-light she studied his features and smiled.

Not bad, she thought. I knew it.

She stopped in the kitchen to grab two apples and a ripe banana. Slipping out the back, she was careful to close the screen door softly. Strom lifted his head when she stepped barefoot onto the dock. Joey stroked his muzzle and whispered, "You're a handsome fella. Maybe someday mean ol' Mick will find you a girlfriend."

As she climbed aboard the skiff, Joey was thinking: This is really rude. The least I could have done was leave him a note.

She untied the ropes and shoved off. As the boat slid lightly away, Joey sat down at the wheel, peeled the banana and waited. She didn't want to crank up the engine too near the island and awaken Stranahan—she felt guilty enough about the way she was leaving.

Inside the steering console was Stranahan's telephone, plugged in with a charger cord; that meant he'd have no way to call the authorities when he discovered his skiff was gone. Again Joey felt lousy, but keeping Mick incommunicado would give her some extra time to do what she had to.

As the boat drifted away, she finished the banana and placed the peel under the seat. In an aft hatch she located the fuel-primer bulb and squeezed until it was hard in her fist. She knew something about outboards—years earlier she had taught her first husband to water-ski, and together they'd bought an Aquasport powered with a 150-horse Yamaha.

Stranahan's boxy old Evinrude started on the third try. Joey nudged the throttle forward and checked over her shoulder. There was no sign of Mick, but the Doberman was watching her from the end of the dock, his ears pricked and his butt wiggling excitedly. She waved at the dog, then took off toward the Miami skyline.

"Not again," Stranahan muttered, kicking at a fallen coconut.

He sat down at the picnic table with a cup of coffee, Strom settling at his feet. Joey wasn't the first woman to take off with Stranahan's skiff, but she was the first he hadn't already slept with, lived with and then driven away in a state of exasperation. When they made up their minds to go, melodrama seemed mandatory.

The last one to try the same stunt had been a successful patent attorney named Susan. She had professed to adore the isolation of the island, but in fact she was going batty because she couldn't uplink her

BlackBerry—whatever the hell that meant—due to unspecified atmospheric anomalies. Possibly other factors contributed to her restlessness, as well, Stranahan had concluded afterward.

One evening at sunset, Susan snapped. After lacing Stranahan's rum-and-Coke with Ambien, she packed her bags, boosted his boat and promptly piled into the submerged rocks off the Ragged Keys. She cracked not only her collarbone but the shaft on the Evinrude, which set Stranahan back eighteen hundred bucks.

"For God's sake, why didn't you just ask me to give you a lift?" he'd said to her later in the emergency room.

"Because I didn't want to upset you," she'd replied. "I know how you are."

That's what they all said—*I know how you are*—and usually they were mistaken. They didn't really know him at all. But since Stranahan wasn't much good at revealing his sensitive inner self, the women who took an interest couldn't be blamed for misreading the signs. The Susan incident had cast him into a mood of frank introspection, but in the meantime he'd taken steps to protect his humble vessel from future hijackings by disgruntled companions.

With a hunting scope he easily located Joey Perrone, adrift less than two miles from the island. "Wanna come along?" he asked Strom, who declined in favor of licking his privates.

Stranahan dragged the yellow ocean kayak from the shed and pushed it into the water. He stripped off his shirt, kicked away his flip-flops and climbed in. He paddled through the light chop with short, hard strokes, and the burn in his shoulders felt good. With the wind behind him, he reached the disabled skiff in twenty minutes.

Joey sat on the bow with her legs dangling. She said, "Twice in three days. How lame is *that*?"

Stranahan pulled himself aboard and secured the kayak to a cleat on the stern. "This one definitely doesn't count as a rescue," he said. "This is purely a fuckup."

"Mick, I wasn't stealing the boat. Honest."

He opened one of the front hatches and with some effort inserted his head and arms inside.

"I was going to leave it tied up at Dinner Key," Joey insisted. "Look, I didn't mean to break the darn thing. I'll pay for the damage, okay?"

From below he said, "What makes you think it's broken?"

"No?"

"Actually, it's working perfectly." He got up, wiped his palms on his khakis and stepped back to the console. The instant he turned the key, the engine rumbled to life.

Peevishly, Joey asked, "How'd you do that?"

"I've got a manual valve on the fuel line, near the tank. Last night I shut it off," he said. "Force of habit, I guess."

"A cutoff valve."

"Exactly. Whatever gas was left in the hose, that's all you had to run on this morning," he explained, "and that's why the engine crapped out."

"Clever." Joey was working her lower jaw.

"See, I've had my boat swiped before."

"That doesn't surprise me."

Stranahan motioned her away from the bow. She moved to the ice cooler and assumed a slump-shouldered pose, watching him as he spun the steering wheel.

He said, "I can't blame you for being disappointed. You were expecting the pale rider and all you got was me."

Joey rolled her eyes.

Stranahan took it easy on the trip back to the island, the kayak bouncing lightly in the backwash of the skiff. Leaning sideways, he said, "I would've gladly taken you to the mainland myself. What the hell were you thinking?"

"I was thinking you're probably going to call the Coast Guard or the police, regardless, and that's not what I want."

"Where were you going?"

"To surprise my husband. To enjoy the look on his face when he saw I was still alive."

"And then what—let him try to murder you again?"

"So maybe it wasn't the smartest idea I've ever had," Joey said. "I'm just so damn furious—I was going to wait 'til he was taking a shower and then sneak in the bathroom and yank open the curtain. I thought maybe I could give him a heart attack."

"Great scene," Stranahan said, "but not a great plan."

"I thought of a better one. Want to hear it?"

"Nope," he said.

"It came to me all of a sudden while I was floating around out here in your boat," she said. "I think you'll approve."

"Doubtful," said Stranahan. "And for what it's worth, I keep my promises. There was no need to run away—I wasn't going to call the cops until you were ready."

Joey tugged the rubber band out of her ponytail. "What if I'm never ready?"

"That's the new plan? You want everybody to keep on thinking you're dead?"

"Mainly my homicidal shitbird of a husband."

Stranahan played along. "And this is so you can disappear to some-place far away, right? Take a new name. Start a new life."

"Oh no," Joey said, "this is so I can ruin his."

"Ah, sweet revenge."

"*Justice* is a better word for it."

"Please." Stranahan laughed. She was a fireball, this one.

"Joey, what about your folks and your family? Your friends? You really want to put them through that sort of agony?"

She informed him that her parents were dead and that her only brother lived on the other side of the world. "Him, I'll tell," she said. "He'll be cool with it."

"And your boss? The people you work with?"

"I quit my job when I got married," she said. "Also, you might as well know I've got money, a ridiculous amount—more than enough to do what I have in mind for Chaz."

"Christ, you're serious."

"Of course. I'm surprised you can't understand." Joey turned away, raising an arm to shield her eyes from the sun.

When they pulled up to the dock, Strom wet himself in exuberance. Stranahan tied off the skiff, stowed the kayak and went inside to make omelettes. Joey changed into somebody's yellow sundress and an oversized straw hat.

Breakfast, which included fresh-squeezed grapefruit juice, was served on the deck under partly cloudy skies. Stranahan waited until they were done before finishing his lecture.

"Listen to me, please. You can't kill your husband and get away with it," he said, "just because everybody thinks you're dead. That kind of nonsense only happens in the movies."

She peered from under the brim of the immense hat, her expression one of broad amusement. "Mick, I don't want to *kill* Chaz Perrone. I just want to screw with him until he screws himself. Can't you see the possibilities?"

Stranahan was alarmed to find himself intrigued by the idea. He hoped Joey wouldn't notice.

She sat forward intently. "Has anyone seriously tried to murder you? Tell the truth."

"Yes, as a matter of fact."

"And what'd you do about it?"

"That was different, Joey. I was in law enforcement."

Triumphantly she banged her hands flat on the table. "I knew it! I frigging knew it!"

"*Was,*" Stranahan said. "Long, long time ago."

"Answer the question, Mick. What did you do to the guy who tried to murder you?"

He took a slow breath before answering. "I killed them."

She sat back as forcefully as if she'd been shoved. "Wow," she said.

"Want a papaya?"

"*Them?* You're talking dead guys plural?"

"I was in the military, too," Stranahan said. "Be right back."

He went to the kitchen and returned with two bagels and a platter of glistening papaya slices.

"Tell me everything," Joey said, her eyes shining.

"Under no circumstances."

Stranahan's two least favorite topics of chat were, in order, the women he'd married and the men he'd killed. Of the latter, Raleigh Goomer, the crooked judge, was the most well known, although others had come before and after. All the killings were by most moral standards justified, from the North Vietnamese Army regulars he'd shot in a firefight to the slow-footed hit man he'd impaled with the sword of a stuffed marlin. They made for colorful stories, Stranahan supposed, but none he wished to share with a young stranger.

Joey said, "I guess I should be scared of you."

He shook his head. "Other way around."

"I told you, Mick, I don't want to kill Chaz. I can't even squish a darn palmetto bug without feeling guilty. But he needs to pay for what he did."

"What have you got against prisons?" Stranahan asked. "Trust me, ten years at Raiford will rock your husband's little world worse than anything you can dream up."

Joey popped a crescent of papaya into her mouth. "Assuming he's convicted," she said, "which ain't exactly a slam dunk. Not without eyewitnesses, or at least a motive. Am I right?"

"There's got to be a motive, Joey. There's *always* a motive."

"Look, I haven't got all the angles figured out. But let me tell you—Chaz is slicker than pig snot on a doorknob, or however the saying goes."

"Close enough," Stranahan said.

"The thought of me against him in court, it's too scary. I can't take that risk."

Stranahan appreciated Joey's misgivings. Trials in South Florida were famously unpredictable.

"Before I met Chaz, he worked for a cosmetics company," she said. "He was their big scientific hotshot, the one they'd trot in to testify how safe their perfumes were. He showed me a tape of himself on the witness stand, and you know what? He was good, Mick. I can totally see a jury buying his act."

Stranahan knew that he should tell her to trust the system, but he couldn't say the words with a straight face. He'd seen more than a few cold-blooded monsters stroll out of a courtroom scot-free.

"So where do we stand?" Joey asked him. "What're you going to do with me now?"

He was pondering a reply when he noticed a blaze-orange helicopter approaching low from the ocean. Strom spotted it, too, and began barking insanely, leaping in circles.

Joey's hat fell off when she tilted her head to see the aircraft, which flew directly over them and slowed to a hover. Stranahan could make out the Coast Guard spotter, positioned at an open door. The man was wearing a white helmet and aiming binoculars, and almost certainly he was searching for Mrs. Charles Perrone, believed lost at sea.

To end it, Stranahan had only to stand up, wave both arms and point toward the woman in the yellow sundress—the one who had hastily ducked back under her floppy hat and was now eyeing him anxiously.

How easy it would be, he thought, and how tempting, too, because honestly he was too old for this shit.

Yet he didn't wave or point or signal to the chopper in any of the usual ways. Instead he reached for Joey's left hand and brought it to his lips, lightly but long enough for the Coast Guard spotter to see him do it.

So that the searcher would conclude, as any observer might, that the woman in the sundress wasn't a castaway but obviously the wife or girlfriend of the lucky middle-aged guy at the picnic table.

And, sure enough, the helicopter buzzed away. They watched until it was a bright dot in the soft blue distance. Satisfied that he'd done his job, Strom stopped barking and curled up. A flock of perturbed gulls materialized overhead.

"Thank you," Joey Perrone said to Stranahan. "Does this mean I can stay?"

"I must be nuts," he said.

Six

The call from the Coast Guard came at noon sharp.

"I can't believe you're giving up!" Chaz said. His bags had been packed for an hour. "My wife's out there in the water somewhere—what if she's still alive?"

"The odds are very slim. I'm sorry, Mr. Perrone."

Chaz checked out of the Marriott and drove home feeling relieved and emboldened. He had committed a flawless crime. Thirty-seven hours had passed since he'd heaved Joey overboard, and not so much as a single hair had been found. The ocean had done its job.

Entering the house, Chaz experienced a wave of—what was it?—not remorse, but more of a carnal longing. The place smelled lightly of Joey's favorite perfume, a scent that never failed to arouse him. It was much more subtle than the fruity slop that Ricca wore, Chaz thought. Maybe I can talk her into switching brands.

He listened to a score of choked-up phone messages from friends of Joey who'd read about her disappearance in the paper. Chaz pondered his good fortune to have wed a woman with practically no family, extended or otherwise, to make a fuss. Chaz had never even met his wife's only brother, and he wondered if the news of Joey's death would dislodge the reclusive Corbett Wheeler from his beloved New Zealand.

At first the sight of Joey's clothes in the closet unsettled Chaz. He felt better after sweeping the hangers clean, and better still after expunging the bathroom of all her soaps, creams, scrubs, moisturizers, exfoliants, lotions and conditioners. Methodically he went around gathering his wife's belongings and piling them on their king-sized bed. He took everything except one intriguing lace bra and a pair of panties, which looked as if they might fit Ricca if she dropped a few pounds. Also exempt from removal was Joey's jewelry, worth at least ten or twelve grand.

. Chaz had no containers large enough to hold all his wife's stuff, so he drove to the delivery bay of a nearby BrandsMart and scored some jumbo cardboard boxes. Upon returning, he saw a gray Ford sedan in his driveway, and Karl Rolvaag waiting on the front step.

To avoid the appearance of embracing widowhood, another murderous spouse might have left the boxes in his car, out of the jaded detective's sight. Chaz, however, was resolved not to let himself be intimidated or thrown off course.

"Whatcha got there?" Rolvaag asked. "Is that one of those new Humvees?"

Wordlessly, Chaz unlocked the front door and backed inside with the boxes. He went directly to the bedroom, the sallow cop following at a courteous distance.

"I can't stand to see all her things here. It's just too damn painful," Chaz said. He began tossing Joey's dresses and blouses into a box that had once held a forty-inch Sanyo. "Everywhere I turn, there she is," he went on somberly. "I can't even bring myself to unpack her suitcase from the cruise."

Rolvaag looked on thoughtfully. "Everyone reacts different to a shock like this. Some people, they won't touch anything in the house. They leave every single item exactly as it was before, and I mean everything—linens, dirty laundry. You'd be amazed. Won't even throw out their loved one's toothbrush—they keep it standing in a cup by the sink. Sometimes for years this goes on."

Chaz continued to fill the box. "Not me. All these things to remind me, I'd be too depressed to get out of bed."

"What're you going to do with all of it?"

"I haven't decided. Give it to charity maybe."

The detective reached in and picked up a tortoiseshell hairbrush. "May I take this?"

"Be my guest," Chaz said automatically. Then, after a moment's thought: "Can I ask what for?"

"Just in case."

"Yeah?"

"In case something turns up later," Rolvaag said, "a body part or whatever. I don't mean to be graphic, Mr. Perrone, but it occasionally happens."

"Oh, I see. You want a sample of Joey's DNA."

"That's right. The hair on this brush should be enough to establish a match, if necessary," the detective said. "Do you mind?"

"Course not." Without missing a beat, Chaz snatched a couple of purses off the bed and dropped them into the box.

Rolvaag slipped Joey's brush into an inside pocket of his suit jacket. He said, "There've been incidents here in Florida where a fisherman hauls in some huge shark and it's flopping around the deck of the boat and all of a sudden it regurgitates part of a human body. And this can be, like, *weeks* after the person has gone missing. Meantime, the shark might've swum two or three hundred miles—"

Chaz interrupted with a queasy grimace: "I get the picture."

"Sorry, Mr. Perrone. You probably studied cases like that at Rosenstiel."

Chaz's gaze flickered briefly from the box to the detective's face. "Yes, we did." He heard an edginess in his own voice. Rolvaag had been checking up on him.

"Take whatever you need," Chaz offered, motioning toward the pile of Joey's things. "I'm willing to do anything if there's a chance to bring closure."

The detective gave a smile that Chaz chose to read as sympathetic. "Closure would be good," Rolvaag said. "Painful sometimes, but still a step forward. I'm sorry to have intruded on your privacy."

Chaz walked him to the door and said, "The Coast Guard called. They quit searching at noon."

"Yes, I know."

With simulated chagrin, Chaz added, "Three thousand square miles and they couldn't find a damn thing."

"Oh, they found something," Rolvaag said, freezing Chaz with one hand on the knob. "Four bales of marijuana. That's it."

Chaz waited for the rush of nausea to subside. "Whoop-de-doo," he said. "I'm sure they're scared shitless down in Colombia."

"Actually, the stuff was Jamaican. But you're right, they'll never figure out who dumped it, or even where. The Gulf Stream probably dragged it all the way up the islands."

Chaz snorted. "From Bermuda, maybe. Not Jamaica."

"What do you mean?"

"The Gulf Stream? It flows from north to south."

Rolvaag's blond eyebrows crinkled. "Not the last time I was out there," he said. "I'm pretty certain it goes the other way, Mr. Perrone. To the north."

Chaz lapsed into an unplanned coughing jag. What if the lame-ass detective isn't wrong? he wondered despondently. That meant the ocean currents had carried Joey's body from the remote perimeter of the search-and-rescue zone into the bull's-eye.

"Heck, you might be right." Chaz cleared his throat. "My brain's so scrambled today, I couldn't tell the sun from the moon."

"I understand completely. You get some rest," Rolvaag said, and headed out to his car.

Chaz shut the door and leaned wearily against it. Of the millions of people who weren't sure which direction the Gulf Stream ran, he was probably the only one to hold an advanced degree in a marine science. He had a fleeting urge to phone one of his former professors and settle the question, but that would have invited scorn that Chaz was in no mood to suffer. It was one of the rare times that he regretted having been such a slacker in school.

Quickly he returned to the chore of removing his late wife's belongings, consoling himself with the knowledge that sharks off the coast of Miami Beach were as indiscriminate in their feeding habits as the ones in the Keys. Joey undoubtedly had been gobbled by one, the strongest evidence being the absence of a corpse.

When Ricca phoned, though, Chaz couldn't restrain himself from asking, "Honey, which way does the Gulf Stream go?"

"Is this a quiz? What are my choices?"

"North or south," Chaz said.

"I got no idea, baby."

"Shit."

"Well, don't get mad at *me*," Ricca said. "Aren't you the one s'posed to be the big-shot scientist?"

Which is exactly what Karl Rolvaag was thinking about Charles Perrone on the way to the Coast Guard station.

Corbett Wheeler had moved to New Zealand at the age of twenty-two, believing that if he stayed in America he'd spend the rest of his youth battling to hide his inheritance from his gummy-fingered aunt.

Corbett had begged his younger sister to flee the States with him, but Joey's heart had been set on Florida. He had not been surprised when she married Benjamin Middenbock, but he was astounded when the stockbroker proved to be an upright, honest fellow with no overt interest in Joey's money. It was only later, after Benny had been flattened by the sky diver, that Corbett learned his sister had never educated her adoring husband about the family fortune. Corbett then began to suspect that Joey could take care of herself.

By that time he'd grown to love New Zealand, which was as vast and glorious as California, though without the motoring hordes. He had developed an improbable interest in sheep farming during a period when the East Friesian breed was being introduced from Sweden. East Friesians were the most prolific milking sheep in the world, and cross-breeding with New Zealand strains produced a bounty of chubby, fuzzy lambs. Corbett Wheeler had done very well for himself, though profit had never been a motive; he simply possessed an innocent fondness for the husbandry of sheep. Nothing gave him more joy than sitting on the porch of his farmhouse, toking on a joint and gazing out upon verdant slopes speckled in pewter with rams, ewes and lambs.

One night, Joey had called excitedly to report that their late mother's twin sister—the avaricious harpy who had raised them—was being sent to prison for authoring fraudulent insurance claims. Dottie Babcock had been working in Los Angeles as a professional accident victim, racking up two or three imaginary collisions per month in league with a crooked physician. For every alias used by Dottie Babcock, there was a corresponding crushed vertebra, shattered hip or detached retina. A newspaper had tracked her down and plastered on the front page a photograph of her Rollerblading with her Pilates instructor in Santa Monica. Authorities had been obliged to take action, and a judge slapped Dottie with eight to twelve years. Joey had delivered this bulletin in the hope that her brother might consider a return to the States, but Corbett had declined. From such a distance (and filtered through the leery eye of the BBC), American culture appeared increasingly manic and uninviting. Moreover, Corbett Wheeler couldn't imagine a life without lambing.

He had come back only once, for Benjamin Middenbock's funeral, and had lasted barely forty-eight hours. The blinding vulgarity of South Florida was too much; total sensory overload. Corbett had flown home to Christchurch, resolved to hunker down and tend his flock. He spoke regularly to his sister, and in that way had learned of her growing doubts as to the faithfulness and rectitude of her second husband, Dr. Charles Perrone. Still, Joey had said nothing in those conversations that even hinted she feared for her safety.

"He actually pushed you off the ship?" Corbett Wheeler's hand was shaking as he gripped the telephone. "How? And why, for God's sake?"

Joey told him the story of what had happened that night. He managed to laugh when she got to the part about the bale of grass.

"Who found you—the DEA?"

"Not even close."

"But you've been to the police, right?"

No reply.

"Joey, what's going on?"

"It would be my word against Chaz's," she said, "and he's a good actor, Corbett. Better than me."

Corbett Wheeler thought about that for a few moments. "So, is there a plan?" he asked.

"There will be. I might need your help."

"You name it," he said. "Where are you now?"

"On some island," she said.

"Oh, that's terrific. Are you alone?"

"I'm staying with the man who rescued me."

"Aw, Joey, come on."

"I trust him," she said.

"You trusted Chaz, too," Corbett Wheeler said. "I'm chartering a jet first thing in the morning."

"No, not yet. Please."

His little sister had her weak moments, Corbett knew, but deep down she was a tough cookie.

"What exactly are you up to?" he asked.

After Joey got off the phone, she went outside and found Mick Stranahan fishing from the seawall, Strom dozing at his side.

"How soon can Chaz have me declared legally dead?" she asked. "We're talking, what—weeks? Months? When there's no corpse, I mean."

"State law says five years," Stranahan said.

Joey was glad to hear it, although she didn't intend to spend that much time stalking an asshole husband. She was looking for something quick and dirty.

"Corbett is calling the sheriff's office," she said, "to tell them it wasn't a suicide or an accident."

"You want the cops leaning on Chaz so soon?"

"The more the merrier. Besides, they can't prove he did it. You said so yourself."

"Not without your testimony, they probably can't."

"So they'll just ask lots of questions and make him a nervous wreck, which is fine by me."

"Him lying awake every night, wondering what's next," Stranahan said.

"Yeah, exactly. Staring at the ceiling."

"But then how does it finally end?"

"I'm not sure," Joey said. "You got any nifty ideas? I'll bet you do."

Stranahan reeled in a snapper and tossed it in the bucket. He said, "You're entitled to some hard feelings. The guy tried to kill you, after all."

"Mostly, I need to find out why," said Joey. "Whatever else happens with Chaz, I can't walk away until I know the reason he did it. Did I mention he was younger than me?"

"No."

"By almost five years. Big mistake, marrying an arrested adolescent." She paused, worrying about one possible implication of what she'd said. Pointedly she added, "That doesn't mean I'm going to suddenly start dating older guys."

"Oh, darn my luck." Stranahan never took his eyes off the water.

Joey frowned. "Sarcasm is not attractive. Chaz specialized in it."

"Grand larceny isn't exactly my idea of a turn-on, either."

"What!"

"You stole my boat, remember?"

"For heaven's sake," Joey said.

She was trying to lay down a few simple rules, that's all. She didn't want Stranahan to get the wrong idea about their relationship. The cornerstones of her revamped approach to men would be candor and clarity, and Stranahan was the first test case.

"Mick, I want to pay you for your help. Plus expenses, of course, including room and board."

"I still can't promise I won't try to sleep with you," he said. "That's how I often behave when I meet someone attractive. It's only fair you should know."

"I appreciate the honesty. I do."

"Don't worry, you'll see me coming about a mile away. I'm not real slick."

"No?"

"French wine, moonlight and Neil Young, strictly acoustic. Don't laugh, I know it's hokey."

"Depends on the wine," Joey said.

She was remembering the way he'd kissed her hand while the Coast Guard spotter was eyeballing them from the helicopter. She was wondering if it had been more than a show.

Stranahan said, "If you were my sister—"

"Or daughter."

"Christ, I'm not *that* old."

"Go on," Joey said.

"If you were my sister—honestly?—I'd tell you to get your butt off this island as fast as possible."

"Because . . ."

"Because for all you know," he said, "I could be president of the Ted Bundy Fan Club. I could be a serial killer-slash-rapist-slash-fill in the blank."

"Now you're just tryin' to sweet-talk me," Joey drawled.

Stranahan pulled in another snapper and declared they had plenty for supper. He got up and whistled for Strom to follow him to the fish-cleaning table.

"He loves to hassle the gulls," Stranahan said.

"You eat fish every night?"

"No. Sometimes it's lobster. Sometimes stone crabs."

"You don't get lonely out here?" Joey asked.

"Makes up for all the years of foolish companionship."

Stranahan unsheathed a narrow curved knife and went to work. It was a delicate enterprise because the snappers were small, but the blade was steady and precise in his large weathered hands. Joey found herself watching with an odd sort of reverence, as if gutting a fish were some sort of mystic rite.

"One night maybe we'll take the skiff up to Key Biscayne," he was saying. "There's a few decent restaurants—"

"Mick, do you have a gun?" she asked.

"This is Florida, darling."

"I'm serious."

"So am I. The head of the Miami Chamber of Commerce used to keep a loaded Uzi under her bed," Stranahan said. "So the answer would be yes, I own a firearm."

"Will you show me how to use it?"

"I don't think so."

"Just in case Chaz gets wise?"

"It's too dangerous."

"Okay." Joey thinking: A half-wit baboon could learn how to shoot.

"What exactly does your husband do for a living?" Stranahan asked.

"I told you. He's a biologist."

"But doing what?"

"He works on the Everglades project for the state water-management district."

"He any good?" Stranahan asked.

"I wouldn't know. Science is another universe to me," Joey said. "I was the jock in the family."

"What do they pay him?" Stranahan tossed a handful of fish entrails into the water. A gull dove on the splat, ignoring Strom's fevered barking.

Joey said, "Chaz's salary is sixty-two thousand a year. The only reason I know is because he got audited by the IRS."

"Can he get to your money? This is important."

She assured Stranahan that her inheritance was safe.

"And Chaz signed a pre-nup anyway. Every so often he'd hint around like he wanted me to tear it up, but eventually he gave up."

"Doesn't that seem strange?"

"No, because he had a nest egg of his own. I didn't pry," Joey said, "because he didn't pry. Money wasn't a huge issue in our marriage, if that's what you're getting at. We split the bills down the middle. Filed separate tax returns."

"Money is an issue in every marriage, Joey. Ask any divorce lawyer." Stranahan lobbed a glistening fish skeleton into the basin. It sank slowly in a wisp of crimson.

"Are Chaz's parents rich?" he asked.

"His dad was the greenskeeper at a country club in Panama City,"

Joey said. "He got sick from all the pesticides and went insane is what Chaz told me. Woke up one day and decided he was Gen. William Westmoreland. Drove down to the docks and attacked a shrimp boat with a Ping putter and a bunker rake. The captain and the crew were Vietnamese immigrants—"

"Whoa. Chaz told you this?"

Joey nodded. "He saved the newspaper clippings. Bottom line, his father's institutionalized. His mother works at Target and she's remarried to a retired fighter pilot from England."

"So where did Chaz's 'nest egg' come from?" Stranahan had finished cleaning the fillets and was hosing off the table. "Is he a big spender?"

"Not usually," Joey said. "But, like, three months ago he went out and bought a brand-new Hummer H2. Not financed, *bought*. Bright yellow, too. Said he needed a four-wheel drive for his fieldwork out in the swamps."

Stranahan chuckled. "Beautiful."

"When I asked how much it cost, he kind of snapped," Joey recalled. "And I wasn't nagging. I was just curious about what he spent. The same way he's curious when I come home with a new dress or a pair of shoes. But this time he told me to mind my own goddamn business. Called me a nosy bitch."

"What'd you do?"

"I told him if he ever spoke to me like that again, I'd reach down his throat and pull out his testicles one at a time," Joey said. "I've got a temper, okay?"

Stranahan promised to keep that in mind.

"So that night we're lying in bed," Joey said, "and Chaz says he's sorry for blowing a gasket. This while he's trying to climb on top of me. Tells me he won a big settlement from being in a car accident."

"When?"

"Long time ago, before we met. He got T-boned by some drunk Kiwanian up in Tampa and seriously screwed up his back. Said he was on crutches for, like, six months."

"And you're married almost two whole years before he mentions this traumatic, life-altering event," Stranahan mused.

"Maybe he thought . . . I don't know." Joey shook her head. "Maybe he was embarrassed because he got the money from a lawsuit."

"I'm sure. Probably wanted you to think he'd won a Nobel Prize, or maybe a MacArthur grant."

She was feeling more foolish than ever. "In other words—"

"Assume everything your husband ever told you was bullshit," Stranahan said. "How much would you guess that new Hummer cost?"

"Nearly sixty grand, with all the bells and whistles. I checked on the Internet."

They heard a yelp and turned around. Strom was floundering miserably in the basin under a swirl of teasing seabirds. Stranahan calmly jumped in the water and gathered the big dog in his arms. Joey hurried to fetch a towel.

Later, while the fish was frying, Stranahan opened a bottle of wine. "Don't worry," he told Joey. "It's from California, not France."

"So this isn't one of your smooth bachelor moves?"

"Give me a little credit."

"But isn't that Neil Young we're listening to?"

"With Buffalo Springfield, that's right. You're pretty darn sharp for a youngster." Stranahan filled her wineglass. "How about tomorrow we get off this rock?"

"Good idea. Wait'll you see that Hummer," Joey said.

"What I'd really like to see," said Stranahan, "is anyone on a state salary who can pay cash for a sixty-thousand-dollar set of wheels."

The petty officer's name was Yancy.

"Here's what I was talking about," she said.

The four bales were laid out in a row on the floor of an empty holding cell. The sodden weed gave off a strong sickly-sweet smell.

Yancy was pointing at the third bale. Karl Rolvaag crouched to get a closer look.

"Weird, huh?" the petty officer said.

The wrapping was damaged in two places. Rolvaag carefully probed at the puckered fabric with the capped tip of a ballpoint pen. Each area was characterized by a series of slender longitudinal furrows, several of which were deep enough to have punctured the burlap.

"Can I ask a favor?" The detective motioned Yancy forward.

The petty officer did as she was asked. Rolvaag lifted her left hand and placed it over one of the divots in the bale. Then he took her right hand and covered the other. The alignment was nearly perfect, each of Yancy's fingers matching a rumpled groove in the cloth.

"How about that," Rolvaag said.

Yancy went rigid. "Sir, it wasn't me. You have my word," she said. "This is what it looked like when we found it."

"Relax," the detective said. "I believe you."

"You asked us to report anything unusual that we saw or found," she said. "Anything out of the ordinary is what you said."

"Yes, and this is very helpful. I can't thank you enough."

"We're glad to be of assistance, sir."

"And whereabouts was this one found?"

"Angelfish Creek," Yancy said.

"No kidding? That's a long haul." It meant that Joey Perrone had gone in the water long before her husband said she did.

"I need two small favors," Rolvaag told Yancy. "You ordinarily burn the grass you confiscate, isn't that right?"

"Yes, sir, we turn all contraband over to the federal task force. They incinerate it," the petty officer said.

"This bale here? Tell them not to," Rolvaag said. "Mark it as evidence and put it in a safe place."

"Evidence. Yes, sir."

"Also, have you got a pair of tweezers and a Baggie?"

"Let me check the first-aid station," Yancy said.

While she was gone, Rolvaag sat down on one of the other bales and blew his nose fiercely. He was afflicted with numerous crop and pollen allergies, and wet marijuana rated a code ten.

The word *Libertad!* had been scratched on a wall of the cell, and the detective wondered who had done it and where the poor bastard had been deported. As much as Rolvaag disliked South Florida, it was useful to be reminded that there were infinitely worse places not so far away; places that made Hialeah look like the Emerald City of Oz.

Petty Officer Yancy returned with the requested items. Using the tweezers, Rolvaag began meticulously exploring each of the finger grooves on the burlap sacking. It didn't take long to dig out the clue he was hoping for.

"Could you open the plastic bag?" he asked Yancy.

"Yes, sir. What'd you find?"

The detective held it up, pinched firmly in the beak of the tweezers, for her to see.

"Is that the tip of a fingernail?" she asked.

"It would appear so. A woman's, I'm almost sure."

"So she was trying to rip open the bale—is that what happened?"

"No." Rolvaag dropped the nail fragment into the Baggie. "She was hanging on for dear life."

As Petty Officer Yancy studied the clawings in the fabric, Rolvaag thought he saw her shiver.

"Sir, was this the woman . . . could these marks be from the woman we were trying to locate? The one missing off the cruise ship?"

The detective said it was possible.

"Weird," Yancy said quietly. "Spooky weird."

"Yes, it is." Rolvaag turned back to the soggy bale. "Let's see if there's more."

Seven

The development was called West Boca Dunes Phase II.

"Dunes?" said Mick Stranahan. "We're fifteen miles from the beach."

"Chaz tried to buy into Phase I because it's on a golf course," Joey Perrone explained, "but they were sold out."

"Every house looks the same."

"Oh, they're identical. All three hundred and seven units in our modern Florida subdivision," Joey said in a mock sales-pitch voice, "except that some feature the master bedroom suite on the east side and some have it on the west. Also, you can get a pool."

Stranahan lowered the binoculars. "But you don't have one."

Joey said, "Chaz hates to swim."

"Not you. That was your big college sport, right?"

"Ancient history," she said.

"Still, it would have been nice for you. A swimming pool."

"Yeah, well."

"How about another fig?" Stranahan asked.

They'd stopped at an outdoor market in Pompano Beach and he had loaded up on fresh produce. Now the car smelled like two tons of Mediterranean fruit salad.

Joey Perrone said, "It's lucky you've got that island thing going for you, Mick, because this"—she patted the dashboard—"ain't exactly a pussy magnet."

"Excuse me?"

"That's a Chazism for a hot car."

Stranahan said, "The Cordoba is an automotive classic. You'll be pleased to know that your butt is sitting on rich Corinthian leather."

"Maybe once upon a time."

For years Stranahan had kept the rusty car under a shady ficus tree near the Dinner Key marina, where he docked the skiff when visiting the mainland. Nothing on the Chrysler worked properly anymore except the enormous engine, which ran like a miracle.

Joey said, "We sit here much longer, somebody will definitely call the police."

Mick Stranahan conceded that the Cordoba didn't blend in with the late-model SUVs gleaming in the parallel driveways of West Boca Dunes Phase II. Joey told him to get busy while she found a place to hide the car.

"I might need to break a window," he said.

"There's a spare key in a bird feeder in the backyard."

"How about an alarm?"

"Broken. See you in ten minutes."

Stranahan wore a short-sleeved work shirt from Florida Power & Light and a white hard hat. He went up to the front door and rang the bell. After a minute he circled to the rear of the house and pretended to examine the electric meter until he figured even the nosiest of Joey's neighbors would have lost interest.

The bird feeder was hung in the only tree in the Perrones' yard, a scrawny black olive. The key was covered with grackle droppings, which Stranahan wiped on the grass. As soon as he entered the house, he scrubbed his hands and put on a pair of rubber kitchen gloves. He was waiting by the front door when Joey knocked.

"So, what do you think of my new look?"

"I'm there," Stranahan said.

She wore a cropped brunette wig and a gray knee-length house-dress, and she carried a worn Bible. All of it came from a thrift shop they'd found down the street from the produce mart.

Stranahan motioned her inside and shut the door. Her shoulders stiffened and she stood in the foyer for several moments without say-ing a word.

He took her by the elbow and said, "It's all right."

"Is there anything I shouldn't see?"

"I haven't taken the grand tour, but this was on the kitchen counter."

It was a section of the *Sun-Sentinel* that had been unfolded to an inside page.

Joey read the headline aloud: " 'Coast Guard Calls Off Search for Missing Cruise Passenger.' Oh my God, there I am! 'Local Woman Feared Drowned.' Do you believe this?"

She dropped the Bible and seized the newspaper with both hands. "I knew it, Mick. He's saying I got drunk and fell overboard!"

"That's not in the story."

"No, but it's the obvious implication. 'Perrone told police that he and his wife had shared several bottles of wine earlier in the evening. The couple had been celebrating their second wedding anniversary.' The prick!"

Joey crumpled the newspaper and slam-dunked it into the trash can. "I'm calling Rose," she said.

"Who's that?"

"My best friend. She's in our book club."

Mick Stranahan waited in the living room, trying to figure out who had decorated the place. The sofa and two reading chairs were comfortable and smart-looking, probably Joey's touch. Chaz's contributions would be the plasma TV and the jet-black Natuzzi recliner. The tragic aquarium could go either way. Stranahan was struck by the absence of books and the abundance of golf magazines. No family photographs were on display, not even a wedding picture.

Joey stalked into the room carrying a cold beer in each hand. She gave one bottle to Stranahan. "Rose almost had a seizure. She thought I was calling from the grave—speaking of which, what's that awful smell?"

"The aquarium, I'm afraid."

Joey groaned as she approached the tank. "That frigging idiot forgot to feed the fish!"

They looked like shiny little holiday ornaments, bobbing in the clouded water. Joey turned away in angry disgust. Stranahan followed her through the house, room by room. Nothing more was said until they reached the master bath.

"Oh, cute. My stuff's gone."

"Everything?"

"My toothpaste, makeup." Joey tore through the drawers and cabinets. "All my lotions and creams, even the tampons. This is unbelievable."

She hurried to the bedroom and flung open the closet door and let out a cry. "My clothes, too!"

Stranahan opened the top drawer of an antique bureau. "Undies," he reported, perhaps too brightly. "These he saved."

"Asshole." Joey slammed the closet door so violently that it came off the track.

Stranahan said, "Personally, I advocate cunning and stealth over mass destruction."

He righted the door and set it back in place. Joey grabbed her bra and panties out of the bureau and sat down stiffly on the edge of the bed. "I'm going to cry now, okay, and I don't want to hear a word from you. Not one damn word."

"Crying is allowed. Go right ahead."

"And don't you dare put your arms around me and stroke my hair and give me all that wise fatherly-brotherly bullshit. Not unless I tell you to."

"Fair enough," Stranahan said.

"This was my house, Mick. My life. And he's just sweeping me out the door like I was dirt."

She closed her eyes and oddly found herself thinking of the night that Chaz had begged to tie her to the bedposts. He had chosen Alsatian scarves but had cinched the knots so tightly that her fingers and toes immediately went to sleep. It had been one of the rare times with Chaz that she'd had to fake it, but what made the night more memorable was that he'd passed out on top of her in a creepy sexual stupor. For nearly an hour he had lain there, snoring between her breasts and drooling like a Saint Bernard, yet remaining solidly erect inside her. Joey had felt as helpless as a butterfly pinned to a corkboard.

Upon reflection she realized that the bizarre interlude had been a telling lesson about her husband: Conscious or unconscious, he was completely dick-driven.

"The guy's an animal and I never saw it," she said disconsolately. "A primitive with a Ph.D. And I was a fool for marrying him."

"Joey?" Stranahan was standing at the bedroom door, spinning his hard hat in his hands.

"Yeah?"

"If you're going to cry, then cry. We need to be moving along."

"Give me five minutes alone."

"You got it," Stranahan said.

"Five minutes. Then come back and put your arms around me and tell me everything's going to be okay. All that cornball crap."

"You sure?"

"Yeah, let's give it a shot. But first, take off those ridiculous gloves."

Later they found the rest of her belongings crammed in three cardboard boxes, stacked in the garage next to her Toyota. As Joey began sorting through the depressing inventory, Stranahan warned her that Chaz might become suspicious if items disappeared.

"And don't even think about taking your car," he added.

Glumly she held up a pale orange handbag. "This is what I brought on the cruise."

Chaz had obviously overlooked her wallet, which contained $650 and an American Express card. "The plastic I'm keeping," she informed Stranahan. "We'll need it."

"The cash, too."

"Come here and dig in." Joey pointed to one of the other boxes.

"May I ask what we're looking for?"

"Something saucy," she said. "Something to catch the eye of my worthless troglodyte husband."

Dawn brought a thunderstorm and the screeching of rats. Karl Rolvaag's pythons had awakened hungry.

For ten minutes the detective stood under a cold shower, a ritual meant to thicken his blood in preparation for the return to Minnesota. Rolvaag believed that living in South Florida had turned him into a weather wimp.

Captain Gallo had told him to take the day off as comp time, but Rolvaag had nothing else to do but work. By the time he'd shaved and dressed, the snakes were finished and Mrs. Shulman was pounding on the door. She lived across the hall in unit 7-G and held the title of acting vice president for the Sawgrass Grove Condominium Association. Her current mission was to evict Karl Rolvaag from the premises.

"Good morning, Nellie," he said.

"I heard it, that god-awful screaming again, you sick bastard!"

"They've got to eat," the detective said, "same as you and me."

"If you weren't a cop, they'd throw you in jail for animal cruelty!"

Mrs. Shulman, who weighed at least ninety pounds, acted as if she intended to punch Rolvaag in the chest. Her bony mottled fists were clenched and trembling.

The detective said, "The condo association paid how much for rodent extermination last year—three or four grand, wasn't it?"

Mrs. Shulman sneered. "Don't get snide with me."

"There's nothing in the rules says I can't keep reptiles."

" 'Dangerous pets,' it's right on page one nineteen."

"Your dog's bitten four people," Rolvaag pointed out. "My snakes haven't hurt anybody."

"Disturbing the peace, then. Those helpless mice screaming and moaning while God's breath is strangled out of them—it's horrible. I had to double up on my Xanax, thanks to you."

"They're big fat rats, Nellie, not Stuart Little. And, by the way, that poison your exterminator uses? It makes their little tummies explode."

Mrs. Shulman wailed, backpedaling.

"Why don't we leave this to the lawyers," Rolvaag said.

"You're a sick, sick, *sick* bastard. No wonder you're not married anymore."

"And no wonder your husband went deaf."

Somewhere in the parchment fissures of Mrs. Shulman's face, her eyes narrowed. "You'll be gone by July, smartass."

"Keep Petunia on her leash," Rolvaag advised, "and you've got nothing to worry about."

After a late breakfast he drove to the office and showed Captain Gallo the letter from the police chief in Minnesota.

"Very humorous," Gallo said. "Where the fuck is Edina?"

"Twin Cities area."

"Didn't they write a song about it? 'Nothing could be finer than to be in your Edina in the morrr-ning!' "

Rolvaag said, "I'm serious about taking the job."

"Cut it out."

"I want to live somewhere normal."

"And die of fucking boredom. Sure you do." Gallo handed him a scrap of paper. "Guy name of Corbett Wheeler called. That's his number."

"Mrs. Perrone's brother."

"One-thirty in the morning, kangaroo time, he's wide-awake," Gallo said. "Wants to talk to someone ASAP. Says it's important."

Rolvaag had been trying to locate Corbett Wheeler since Saturday afternoon. "I'll call right now," the detective said.

"Make it collect."

"You're kidding."

Gallo shrugged. "That's what the guy said—'Be sure and call collect.' "

Somewhere in the hills of New Zealand, Joey Perrone's brother picked up on the first ring. Karl Rolvaag half-expected him to sound like the flaky Aussie who wrestles crocodiles on TV, but Corbett Wheeler hadn't lost his flat American accent.

"Are you the one in charge of the case?" he asked.

"That's right," Rolvaag said.

"Then listen up: My little sister did *not* get drunk and fall off that cruise ship," Corbett Wheeler declared, "no matter what her husband told you. And she didn't take a dive, either."

The connection was fuzzy, and Rolvaag heard his own voice reverberate when he spoke. "I understand this must be hard for you. Would you mind a few questions?"

"It was in the Boca newspaper. That's how I found out—a friend of Joey's called to tell me."

Rolvaag said, "We've been trying to get hold of you since Saturday. Your brother-in-law gave me a couple of phone numbers, but they were no good."

"Just like my brother-in-law," Corbett Wheeler said. "He is a fuckwit and a reprobate."

"When's the last time you saw him?"

"Never met the man, or even spoke to him. But Joey's given me an earful—I wouldn't trust the guy alone with my bowling ball, that's what a horndog he is."

Rolvaag had heard similar opinions from Joey's friends, though none of them hinted that Charles Perrone was deeply involved with anybody but Charles Perrone.

"You're suggesting that Chaz had something to do with your sister's disappearance?"

"Bet the farm on it," said Corbett Wheeler.

"It's a long way from adultery to homicide."

"From what Joey told me, he's capable of anything."

Rolvaag heard sheep lowing in the background.

"Maybe we should talk in person," he suggested.

"Honestly, I don't travel much," said Mrs. Perrone's brother, "but I'd fly all night to see that little whorehopper strapped into the electric chair and lit up like Dodger Stadium."

"These days most of them opt for lethal injection."

"Are you telling me they get a choice?"

"I'm afraid so," Rolvaag told him. "What's that noise?"

"One of my ewes, trying to pop triplets."

"Can I call you back?"

"No, I'll call you," said Joey Perrone's brother, and the line went dead.

Fuckwit, reprobate, horndog, whorehopper—an impressive litany of contempt for Chaz Perrone. Rolvaag reported Corbett Wheeler's suspicions to Captain Gallo, who shrugged and said, "Hey, nobody wants to believe their little sister was a clumsy lush. Did he know about the DUI?"

"I didn't ask." Rolvaag could name plenty of friends who'd been busted for drunk driving, and not one had ever fallen off a cruise ship. "What if Wheeler's right about Perrone?"

"Then you'll figure it out, too, and make us all look like geniuses," said Gallo, "hopefully by Friday."

Rolvaag knew better than to mention the nail marks on the marijuana bale until the DNA testing was complete. The procedure wasn't inexpensive, and the captain would be miffed that Rolvaag had ordered it without his approval.

Gallo handed him the letter from the Edina police chief. Rolvaag folded it back into the envelope. "Is three weeks enough time?" he asked.

"Didn't you hear what I just said? Friday, Karl, and then we move on."

"I'm not talking about this case," said the detective. "I'm giving my notice. Is three weeks enough?"

Gallo sat back and grinned. "Yeah, whatever. I'll play along."

Chaz Perrone parked his Hummer on the levee, a half mile from the spillway. He kept the AC running and slurped coffee as he stared blankly across miles and miles of Everglades. A breeze fluffed the saw grass and combed ripples in the dark water. Coots tiptoed through the hyacinths and lilies, a young heron speared minnows in the shallows and a small bass went airborne to take a dragonfly. The place was thrumming with wildlife, and Chaz Perrone was miserable.

Nothing about nature awed, soothed or humbled him—not the solitude or the mythic vastness or the primordial ebb and flow. To Chaz, it was all hot, buggy, funky-smelling and treacherous. He would have been so much happier on the driving range at Eagle Trace.

Red Hammernut was the one who had insisted that Chaz stick to the program, in case Chaz's supervisors at the water-management district decided to check up on him. It was also Red who'd bought him the Humvee, after Chaz had griped for months that the dirt roads were tearing up the shocks on his midsize Chevy.

Chaz had chosen bright yellow for the Hummer on the theory that such an intrusive color would freak out any panthers that might be lurking in the sector of the Everglades to which he was assigned. Chaz was terrified of being ambushed by one of the big cats, despite the fact that no such attack on humans had ever been recorded. Furthermore, the animals were nearly extinct, perhaps only sixty or seventy remaining in the wild.

When a fellow biologist reminded Chaz that the odds of being mauled by a Florida panther were roughly the same as being struck by a meteorite, Chaz announced he was taking no chances. When informed that the cats were color-blind and would therefore be oblivious to the blinding hue of his Humvee, Chaz wasn't entirely disappointed. Girls seemed to go for the yellow.

He climbed out of the driver's seat and was promptly engulfed by mosquitoes. Grunting and flailing, he struggled to insert himself into the heavy rubber waders that he'd purchased from a high-end hunting catalog. The commotion spooked a turtle off a rock, the splash causing Chaz to spin around and glare at the telltale rings on the surface. When he was seven, his mother had presented him with a baby dime-store terrapin, which he'd named Timmy and later flushed down the toilet in disapproval of its casual potty habits.

As he sloshed reluctantly into the marsh, Chaz wasn't worried about a turtle attack, as turtles had no teeth. What he dreaded were the alligators, brazen and plentiful. Not a single scientist had been devoured or even maimed by a gator while working in the Everglades, but Chaz believed it was only a matter of time. He would have carried a high-caliber rifle except that it was strictly forbidden, and he couldn't risk getting fired, demoted or transferred from the sampling sites. That would ruin everything, including his profitable association with Red Hammernut.

Consequently, Chaz's sole instrument of defense was a boron-shafted two-iron, which in his hands was far more efficient at scaring off aquatic reptiles than striking a golf ball. Chaz swung the club haphazardly and yowled like a hemorrhoidal bobcat as he hacked a soggy trail through the saw grass. Nature recoiled as he threshed the water, launching clumps of algae and splintered twigs and shredded lily pads. In the cumbersome waders Chaz clomped and teetered like the Frankenstein monster, but the desired effect was achieved: every living vertebrate within a hundred yards of the dike fled the scene.

Only the mosquitoes and horseflies lingered to harass Chaz Perrone, and their impassive humming was all he heard when he finally reached the pond where the first monitoring station stood. Otherwise the swamp had gone mute and lifeless, which was how Chaz preferred it. He stood at the edge of the deeper water, catching his breath and waiting for the wavelets he'd made to subside.

Here Chaz was required to immerse up to his armpits, surrendering what little mobility he had. The stiff rubber leggings that protected him so reliably from the razor-sharp saw grass and lethal moccasin fangs were not designed for swimming, and would in fact fill up and drag him down like an anchor if Chaz wasn't careful.

So he waited for the water to calm, intently scanning the surface for ominous log-like snouts. In his nightmares this is where the gators always nailed him—in the pond—because he was exposed and helpless, a sitting duck. On more than one occasion Chaz had retreated in a blind froth from the monitoring station, certain he was being pursued by one or more of the flesh-eating saurians. Today the only specimen to be seen was a vividly banded newborn that would have fit easily in a shoe box. Chaz bravely stepped forward and whaled away with the two-iron, failing (as usual) to land a blow. As soon as the baby alligator was gone, Chaz made his move.

Wielding the golf club over his head, he skated his feet heavily across the muddy bottom. He was prepared to clobber anything that came to the surface, no matter how small or harmless, but nothing rose to challenge him. Along the way, he diligently paused to uproot several fresh sprouts of cattails, a small act of tidiness that Chaz believed was crucial to his future wealth and comfort.

It took only three minutes to remove a water sample from the monitoring station. Chaz made it look good, even though he was fairly certain that nobody from the district was within thirty miles of the site. Red Hammernut said they sometimes sent up helicopters to spy on the biologists in the field, but privately Chaz was doubtful. He acted out the charade of sample collecting only because it was Red's wish, and Red was the last person on earth Chaz wanted to cross.

Following his freshly cut path, he crashed and howled his way back to the levee without incident. After placing the quart-size container upright in the back of the Hummer, he kicked and wriggled out of his waders, which stunk of sweat and ripe muck. He grabbed a mango-flavored Gatorade from the cooler and sat on the bumper, the two iron propped within lunging distance. With a dirty shirtsleeve Chaz mopped the perspiration from his brow, thinking: What a steaming shithole this is! To think that the taxpayers of America are spending 8 billion bucks to save it.

Suckers, Chaz thought. If they only knew.

With the binoculars he checked in both directions along the rutted embankment. No other vehicles were visible. He squinted up at the sky and saw the omnipresent buzzards, circling clockwise, but no choppers or planes.

Satisfied, Charles Regis Perrone finished off the Gatorade and lobbed the bottle into the saw grass. Then he unscrewed the lid from the sample jar and poured the tea-colored water into the dirt at his feet.

River of grass, my ass, he thought.

Eight

Chaz was sitting in the bathtub, scrubbing off the swamp grime, when Ricca showed up.

"Are you nuts?" he said.

"Nope. Just lonely." She stepped out of her oxblood heels.

"Did anybody see you drive up? Where'd you park?"

Ricca unfastened her hoop earrings and set them next to Chaz's stick deodorant on the vanity. "What are you so jumpy about? I thought you'd be happy to see me."

In a moment she was out of her clothes, straddling him imperiously.

"But I'm not finished," Chaz said.

"Damn right you're not."

Ricca placed her palms against his chest and pushed. Chaz took a quick breath, squeezing his eyes closed as he submerged. Being a clean freak, he was concerned about the health risks of rough sex in dirty bathwater. Who knew what pernicious tropical microbes had hitched a ride back from the Everglades?

It was too late to protest. He felt like he'd been thrown into a blender with a live coyote. The bare tile amplified Ricca's feral yips and howls to soul-chilling decibels, the racket seeming louder every time Chaz came up for air. Meanwhile she was pounding against him with such zest as to generate a seismic rhythm of concussive smacks. Chaz feared that his eardrums might blow out underwater. With both arms he helmeted himself, not only to save his hearing but to prevent his skull from cracking against the brass drain plate. Ricca was as speedy as she was rambunctious, and Chaz was confident that he could outlast her, providing he didn't drown.

True to form, she was done in less than four minutes. Chaz disentangled and stork-stepped out of the bathtub, which by then was nearly empty. He grabbed a couple of towels and began mopping up the floor and the walls.

"You're somethin' else," Ricca gasped.

She was splayed in the tub like a broken doll, one foot hooked on the soap tray and the other braced against the spigot. Jet-black hair fell in a dripping tangle across half her face.

"My God, Chaz. That was fantastic."

He said, "Yeah. You damn near killed me."

"Hey, you're still hard. What's the matter?"

"Not a thing." He snatched a robe off the hook on the door.

"Didn't you come?"

"Sure I did," he lied. "All over the place."

"So that means"—Ricca pointing—"you're ready to go again? Already?"

He shrugged. "Let's get some dinner."

"You are seriously amazing." She stood up and wrung out her hair. "Wanna b.j. or something?"

Chaz peered quizzically at her crotch. "What'd you do to yourself?"

"It's a shamrock. You like it?"

"A shamrock." He hadn't noticed earlier.

"For good luck," Ricca explained. "I wanted four leaves, but I only had enough pubes for three."

Chaz was trying to remember if she was Irish.

"It took, like, an hour to do. With two mirrors," she added.

"And they make green hair dye these days?"

"You bet."

"Well, I'm impressed," Chaz said.

"Then we're even. Come here, lemme take care of that."

Chaz was unnerved to realize that he wasn't in the mood. He glanced down at himself and wondered: What the hell's the matter with me?

"I think I heard the phone," he said, and hurried to get dressed.

A few minutes later, Ricca found him slouched on a corner of the bed. He wore one brown sock and a misbuttoned shirt, and he was staring dully into an open closet.

"What's wrong?" she asked, touching his shoulder.

He shook her off dismissively.

"Baby, I was thinking," she said. "Are you gonna have a service for Joey? You probably should."

"I hate funerals. Besides, there's no body to bury."

Ricca said, "A memorial service, I mean. They do it all the time for people who get burnt up in plane crashes, or when a ship sinks and everybody's lost at sea."

Chaz insisted there was no point. "Joey's only family is some hermit brother who lives on the other side of the world."

"What about her friends?"

"So, I'll put a notice in the paper. They can make donations to the World Wildlife Mission. Save the endangered yaks or whatever."

Ricca smoothed her skirt and sat beside him on the bed. "What happens next? I guess you've gotta have her declared legally . . . you know . . ."

"Dead?"

"Right."

"Christ, Ricca, it's only been a few days."

"Eventually, I mean."

"There's no rush," Chaz said.

That damn detective, Rolvaag, would be scrutinizing him for a while. Chaz didn't want to appear in a hurry to be single.

"How long, then?" Ricca asked.

"What's the difference? I'm not getting any of her money anyway," he said. "The fucking yaks can wait."

"Well, suppose I can't?"

Chaz pretended not to hear. He approached the closet and focused once more upon the sheer black dress. It was scooped in the front and featured a racy slit up one side.

He took it out and showed Ricca. "Did you bring this with you tonight? Because Joey had one just like it, I mean identical."

Ricca was peeved. "It's not mine, Chaz. Not unless I've grown three inches taller and dropped ten pounds."

"Aw, come on."

"*It's not mine.*"

"Okay, okay." He yanked the dress off the hanger, rolled it up and tossed it in a corner. "I swear I packed that away yesterday."

Ricca glanced uneasily around the room. "To be honest, this *is* kinda freaky, being in the house with your wife dead."

"What—it was easier when she was alive?"

"No, it's just very sad, what happened to her," Ricca said. "Can we get outta here?"

Chaz went to the dresser and pawed through the drawers one by one. He couldn't find Joey's panties and bra, the ones he'd meant to save for Ricca. He wondered if he was cracking up.

"Lookin' for your other sock? It's right there on the floor, under the nightstand."

"So it is," said Chaz. "Thanks."

As soon as Ricca went to fix her makeup, he slipped out the kitchen door and into the garage. The cardboard boxes containing Joey's belongings were exactly where he'd left them, piled next to the Camry. The boxes didn't appear to have been touched, causing Chaz to think that he had somehow forgotten to collect his wife's black dress. As for the missing undergarments, perhaps he'd moved them to another place.

In the living room he was gratified to see that the stinking dead fish had not re-materialized in his aquarium since he'd flushed them down the toilet. Chaz made himself a drink and began scanning the alphabetized-by-artist CD rack, looking for some kick-ass driving music. What he found while thumbing through the *T*'s gave him a chill. *Bad to the Bone* was missing. So was *Move It on Over.* Even the *Anthology* was gone.

Ricca appeared, looking spectacular but troubled. She said, "I hope you don't mind—I borrowed some of Joey's lipstick."

Chaz felt the hairs prickle on his neck. "That's impossible."

"I left mine in the car. I'm sorry."

"You don't understand. I threw out all her lipstick," he said. "I went through the whole goddamn bathroom and tossed out every goddamn thing of hers."

"But it was right there, Chaz. In the vanity—"

"No! Not possible."

Chaz felt a bloom of cold sweat under his arms. He stalked up to Ricca, grabbed her chin and turned her mouth toward the light so that he could examine the color.

"Shit," he muttered. It was definitely Coral Tease, Joey's favorite.

His favorite, actually. Just like that slitted black dress, the one she'd worn at his request to Mark's on Las Olas for their first anniversary.

He let go of Ricca's face and said, "Something's fucked up around here."

"Why would I lie about lipstick?" Rubbing her jaw, she was bewildered and angry.

"You're right. I'm sorry," he said.

"Can we get outta here, like, *now*?"

"Absolutely," Chaz told her. "Right after I make a call."

"Swell. I'll be in the bathroom." She shut the door forcefully behind her and fumed for a minute.

"Where's your razor?" she called out, but Chaz was already on the phone.

Joey Perrone and Mick Stranahan were watching the house from a neighbor's driveway halfway down the block. Joey said it was safe because the neighbors had gone to upstate New York for a month and possibly longer.

"Dodging subpoenas," she explained. "They run a telephone boiler room, selling ethanol futures to senior citizens. Every time the feds shut 'em down, they dash off to their lodge in the Adirondacks."

"It's a great country," Stranahan said.

"What're you doing?"

"Trying to figure out the damn CD player."

For surveillance purposes, Joey had rented them a dark green Suburban with tinted windows.

She said, "Mick, please don't."

He was sorting through the George Thorogood discs that Joey had swiped from her husband's collection. "What, you don't like the slide guitar?"

"I don't like the memories," she said.

Joey meant to drop the subject, but then she heard herself saying, "We'd be going along in the car and whenever he'd put on 'Bad to the Bone,' that was the signal he wanted me to, you know . . ."

"Gotcha." Stranahan tossed the CDs into the backseat. "So he imagines himself a wit, Mr. Charles Perrone, and a sex machine to boot."

Joey recited the ten things that Chaz disliked most about her, with hiding Thorogood being number six.

"That's not why he tried to kill you. Believe me," Stranahan said.

"See, this is what's driving me crazy," she said. "I can't figure out why he would do what he did."

"Money's my guess."

"But I told you, he's not getting a dime if I'm dead."

Stranahan fiddled with the radio dials. "Most murders come down to lust, anger or greed," he said. "From what you've told me about your husband, I'm betting on greed. If this isn't about your money then it's about somebody else's."

Joey said that, in a way, she hoped he was right. "I'd hate to think he threw me off that ship just so he could be with *her*." She shot a glare toward the house.

"Not likely," said Stranahan.

"I wish you could've met Benny, my first husband. He was a sweetheart," she said fondly. "Not exactly a firecracker in certain departments, but a good honest guy."

Stranahan aimed the binoculars at the bay window of the Perrone residence. The lights had come on, though the curtains remained closed. It had been an hour since the dark-haired woman had arrived, parking a blue Ford compact next to Chaz's Humvee.

"You don't know who she is?"

"No idea. It's pitiful," Joey said. "He's got so many bimbos, you'd need radio collars to track them all."

Stranahan secretly was pleased that Chaz Perrone was entertaining female company only three tender days into widowhood. Such a boggling lack of self-restraint could open a world of squalid opportunities for someone seeking to mess with Chaz's head.

"Let's call it a night," Stranahan suggested.

"Honestly, did she look that smokin' hot to you?"

"The longer we stay, the riskier it gets."

"This is what the Secret Service drives. Chevy Suburbans."

"Joey, we're not the Secret Service. I'm supposed to be retired and you're supposed to be deceased."

"Hey, we should copy the license off her car!"

"Done." Too tired to trust his memory, Stranahan had jotted the tag number on the inside of his wrist.

"Fifteen more minutes," she said. "Then we can go."

"Thank you."

Earlier, after leaving the car-rental agency, they had, over Stranahan's objections, stopped at an outlet mall. Joey had decided that she couldn't continue wearing the clothes of his ex-wives and girlfriends, and noted as an example that their bras were all too large. Grimly,

Stranahan had trailed after her as she accumulated $2,400 worth of slacks, tops, skirts, shoes, cosmetics and other personal items. She was the most ruthless and efficient shopper that he'd ever seen, but the experience had exhausted him so thoroughly that his senses now seemed cauterized.

Or perhaps that's how everyone came to feel in West Boca Dunes Phase II.

"You didn't even ask about the black dress," Joey was saying. "There's quite a naughty history there."

"I was letting my imagination run wild."

"Whatever he's doing with her tonight, he's thinking about *me*. That I can guarantee. And wait'll he finds the lipstick!"

Stranahan leaned his head against the window and shut his eyes.

"Don't you dare go to sleep," Joey said.

"I miss my dog. I want to go back to the island."

She poked him in the shoulder. "There they are!"

Two figures emerged from the Perrone house, a man and a woman, hurrying down the walkway. In the darkness Stranahan couldn't make out their faces but undoubtedly it was Joey's husband and his guest. As they got into the blue Ford, their expressions were briefly illuminated by the dome light. Both of them appeared soberly preoccupied, and not exactly radiating the afterglow of love.

Joey said, "He's driving. You know what that means."

"No, what?"

"He's been doing her," she said. "Guys never ask to drive your car until after they've slept with you at least twice. That's what Rose says, and she's been with, like, forty-nine men."

"Sounds like it's time for an oil change."

"Hey, let's follow 'em," Joey said.

"Let's not. Let's assume he screwed her and he's taking her to dinner and then he's sending her on her way."

"I'm going back inside my house."

"Bad idea," Stranahan said. "You've creeped him out enough for one night."

"Give me ten minutes. I've got to use the bathroom."

Joey hopped out of the Suburban and jogged down the street. When she returned, "Move It on Over" was blasting from the speakers.

She frowned at Stranahan. "That's cold."

"It's not the CD. It's the radio." He twisted the volume down. "I lucked into classic rock."

"What's so funny?"

"At my age I'm a sucker for ironies. Buckle up."

Joey didn't speak again until they were southbound on the interstate. "Chaz definitely noticed the dress in the closet, because it was gone when I went back."

"Excellent."

"But I found something really weird in the sink."

"What?" Stranahan was thinking maybe Jell-O or whipped cream.

"Pubic hair," Joey reported indignantly. "Kelly-green pubic hair. That nasty woman shaved herself all over my vanity."

Mick Stranahan reached over and squeezed her hand. "Nobody said this was going to be easy."

The man called Tool lived in a trailer outside of LaBelle, not far from Lake Okeechobee. The trailer had come with a half-acre parcel upon which the previous owner had cultivated tomatoes, a crop despised by Tool since his days as a crew boss. The day he moved in, he hitched an old Pontiac engine block to his truck and dragged it back and forth across the tomato patch until all that remained was churned dirt.

In place of vegetables Tool began planting highway-fatality markers that he collected on his travels throughout southwest Florida. The small homemade crosses often displayed colorful floral arrangements, which Tool found pleasing to the eye. Whenever he spied one of the markers along a road, he would yank it from the ground and place it in the back of his truck. Often this act was witnessed by other motorists, though nobody ever attempted to interfere.

Tool stood six three and weighed 280 pounds and owned a head like a cinder block. His upper body was matted so heavily with hair that he perspired copiously, even in cold weather, and found it uncomfortable to wear a shirt. Nearly a year had passed since Tool had been shot in broad daylight by a poacher who had mistaken him for a bear. No entry wound had been visible, as the slug had uncannily tunneled into the seam of Tool's formidable buttocks. Because bleeding was minimal, he elected to forgo medical treatment—a decision that would come back to haunt him.

Soon the pain became so unbearable that he gave up his job as a crew boss, no longer physically able to harass and abuse migrant farm-workers for twelve hours at a stretch. Such was his misery that a concerned dope-addict friend recommended fentanyl, a high-octane painkiller used during surgery but also available in a convenient skin patch.

Tool had no prescription for the medicine, but he did have a lock-pick. Once a week he'd drive to Fort Myers, break into a nursing home and meticulously peel the fentanyl patches from torsos of sedated cancer patients. In no time Tool was hopelessly hooked, his dosage escalating to levels that would have euthanized a more highly evolved organism. The only serious obstacle to his drug habit was his excess of body hair, so dense and oily as to defy conventional adhesives. Daily cropping was required, often in checkerboard patterns to accommodate multiple stolen patches.

That was how Red Hammernut found him, buck naked in a rusty washtub behind the house trailer, scraping brutally at his shoulder blades with a disposable razor.

"Hey," Tool said. "Long time no see."

"I been to Africa after them tarpon." With a groggy sigh Red Hammernut lowered himself into a tattered lawn chair. "Just got back to Tampa this morning and I'm jet-lagged outta my skull. May I ask what in the name of Jesus P. Christ you're doin'?"

"You got a job for me?"

That was one thing Red Hammernut admired about Tool—the sumbitch got right to the point.

"Go on and finish your bath. We'll talk after," Red said. "Mean-time, where's my ole friend Mr. Daniel?"

"They's a bottle in the bedroom somewheres."

Tool's bedroom was the last place that Red Hammernut yearned to explore, so he took a beer from the refrigerator instead. When he came back outside, Tool was hosing himself off.

Red pointed at the field of white fatality markers behind the trailer. "How many you got now?"

"Sixty odd. Mebbe seventy." Tool shook himself like a drenched buffalo. "Say, Red, throw me that damn towel."

It was a wadded scrap stained with what appeared to be transmission fluid. Red Hammernut tossed it to Tool, who fashioned a do-rag crookedly around his head.

"I still can't understand why you save those damn things. It's pretty fuckin' depressing, you ask me," Red said.

Tool turned to contemplate the orderly rows of crosses. He didn't give a shit about the car-crash victims, but he liked the visual symmetry of his design. "It's sorta like that famous soldier graveyard up in Washington—what's it called?"

"Arlington?"

"Yeah. Sorta like a mini Arlington!"

"Christ, I'm sure."

"Well, it's better'n goddamn tomatoes."

"You're right about *that*." Red Hammernut laughed.

The two men had met four years earlier when Red Hammernut's company purchased the vegetable farm where Tool was running crews of pickers and packers. After observing Tool's specialized management techniques, Red had recruited him for side jobs that required muscle and a lack of conscience. Red had found him to be reliable and focused in the way of a natural predator, though not as ruthlessly gung ho as his precedessor, Crow Beacham. It was Crow who had eagerly volunteered to dispose of that foolish young Mexican, the one griping about the curdled toilets and brown-running water at the migrant camps. Barely nineteen, the boy had marched his complaint to the faggot Communist lawyers at Rural Legal Services, who were preparing to share it with a federal judge, when their star witness vanished. It was almost two years before they'd found the Mexican kid's skeleton, in a phosphate pit a hundred miles away, but by then Crow Beacham was dead from syphilis and tapeworms. Tool took better care of himself, Red Hammernut noted, though not much.

"What's the work," Tool asked, "and how much does it pay?"

"Five hundred a day."

Tool looked amazed, and doubtful. "Do I gotta kill somebody or somethin'?"

"I doubt it."

"Don't be jerkin' me around, Red, I ain't in the mood. Not with a bullet in the crack of my ass." He lumbered indoors and banged about for a few minutes. He emerged wearing black denim overalls and carrying a pizza that was frozen solid. When he took a bite, it sounded like the crack of a .22.

Red Hammernut decided not to ask about the three flesh-colored patches that Tool had attached to the shaven areas on his back. The less known about the man's personal habits, the better.

"Let's have it," Tool said.

"Okay, here's the deal. I got a boy does some work for me, he lost his wife a few days back. He's a little shaky right now and I need you to keep a eye on him."

"How'd she die?" Blood was trickling out of Tool's mouth from where the pizza crust had lacerated his gums.

"She fell off one a them cruise liners out in the ocean."

"No shit? Was she some kinda retard or somethin'?"

"Not hardly." From experience Red Hammernut knew it was best not to clutter Tool's brain with a surplus of information.

"Anyway, the boy's nerves are 'bout fried on account of her bein' lost at sea and the cops askin' questions and so forth. This mornin' I get a message on my machine. Now he thinks somebody's sneakin' into his house and movin' shit around and generally tryin' to freak his ass out. Personally, I got a feelin' it's all in his head. Either way, he needs a guardian angel, and that would be you."

Tool nodded, chewing savagely. "You say he works on the farm?"

Red Hammernut raised his arm in time to deflect an errant chunk of pepperoni. "Nope. He lives over in Boca Raton."

"Oh fuck, Red."

"I know, it's hor'ble. That's how come the five hundred a day."

Tool spat again, this time intentionally, and stomped back into the trailer. He came out with a bag of beef jerky sticks.

"Gimme one a them bad boys," Red Hammernut said, helping himself.

"Boca! I swear to God, Red."

"I'm really sorry, man."

"What kinda work he do for you, this guy?"

"Nuthin' I want advertised, unnerstand? You notice any funny bidness, I spect you to call me."

"Sure thing," said Tool.

"And don't hurt nobody," Red Hammernut said, "less I say so."

Once, when the feds were investigating potentially damaging (though well-founded) accusations that Red was holding farm laborers as indentured slaves, he sent Tool to discourage the aggrieved workers from cooperating with the authorities. While nobody disappeared or died, the few workers who dared to testify unanimously portrayed "Mr.

Hammernut" as a saintly, paternal figure who'd plucked them from a life of aimless destitution and given them a bright future in modern agriculture.

Based on what he'd seen in the labor camps of Immokalee and Belle Glade, Red felt confident that Tool would have no trouble handling a weak, pampered white boy like Chaz Perrone.

With a grunt Red stretched his arms and announced he was going home to sleep for about four days. Tool followed him out to the paved road, where the gray Cadillac waited. As usual, Red's driver had kept the engine running and the thermostat set at sixty-eight degrees.

"She a pretty girl?" Tool asked.

"Who—the wife? Yeah, she was."

Tool scratched at his neck. "Maybe he kilt her."

"I don't care," said Red Hammernut, "and neither do you."

Nine

One spring evening in 1896, a prominent Pennsylvanian named Hamilton Disston blew his brains out in a bathtub. He had become gravely depressed after depleting his inheritance on a grandiose campaign to drain 4 million acres of Florida swamp known as the Everglades.

Although Disston died believing himself a failure, he was later proven a pioneer and an inspiration. In the years that followed, one version or another of his rapacious fantasy was pursued by legions of avaricious speculators—land developers, bankers, railroad barons, real-estate promoters, citrus growers, cattle ranchers, sugar tycoons and, last but not least, the politicians they owned.

Those wetlands that could not be dried, paved or planted were eventually trenched out and diked into vast reservoirs by the U.S. Army Corps of Engineers. Billions of gallons of freshwater that for eons had flowed freely as a broad marshy river toward Florida Bay was now held captive for siphoning by agriculture, industry and burgeoning municipalities. First one cross-state highway and then another transected the southern thumb of the peninsula, fatally interrupting the remaining southbound trickle from Lake Okeechobee. What precious water made it to the heart of the marsh often arrived tainted by pesticides, fertilizers and mercury.

To protect farms and subdivisions from frequent flooding—the unsurprising consequence of having occupied a bog—hundreds of miles of canals were dug to carry the overflow out to sea during the rainy summer months. Engineers employed a string of pumping stations to manipulate the water levels according to whim and weather, heedless of the historic natural cycles. Inevitably the Everglades and all its resplendent wildlife began to die, but nobody with the power to prevent it considered trying.

It was, after all, just a huge damn swamp.

Toward the latter part of the twentieth century, a series of severe droughts shattered the cocksure assumption that there would always be plenty of water to steal. Those whose fortunes depended on luring home buyers and tourists to South Florida now contemplated the dreadful possibility that the infernal granola-head environmentalists had been correct all along. If the Everglades dried up or succumbed to pollution, so might the vast underground aquifer that supplied drinking water from Palm Beach to the Keys. Growth would come to a gagging halt, and the dirty fortunes that accompanied it would evaporate faster than jizz on a griddle.

This apocalyptic scenario was laid out before Florida's politicians, and in time even the most slatternly among them were extolling the Everglades as a national treasure that must be preserved at all costs. Officeholders who had for decades abetted its destruction now delivered quavering oratory lamenting its demise. During election campaigns, they shamelessly contrived to be photographed kayaking around the East Cape or hiking Shark Valley, drowsy alligators and snowy egrets prominent in the background. Saving the Everglades became an apple-pie cause embraced by both political parties, and voters responded avidly.

Sadly, there wasn't much left to save. Ninety percent of the original 'glades already had been developed, converted to agriculture or otherwise debauched. The only untrampled remnant was a national park, the waters of which were of dubious purity. Nonetheless, in the late 1990s the United States Congress and the Florida Legislature allotted a boggling $8 billion to restore a natural and unpolluted flow to the fabled river of grass. Many decent and well-meaning people believed this to be a moral imperative.

Then there were those such as Samuel Johnson Hammernut, whose sole interest in sustaining the Everglades was to make sure that his thirteen thousand acres of lettuce, cabbage, sweet corn, tomatoes, radishes, escarole and parsley would have cheap and unlimited irrigation forever. Red Hammernut cared only slightly less about the imperiled wildlife than he did about the wretched souls who toiled for dirt wages in his crop fields, held captive to his employment with imaginary debts imposed by violent crew bosses.

As for the pollution issue, Red Hammernut intended to continue using the vast marshlands as a latrine, and to hell with the law. A pragmatic fellow, he'd watched closely as the bureaucracy of the Everglades restoration project evolved, and he had taken measures to safeguard his stake. Eight billion dollars was an unholy shitload of dough, and Red Hammernut calculated that no less than a third of it would be ripped off by lobbyists, lawyers, consultants and bid-riggers favored by well-placed politicians. The remaining windfall would be spent more or less earnestly, if not efficiently, by a phalanx of municipal, state and federal agencies that would seldom communicate with one another.

Prominent among these was the South Florida Water Management District, which was recruiting field biologists to test for harmful substances in farm runoff. It was a specialized mission, one that held some potential to complicate Red Hammernut's life.

Conveniently, the members of the water board had been appointed by the governor, to whose re-election campaign Red Hammernut had donated large sums of money and the use of a Cessna Citation. Therefore it was no surprise to Red Hammernut that his phone call to the water board was so genially received, or that his recommendation of a bright young job applicant was so promptly acted upon.

After that, it was easy arranging for the newly hired biologist to be assigned to the same water-testing district in which certain large vegetable farms were located.

On paper, Dr. Charles R. Perrone looked like the real deal.

Red Hammernut had his mole in place.

"It's good you're staying busy," Karl Rolvaag said.

Chaz Perrone nodded stoically.

"Your supervisor said she told you to take the whole week off, even longer if you needed."

Chaz frowned. "You spoke to Marta? What for?"

"Just routine," said the detective. "Anyway, she said you insisted on coming back to work, and I told her it could actually be a healthy thing."

"Well, what else am I supposed to do—hang around the house all day and get morbidly depressed? No thank you."

They were standing in the kitchen, Chaz with a Budweiser in his hand and Rolvaag sipping a Sprite. The detective had shown up at the front door not five minutes after Chaz had returned from work.

"I'm really beat," Chaz said for the third time.

"Yeah, it was a scorcher out there today." Rolvaag had seen on the news that an early spring snowstorm had hit the Twin Cities; he sitting in air conditioning in Florida. It was fairly astounding.

He said, "Marta explained what you do on your job, and it sounds real interesting. I bet you run into plenty of snakes out there."

"Well, I run *over* plenty of 'em with my truck." Chaz, unable to resist the smartass quip. "Look, I'm not trying to be rude, but, man, I am seriously whipped."

"Of course. I understand." The detective finished off the soda and raised the empty bottle. "Do you recycle?"

Chaz made a dunking motion toward the trash can. "Let God sort 'em out," he said.

Rolvaag placed the bottle on the counter. "There was just one point I needed you to clarify about that night on the *Sun Duchess.*"

"You know who you remind me of? That TV cop, Columbo. He never quit with the questions," Chaz said. "I bet that was your favorite show, am I right?"

"To be honest, I never watched it."

"But I'm sure other people must've told you the same thing—that you remind them of Columbo. Not the way you look, but how you never let up. In a nice way, though."

Rolvaag said, "What night is the show on? I'd like to see it."

Chaz shook his head. What a hopeless dweeb. "It was canceled, like, a hundred years ago. Anyway, what did you want to ask me about?"

The detective seemed relieved to get back to business. "Just one thing, really. Are you certain about what time Mrs. Perrone left the stateroom?"

Chaz experienced a disconcerting twitch in his colon. "Three-thirty in the morning, like I told you before. I remember looking at my watch."

"And there's no chance your watch was wrong?" Rolvaag's tone was unbearably neutral. "The reason I ask, we've found some evidence raising the possibility that your wife went into the water a few hours earlier than you told us."

The detective was leaning against the countertop, his hands shoved casually in his pockets.

Chaz said, "That's impossible."

"I'm sure there's an explanation."

"What kind of evidence did you find?"

Rolvaag winced apologetically. "Afraid I can't discuss it."

Locked in his desk at the office was the test confirming that the fingernail tips removed from the marijuana bale belonged to Joey Perrone.

Chaz said, "This is my wife we're talking about—and you're saying you can't tell me?" He felt his cheeks redden, but that was actually a good thing; he was supposed to look angry. "Did you find her body or not? Goddammit, I've got a right to know!"

Rolvaag said, "No, sir, we didn't recover a body. That I can tell you for a fact. Or even a body *part*."

"Then what the hell was it?"

Chaz was racking his brain. Joey hadn't been carrying her purse, so it had to be a piece of clothing that had washed ashore somewhere at odds with the computer model of where her body should have floated, factoring in that night's currents and wind.

"Is this why you wanted a DNA sample?" Chaz demanded.

"It's an active investigation. Certain aspects must remain confidential for the time being," Rolvaag said. "I'm sorry, Chaz."

It was the first time the detective had used Charles Perrone's nickname, and the sudden informality only heightened Chaz's anxiety. He'd seen enough TV homicide shows to know you were in deep trouble when cops started acting like they were your asshole buddies.

"I've lost my wife and you're playing head games," Chaz said, acting hurt and disappointed. "Just come out and say so if you think I'm lying."

"I think people make mistakes."

"Not this time."

"But you'd been hitting the wine pretty hard that night is what you told me. That's not always good for the memory," Rolvaag said.

Chaz twisted the cap off another beer and drank slowly, stalling to let his emotions settle. It occurred to him that the detective had unwittingly provided a way out. The Coast Guard had ended its search for Joey, so what was the point in arguing about when she'd gone overboard? If there was anything left of her, which was unlikely after four days at sea, it wouldn't really matter how far south she was found. One could always blame a shark or some other deep-water scavenger for carrying her remains out of the search grid.

Chaz hung his head. "I was pretty hammered, that's true. Maybe I did get confused about the time Joey left. Or maybe I misread my watch." For effect he tapped the crystal of his inexpensive Timex, which he wore only on sampling days in the Everglades.

As usual, Rolvaag's expression was unreadable.

"Those are two possibilities," the detective said. "Something to think about anyway. Thanks for the pop."

Chaz laughed. "The what?"

"The cold drink," Rolvaag said. "By the way, somebody's staking out your house—some big hairy guy in a minivan, parked down by the corner. The tag comes back to a rental agency."

"Oh?" Chaz thinking: Wait until I tell Red.

"Any ideas?"

Chaz poked his head out the doorway and looked down the street. "I've got no earthly clue who that man is," he lied. "How do you know that it's me he's watching?"

"Wild guess." Rolvaag smiled. "You've got my card. Call if you need anything."

"Right," said Chaz. When goats learn ballet.

He stood at the bay window and watched the prying detective drive away. When the phone began to ring, he almost yanked it out of the living room wall.

What the hell's happening? he wondered dismally. Wasn't I supposed to be home free by now?

Off the hook.

Cruising.

Instead, that goddamn cop is still snooping around, some sadistic perv is sneaking into my house and messing with Joey's stuff—and now I've got to deal with some knuckle-dragger of a bodyguard that Red's dredged out of a sinkhole somewhere.

When Chaz answered the phone, the man named Tool was on the other end.

"That guy that just left?"

"What about him?" Chaz said.

"Want me to go after him?"

"And do what?"

Tool grunted. "I dunno. Bust his spleen."

Chaz sighed. "He's a cop."

"Yeah, so?"

Unbelievable, Chaz thought. "Leave him be, please."

"It's your party," said Tool. "Hey, I gotta go take a dump. You gone be all right?"

"I think I can manage."

Chaz stripped off his clothes and propped himself under a hot shower for twenty minutes. Try as he might, he still couldn't see where he'd made a single mistake in the plan, not one wrong move.

The crime was perfect. It was the rest of the world that was fucking up.

"I lied," Joey Perrone said.

This was after a day of doing largely nothing; swimming, sunning, losing herself in a John D. MacDonald paperback that she'd found in Mick Stranahan's tackle box.

"I lied to you," she said again.

Stranahan didn't look up. He was cracking stone crab claws by whomping them with the flat side of a spoon. It was all in the wrist, he'd explained. Fragments of shell were flying around like shrapnel.

"Lied about what?" he asked.

"About not touching anything in the house when I went back inside to take a pee. There was a stash of pictures in the hall closet."

"Wedding pictures, that sort of thing?"

"Wedding, honeymoon, vacations. All shots of Chaz and me," Joey reported, "in happier times."

"Why were they in a closet?"

"Because my shitheel husband pulled 'em off the wall," she said, "probably within five minutes after he got home from the cruise. I guess he couldn't even stand to look at my face."

Stranahan brushed an orange fleck of crab claw from her cheek. "Tell me what you did."

Joey spun away. "Another glass of wine, sir. Please."

"What did you do with the photos?"

"Not all of them. Just one," she said. "All I did was take it out of the frame and slip it under his pillow."

"Oh Christ," Stranahan said.

"But first I took cuticle scissors—"

"And cut your face out of the picture."

Joey blinked. "How'd you know?"

"No comment."

"Wife or girlfriend?"

"Spouse number three, if memory serves," he said.

She sighed. "Next time I'll try to be more original."

They ate inside, Strom whining for handouts through the screen door. Stranahan was quiet, and Joey began to worry that she'd done something foolhardy, something that might ruin the plan, whatever that was.

Firmly she set down her wineglass. "If you want to yell at me for cutting up that picture, go ahead. Just remember, it's my house, too. My stuff that he's throwing away."

Stranahan said, "There was no car accident in Tampa involving Chaz and a drunk driver."

"How do you know?"

"Checked with the Highway Patrol. There wasn't any lawsuit, either," he said, "according to the court files. And no big settlement, obviously."

"Meaning no nest egg," Joey said quietly.

"Highly unlikely. You want to hear our plan?"

"If it'll cheer me up, sure."

"We're going to blackmail your husband," Stranahan said.

"I see."

"Actually, we're only going to make him *think* he's being blackmailed." Stranahan dipped a jumbo claw into a cup of drawn butter.

"Blackmailed by who?" Joey asked.

"Somebody who knows that Chaz murdered you." Stranahan smiled and took another bite of crab. "Somebody we'll have to invent, of course."

Joey adored the idea even though she didn't entirely get the point.

"Misdirection," he explained. "Chaz is probably freaking out that he's being harassed by some mysterious intruder. I'm assuming you don't want him to figure out it's you, at least not yet. Correct?"

She nodded emphatically.

"No offense," Stranahan said, "but these clever little messages you've left for him—the dress in the closet, the lipstick in the drawer, the photograph under the pillow—those are estranged wife–type moves. Too much of that and he'll put it all together."

"Yeah, you're right."

"So we need to make him believe it's somebody else who's screwing with his head."

"How about somebody who saw him push me off the ship?"

"Now you're talking."

"A secret witness who gets greedy," Joey said eagerly. "That would be cool. But who could we make up, Mick? And how would this imaginary person know how to find Chaz? Wait a minute—how would he get into the house unless he had a key?"

"Whoa, slow down," Stranahan told her. "I've got an idea how to set this up."

"I'll bet you do." Joey Perrone felt better than she had in days, and not just because of the wine.

"But first it would really help to know why Chaz wanted you dead," said Stranahan. "It would open up some creative opportunities, blackmail-wise."

Joey shrugged helplessly. "That's all I think about, night and day."

"Don't worry. We'll figure everything out," he said with a wink. "This might actually be fun."

Ten

Chaz didn't find the photograph under his pillow until Tuesday night, because he'd spent Monday night at Ricca's apartment in self-prescribed sexual therapy. He had blamed Joey's lingering aura for impeding his finale in the bathtub, but leaving the house they shared had failed to solve the problem. Even in Ricca's jasmine-scented bedroom Chaz couldn't shake the image of his dead wife's slinky black dress in the closet, or the wanton memories it conjured.

Ricca had worked on him as deftly as a sculptress, but the results had been unsatisfactory. For the first time in their relationship—in *any* relationship—Chaz had heard that most hollow and dreaded of consolations:

"Don't worry, baby, it happens to everybody."

In a panic he'd dragged Ricca to a nearby music store and purchased a replacement copy of George Thorogood's greatest hits, to no avail. Even digitally remastered, "Bad to the Bone" could not rally Chaz's bone to its usual badness. The gloom of failure followed him all the next day as he drove up and down the levees of the Everglades. It weighed on him still when he returned home, although Rolvaag's visit had offered a brief, though grating, diversion.

Toppling into bed that night, Chaz was emotionally unprepared for yet another ghoulish shock. He stared at the picture and absently poked a finger in the scissored hole where his wife's pretty face had been.

Too vividly he remembered the circumstances of the photograph, which had been taken the previous New Year's Eve at a ski lodge in Steamboat Springs. He and Joey had just emerged from their room after one hour and seventeen minutes of spectacularly rowdy sex. It was the only time Chaz had ever tired before his wife, and he'd signaled breathless surrender by making a T with his hands in the manner of a sacked quarterback. He and Joey were still laughing about it later when they'd handed the camera to the bartender.

Now, hunched over the photo, Chaz should have been worrying about who had retrieved it from the closet and, literally, defaced it. He should have been wondering when the act of venomous mischief had occurred, and how the perpetrator had entered the house without breaking a window or prying a doorjamb. He should have been summoning the hulking hairy bodyguard, Red's goon, to find out if any suspicious persons had been lurking in the neighborhood.

But instead Charles Regis Perrone found himself thinking of that night only four months ago in Colorado, reliving in erotic detail how the woman he fondly once called "my monster blonde" had turned him inside out. Soon Chaz found himself saluted by a formidable hardon, which sent him scampering in unwarranted optimism to the bathroom. There he labored doggedly, his face crimson and contorted, until one and then both of his fists cramped. No relief would be forthcoming.

Chaz glared down at himself and cursed. My cock was never faithful to Joey while she was alive, he thought, so why all of a sudden now? It was crushing to consider that whatever puny conscience he possessed might manifest itself in such a humiliating way.

"I didn't want to kill her!" he shouted at his chafed and shrinking tormentor. "She gave me no choice!"

Chaz tore the photograph to shreds over the toilet bowl. After checking the doors and windows, he gobbled a half dozen Maalox chewables and collapsed on the living room sofa. Tomorrow he'd get the locks changed and call the alarm company and move Joey's jewelry to his personal safe-deposit box at the bank. Afterward he would scour the house one more time until nothing remained of his deceased spouse, not one blond eyelash, to arouse him against his will.

Then, on the way back from the county landfill, he'd stop at Wal-Mart and buy himself a gun.

"You wouldn't happen to have herbal tea, would you?"

"The best I can do is coffee," Karl Rolvaag said.

"Poison," said Rose Jewell with a frown. "No thanks."

She was about forty years old and fearlessly attractive. The detective office had come to a standstill when she'd walked in—white cotton pullover, tight stonewashed jeans, high heels. Her hair was a wattage of blond unknown in Minnesota, the land of blondes. Even Rolvaag was slightly nervous.

"I'm Joey's best friend. *Was* Joey's best friend," Rose said, "and I just want you to know, she would never, ever kill herself. If that's one of your theories."

"It's too early for theories," Rolvaag said, which wasn't true. He was certain that Charles Perrone had pushed his wife off the *Sun Duchess*. He was equally sure that proving it would be impossible without a corpse, evidence or eyewitnesses.

Captain Gallo had thought it interesting that Mrs. Perrone's fingernails were found embedded in a bale of marijuana, but he said it proved only that she'd survived the plunge—not that she had been shoved. Her husband giving the wrong time she'd left their room was suspicious, Gallo agreed, but it wasn't enough on which to file charges.

"And she didn't get bombed and fall off the ship, either," Rose was saying. "I saw that business in the newspaper about her having all that wine—what a bunch of bull! I've never seen Joey drunk, not even *close* to drunk. Not since her DUI."

"How was her marriage?"

"Chaz Perrone was a total slut. He cheated on her all over town."

"Did he ever try with you?" Rolvaag asked, somewhat startled at his own nerve. Perhaps Rose's frankness was contagious.

She smiled and crossed her legs in a way that made the detective feel like a fumbling teenager. "If Chaz ever laid a hand on me," she said sweetly, "I would've kicked him in the raspberries. But no, I never even met the guy."

Rumors of multiple infidelities did not, in Captain Gallo's biased view, automatically make Charles Perrone a murder suspect. In three weeks Rolvaag would be heading back to Minnesota, and it was dismaying to know that his final case in Florida would end in failure—a cold-blooded killer escaping justice. The captain had made it plain that he saw the Perrone investigation as a dead end and that no more time or manpower would be committed.

Often Rolvaag imagined Mrs. Perrone alone in the ocean, clinging so fiercely to that floating bale that the tips of her nails snapped off one by one. The daydream was more haunting for its detail, since Chaz

Perrone had provided a snapshot of his wife to the police and Coast Guard. In the photograph, taken on a beach somewhere, Joey Perrone was dripping wet. The morbid irony had been lost on her husband but not on the detective, who could now envision Chaz's victim—her blond hair slicked back, her cheeks sparkling with beads of water—as she must have looked when she burst to the surface after that long, harrowing fall.

Except for the smile. Joey Perrone would not have been smiling after her husband threw her overboard.

Rolvaag said, "What do you think happened on that cruise, Miss Jewell?"

"I know what *didn't* happen. My friend didn't jump and she didn't fall." Rose stood up and slung her handbag over her shoulder. "I just wanted somebody to know, that's all. I wanted it written down in a file somewhere."

"It will be. I promise."

Rose touched his arm. "Please don't give up on this case," she said, "for Joey's sake."

Rolvaag didn't have the heart to tell her that it would take a miracle for him to nail Charles Perrone.

On the way home, the detective stopped at the downtown branch of the library to read up on the Everglades. It seemed peculiar that a man so openly averse to nature would study biology and then take a job in a humid, teeming swamp. That Perrone didn't even know which way the Gulf Stream flowed betrayed a certain flimsiness in his academics. His ideals were no less murky and suspect. Rolvaag was particularly bothered by Perrone's casual comment about running over snakes with his gas-sucking SUV, and also by the flippant manner with which he'd dismissed the notion of recycling a pop bottle. Was this a guy who cared about the fate of the planet?

How odd that Chaz Perrone had aimed his career toward the study of organic life when he displayed no concern for any other than his own. However, if a clue lay in the sad and complicated story of the Everglades, Rolvaag couldn't find it. Perrone's connection to such inhospitable wilderness remained a riddle, and time was running short.

Driving back to his apartment, Rolvaag recalled his own failed marriage and found it impossible to imagine a scenario under which murder would have been an option. In this exercise the detective felt handicapped by his heritage—Norwegians were natural brooders, not given to the sort of volcanic emotions associated with domestic homicides. But then, Rolvaag hadn't understood the majority of criminals he had sent off to prison, regardless of their crimes. Shooting an ice-cream vendor for thirty-four bucks and change was no more comprehensible to him than launching one's attractive (and, by all accounts, faithful) spouse over the side of a cruise liner.

Why had Perrone done it? Not for money, as there was no insurance payoff, no inheritance, no jackpot whatsoever. And not for love, either—if Chaz had wanted to dump his wife and run off with one of his girlfriends, divorce would have been relatively easy and painless. Florida was a no-fault jurisdiction that dealt perfunctorily with short, childless marriages. Moreover, Mrs. Perrone's substantial personal wealth made her an unlikely candidate for alimony.

Gallo's right, Rolvaag thought. I've got zilch for a motive.

When he arrived home he saw that a newspaper clipping had been slipped under his door. It was the story of a man in St. Louis who had been strangled and then nearly devoured by an enormous pet python, which he had foolishly neglected to feed for several months. The snake's gruesome repast had been interrupted by a concerned neighbor, who scampered for help. Paramedics skilled with the Jaws of Life arrived and retrieved the victim's grossly elongated body, dispatching the sated reptile in the process. Above the headline, in violet ink, was a familiar spidery scrawl: "This should happen to you!"

Rolvaag chuckled, thinking: That makes two people who'll be happy to see me go—Chaz Perrone and Nellie Shulman.

The detective's own two snakes were coiled together in a large glass tank in the corner of the living room. They were not pure white in the way of some albinos, but rather a creamy hue with exotic tangerine saddle marks. In the urban outdoors their unnatural brightness could have been a fatal trait, but the pythons were safe in Rolvaag's apartment. They displayed no gratitude whatsoever, and seldom moved a muscle except to eat or re-position themselves in a shaft of sunlight. Still, Rolvaag enjoyed observing them. That a twerp like Perrone would purposely kill something so primal and perfect angered the detective in a way that surprised him.

He shoved a frozen lasagna into the oven and picked through the papers in his briefcase until he found the scrap he was looking for. He dialed the Hertz office in Boca Raton and identified himself to an assistant night manager, who was exceptionally cooperative. By the time

Rolvaag hung up, he had obtained the name of the hirsute thug in the minivan staking out the Perrone residence, and also the name of the company that was paying for the rental.

Red's Tomato Exchange, whatever *that* was.

Joey Perrone shook Stranahan awake. "Mick, I just thought of something!"

He sat up on the couch and rubbed his eyes. "Time?"

"Five-forty-five."

"This better be good." He reached for the lamp, but she grabbed his arm.

"I'm not dressed," she said.

Even without lights the house wasn't that dark. Joey was wearing a white cutoff T-shirt and bikini-style panties, the sight of which mitigated Stranahan's grumpiness.

"Tell me what you remembered," he said.

"A fight that Chaz and I had about two months ago. I was supposed to fly to L.A. for a wedding but the weather at the airport was horrible, so I turned around and drove home. I won't get on a plane if there's a cloud in the sky."

Joey said she'd walked in and found her husband at the dining room table, entering numbers on a chart. "I was looking over his shoulder and all I said was, 'How do you remember them all?' Because he wasn't using any notes, just jotting down the figures one after another. So it was like, 'Wow, how can you remember them all?' Completely innocent and friendly—and he nearly jumped out of his chair. Went absolutely batshit."

"That's all you said to him?"

"It was the craziest thing. He started screaming, stomping around, waving his arms. Told me to quit spying on him and mind my own damn business," Joey said. "It was just like the day I asked about the new Hummer—only this time he called me the *c* word. That's when I decked him."

"Excellent."

"A right cross to the chops. Chaz isn't exactly tough as nails."

"But you seeing those charts set him off. Do you know what the numbers meant?"

"He never told me. But part of his job is measuring stuff in the water out there, some type of pollution," Joey said. "I'm guessing it had something to do with that."

"You really slugged him?" Stranahan asked.

"Maybe I shouldn't have. Maybe that's what did it, Mick."

"Did what? Make him decide to kill you?"

"Maybe it was too much for his ego."

Stranahan told her not to mistake arrogance for pride. "A guy like Chaz can revive his ego with the palm of his hand."

"Still, I never saw him freak like that before," Joey said.

"It's important. I'm glad you told me."

"Hey, are those genuine Fruit of the Looms?" She reached over and tweaked the waistband.

Stranahan slapped a pillow over his lap. Obviously Mrs. Perrone was overcoming her shyness.

She said, "The sun's almost up. How about a swim?"

"Ha-ha."

"Three laps around the island. Come on, I'm serious."

"I thought you were terrified of sharks," he said.

"Not if there's two of us in the water."

"And one of us is old and slow. I get the picture."

"Oh, don't be such a pussy," Joey said.

"Excuse me?"

But off she ran, barefoot in her underwear. Stranahan heard the bang of the screen door, followed by a splash. When he reached the dock, there was nothing to do but dive in and try to catch up. Strom watched quizzically but made no move to join them.

Halfway around the island, Joey said, "You're in pretty good shape for a geezer."

Stranahan stopped midstroke and treaded water.

"What's wrong?" she called out.

Ominously he pointed at the waves beyond her. Joey spotted the three gray dorsals cutting the surface and let out a shriek. She kicked backward, straight into Mick's arms.

"Don't slug me," he whispered after a few moments, "but those are just dolphins."

Slowly she exhaled, blinking the salt from her eyes. "So this is how you get your thrills," she said.

"I'm fairly harmless. You can ask around."

The dolphins rolled away, and Stranahan lost sight of them in the sun's glare. Joey kept her arms around his neck, which surprised him.

"That was pretty wild," she conceded. "Better than the Seaquarium."

"I see them playing out here all the time. You want to keep going?"

"You mean with the swimming, or the groping?"

"I'm not groping," Stranahan said, "I'm trying to keep us afloat."

"Your hand is on my ass."

"Technically that's a thigh, and it's the easiest place to get a grip."

"Oh, nice," she said. "How much do you think I weigh?"

"Not with a gun to my head would I answer that question." He ducked out of her grasp and pushed away.

"A hundred and thirty-one pounds," Joey announced, smoothing the water from her hair. "But I'm tall. Almost five ten."

"You look terrific," he said. "So shut up and let's swim. This was your brilliant idea, remember?"

Forty-five minutes later they were dry and dressed. He was fixing waffles and she was brewing coffee and the dog was baying at a boat full of snapper fishermen drifting past the island.

Joey said, "Tell me more about the blackmail plan."

"Oh, that reminds me." He left the kitchen for a minute and returned with the cell phone, which he handed to her. "Dial your house."

"No way!"

"You don't have to talk to him. Just dial the number and give me the phone."

"He's got caller ID. He'll see your name," Joey said.

"Then do star sixty-seven to block it."

"Mick, what are you going to say to him?"

"Just do it, please."

"Aye, aye, sir."

Stranahan wedged the receiver under one ear as he tended to the waffles. He spoke in a stage voice that caused Joey to stifle a giggle.

"Is this Charles Perrone? Chaz, we don't know each other yet, but soon you'll be giving me a shockingly large sum of money. . . . No, this isn't the cable company. This is the person who saw you push your lovely wife off the *Sun Duchess* last Friday night. . . . That's correct. At eleven p.m. sharp, in a drizzling rain. You grabbed her by the ankles and chucked her overboard. Chaz, you still there? Oh, Cha-az?"

Joey applauded after Mick hung up. "That was Charlton Heston you were doing, right? Back in college we got stoned one night and watched *The Ten Commandments* and *Planet of the Apes* back-to-back."

Stranahan said, "I believe I've ruined your husband's morning."

"What'd he say?"

"At first he thought I was trying to sell him digital Pay-per-View. Then he accused me of being somebody named Rolvad or Rolvag, playing a sick trick on him. Toward the end it was more of a gurgle, really. Like he'd swallowed some bleach."

"What you just did, is that legal?" Joey asked.

"Possibly not. I'll run it by Father Rourke the next time I go to confession."

"You certainly seem to be enjoying yourself."

"Chaz deserved a hot little rocket up the ass."

"Well, I admire your style."

"Now, please tell me again," Stranahan said, "why you married a jerkoff like that."

Joey's smile evaporated. "You'd never understand."

"It's also none of my business, I admit."

"No, I'll tell you why. Because three guys in a row had dumped me for somebody else, okay? Because Chaz sent a single long-stemmed pink rose to my house every day for two weeks after our first date. Because he wrote me mushy notes and called me when he promised and took me out for romantic dinners. I was lonely, and obviously he was a pro at that sort of thing," Joey said. "And I said yes the second time he asked me to marry him, because honestly I didn't want to get dumped again. By the way, this is an unbelievably humiliating subject."

Stranahan said, "For God's sake, you're not the first woman to get conned. But then once you realized it was a mistake—"

"Why did I stay married to him? Mick, it was only two years," she said, "and not all of it was horrible. Let me try to explain this without sounding like a bubblehead—Chaz was good in bed, and I confess there were times when that canceled out his less admirable qualities."

"I understand perfectly," Stranahan said. "Hell, that's the story of my life." He stacked three waffles on her plate. "Several of my worst marriages were based on dumb lust and not much else. You hungry?"

Joey nodded.

"Me, too," Stranahan said. "Maple syrup, butter, or both?"

"The works."

"Thattagirl."

They were interrupted by Strom yelping in pain. Stranahan ran outside, with Joey close behind. The dog lay at the end of the dock, pawing at an angry knot on his snout. Joey sat down and pulled the whimpering animal onto her lap.

In the water, no more than a hundred feet away, was the boat with the snapper fishermen; four of them, chuckling as they pretended to tend their baits. Stranahan spotted an egg-shaped piece of lead on the dock, and slowly he bent to pick it up.

"What's that?" Joey said.

"Two-ounce sinker."

"Oh no."

Stranahan called out to the men in the boat. "Did you guys throw this at my dog?"

The fishermen glanced over, murmuring among themselves, until finally the largest one piped up: "Damn thing wouldn't shut up, bro."

Bro? Stranahan thought. So that's what I'm dealing with. "Come over here," he said. "We need to talk."

"Go fuck yourself!" shouted another of the fishermen, a smaller version of the first. "And your *puta* girlfriend too." Defiantly he swung back his fishing rod and cast a heavy yellow jig at the dock. It landed short, making a hollow *plonk* in the water.

Stranahan said to Joey: "Please take Strom inside the house."

"Why? What're you going to do?"

"Go."

"No way am I leaving you alone out here with those morons."

"I won't be alone," he said.

Stranahan counted three separate breaches of etiquette for which the fishermen deserved rebuke. The first was the casual manner in which they'd violated his privacy by coming so close to the island. The second was their contemptible assault on a rather dull-witted beast that was merely doing its job. The third was the coarse insult directed at Joey Perrone, who had done nothing to provoke it.

From the kitchen window, Joey could see the boat motoring toward the dock, all four of the fishermen now standing in anticipation of a fight. Stranahan disappeared briefly inside the shed. He emerged with what he later would identify as a Ruger Mini-14, a semi-automatic rifle of formidable caliber.

The intruders' boat was equipped with a ninety-horsepower Mercury outboard, into which Stranahan methodically fired three rounds. The men could be seen throwing their arms high in frantic gestures of surrender, and their fearful pleas were audible to Joey even through the closed windows. She couldn't make out Stranahan's precise instructions, but the fishermen dropped to their knees, leaned over the gunwales and began paddling with their arms. The visual effect was that of an addled centipede in a toilet bowl.

Joey tied Strom's leash to a leg of the kitchen table and hurried outside. Stranahan stood with the rifle on one shoulder as he watched the boat laboring crazily toward the mainland.

"So, that's your gun," Joey said.

"Yes, ma'am."

"I'm impressed."

"They were, too."

"What you did just now, was it legal?"

Mick Stranahan turned to look at her. "Please don't ask me that question again."

Eleven

Tool twisted the AC knob to maximum high and it still felt like a hundred damn degrees inside the minivan. American-made, too, which he thought was disgraceful. Florida, of all places, you don't rent out vehicles with cheap-ass air conditioners.

Not even nine in the morning and already Tool was sweating off the fentanyl patches. To cool down, he removed his boots and overalls, then chugged a liter of Mountain Dew that he'd picked up at the Circle K on Powerline. Fiddling with the radio, he miraculously located a decent country station. Shania Twain was singing about how much fun it was to be a woman, though Tool couldn't see how that could be true. Just about every female he'd ever known, starting with his mother, seemed perpetually pissed off at the human race. Or could be it was just me in particular, Tool thought.

At half-past nine, the man he was bodyguarding emerged from the house and hurried up the street toward the minivan. Up close he looked shiny and clean-cut—awful damn young to be a widower, Tool mused. You couldn't help but wonder what had happened to the guy's old lady.

Charles Perrone motioned him to roll down the window. "Have you seen anybody strange hanging around?"

"Whole goddamn place is strange, you want my opinion," Tool said. "But no, I ain't seen nobody ain't supposed to be here."

"You sure? Because I think they got into my house again."

"Not while I was here they didn't."

The man looked as if he hadn't slept all night. "Somebody mutilated one of my favorite pictures," he said.

Tool was skeptical. "You want, I'll follow you to work and hang close today. Just in case."

Charles Perrone said he wasn't going to work. "How come you're not wearing any clothes?" he asked Tool.

" 'Cause inside this van it's hotter'n a elephant fart. Hey, Red says you're a doctor."

Charles Perrone seemed pleased. "That's right."

Tool pivoted his immense mass to display the two remaining patches on his back. "Can you get me some more a these?" he asked.

The doctor seemed put off by the damp wall of flesh before him.

"Stick-ons," Tool said. "They's medicine."

"I know, but—"

"Duragesic's the brand name. Can you write me a scrip?"

"No, I'm afraid not," Charles Perrone said.

"It's for super bad pain," Tool explained. "See, there's this bullet slug up the crack a my ass—I'm dead serious."

Charles Perrone blanched and stepped back from the minivan. "Sorry. I don't do prescriptions."

"Now hold on a second."

"I'm not that kind of doctor." He spun around and strode back to his house at an accelerated pace.

Tool grunted. That's one lame-ass quack, he can't even write scrips.

Two doors down, a middle-aged woman in a yellow linen robe came outside, leading two small animals on leashes. Tool guessed that they were dogs, although they resembled none he'd ever seen. Their roundish wrinkled faces were flattened, as if they'd run full bore into a cement truck. The woman herself had a fairly spooky mug, all slick and stretched out like a Halloween mask that was too small for her head. Tool was treated to a close-up view as she walked the strange pinch-faced dogs down the sidewalk. The woman must not have spotted him inside the minivan, for she nonchalantly allowed her critters to pee all over the right front tire.

Tool's instant response was to punch out the passenger window, raining glass upon the woman's sandaled feet. She bleated in fear as he stuck his head out the window and instructed her in the crudest terms to clean up the damn mess.

"What!" She yanked the dogs away from the van and gathered them into her arms. "Just who do you think you are, mister?"

"I'm the sumbitch gonna butt-fuck those puppies, you don't clean the piss off my tar."

He cracked the door enough for the woman to see all she needed. In a heartbeat she was on her knees, furiously dabbing at the wet tire with a wad of pink tissue while her pets whined and scrapped nearby.

When she was finished, Tool said, "I didn't hear no 'pology."

The woman made a spiteful sound and her cheeks turned red, yet her expression never changed. The skin from her forehead to her chin was so tight and glossy that Tool wondered if she might split open like a bad mango.

"Beat it," he said, and she did, sandals slapping in retreat. The accordion-faced dogs could barely keep up.

Minutes later, the doctor reappeared.

"What did you do to Mrs. Raguso?" he demanded.

"She let her damn mutts take a leak on my tar!" Tool protested. "I thought this was 'posed to be a class neighborhood, what they call 'upscale.' Hell, I live in a trailer and I wouldn't let *my* dogs pee on summon else's personal vee-hicle."

Charles Perrone said, "You'd better get out of here. Carmen Raguso is probably calling the police right this minute."

"What for? She's the one started it."

"You flashed her! I was watching from the living room." Charles Perrone had got himself quite worked up. "I don't want to deal with any more cops, you understand? Now hurry up, before she gets your license tag."

"But who's gonna watch your house?"

"Just keep driving," Charles Perrone said, "until you hear from Mr. Hammernut. He'll tell you what to do next."

"Shit," said Tool, and started backing down the street. At the corner he wheeled the minivan around, then shot forward at high speed toward the exit of West Boca Dunes Phase II. More than an hour passed before the cell phone rang, but by then Tool had scored two more fatality markers from the grass median of the Sawgrass Expressway. The flowers had rotted down to the ribbons, yet the crosses themselves were in mint condition. Consequently, Tool's outlook was much improved by the time Red Hammernut called.

"On this bodyguard thing," Red said, "the trick is, you gotta blend in."

"I never been too good at that."

"Okay. Lemme work up another plan."

"Meantime, can I swap out the minivan?" Tool asked.

"By all means."

"Get me somethin' with a decent AC."

"You bet."

"By the way, your boy ain't much of a doctor."

Red Hammernut chuckled. "Don't you dare tell a soul."

Mick Stranahan and Joey Perrone were surprised to see Chaz's yellow Humvee when they came around the corner at ten-thirty.

"Guess who's taking a sick day," Joey said.

Stranahan positioned the Suburban in the driveway of the fugitive telemarketers, same as the last time. Moments later, a panel truck turned onto the street and drove past the Perrone house, then braked, reversed and pulled in beside the Hummer. Painted in red lettering on the sides of the truck: SUNSHINE LOCKSMITH.

"Damn," Stranahan said. "He's changing the locks."

"So what?"

"So the spare key in the bird feeder won't fit."

Joey raised an eyebrow. "Wait and see."

Soon another truck appeared. It was a small white pickup with magnetic signs on the doors: GOLD COAST SECURITY SYSTEMS.

"Now what?" Stranahan grumbled.

"He's reconnecting the alarm."

"Terrific."

"Would you please stop worrying?" Joey said.

"Just so you know, I'm not keen on B-and-E's."

"Translation?"

"Break-ins. They're messy," Stranahan said, "and very hard to explain if the cops show up. Are your window screens wired?"

"No, but there are motion detectors in the hallway and bedrooms. I suppose Chaz could put in more, depending on how spooked he is."

"I would say plenty spooked," said Stranahan, "based on what we're seeing."

"It was your phone call, Mick. The Moses impersonation."

"Let's not forget the snapshot under his pillow."

"Oh yeah." Joey would have given anything to see her husband's face when he found it.

By noon the locksmith and the alarm technician were gone, but Charles Perrone hadn't come out of the house. Joey was restless, ready to roll. She had tucked her hair under a Marlins cap and costumed herself in long pants and a loose-fitting work shirt. Instead of a Bible, her prop this time was a toolbox. Someone watching her come down the sidewalk might have mistaken her for a man, because of her height and long athletic stride.

"What if he's really sick in bed?" she said.

Stranahan was scanning the place with the binoculars. "Give him one more hour."

A blue car turned the corner and approached the Perrone residence. It was the Ford compact belonging to the woman with the kelly-green pubic hair.

Joey groaned. "You've got to be kidding."

"Take it easy, now."

"What, he can't even make it past lunch without getting his rocks hauled?"

Stranahan said, "Looks like she's not going in."

Two short honks came from the Ford, then the front door of the house opened. Out came Charles Perrone, carrying a brown paper bag.

"See that golf shirt he's wearing? I gave him that for his birthday," Joey said. "New set of irons, too."

Chaz got in on the passenger side and the blue car pulled away. Joey noted that the woman was wearing large Jackie Onassis–style sunglasses—"probably so she won't be recognized from her porno flicks."

Stranahan advised Joey to stay focused on her no-good husband. "What do you want to do?"

"I want to go back in the house. *My* house."

"But how?"

"Wait here," she said, "until you see the sprinklers come on."

Stranahan touched her wrist. "The second the alarm goes off, I'm rolling. Be sure to come out the front door, not the back, then walk very calmly to the street."

"Mick, don't you dare leave me stranded here. That would really suck."

"Come to think of it, I still owe you one."

"Not the stolen boat thing again." Joey sighed as she hopped out of the Suburban. "How many times did I say I was sorry? Like a dozen?"

Stranahan had been underestimating women for about forty years, so he was not flabbergasted to see the lawn sprinklers bloom at the former residence of Joey Perrone. He would have congratulated her merely for getting past the new locks; that she'd also thwarted the security alarm was truly impressive.

When she met him at the door, he asked, "Were you a burglar in a previous life?"

"No, a wife," Joey said. "Chaz hid the new key in the same bird feeder, just like I knew he would."

"Because . . ."

"See, it was his idea the first time. He was so proud of himself, thought he was so darn clever. And since I'm the only other person who knew about the hiding place—"

"And he thinks you're dead—"

"Exactly. Why not hide it there again?" she said. "He probably figures that whoever snuck into the house scored the old key from our cleaning service, or maybe the guy who does the aquarium."

"Okay, but how'd you disarm the alarm?"

"Now, Mick, put on your thinking cap."

He grinned. "Don't tell me Chaz used the same keypad code as before."

"Yup," Joey said. "Two, twenty-one, seventy-two."

"Sounds like a birthday."

"Bingo. I knew he'd be too lazy to make up a new sequence."

"Still, that's quite a gamble you took," Stranahan said.

"Not really. Not knowing him the way I do."

They sat in the dining room, Chaz's mud-smeared backpack on the table. Joey said she'd once bought him a nice leather briefcase, but he had told her it was impractical for working in a swamp. Stranahan unfastened the backpack's many buckles and zippers and emptied the contents pocket by pocket: a sheath of loose papers and charts, a handful of mechanical pencils, two aerosol cans of insect spray, a snakebite kit, tape and gauze, a pair of heavy cotton socks, canvas gloves, rubberized gloves, chlorine tablets, a tube of antibiotic ointment, a rolled-up Danish skin magazine, a bag of stale chocolate doughnuts, a pound of trail mix and a plastic bottle of Maalox tablets.

"Your husband has a nervous tummy. That could be helpful," Stranahan said.

Joey leafed through the papers. "This is the same kind of stuff he was working on the day he got so mad at me."

"You were right. They're charts for water samples." Stranahan removed a blank form, folded it up and slipped it in the pocket of his Florida Power & Light shirt.

"That's all we're taking?" she asked.

"For now, yes."

He carefully replaced each of the other items in the backpack. "That was a nice little bonus. Now—where does Squire Perrone hide his checkbook?"

"Be right back." Joey disappeared down the hallway, and returned carrying at arm's length a crusty, soiled sneaker. "Never been washed," she reported distastefully.

A clever idea, Stranahan had to admit. Even the most desperate of thieves avoid rancid footwear. Joey turned the shoe upside down and the checkbook dropped out. Flipping through the register, Stranahan found no unusual transactions; the only deposits were Chaz Perrone's bimonthly paychecks from the state of Florida.

"When did you say he bought the Hummer?" Stranahan asked Joey.

"Middle of January."

"There's nothing here, not even a down payment."

"Maybe he's got another account I don't know about," she said.

Or maybe he didn't pay for the Hummer himself, Stranahan thought. "What about Chaz's so-called nest egg?" he asked.

Joey shook her head weakly. "Stocks and bonds?"

"Then he should get brokerage statements in the mail."

Joey admitted that she'd never seen any. Stranahan stood up and said it was time to go, before Chaz returned with his lady friend.

"Wait. Let's leave him another present." Joey was eyeing one of her husband's umbrellas, which was leaning in a corner.

"Absolutely not," Stranahan said.

"Mick, come on."

"He's already a nervous wreck, I assure you."

Joey feigned a pout as she followed him to the door. "At least can I leave the sprinklers running?"

"Is the timer box outside?"

She nodded. "On the wall outside the utility room. He'll have no reason to think that we actually got into the house."

"Then, sure, what the hell," Stranahan said. "If it makes you feel better."

"It'll do for now," said Joey, and reset the alarm.

Ricca remarked that Chaz looked dreadful.

"I didn't sleep much," he mumbled.

"That's because *I* wasn't there to tire you out."

"Some crank called first thing this morning."

"A breather?" Ricca asked. "I get those all the time."

"No. Just a crank." Thinking about the mystery phone call, Chaz felt his palms go damp.

Ricca asked if he had given any more thought to holding a memorial service for Joey.

"What is it with you?" he said irritably. "I already told you I hate funerals. Light a goddamn candle if it makes you feel better."

Ricca said, "Doesn't have to be a major production. Rent a chapel, get the priest to say a few words. Maybe some of Joey's friends would like to share their feelings, too."

Chaz stared out the window.

"It's important, baby," she said. "For closure."

He exhaled scornfully, blowing invisible smoke rings.

"One chapter of your life has ended," Ricca went on, "and another is just beginning."

Jesus, Chaz thought. She's about as subtle as a double hernia.

"Besides, it'll look bad if you don't do *something* in Joey's memory. It'll look like you don't even care that she's dead."

Ricca had a point. Eventually he might have to stage a service for the sake of appearances. He was surprised that Detective Rolvaag hadn't called him on *that*, too.

The crooked, blackmailing sonofabitch. It had to be him, the voice on the phone.

"Chaz, are you listening to me?" Ricca said.

"Do I have a choice?"

She made a sad-sounding noise. "Baby, I'm just trying to be here for you."

Right, thought Chaz. Here, there and everywhere.

He said, "Maybe I'll arrange a memorial for later. In a couple weeks." Thinking: After all this heavy-duty shit is behind me.

Ricca remained in the car while he went inside the bank. Later, at lunch, she got around to asking what was in the paper bag.

"It was jewelry," Chaz said. "I was putting it in a safe box."

"Your wife's jewelry?"

"No, Liz Taylor's. She asked me to hold it for her."

"Don't have to get snotty," Ricca said.

Chaz mustered an apology. "I've got a jillion things on my mind."

"You wanna stop over my place for a fashion show? I just got a new box of thongs from Rio."

"Not today, sweetie. I've got to haul a major load of trash out to the county landfill."

Ricca froze, a forkful of linguini halfway to her mouth. "Let me get this straight: You'd rather go to a garbage dump than get laid?"

Chaz said, "Come on. It's not that simple."

At least he hoped it wasn't.

Twelve

On the drive back to Miami, Joey started thinking about the last time she and her husband had had sex—in their cabin aboard the *Sun Duchess*, less than five hours before he tossed her overboard. She couldn't recall that Chaz had behaved any differently in bed; his performance had been typically voracious and unflagging. It infuriated her to think he could have enjoyed himself with such abandon, knowing that before midnight he would murder his partner in pleasure.

"I need you to explain something about men," she said to Mick Stranahan, "because I truly don't understand."

"Fire away."

"Chaz and I did it on the ship while we were getting ready for dinner. This is the night he tried to murder me!"

"As if everything was hunky-dory."

"Exactly," Joey said. "How could he even get it up?"

"I believe it's called 'compartmentalizing.' "

"And you've done this yourself?"

"On rare occasions," Stranahan said.

"Examples, please."

He answered hesitantly. "Well . . . there was one time I made love to a woman forty-five minutes before I moved out."

"And you knew you were leaving?"

"Yep. I'd already rented my own place."

"And she had no clue? None whatsoever?"

"Evidently not," Stranahan said, "judging by her reaction."

Joey was watching him closely. "Well? Don't stop now. Going to bed—was that your idea or hers?"

"They say it relieves stress, and God knows I was stressed."

"Oh please," she said. "You just wanted one last taste."

"I suppose that's possible."

"Men are such slugs."

Stranahan kept his eyes on the traffic. "For what it's worth, I would never toss a woman off a ship after having wild sex with her. Or even tame sex."

"Spoken like a true gentleman."

"And may I submit that your husband—"

"Don't call him that anymore. Please."

"All right," Stranahan said. "May I submit that Chaz is light-years beneath common male slugdom. He is one coldhearted prick, and let's not forget it."

Wearily, Joey slid down in the seat. "What's it called when you start hating yourself?"

"A waste of energy."

"No. Self-loathing, I think. All these questions keep banging around my head. *What the hell were you thinking, Joey? Why didn't you see through this guy? How come you put up with all his whoring around?* Mick, we're talking about a serious deficiency of self-esteem here."

She felt a hand lightly brush one of her cheeks. He was checking for tears. "Don't worry," she said, "I'm so over that."

"Figure we've got almost one healthy ego between us. That ought to be enough."

"Why are you helping me?" Joey heard herself ask.

"Because I miss chasing after guys like Chaz. It was the best part of my job, sending shitheads up the river."

"You're not just trying to get in my pants?"

Stranahan drummed his fingers on the steering wheel. "You know, I'd be just fine if you didn't keep bringing up the subject."

"God, I'm starved. Let's grab something to eat."

"We'll be home in an hour," he said.

Joey didn't argue. She knew how much Mick hated the city.

"Sometimes I think about killing Chaz. Seriously," she admitted. "Last night I dreamed I beat him to death with one of his umbrellas. Is that crazy?"

Stranahan said she'd be crazy not to feel angry. "But this is a much smarter way of dealing with it. With any luck, neither of us will end up in prison or the nuthouse."

"Did we really accomplish anything today? I mean, besides watering the lawn."

"Definitely." Stranahan patted his breast pocket. "The chart I took from Chaz's backpack is used for recording phosphorus levels at water-sampling stations. Those were probably the numbers he was writing down that day he wigged out on you."

"Phosphorus—is that the same as phosphate?" Joey asked. "Like in fertilizer."

"Yes indeed."

"Not good for the Everglades."

"Not according to what I've read, no," Stranahan said.

Joey was struggling to make it all fit. "Okay, say Chaz was slacking at work. Instead of schlepping out to the boonies, he sneaks off to play golf. Later he cooks up a bogus water chart to fool his boss."

"Sounds like our boy."

"Then I come home unexpectedly, ask one innocent question," Joey said, "and he's so paranoid that he thinks I've figured out the whole scam. Caught him red-handed."

"And then he loses it."

"Yeah, but hold on. Do you really believe he tried to kill me over *that*? Over fertilizer?"

"I'm not saying this is the whole answer. It's just a piece of the puzzle," Stranahan said.

Joey was skeptical. It seemed entirely possible that Chaz's tantrum two months ago had nothing to do with what had happened last week on the cruise ship. Even if he'd been fudging some scientific data, the guy wasn't exactly trading in atomic secrets.

She said, "Before this is over, I want a one-on-one with him. Can you make that happen?"

"Joey, it all depends."

When they got to Dinner Key, Stranahan parked the Suburban next to the old Cordoba under the ficus tree. A chilly rain started falling as they reached the skiff, and they shared a poncho on the choppy ride out to the island.

Karl Rolvaag drove north on U.S. 27, the glistening sedge of the Everglades giving way to cane fields as far as he could see. At Lake Okeechobee the detective headed west on State Road 80, toward the town of LaBelle. He was taking his time, enjoying the wide-open drive. The flat farmlands checkered in shades of green reminded him of western Minnesota in the summer.

The address of Red's Tomato Exchange turned out to be the same as that of Hammernut Farms. Rolvaag followed a straight gravel road for a half mile until it dead-ended at a modern brick complex that belonged in a suburban office park. The receptionist peered at Rolvaag's badge, made a quiet call and then offered him coffee, soda or lemonade. A woman identifying herself as Mr. Hammernut's "executive assistant" appeared and led the detective to a conference room overlooking a stagnant though perfectly circular pond. On the paneled walls of the room were framed photographs of governors, congressmen, Norman Schwarzkopf, Nancy Reagan, Bill Clinton, the three Bushes and even Jesse Helms—each posing with a shorter, reddish-haired man, whom Rolvaag assumed to be Samuel Johnson Hammernut. Undoubtedly the pictures were displayed to remind Hammernut's guests that they were dealing with a heavy hitter. From his own hasty Internet research, Rolvaag had learned that Hammernut's enterprises extended well beyond Florida; soybeans in Arkansas, peanuts in Georgia, cotton in South Carolina. Plainly he made important friends wherever he chose to do business. He'd also gotten into occasional trouble for brutal labor practices and a casual disregard for pollution laws. That he had skated away with only comical fines was hardly surprising to Rolvaag, considering Hammernut's deep-pocket connections with both political parties.

"Call me Red," he said after a sniffling and somewhat unimposing entrance. "Damn allergies get me every spring. What can I do you for?"

The detective told Hammernut about the unusual man in the minivan at West Boca Dunes Phase II. "The license tag came back to a Hertz agency. They said the rental was billed to a corporate credit card—Red's Tomato Exchange."

Hammernut nodded. "I own that company, yessir. And half a dozen others."

"You know a person named Earl Edward O'Toole?"

"Not off the toppa my head. Did he say he worked for me?"

"I didn't speak with him personally, but I got a good look. He's a very distinctive individual," Rolvaag said.

"How so?"

"Sizewise."

"We hire lotsa large fellas out here. Lemme ask Lisbeth." Hammernut leaned across the table and poked a button on the speaker phone. "Lisbeth, we got anybody on the payroll name of Earl Edward"—he turned back to Rolvaag—"what was it again?"

"O'Toole. That's what was on the car-rental contract."

"O'Toole," Hammernut repeated for Lisbeth, who said she would check. Less than a minute later the phone buzzed. This time Hammernut turned off the speaker and snatched up the receiver.

"Hmmm. Okay, yeah, I think I 'member him. Thank you, darlin'."

The detective opened his notebook and waited.

Hammernut hung up and said, "That big ole boy used to be a crew boss round here, but not for some time. I don't know how he come to get hold of that credit card, but I aim to find out."

"Do you know where he works now?"

"Nope. Lisbeth says he left on account of medical problems," Hammernut said. "It's hard, runnin' a crew. Maybe he just got broke-down and wore-out."

Rolvaag went through the motions of scribbling in his notebook. "Can you think of any reason Mr. O'Toole was hanging around that particular neighborhood in Boca? He didn't hurt anybody, but still it's a matter of concern for some of the residents—you can understand."

"Oh hell yes," Red Hammernut said. "If he's the same ol' boy I'm thinkin' of, he could scare hot piss out of an igloo."

Rolvaag managed a chuckle. "Mind if I take a look at his personnel file?"

"What file? Ha!" Hammernut roared. "We got, like, index cards. Half these fellas, we're lucky they cop to their real names. That's a problem with your itinerant labor."

The detective nodded commiseratively. "You'd tell me, I'm sure, if your records showed that Mr. O'Toole had a history of violence or mental instability."

Hammernut sneezed and groped in his pockets for a handkerchief. "Psychos ain't much use on a farm operation like mine. Somebody turns out to be a goony bird, he don't last long."

"But you get all kinds, I bet," Rolvaag said.

"You say this boy hasn't hurt nobody, right? I'm curious how come you drove all the way from Broward County to check up on him. Is he what you call 'under investigation'?"

The detective had no intention of telling Red Hammernut the truth—that he was fishing for leads in a possible homicide; that he had nothing better to do than track down some dumb gorilla who seemed to be surveilling his prime suspect; that he needed an excuse to get out of the office anyway, before Captain Gallo tossed a new case in his lap.

"No, but you're right. Normally this is worth a phone call," Rolvaag said, "or even a fax. But some of the folks who live in that neighborhood where Mr. O'Toole was seen . . . how can I put this? They've been very loyal supporters of our sheriff—"

"Meaning they give serious bucks to his re-election campaigns," Hammernut cut in, "so when they got a problem, the sheriff, he takes a personal interest. Right?"

"I'm glad you understand." Rolvaag let his gaze wander appreciatively across the photographs on the wall. "I had a feeling you would."

Hammernut smiled sagely. "Works the same way everywhere, don't it? Politics, I mean."

The detective smiled back. "Anyway, I'm supposed to make sure this O'Toole character isn't some sort of serial killer waiting to pounce on unsuspecting Republican housewives."

Another cataclysmic sneeze erupted from Hammernut, who swabbed daintily at his florid nose. "You go on home and tell your sheriff not to worry about ol' Earl Edward whatever. He won't bother nobody. I'll see to it."

Rolvaag put away his notebook and rose to leave. He considered tossing out the name of Charles Perrone to see what reaction it might elicit, but he changed his mind. Red Hammernut was too sharp to admit having a connection to the scientist, if there was one.

The detective said, "You can prosecute Mr. O'Toole for using that credit card."

"I could do that. I could also get him some, whatchacallit, private counselin'." Red Hammernut winked. "Big and hairy as he is, I got some boys even bigger and hairier. Know what I mean?"

The detective had not mentioned O'Toole's startling pelt, which meant that Hammernut plainly remembered the man more clearly than he'd let on.

At the door, the bantam tycoon slapped a hand on Rolvaag's shoulder and asked if he wanted to take home a crate of fresh-picked escarole. Rolvaag said leafy greens gave him indigestion, but he thanked Hammernut just the same.

Driving back toward the highway, the detective swerved to miss a baby snake that was sunning itself on the gravel. It was a speckled king, the size of a child's necklace, and right away the detective noticed it was grossly deformed. The snake had been born with only one eye, and on the ebony tip of its nose was a growth the size of an acorn. Rolvaag knew it probably wouldn't survive much longer, but he released it in a nearby grove anyway.

Thinking: Poor little guy. What a lousy roll of the dice he got.

Red Hammernut remembered the day he first met Charles Perrone. Lisbeth had fluttered into his office, saying there was a young man wanting to see him about a job; a persistent young man, she'd said, wouldn't speak to anybody but the boss himself. Red Hammernut's first impulse was to call security and have the impertinent punk heaved off the property, but then he glanced at the man's résumé and said what the hell, give him five minutes. Red Hammernut was curious to know why anybody with a master's degree in marine biology was so keen on working for a vegetable farm.

Chaz Perrone walked in wearing a blue blazer, tan trousers and a club tie. He pumped Red Hammernut's hand, installed himself on the other side of the desk and started yakking like he was pushing time-shares. His cockiness was so annoying that Red Hammernut couldn't help interrupting now and then with a belch, but after a while the young man started making a certain amount of sense.

Perrone opened a file and took out a recent newspaper clipping that Red glumly recognized, the headline reading LOCAL FARM CITED AS GLADES POLLUTER. The article was about a series of water samples taken downstream from Red Hammernut's vegetable operation. Phosphorus had been measured in suspension at 302 parts per billion, nearly thirty times higher than the legal limit for runoff into the Everglades. By itself, Hammernut Farms was flushing more fertilizer per gallon into South Florida's water than the state's largest cattle ranch and sugarcane grower combined, an act of pollution so egregious that even Red Hammernut's powerful cronies in Washington dared not intercede.

It was Chaz Perrone's opinion that Hammernut Farms would continue to face harsh scrutiny from regulatory agencies as well as the news media, which is why he was generously offering his services as an environmental consultant. When Red Hammernut pointed out that Perrone had no background whatsoever in agricultural waste treatment, Chaz replied that he was a quick learner. He described his experience defending his current employer, a renowned cosmetics firm, against charges that their products contained carcinogens and industrial corrosives. Proudly he recalled the time that his testimony had cast critical doubt upon that of a female plaintiff whose cheek-bones had mysteriously delaminated after an application of designer blush. Chaz asserted it was important for corporations to have their own experts, people who could credibly challenge accusers on points of science, or at least muddle the debate.

Red Hammernut liked Chaz Perrone's attitude. It was a pleasure to encounter a young biologist so unfettered by idealism, so unabashedly sympathetic to the needs of private enterprise. Morever, Chaz wasn't nerdy and soft-spoken like some of the scientists Red Hammernut had hired in the past. He was sharp-looking and glib, and would come across credibly on TV. Unfortunately, a master's degree in sea lice wouldn't cut it. "You need a Ph.D. on swamps and such," Red Hammernut had informed Chaz, "else these enviros gonna eat you for breakfast."

And so it unfolded that Charles Regis Perrone was enrolled in a doctoral program at Duke University's Wetland Center. His improba-ble acceptance at such a lofty institution coincided with a substantial cash endowment from Mr. S. J. Hammernut, who also happened to be paying Chaz's tuition. Red Hammernut guessed correctly that, being in the heart of tobacco country, Duke would have no qualms about accepting phosphorus-tainted farm dollars.

Unlike during his stay at the University of Miami, Chaz Perrone required no whip cracking on his quest for a Ph.D. Although he didn't distinguish himself academically at Duke, he didn't embarrass himself, either. This time he was self-motivated; this time he smelled real money down the line. Upon graduation he expected to be presented with a lucrative consulting contract for Hammernut Farms, but Red had other plans. After pulling a few strings, he'd landed Chaz a gig as a state biologist, testing water purity in a particular sector of the Everglades Agricultural Area. The young biologist was profoundly disappointed, but Red assured him that a six-figure position (and an air-conditioned office) awaited—if he proved himself in the field.

And that Chaz was doing. Less than six weeks after he took the job, phosphorus levels in the runoff from Hammernut Farms were recorded at 150 parts per billion, a startling reduction of more than 50 percent. Two months later, the figure dropped to 78 ppb. Six months after that, field surveys showed the phosphorus discharge holding steady at about 9 ppb, a level so low that regulators removed Hammernut Farms from their target list of outlaw polluters. The local Sierra Club even gave a plaque to Red Hammernut, and planted a cypress seedling in his honor.

Red was pleased by the positive publicity, and he was glad to get those goddamn tree-huggers off his case. More important to the bottom line, however, was that the fictitious phosphorus readings allowed Red Hammernut to escape the costly inconveniences being imposed on his neighbors in the name of wetlands restoration. Unlike other farms in the area, Red's operation wasn't forced to cut back on the potent amounts of fertilizer it was dumping on crops, for example, or made to spend millions building filtration ponds to strain out the phosphate crud. Thanks to the innovative fieldwork of Dr. Charles Perrone, Hammernut Farms could continue using the Everglades as a cesspit.

Of course it was imperative that the corrupt arrangement between Chaz and Red remain secret, and in that regard Chaz's serial philandering proved to be a continuing source of concern. More than once Red Hammernut reminded Chaz that his fortunes would take a radically negative turn if he told any of his girlfriends the name of his true employer. Ironically, the woman about whom Red Hammernut worried least was Chaz's wife, because it seemed that Chaz didn't tell her much of anything.

Then came the phone call, Chaz jabbering frantically that Joey had caught him forging the water data. Red asking over and over: "You sure she knows what it is?" Chaz saying that he couldn't be certain, because Joey had just dropped the subject afterward. Over the phone, though, he had sounded suspicious. Definitely spooked. Red Hammernut had urged him to stay cool: "Don't assume nuthin'. Wait and see what she says about it."

And Joey Perrone hadn't said anything, not a word. Still, Chaz had remained anxious, and it rubbed off on Red. What if wifey had figured out the Everglades deal and decided to keep quiet and bide her time? In Red's worst nightmare, Joey would catch Chaz with his weenie in the wrong bun and become so enraged that she'd blab to the water district about his phony samples. Trying to buy her silence would be useless because she didn't need the dough—according to Chaz, Joey was worth millions.

As the days had turned into weeks, Chaz seemed to calm down. He hadn't talked so much about his wife or what she might suspect, so Red Hammernut had assumed that the situation on the home front had ironed itself out. Suddenly Joey Perrone was dead, and now somebody was trying to blackmail Chaz. Or so he said. Red Hammernut couldn't rule out the possibility that the young man might be trying to rip him off; it would not be entirely out of character.

"You're sure it's the detective?" Red asked.

"Who the hell else could it be? He's the only one who's been hassling me about Joey." Chaz was waving his hands in agitation. "He tried to disguise his voice over the phone and make like he was Charlton Heston!"

Tool grunted quizzically.

"That NRA guy," Red explained. "The one's got old-timer's disease."

"He's also in the movies," Chaz said thinly.

"You know who does a funny 'personation of Heston? That Robin Williams fella—"

"Red, are you even listening to me?"

"Course I am, son. This detective who does voices of movie stars, you think he's the same guy that's been sneakin' into your house?"

"Absolutely. It'd be damned easy for a cop," Chaz declared. "Know what he did today? Turned on my sprinklers. Pouring rain when I get home, and the sprinklers are running like Niagara fucking Falls! Dumb shit like that, it can make you nuts."

Red Hammernut thinking: He must be readin' my mind.

They were squeezed together like nuns in the back of the gray Cadillac—Red stinking like a knockoff Montecristo; Tool like a wet bull; and Chaz Perrone like the county dump where he had just tossed several boxes of his wife's belongings.

Red Hammernut had sent his driver into the doughnut shop in case Chaz blurted out something stupid or incriminating. It was a conversation that had to be managed carefully, as Red didn't wish to be taxed with unnecessary details. Whatever had happened between Chaz and Joey Perrone aboard the cruise ship was a private matter and ought to stay that way.

Eyeing Chaz now, Red had trouble picturing him tossing anybody overboard—especially Joey, who was a big strong girl. Tool could have handled her, no problem, but Chaz?

Maybe he's tougher than he looks, Red thought.

He said, "Son, you wanna hear somethin' wild? I met him this morning. Your cop."

"Rolvaag!" Chaz turned ashen. "Christ. How?"

"Drove all the way up to the farm to ask me about a rented minivan." Red shot a sideways glance at Tool, who was absently picking a scab on his neck.

"Did he mention my name?" Chaz asked anxiously.

"He did not. Gave me a bullshit story, which I believed at the time, about Tool's good looks scarin' some friends of the sheriff. Needless to say, I didn't know it was the same detective that's been ridin' your ass."

Tool spoke up. "Red, I was ready to take care of him. Your boy here tole me not to."

"He was right," Red Hammernut said. "You can't deal with cops the same way you deal with beaners. That's a damn fact."

Chaz sighed dispiritedly. Tool cracked his knuckles and said, "I don't get how anybody can do a blackmail if your boy here ain't committed no crime."

Red laughed to himself. Once again, the man had gotten straight to the nut of the matter.

"The guy on the phone says he saw me throw Joey over the side of the ship. That's just not true," Chaz said.

Tool crinkled his brow. "What's not true? You didn't do it, or you *did* do it and nobody saw?"

Chaz opened his mouth to respond, but a sickly quack came out.

Red Hammernut quickly changed the subject. "This Rolvaag, he didn't strike me as the type to be runnin' his own game. I been around long 'nough to know a crook when I see 'em."

"And I'm telling you, he's the only one it could be." Chaz didn't sound as certain as Red would have liked. If Chaz had in fact thrown his wife off the ship, some stranger could have witnessed it; another passenger, a cabin boy, whoever.

"This blackmailer fella, let's make sure who he is and how much he wants," Red said to Chaz. "Could be some smartass just saw the story on the news and got the bright idea to shake you down. That kinda shit we can handle." He nodded confidently toward Tool. "But if it's really the cop, like you say, then we gotta be extra careful. He can cause all sorta problems, even if you ain't done nuthin' wrong."

Through clenched teeth, Chaz said, "I haven't, Red. Like I said, it was an accident."

"Take it easy, son. I believe you."

Tool, who was probing a hangnail with a rusty fishhook, snorted doubtfully.

"Next time this sumbitch calls," Red Hammernut said, "you try and set up a meeting."

"Christ, Red, you mean face-to-face?" Chaz whined. "But why? What're we going to do?"

"Listen politely to whatever he's got to say," Red said. "And, son, let's be clear on this. It ain't 'we.' It's 'you.' "

Thirteen

Mick Stranahan phoned Charles Perrone at 5:42 a.m.

"Good morning, dipshit," he said, this time doing Jerry Lewis. The Mexican writer who owned the island adored *The Nutty Professor*, and Stranahan had watched it often on the VCR. There were worse ways to get through a tropical depression.

At the other end of the line, Joey Perrone's husband needed a few moments to rouse himself. "Are you the same guy who called yesterday?"

"That's riiii-ghht."

Chaz Perrone said, "We should get together, you and me."

"Why?"

"To talk."

"We're talking now," Stranahan said. "You tossed your beloved into the Atlantic Ocean. I'm curious to hear an explanation."

"I didn't push her. She fell."

"That's not what I saw."

"Listen to me," Perrone pleaded, but his voice trailed away.

"Yoo-hoo? Chaz?"

"We should do this in person."

"Do what? There's eighteen hundred dollars in your checking account," Stranahan said. "That's pitiful."

"I can get more," Perrone blurted. Then, warily: "How'd you know what I have in the bank?"

"Pity-full."

"Don't hang up. Don't!"

Stranahan said, "How would you ever get enough money?"

"People owe me."

Stranahan laughed. "Are you a biologist or a loan shark?"

"Okay, Rolvaag. Tell me how much you want."

Again with the "Rolvaag" stuff, thought Stranahan. "I haven't decided on an amount," he said.

"Okay, when can we get together? I'm serious."

"Bye-bye, Chaz."

"Wait," Perrone said, "I've gotta ask—that voice you're doing?"

"Yeah?"

"Jim Carrey, right?"

Stranahan said, "Mister, my price just doubled."

Tool filled the bedroom doorway, demanding to know who the hell was calling so early in the morning. When Chaz Perrone said it was the blackmailer, Tool swore groggily and lurched back to bed. It had been a long, fitful night, the fentanyl patches having dried up one by one, dying like flowers. The so-called doctor had been no help whatsoever—obviously he hated the idea of Tool staying inside his house, and the feeling was mutual. But Red was the boss man, and Red said he didn't want Tool out on the street, freaking the neighbors. He was to remain with the doctor, and make sure nobody else broke in. Chaz Perrone grudgingly had surrendered the guest bedroom. Later Tool had attempted a shower, but within five minutes he shed so much tarry body hair that the drain clogged. Chaz had cleaned it out with a coat hanger; not saying a word, but Tool could tell he was ticked.

For breakfast Tool prepared an omelette, using nine eggs, a pint of clotted cream, a half pound of cheddar, assorted peppers, a pawful of pitted olives and four ounces of Tabasco. As Tool slurped down the pungent creation, the doctor reeled from the kitchen in disgust.

Afterward Tool announced he was heading out in search of medicine. "Where's the closest hospital?" he asked Chaz Perrone.

"Are you out of your mind? You can't sneak into a hospital and steal that stuff."

"Wherever they's a hospital, they's a nursing home close by. Or else a whatchacallit—a place where they put, you know, the terminals. Them that's gone die."

"You mean like a hospice."

"Right," Tool said, "where the people are too sickly to make a fuss."

"And then?"

"I look around till I find the ones with stick-on patches."

"Jesus." The doctor suddenly got quiet.

"Well?" Tool demanded.

"Does Mr. Hammernut know you do this?"

"Red don't pry hisself into my bidness."

"Smart man." Charles Perrone reached for a pen. "The nearest hospital is Cypress Creek. I'll write down the directions."

"Draw me a pitcher instead."

"A map, you mean."

Tool smiled. "Yeah, that'd be good."

He had dumped the minivan at Hertz and defected to Avis for a black Grand Marquis. The extra legroom was a treat, and the air conditioning was purely glorious. Once Tool located the hospital, he began scouting adjacent neighborhoods for likely targets. The first place was called Serenity Villas, but he backed off as soon as he realized it was an assisted-living facility. That meant that the old folks were still hoofing around pretty good, and in Tool's experience they did not part easily with their medications.

His next stop was Elysian Manor, a convalescent home run by a local church. Tool put on the size XXXL lab whites that he always carried, and entered through a rear service door. For a large man he moved unobtrusively, checking one bed at a time. Some of the patients, as frail as baby sparrows, were sound asleep; those Tool gently rolled over to inspect for patches. The patients who were awake behaved cooperatively, although one launched into a fractured monologue that Tool couldn't sort out—something about a sellout in Yalta, wherever the hell *that* was.

The lack of visitors was one reason that Tool favored nursing homes over hospitals. Why people spent so little time with their ailing mothers and fathers, he didn't know, but it was a bankable fact. In only one room at Elysian Manor did Tool encounter a relative perched at a patient's bedside—Tool excusing himself with a wave, and moving on down the hall. Nobody in authority displayed the slightest interest in his presence; the harried nurses assumed he was a newly hired orderly, turnover being universally rampant at geriatric facilities.

He hit pay dirt in no. 33, a private room. The patient, a bony-shouldered woman with permed silver hair, was curled up, sleeping with her face to the wall. The back of her cotton gown was untied, revealing on her papery gray skin a crisp new patch of fentanyl. Tool crept forward and began to peel it off. The woman spun violently, her knobby right elbow nailing him like a cudgel between the eyes. Rocking backward, Tool groped for the bed rail to steady himself.

"What're you up to?" The woman's fierce blue eyes were clear and alert.

"Changin' out your patch," Tool mumbled.

"But they just gave me a new one an hour ago."

"Ma'am, I just do what they tell me."

"I believe that's a load of bull crap," she said.

This is no good, Tool thought. She's too damn ornery.

"They'll bring you more," he said. "Come on now, roll over."

"You're sick, too, I can tell. Is it cancer?"

Tool fingered the rising lump on his forehead. "I ain't sick," he said, glancing at the door. He expected somebody to barge in any second.

"I'm Maureen." The woman pointed at a straight-backed chair in the corner. "Pull that over here and sit. What's your name?"

Tool said, "Nice and easy now. Lemme take off that patch, then you can go back to sleep."

Maureen sat herself up, plumping a pillow behind her head. "I must look terrible," she said, touching her hair. "I wasn't sleeping, for your information. In my condition, who could sleep? Pull up that chair, I'll give you what you want."

All Tool could think about was the warm embrace of the drug, deep and delicious. He dragged the chair over to Maureen's bedside and sat down.

"You're in pain, aren't you?" she inquired.

"Damn straight. I gotta bullet up the crack a my ass."

"Yow."

"That's how come I need the dope," Tool said. "So, what d'ya say?"

He didn't want to take it by force. She was a scrapper and he'd have to get rough, maybe even strangle her. . . .

"How did you happen to be shot?" she asked.

"Huntin' accident."

"And they couldn't remove it surgically?"

"Guess not," Tool said.

"My late husband was a police officer in the city of Chicago, Illinois. He shot a man once."

"Not up the ass, I bet."

"It was in the shoulder," Maureen said. "The fellow was a hardened criminal. He robbed a gypsy cab. Are you a criminal?"

"Not to my way of thinkin'." Tool was perspiring through his medical whites. He fought the urge to tear the patch from the old coot's hide and bolt for the door.

Maureen said, "All right. I can see you need the medicine more than I do." She turned and presented her bare back, gesturing over one shoulder. "Go ahead and take it, but please be careful. I tend to bleed for no darn reason these days."

Tool started at a top corner of the patch and peeled carefully downward, as if removing a decal. "They'll bring you more," he assured Maureen. "Tell 'em it come off while you was in the bath."

"I don't have a tub, young man. They bathe me with a sponge."

"In bed? Don't that make a mess?"

Maureen said, "I miss my privacy, I really do."

After Tool was done, she rolled over to look at him again. "I'm eighty-one years old, but I feel like a hundred and ten. Please tell me your name."

"Earl." Tool scarcely recognized his own voice. Nobody left on earth called him Earl.

"Is your mother still alive?" Maureen asked.

"Nope. Not my daddy, neither."

"I'm sorry, Earl. I hope it wasn't cancer."

"That's what you got?"

Maureen nodded. "But some days I feel pretty chipper. Some days I surprise myself."

Tool stared at the flesh-colored patch in his hand, thinking: Why couldn't she have been asleep? Or at least a veggie?

"No, you keep that," Maureen said, patting him on the arm. "I want you to feel better."

" 'Preciate it."

He was three steps toward the door when he heard: "Earl, could you pop in and visit me again sometime?"

Tool stopped and turned. "Ma'am, I . . . I don't really work here."

"Oh, I know." Her blue eyes were dancing. "What do I look like, some sort of nitwit?"

Rolvaag was working on his resignation package when Captain Gallo came over and said, "Tomorrow's the last day you waste on Perrone."

"Yes, I remember," Rolvaag said.

"Reason I mention it, I got a call from the man."

"No kidding."

Gallo always referred to the sheriff as "the man."

"He asked what you were doing up in LaBelle yesterday, and I didn't have a real swift comeback," Gallo said, "seeing as how I've been in Florida thirty fuckin' years and never had a reason to go there."

Rolvaag explained that he'd been tracking a lead in the cruise ship case.

"And that took you to the office of Mr. Samuel Johnson Hammernut," Gallo said. "I hope you know who he is."

"A farmer," the detective said.

"No, a millionaire CEO farmer with heavyweight clout. Soon as you leave, Hammernut calls his asshole buddy, the sheriff of Hendry County, who right away calls the sheriff of Broward County—that would be my boss and yours—and wants to know who the hell's this Karl Rolvaag? Next thing I know, I get a call asking how come you're hassling a fine upstanding citizen like Red Hammernut?" Gallo spread his arms as if awaiting crucifixion. "And what is my response, Karl, besides stuttering like some sort of mental defective? What can I possibly say to the man?"

Rolvaag capped his pen and sat back. "It's interesting that Hammernut would react that way. Don't you think?"

"Are you dicking with me, Karl?"

"No, sir. I'm only trying to finish my resignation papers."

Gallo said, "Aw, knock it off."

"I'm serious about the job in Minnesota."

"Yeah, whatever," the captain said. "Just tell me how a rich Cracker like Hammernut could possibly fit into your case—and I use the word loosely."

Rolvaag informed Gallo about the man staking out Perrone's house. "He used one of Hammernut's credit cards to rent the minivan."

"And that's all?"

"So far. But it's strange, you've got to admit. Why would anyone be tailing a recently widowed man?"

"Karl, we can't go to a grand jury with strange. The whole damn human race is strange," Gallo said. "You and your choice of roommates, for example. Some people would say that's slightly shy of normal."

Rolvaag said, "Lots of folks keep pet snakes."

"I'll explain to the man it was just a dry hole, your road trip to LaBelle."

"Okay. If it'll make your life easier."

"What about you? And don't give me any more horseshit about moving back north," Gallo said. "Just tell me what you want, Karl. A raise? Weekends off? I can't promise anything, but sometimes miracles do happen."

The detective said, "I think Mr. Perrone pushed his wife off that ship. I probably can't prove it in the short time before I leave here, but that's what I believe. Could you give me a couple more days to work the case?"

What bothered Rolvaag the most were the broken fingernails that he'd found in that bale of grass. He couldn't stop thinking of Joey Perrone, desperate and terrified, trying to hang on in the waves, all the while pondering the dreadful thing that her husband had done; hanging on in the chill and the darkness until finally her arms went numb and she slipped into the sea.

"No way," Gallo was saying. "Sorry, Karl, I'm pulling the plug."

"Suppose I came up with the motive."

"In the next, what, twenty-four hours?"

"You betcha."

"Then I'd have to reconsider. Sure I would," Gallo said. "But it'd better be fucking brilliant."

"Maybe I'll get lucky." Rolvaag sounded far more confident than he felt, having no theory, no hunch, not even a wild guess as to why Chaz Perrone had so casually murdered his wife.

The generator broke down before Stranahan could start breakfast. He was still working on it when Joey Perrone awoke and came outside.

"The joys of island living," she said.

"Old Neil was right. Rust never sleeps."

Stranahan was wearing cutoff jeans and no shirt; dripping sweat, grease smeared like war paint on his face and chest. Joey asked if he wanted some help, and he said what he really needed was dynamite.

"That bad, huh?"

"I'll fix it eventually," he said, twirling a mallet. "In the meantime there are some delectable bran flakes in the cupboard."

Joey asked to borrow his cellular. He pointed to the boat, where the phone was recharging on the battery plug, and went back to banging on the generator. Twenty minutes later, Joey returned with a pitcher of tea and a bowl of fruit from the kitchen. They walked down to the dock and sat down, Joey tickling the water with her toes. Strom blinked at them from the shade of his favorite palm.

"I'm getting worried about using my credit card," Joey said.

Stranahan assured her that American Express didn't know that she was missing, and didn't care as long as the payments got made. "They don't read the newspapers. Unless somebody calls up and cancels the card, it stays active," he explained.

"The balance is automatically deducted from a private money-market account, but the monthly statement is mailed to the house. What if Chaz gets nosy?"

"Another reason we should work fast," said Stranahan, "before the billing cycle ends. He'll probably just toss the statement into the trash, but if he opens it, then we've got a problem. He'll see that you're continuing to spend money."

"Yeah. Neat trick for a corpse." Joey turned her face upward and squeezed her eyes closed. "The sun still hurts."

"It hasn't even been a week. Next time we go to the mainland, we'll find you some cool shades."

She said, "I dreamed about Chaz again last night."

"Killing him?"

"Worse." Joey rolled her eyes. "Can you believe it, Mick? Even after what he's done, I'm still having sex with the guy in my sleep."

"It's emotional withdrawal, that's all. Like when you try to kick caffeine, suddenly the whole damn world smells like Folger's."

Joey worked her lower lip. "Maybe I actually loved that creep up until the end. Maybe it was more than physical, and I can't admit it."

Stranahan shrugged. "Don't look at me, I'm the crown prince of dysfunctional. What's important is figuring out how you feel about him here and now, before we make another move."

The dog ambled over and stretched out on the warm planks beside Joey. "That was my brother I called earlier," she said. "The people who take care of my money contacted him because someone saw in the paper that I was lost at sea. Corbett told them to sit tight. They can't do anything without a death certificate anyway."

"Chaz hadn't called to snoop around about the trust?"

"Nope. My brother was surprised, too." Joey smiled ruefully. "In a weird way, I wish Chaz *had* done it for my money. Then I could almost understand," she said. "But killing somebody just to be rid of them—man, it's hard not to take it personally."

"That's not why he did this, Joey. You'll see." Stranahan put an arm around her, and she let her head drop lightly against his shoulder. "What does Corbett think you should do?"

"He likes the idea of me driving Chaz clinically insane," she said. "Float around like a ghost, he says, until the bastard loses his marbles."

"It could happen."

"Oh, guess what else?" Joey lifted her head. "This detective keeps calling Corbett to talk about Chaz—the same guy Corbett spoke with on Monday, and now he's calling back, leaving messages."

Stranahan said, "So the heat's on, just like you wanted."

"It would be fun to think so."

And one more reason to be careful, thought Stranahan. The trick would be putting the cop into play without exposing themselves. "Did your brother tell you the detective's name?" he asked.

"Rolvaag. Karl Rolvaag," she said, "with a *K*, not a *C*."

"I'll be damned."

"I even wrote down the phone number," she added, "in lipstick, unfortunately, on the deck of your boat."

"No problem," Stranahan said cheerfully.

"What's so funny?"

"Chaz. He thinks the cop is the blackmailer. On the phone this morning he even called me Rolvaag."

Joey was delighted. Then: "Hey, wait a minute. You talked to Chaz and you didn't even tell me?"

"You were sleeping," Stranahan said.

"So what!"

"In a languid state of undress. Frankly, I was intimidated."

"Mick."

"That's a compliment, by the way."

"Was I snoring?"

"Moaning, actually. If I'd known you were dreaming about Chaz, I would have thrown you under a cold shower."

Joey took a playful swing and he caught her fist with the palm of his hand. "Go wash up. I got you all grimy."

She said, "Buddy, if you're not careful . . ."

Giving Stranahan a look that reminded him of Andrea Krumholtz, his very first girlfriend, on the night she'd slipped off her bra and tossed it out a window of Stranahan's father's car. For Mick, sixteen at the time, it had been a sublimely instructive moment.

To Joey he said, "Guess I'd better get back to work."

"You sure about that?"

"There's five pounds of lobster in the freezer. It would be a mortal sin to let it spoil."

She said, "Okay. Go fix your stupid generator."

Stranahan finished the job two hours later, arms aching, knuckles raw. He went looking for Joey to give her the news, but she wasn't reading in bed, or sunning on the seawall, or roughhousing on the dock with the dog. In fact, she wasn't anywhere on the island.

Strom wagged his nub but offered up no information. The Whaler was still tied to the pilings, so Stranahan wasn't completely shocked to throw open the doors of the shed and find the yellow kayak missing. By then Joey was so far gone that the hunting scope was useless in spotting her. He climbed the roof to better scan the water, but all the bright specks turned into sailboats and Windsurfers and water bikes. He thought about taking the skiff and hunting her down, but he also thought about how bone-tired and grungy he was, and how good a cold beer would taste.

As soon as he hopped off the roof, the Doberman started yipping and whining reproachfully, nipping at his heels all the way to the kitchen.

"Oh, shut up," Stranahan said. "She'll be back."

Fourteen

Mick Stranahan's sister was married to a lawyer named Kipper Garth, inept in all aspects of the profession except self-promotion. He had been one of the first personal-injury hustlers in Florida to advertise on television and billboards, attracting a stampede of impressionable clients whose cases he dealt out like pinochle cards to legitimate attorneys in exchange for a slice of the take. As even his rivals conceded, Kipper Garth helped to pioneer the preposterous notion that finding a good lawyer was as easy as dialing up a plumber in the Yellow Pages.

It pained Stranahan that his sister Katie had fallen for such a shyster, and that she'd stayed with him despite serial philanderings, scalding IRS audits and a ruinous gambling addiction. A cranial injury inflicted by a jealous husband had forced Kipper Garth into an early retirement, and in short order he'd burned up the family savings wagering on British cricket, a sport he never bothered to understand. In the face of bankruptcy he had reopened his practice, inspired by advanced pain medication and a fresh marketing angle. A new series of TV commercials featured him tooling around a law library in the same wheelchair to which he had been confined during his homebound rehabilitation. The aim was to present himself as both lawyer and victim, qualified by empathy (if not expertise) to specialize in disability litigation.

Always a trend hound, Kipper Garth had come across a newspaper article about a pair of lawyers who drove around South Florida scouting restaurants, shops and office buildings for wheelchair accessibility. If a place didn't have the required ramps or lifts, the lawyers would recruit a disabled person—often a friend or relative—to sue. Typically the case would settle before trial, the owners of the building eager to avoid headlines implying they were callous toward the handicapped. The scheme was perfectly suited to Kipper Garth's singular talent and soon he was back in tall cotton, overseeing half a dozen runners who scoured the tricounty area for wheelchair-ramp violations.

Throughout good times and bad, Mick Stranahan contrived to avoid his sister's husband, and timed his visits to Kate's house on days when Kipper Garth was gone. Kate was always happy to see Mick, though she maintained a long-standing ban against discussing Kipper's multiple character flaws. Theirs was one of those marriages that Stranahan couldn't hope to understand, but he had come to accept it as unbreakable. He saw no reason to inform Kate that he now required her husband's slithering assistance.

"Sorry, Mick," Kipper Garth told him. "No can do."

Stranahan was skeptically inspecting the wheelchair slanted in a corner of his brother-in-law's spacious bayfront office.

"I still need it on occasion," Kipper Garth said preemptively. "I get spells."

A putter was propped against one of the wheelchair's tires; three shiny new golf balls were lined up on the carpet.

Stranahan sat down in front of the desk. "Does the bar association know you can walk? Or is there no rule against impersonating a cripple on TV?"

Kipper Garth bristled. "It's what they call a 'dramatic re-creation.' "

"Try 'misrepresentation,' " said Stranahan, "with the stink of fraud. How about it, jocko? Are you going to help me, or do I make the phone call?"

"Katie would never forgive you."

"She did the last time."

Kipper Garth's neck turned crimson. Many years earlier, Stranahan had voluntarily testified against him in a grievance hearing that had unfolded poorly for the lawyer. Disbarment had seemed inevitable, until a cuckolded husband had beaned Kipper Garth with a jai alai ball, knocking him out of action and thereby sparing the Florida Bar a mountain of paperwork.

"Mick, this really isn't up my alley." Kipper Garth, smoothing his necktie and brushing invisible lint from his lapels. "Here"—he reached for his Filofax—"let me give you some names."

Stranahan leaned over and grabbed his wrist. "It's boilerplate, jocko. A first-year law student could do this blindfolded."

Kipper Garth pulled his arm away, though not too assertively. He knew enough of his brother-in-law's volcanic history to avoid physical confrontation. He also knew that the wheelchair caper was but one of many transgressions that Mick had learned about and, strategically, kept to himself.

Stranahan unfolded a yellow piece of lined paper and pushed it across the desk, saying, "That's everything you'll need."

The information seemed innocuous and straightforward. Kipper Garth was sure that his secretary could format a suitable document with the office software. "All right, Mick, I'll do this for you," he said, motioning toward the double doors. "Go ahead and bring her in."

"Who?" Stranahan said.

"The client."

"Oh, she's not here."

Kipper Garth looked puzzled. "Why not?"

"Because she's missing."

"Excuse me?"

"Well, she is and she isn't," Stranahan said.

"You mean, like, Amelia Earhart–type missing or escaped prisoner–type missing?" Kipper Garth was clutching to the hope that his brother-in-law was joking.

"It's complicated," said Stranahan.

"But I'll need a signature, obviously."

"Tell you what. Just leave that part blank."

Kipper Garth felt his gut tighten. "The signature is supposed to be witnessed."

"I was counting on the blind loyalty of your secretarial staff. Hey, I almost forgot—date it in early March, would you?"

"For next year?"

Stranahan said, "No, this year. Date it four weeks ago."

His brother-in-law's voice deflated to a plaintive rasp. "Mick, come on, I could get *prosecuted* for this."

"Aw, they wouldn't do that to a man in a wheelchair."

"I'm serious! The shit hits the fan, I'll deny everything."

"I would expect no less," Stranahan said.

Kipper Garth held up the yellow paper and shook it. "What the hell's this all about? What have you got yourself into?"

Mick Stranahan glanced impatiently at his wristwatch. "We're wasting precious time, jocko," he said. "Chop chop."

For the second day in a row, Charles Perrone called in sick to the water district. Ricca came over and brought him lunch—a ham sandwich, nacho chips and a lobster salad. What the neighbors might think of his voluptuous female visitor was no longer high on Chaz's list of concerns; he had more urgent problems.

"What's the matter?" Ricca asked.

"You name it."

"Wanna talk?"

"Nope."

He led her to the bedroom and undressed her. Twenty-five minutes later she rolled wearily off the mattress and re-fastened her bra. "I'm sorry, baby. I gotta get back to work."

Chaz Perrone flicked at himself, as slack as a noodle, under the sheets. "I can't fucking believe this."

"Hey, it happens to all guys. Like I said before." Ricca was in the bathroom, trying to sound as if she wasn't disappointed. She emerged brushing her hair with military briskness. "You'd tell me if there was someone else, wouldn't you, Chaz?"

"Jesus."

"I don't want to be the last to know."

He said, "Keep talking and I'll be shopping the Internet for an implant."

She picked up her handbag and kissed him on the nose. "You'll be okay, baby. You're just having a tough time moving on, that's all."

"Don't start. I'm begging you."

"After the memorial, you'll be good as new," Ricca said. "Once you say good-bye to Joey, it's back to your old studly self."

Chaz scowled. "I already said good-bye."

"I don't think you have. I think that's the problem."

Minutes after Ricca departed, Chaz heard Tool come in the front door. He poked his anvil-size head in the bedroom and asked with dull indifference if everything was cool.

"Yeah. Peachy."

"Who was the girl? I seen her car here before."

"Grief counselor," Chaz said.

Tool eyed the doctor's trousers and boxer shorts, which were crumpled in a heap by the bed. He said, "When my momma passed, they sent a Pentecostal preacher by the house."

"Everybody's got their own way of coping. Did you find your stick-ems?"

"Just one so far. But it's brand-new." Tool pivoted to exhibit the shaved spot where he'd slapped the fentanyl patch on his shoulder blade. "Maybe I'll go crash for a spell," he said.

Charles Perrone waved. "Sweet dreams."

He waited until Tool disappeared into the guest room, then reached into the nightstand and took out his new gun. Overwhelmed by the selection at Wal-Mart, he'd gone to a pawnshop in Margate, where an imaginatively tattooed neo-Nazi had sold him a basic Colt .38. Sitting in bed now, Chaz hefted the blue-plated pistol from one hand to the other and wondered about its murky provenance. For all he knew, it could have been used in some vicious robbery, or even to kill a person. There was a box of hollow-point bullets in the drawer, but Chaz was hesitant to load the weapon. He'd once heard on CNN that homeowners who buy guns for protection are about fifty times more likely to shoot themselves, or be shot, than they are to cap an intruder. Since he'd never fired anything more powerful than a BB rifle, Chaz inserted the bullets with the utmost care.

After returning the .38 to the drawer, he sank into a melancholy rumination. What if flaky Ricca was right? He'd purged every remnant of his dead wife from the house, and still his pecker remained obstinately on strike. Although he'd never confess it to Ricca, the only time Chaz experienced the slightest twitch of spontaneous lust was when he thought about Joey. That morning in the shower, for example, he'd been going over the crime moment by moment in his head—why, he didn't know. Remembering the tang of the ocean; the drizzling rain on his face; the amber lights lining the rails of the deck; the low, heavy drone of the ship's engines.

And Joey's ankles. That's what had done it for him—remembering how silky and warm her ankles had felt when he'd grabbed them. God, what outstanding legs!

Feeling a blissfully familiar pulsation, Chaz had peeked down to greet his little perpendicular accomplice. Avidly he had hunched over on himself, kneading and tugging to no avail, until finally the hot water ran out and all was lost.

So, it's possible that Ricca is right, he thought. Maybe his subconscious hadn't yet let go of Joey, though it was only the sexual part of the marriage that he missed. Otherwise I'm as steady as an ox, Chaz assured himself; I did what had to be done. Sooner or later his wife would have caught him screwing around and, out of spite, ratted on him for faking the Everglades data. She would have ruined everything—his credentials as a biologist, his secret pact with Red, his whole golden future.

Because she knew the truth. Of course she did. Hadn't she seen it with her own eyeballs, him forging the water charts?

I only did what was necessary, Chaz thought, and I could do it again.

On impulse he snatched the phone and dialed a golfing buddy, a well-known wild man on the weekend club scene. "You know those pills you tried to feed me at Richardson's bachelor party? I've got a friend wants to try the stuff."

"A friend. Sure, Chaz."

"Jesus, they're not for me! My wife just died, in case you hadn't heard. What kind of a heartless prick do you think I am?"

"Sorry, man. I'm really sorry. How many does he want? Your friend."

"I don't know—what's in a starter kit?" Chaz asked. "Half a dozen?"

"No problemo."

"And you said they're stronger than what doctors give out?"

"Oh yeah. The FDA definitely would not approve."

"Where you at now? Have you got 'em on you?"

"I'm hitting a bucket of balls at Boca Pines North. Your friend's in a hurry, huh?"

"Yeah. I think he's got a hot date."

"Meet me at the clubhouse in, like, an hour."

"Perfect," Chaz said. "I owe you one."

"Hey, don't worry about it." Then, after a discomfited pause: "Man, it's really terrible what happened to Joey—that's gotta be *so* fucking rough. How you hangin' in?"

"Oh, some days are better than others," said Chaz Perrone.

After leaving Kipper Garth's law office, Mick Stranahan went back to Dinner Key to see if Joey had returned to the marina. There was no sign of his kayak or the rented Suburban.

Stranahan didn't feel like driving up to Boca, but he couldn't wait in Coconut Grove all afternoon; these days he had no patience for anything but fishing. From his billfold he retrieved a scrap of paper on which he had written the tag number of the blue Ford belonging to Chaz Perrone's mistress of the moment. Only two investigators at the State Attorney's Office remembered Stranahan favorably enough to help, and he phoned one of them as he headed north on the interstate. By the time he passed the county line, Stranahan had a name, age, address, marital status and occupation.

Ricca Jane Spillman held a cosmetology license from the state of Florida, so it was simply a matter of figuring out where she worked. Stranahan made a pit stop in Hallandale to find a pay phone, ripping a sheaf of beauty salon listings from the Yellow Pages. He narrowed his search to the western suburbs of northern Broward, and after only fifty-five minutes of blind calling he located Chaz's girlfriend. She was a senior stylist/colorist at a shop called Hair Jordan, and by chance she happened to have an opening at 5:30 p.m.

Like many of Boca's finest establishments, the salon was shoe-horned into a coral-colored strip mall. Mick Stranahan parked the rust-eaten Cordoba in the rear, where it was less likely to draw stares. He drew a few himself as he walked through the door of Hair Jordan in his grease-stained shirt, faded khakis and scuffed Top-Siders. Taking cover behind a magazine, Stranahan attempted to immerse himself in the travails of Eminem, a deep though conflicted young man. Apparently wealth, fame and unlimited sex are nice, but true spiritual happiness must come from within.

"Mr. Smith? Hi."

It was Ricca, motioning for Stranahan to follow her. "You can bring the magazine if you like."

He was somewhat embarrassed by his hair, which was tacky with salt and piled oddly to one side, a result of the windy boat ride across Biscayne Bay. Ricca said nothing about it, but during the shampoo she commented admiringly on his deep tan. Stranahan said that his job kept him out in the sun.

"Yeah? Where do you work?" she asked, lightly toweling his head.

"On a cruise ship."

"Oh."

Stranahan watched her expression closely in the mirror. "You ever been on one?"

"A cruise? No," Ricca said, less bubbly than before.

"The ships are like a city, they're so big."

She removed a pair of shears from the sterilizer. "How short do you like it—tops of the ears?"

"I was thinking of a buzz cut, like Clint Eastwood had in that Grenada movie."

"Okay."

"Just kidding," Stranahan said. He let her work in silence for a few minutes—Ricca obviously distracted—before he started up again. "Do you get seasick? Lots of people do."

"Sometimes," she said. "What exactly do you do on the ship? Your job, I mean."

"Security."

"Oh wow."

Stranahan bowed his head to accommodate the arc of her trimming. "As I said, it's like a city. Good citizens, bad citizens."

"But it's mostly drunks, right? They don't have, like, serious crimes out there."

"You'd be surprised," he said. "Just the other night, some guy pushed his wife overboard."

The *snip-snip-snip* of the shears ceased. Ricca's eyes locked on Stranahan's in the mirror.

"That's not funny, Mr. Smith."

"Oh, I'm dead serious," he said. "Took her by the legs and flipped her over the rail."

"Oh my God."

Stranahan put on an apologetic smile. "Here I am, trying to talk you into a tropical cruise, and I end up scaring you with some awful story. I'm sorry, I really am."

"No, it's my fault for asking."

Ricca's hands were trembling so badly now that she slapped the scissors down on a tray; picked up a comb and started dragging it mechanically through his half-cut hair.

Stranahan felt sorry for her. He felt sorry for any woman who'd bought into Charles Perrone's bullshit.

In a small voice she asked: "What'd they do to the guy?"

"He got away, believe it or not."

"B-but . . . how?"

"At least he *thought* he did." Stranahan winked. "The sonofabitch didn't know that someone saw the whole thing. Me."

By now Ricca was in no condition to handle sharp instruments, so Stranahan removed the shiny barber's sheet from around his neck.

Stepping back from the chair, Ricca said, "Who are you?"

Keeping her voice low so that Mr. Jordan, the owner, wouldn't know that something was wrong.

Stranahan took out a twenty and placed it on the tray beside the scissors. "Chaz didn't tell you how it went down?"

She shook her head stiffly. "He said it was a accident."

"Oh no, it was murder. Premeditated."

"Why d-didn't you, like . . . stop him?"

"Happened too fast. One second she's standing there, the next she's shark chum. Just like *that*!" Stranahan snapped his fingers sharply.

Ricca jumped. "No way. Chaz said he was sleeping when it happened."

"He's lying to you, Ricca," Stranahan said. "He's an extremely bad person. A coldhearted killer, if you want the truth. My advice is to find yourself a new boyfriend."

"Who the hell *are* you?"

"Chazzie's future business partner. Tell him I dropped by."

"How'd you find me? You'd better go right now."

"Sure," Stranahan said. "But you should know that Dr. Perrone's life is about to get infinitely more complicated. Keep the car running."

"Get out!" she whispered.

Stranahan ate dinner at a Thai joint at the other end of the mall. Ricca's blue Ford was gone when he passed the salon on the way out. Either she was on her way to confront Chaz or was hurrying home to bolt the door, fix herself a drink and contemplate the disquieting fact that she was dating a murderer.

The short drive to West Boca Dunes Phase II took nearly thirty minutes in rush hour traffic. Stranahan was homicidal by the time he turned down Chaz Perrone's street, but he grinned at the sight of the rented Suburban—his yellow kayak strapped to the racks—parked in the driveway of the fugitive telemarketers. He pulled in next to the green barge, rolled down the window and waited for Joey to do the same. Nothing happened. Peering through the tinted glass, Stranahan realized with a pitching heart that the Suburban was empty.

"Hell," he said, and turned his gaze on the Perrone residence. Joey had snuck inside again, which was problematic, since her husband's yellow Hummer was parked out front. So was a dark sedan, either a Grand Marquis or a Crown Vic.

Stranahan was out of his car and moving quickly when a third vehicle rolled up behind the Humvee. It was a white Toyota or possibly an Audi—Stranahan couldn't be certain in the twilight. He shoved his hands in his pockets and slowed to a casual stroll, watching as a woman with frizzy red hair and wind-chime earrings got out of the car.

As Stranahan neared the house, the front door swung open and there was Charles Perrone, holding what looked like a bottle of wine. With the other hand he beckoned the red-haired woman inside.

So it's a party, thought Mick Stranahan. How nice.

Fifteen

Joey Perrone had planned nothing more sinister than a shopping trip. At Dinner Key she hauled the kayak out of the water and tied it on top of the Suburban. Then she drove to Merrick Park, where she purchased a shoulder bag, a bikini, four pairs of Italian shoes, a canvas ball cap and hilarious Versace sunglasses. She was feeling almost human by the time she stopped at the Andalusia Bakery in search of a Key lime tart.

Then out of nowhere it hit her again, the fact that her husband had very nearly murdered her. If she hadn't known how to dive, she wouldn't be alive to enjoy the sunshine on her bare arms, Norah Jones on the radio, the scent of new purse leather. It had been Chaz's wish for her to end up in the steaming belly of a shark, or nibbled to pieces by crabs and needlefish.

That asshole, thought Joey, and headed straight for the interstate. Fifty minutes later she was removing the spare key from the bird feeder in her backyard. She entered the house through the rear door and turned off the alarm. A heavy chill took hold of her as she prowled through the familiar rooms; there was no trace of her anywhere.

From past incursions Joey was aware that Chaz had removed the obvious reminders—photographs, clothes, CDs. Now, though, even more was missing. Paintings and pencil sketches that she had picked out were gone from the walls. A crystal figurine of a dolphin that she'd given him for Valentine's Day had been taken from the bookcase. Four silver candle holders, a wedding present from her brother, had disappeared from the china cabinet. Her antique jewelry box was nowhere to be found.

Even in the kitchen, Chaz had expunged all traces. Where was the orchid that had hung in the window? Her coffee mug? The copper pot she'd bought for boiling his precious fucking spaghetti? It was as if she had never lived there, never been there, never existed.

Joey took a steak knife from a drawer and stalked to the bedroom with the notion of slashing his new silk sheets, which smelled like they'd been laundered in stale sangria. Chaz, so particular about Joey's perfumes, evidently let his bimbos drench themselves with any maggot-gagging aroma that happened to be on sale.

She raised the knife over her head, but that was as far as it got. This is pathetic, she thought, and not very original. She dropped the knife and flopped down on the bed—*her* side of the bed. She stared at the popcorn ceiling as she had hundreds of nights before, only now she felt like an intruder.

Which she was.

She had to give Chaz credit. He had thoroughly erased her from the home that had once been theirs. Joey's shoulders started shaking and her knees drew up, and she realized she was sobbing. It made her angry—no, furious—to be crying over a man who wanted her dead.

Just stop it! she told herself. Stop right now.

This isn't about losing Chaz. This is about pride and self-image and all that Dr. Phil crapola. *How could my own husband come to hate me so much? What did I ever do to him?*

"Nothing."

This Joey stated aloud, between sniffles.

"Not a damn thing."

She sat up, dabbing at her eyes with the top sheet.

"So, to hell with Chaz Perrone."

Joey slipped into the bathroom, wincing at her reflection; the puffy eyes and tear-streaked cheeks. She sat down to pee, and to figure out what to do next. On the vanity was a jumbo bottle of Maalox chewables, the sight of which buoyed her spirits. For Chaz an ulcer would be excellent, she thought; a burning, bleeding ulcer the size of a tortilla.

Normally he didn't return from work until six o'clock, so Joey assumed that the slam of the car door had come from another driveway. When a key began jiggling the front doorknob, she tugged up her jeans, shot out of the bathroom, snatched the steak knife off the carpet and rolled beneath the bed.

Footsteps that seemed heavier than Chaz's plodded through the living room and then up the hall. Joey held her breath, thinking: Damn, I didn't flush. If he notices, it's all over.

She switched the knife to her right hand and tested her grip, the footfalls now approaching the bathroom doorway.

Of all the dumb ways to get caught, Joey thought morosely. The one time I forget to flush.

Life was so much simpler bossing a farm crew. You needed money, all you had to do was steal out of their pay. Most of the time they never said boo, they was so afraid you'd turn their asses over to the INS. Ship 'em back to Haiti or the D.R. or whatever godforsaken hellhole they come from. Adios, motherfuckers, do not pass Go.

The fentanyl had taken care of Tool's pain but not the sense of displacement. He stared at the seeping tooth marks on his knuckles and thought: I hate the city.

Partly it was Red's fault for not fronting him some cash. Tool had forgotten how tough it was to pry a dollar bill out of that rich little peckerwood. If Tool had been carrying even a ten spot, why, the driver of that soda truck wouldn't be on his way to the emergency room with his face stoved in like a rotten pumpkin.

Tool shook his head in exasperation. Hadn't he asked like a gentleman?

Hey, son, how 'bout a case of that Mountain Dew?

The driver had chuckled and said he couldn't sell straight off the truck; said so in a tone that Tool took as rude and belittling. The man hitching his eyebrows and asking, "How much is it worth to you, pops? Maybe I can make an exception."

Him not knowing, obviously, how desperate for refreshment a person under the influence of hospital-grade painkillers could be.

Tool didn't believe in beating around the bush, so he'd let the driver know that he wasn't in a position to pay for the case of Dew, on account of he had no money. Promised the guy he'd catch up with him later, though, next time the minimart was due for a soda delivery.

That got the driver laughing so hard that his head started bobbing up and down like a goddamn parrot, which Tool didn't care for one bit. Out on the farm, nobody laughed at him. Nobody dared to look even slightly happy when he came around.

The truck driver was a younger fella, broad and muscle-bound and

full of hisself. Most men would've thought twice about doing what
Tool done, but Tool right away marked the guy as a gym pussy. It was
the smile that give him away, all those teeth so white and square, like
the tiles in the john at the Greyhound depot. The driver, talking down
to Tool like he was some sorta retard, Tool studying them shiny perfect
teeth and thinking: This fucker's never taken a serious punch his entire
life.

Then proceeding to hit the man square in the face, shattering to
pieces that movie-star smile and the nose it was hung on. Down went
the truck driver, and off walked Tool with a whole pallet of unrefriger-
ated Mountain Dew—them two-liter jumbos, which he greatly favored.
Driving back to the doctor's house, he guzzled a whole bottle warm,
that's how blessed thirsty he was.

Now he stood belching in the hallway, trying to decide whether to
take a leak or lie down or maybe call Red and make a pitch for some
dough. The guys that bodyguard the president and movie stars and
such, they get spendin' money. Tool was sure of it. He went in his
room and kicked off his overalls and sat down bare-assed on the bed.

The cell phone that Red had loaned him had the speed-dial function pre-set to call Red's office in LaBelle. Lisbeth said that he was in a
meeting, but she promised to pass along the message about Tool needing some cash ASAP.

Tool wiped his bloody hand on the blanket. I don't belong here, he
thought. I'm not a city man.

He clicked on the television and there was Oprah, that black lady
what had her own show. Tool had heard on Christian radio that Oprah
was richer than some of the richest white people on earth, so he
decided to tune in for a while and see what all the fuss was about.
Damn if Oprah wasn't yakking with three movie actresses about what a
hassle it was to be famous and have photographers snooping around,
following you to the grocery and the ATM, whatever. Tool didn't feel
one tiny bit sorry for her and them other gals, on account of they was
rich enough to build twenty-foot walls around their mansions if they
wanted. Butlers, bodyguards, the best of everything.

Tool found himself thinking about Maureen, the old lady at
Elysian Manor, alone and dying of God knows what kind of rotten
cancer. Damn nurses won't even let her out of the sack to take a shower
or go to the can. There's somebody would trade places with them
actresses in a heartbeat, Tool thought, Maureen would. She'd be

smilin' and wavin' at them photographers, she'd be so grateful not to be sick.

He turned off the TV and trudged to the kitchen, where he emptied the refrigerator and started repacking it with Mountain Dew. Before long, the doctor walked in the door and asked Tool what in the name of God Almighty he was doing.

"What's it look like?" Tool said.

"But I'm expecting company!" Charles Perrone pulled a bottle of white wine out of a brown bag.

"It'll fit," said Tool. He held up his throbbing hand. "Hey, take a look here. See if it's infected."

Charles Perrone reacted as if a tarantula had been thrust in his face. Stumbling backward, he said, "I told you, man, I'm not that kind of doctor."

"Then what hell kind *are* you?" Tool advanced upon him, snatching the bottle of wine.

"I'm a biologist, not an M.D.," Charles Perrone said. "I study water pollution." He grimaced when the goon presented his punctured knuckles for inspection.

Tool said, "Some guy's mouth ran into my fist. Don't it look infected?"

"There's bandages and antibiotic cream in my backpack. I'll get some for you."

" 'Preciate that."

As Tool cleared a space in the freezer compartment for the wine, he wondered why a doctor of water pollution would need a bodyguard.

His voice calmer now, Charles Perrone said, "See, I've got a friend coming over in a little while."

Tool shrugged. "Goodie for you."

"What I meant is, maybe you could put on some clothes."

Tool glanced down at himself. "Actually, I'm pretty damn comfy as is. Mebbe I'll just go to bed."

"Thank you," said the doctor. "Thank you very much."

Chaz went into the bathroom, shut the door and dug the blue pills out of his pocket. His golfing buddy had said it would take about an hour; said to go easy the first time, figure out your tolerance level. Chaz gulped two of the tablets and washed them down with tap water. In the mirror he saw that Tool had pissed in the toilet bowl with the seat down and hadn't bothered to flush.

"Pig," Chaz grumbled. He swathed one hand in tissue and vehemently pressed the lever.

What was that moron doing in here anyway? Chaz wondered. He probably clogged the toilet in the guest bath with all that goddamn oily hair.

After a hurried shower, Chaz phoned Ricca and asked her to come over.

"Have I got a surprise for you," he said.

"I'm not in the mood."

"Oh, come on."

Ricca said, "I don't feel good. I'm going to bed early."

Chaz Perrone wasn't particularly astute at reading women, but he picked up on the fact that Ricca was upset.

"We'll talk when you get here," he said. "I'll make it all better."

"I told you, Chaz. I'm staying home."

"Not tonight. Please? Don't do this to me."

"Call me over the weekend."

"Wait, Ricca—if it's about what happened at lunch? Everything's back to normal, honey, that's what I'm trying to tell you. Bigger and better than ever, I promise—"

"You're not listening," she said curtly. "I'm whipped. I've had a shitty day, and now I'm saying good night."

The line went dead. Chaz Perrone cursed and slouched on the bed. It was for Ricca that he'd purchased the blue pills. He had wanted to demonstrate to her (and, admittedly, himself) that his problem was temporary and easily surmountable.

Now there was movement inside his underwear; slow but deliberate, the way an awakening snake uncoils. Anticipating the mother of all erections, Chaz despaired at the prospect of having no one with whom to share it. The clock was ticking inexorably toward readiness, but the possibilities for a partner were woefully limited. Unlike some of his friends, Chaz had no female fuck buddies to call upon in times of sudden need. The women with whom he had sex typically stopped associating with him as soon as the seedy core of his character came to light, usually within two or three months of the first assignation. Consequently, the names in Chaz's little black book fell into two categories:

former girlfriends who detested him, and current girlfriends who would eventually detest him.

With Ricca mysteriously out of commission for the night, Chaz's only backup was a dippy New Age reflexologist who went by the name of Medea. He'd met her during a round of golf at Boca North, where she offered massages at a juice bar between the ninth green and the tenth tee. Chaz had slept with Medea only three times, with mixed reviews. While she was avid enough as a lover (and as lithe as a howler monkey), she owned several annoying habits, including a proclivity to hum during intercourse. Her favorite tune was called "Tribal Dream," which Medea claimed had been written secretly for her by a man named Yanni. Another unendearing trait was the ritualistic lathering of her unclothed self (and, by contact, Chaz) with warm patchouli oil, the minty stink of which clung to the skin as obstinately as gum turpentine. No less distracting was her flamboyant taste in fashion. Chaz shuddered, recalling the night that her earrings (which could have doubled as hang gliders) first snagged and then painfully uprooted a tuft of his chest hair.

Finally, there was her goofball devotion to reflexology, which she insisted on practicing upon him before every sexual encounter; brutishly wrenching his limbs and fingers, clumsily corkscrewing his neck. For days afterward, Chaz would gulp Advils like popcorn.

That was Medea. She couldn't have sounded any happier to receive his phone call.

When she arrived at the house, Chaz was waiting at the door with the bottle of wine and a world-class boner.

Joey's memories of her family had lost detail over time, but in her mind she carried an indelible image of her parents arm in arm and smiling. That was how they appeared in most of the photographs she had saved—a close, contented couple. She remembered constant laughter in the house; her mother, in particular, found abundant humor in everyday life. Such an outlook must have been useful for operating a casino, a factory of human folly.

Now Joey imagined Hank and Lana Wheeler looking down from heaven and whimsically wondering if their only daughter had gone off the deep end. There was no denying the comedy of her predicament—

hiding under the bed while her husband was trying to line up a hot date.

"Have I got a surprise for you," Chaz was saying into the phone.

Apparently the unflushed toilet had not alerted him to the presence of a hostile intruder. Joey watched his pale, blue-veined feet pace the carpet. How easy it would be to reach out with the steak knife and spear one of those plump, hairless toes.

"Oh, come on," Chaz urged, in a tone well familiar to his unseen spouse. "We'll talk when you get here. I'll make it all better."

Joey studying her husband's toenails, hoping that some exotic swamp rot from the Everglades was pullulating invisibly beneath them.

"Not tonight. Please?" Chaz, turning it on. "Don't do this to me."

Ha! thought Joey. She's blowing him off.

"Wait, Ricca—if it's about what happened at lunch? Everything's back to normal, honey, that's what I'm trying to tell you. Bigger and better than ever, I promise—"

Now Joey had a name to attach to the presence at the other end of the line. *Ricca*. It rang a bell. Wasn't that the name of his hairstylist? Mrs. Charles Perrone idly flexed her fingers around the wooden handle of the steak knife.

"Shit," Chaz muttered, Ricca evidently having hung up on him. The box spring squeaked as he sat down heavily on the bed.

Sulking, Joey surmised. She eyed his bony pink ankles with their faint circumscribed tan lines. One bare heel displayed a nasty blister, the result of an ill-fitting golf shoe. The blister looked raw and quite painful, Joey thought, absently testing the point of the blade against her thumbnail.

There had been an earlier opening to make a break, a ten-minute window of opportunity when Chaz was in the shower and his male houseguest—the one with the elephant footsteps—had clomped into the guest room. For an instant Joey had considered slipping away; crawling from beneath the bed and darting out the back door. That would have been the wise move, and she'd seriously thought about it. But, then, when would she get another chance to observe her cheating, murderous husband at play?

She heard a sequence of beeps on the telephone keypad; Chaz punching in a new number.

"Medea?" he said.

Joey thinking: Oh, this ought to be rich.

"What're you doing tonight, hon?" he asked. "Wanna come over and listen to some music? Yeah . . . my place."

My place? Joey felt her jaws start to grind. She observed that Chaz was unconsciously tapping his feet; the bastard, feeling cocky again.

"Here's the address," he was saying. "Got a pencil?"

Joey listened intently as he dressed and groomed. She knew the whole sound track of his routine: the brisk uncapping of his stick deodorant, the soft rotary whine of the nose-hair clippers, the rhythmic plucking of floss through molars, the plangent yodel of his gargling.

Realizing what lay ahead, Joey should have felt trapped, if not panicky, for she truly had no desire to hear her husband heaving and snorting on top of another woman. Yet she remained strangely calm and anticipatory. Wouldn't it be the ideal occasion on which to return her wedding band, which she'd been carrying around like a bad penny since Mick Stranahan had rescued her? The timing of such a symbolic gesture would be critical, as Joey hoped for the ultimate effect upon Chaz Perrone and his visitor.

Whose name, it turned out, actually *was* Medea.

Joey heard her husband open the front door, a bit of cordial chatter in the living room, the pop of a cork. Then came the music—Celtic folk ballads, of all things, irrefutable proof of Chaz's wanton desperation.

It took him less than fifteen minutes to draw Medea to the bedroom. Scented candles and sticks of incense were lit, Joey forced to swallow a sneeze. As Medea fluttered about, preparing the love chamber, Joey appraised what little she could see—a gold ankle bracelet with a turquoise charm; a rudimentary tattoo of a rose; toenails glossed lavender; feet well tanned, though not dainty.

"I brought something," Medea said to Chaz, and within moments their clothes began hitting the floor in separate piles. Joey stole a peek at the tag in the peasant-style dress (size 10) and wondered if the woman was as tall as she was.

When Chaz dropped his pants, Medea said, "Well, hello there!"

"I told you we missed you." Chaz, insufferably pleased with himself.

"Here." Medea, patting the bed. "Let me give you a rub."

"That's okay. I'm plenty relaxed enough."

"Now, don't argue. Momma knows best."

Joey covered her mouth to keep from laughing.

"But I'm already ready," Chaz said impatiently.

"And you'll *still* be ready when we're done flexing," Medea told him, "and I'll be ready, too. Now be a good little soldier and lie down while I warm up the oil."

"Honey, please. These sheets are a hundred percent silk."

"Oh hush."

As Chaz stretched out, the springs of the bed emitted sparrow-like peeps. Nervously Joey wondered how much Medea weighed; her calves hadn't looked chubby, but that was no guarantee. And what about that large stranger in the house? Joey hadn't been able to hear what he and Chaz were discussing earlier in the kitchen, but she couldn't rule out the possibility that her husband was acting upon his long-cherished fantasy of arranging a threesome.

What a pitiful irony, Joey thought, if the bed collapsed and I was crushed to death by an orgy.

"Wow," she heard Medea say.

"Yeah," Chaz agreed proudly.

"Is that normal?"

"Tell me you're not complaining."

"No, it's just . . ." Medea began, sounding hesitant. "I don't remember it being quite so—"

"Happy."

"Yeah, boy."

Chaz must be in hog heaven, Joey thought. He could chat about his penis all night long.

Joey cringed as Medea climbed on the bed, but there was no seismic aftermath. The conversation abated for a minute or two, then suddenly Chaz yipped in pain. "Geez, you're killing me!"

"Why so tense?" Medea, in the sedated tone of a yoga instructor. "Tell me what's the trouble, sweetheart."

"It feels like you're trying to unscrew my feet. Can't we just skip this part?"

"Not our limbering-up exercises. No, baby."

Joey regretted that her supine alignment afforded no view of the mirror on the bedroom wall.

"There's only one part of me that needs exercising," Chaz was saying, "or else it's gonna explode."

"Okay, okay. Chill out."

Communications between Chaz and Medea became less verbal, and soon the commotion above Joey attained a familiar martial rhythm. Whatever jealousy or revulsion she might have felt soon was displaced by concern for her own safety. As Chaz's exertions grew more forceful, Joey braced her palms and knees against the cross slats of the bed frame. From experience she expected this part of the proceeding to last between ten and twenty minutes, depending on how much wine her husband had consumed. Joey shut her eyes and tried not to visualize what was taking place an arm's length away. Her plan required clear-headed calculation. She intended to wait until Chaz was on the verge of climax before making her surprise entrance, the cue being a low lupine growl that always preceded his seminal moment.

A melody, gaseous and discordant, rose from the bed and wafted through the room—Medea was humming, with Chaz's grimly delivered grunts providing the percussion. Was it some sort of weird tantric mantra, Joey wondered, or merely an off-key rendering of an intrinsically awful song?

Suddenly she heard her husband gasp. "Christ, why can't I feel anything?"

Medea interrupted her humming. "Huh?"

"I said I can't feel a damn thing!" Chaz, panting furiously.

"Don't you dare stop now. Come on, sweetheart."

The bed springs creaked dolorously as he pulled away. Joey couldn't imagine what might be wrong—once her husband got going, nothing short of a thermonuclear event would prevent him from finishing.

"I'm numb," he said.

"Aw, it's just fine. Come on," Medea implored.

"Fine for you maybe."

"Here, sweetheart, let me help—"

"No! Don't!"

"For heaven's sakes." Serene Medea was beginning to sound annoyed.

Joey heard a muted thump and found herself staring at Chaz's bare legs; he'd taken the radical step of vacating the bed.

"What perfume is that?" he demanded of Medea.

"I'm not wearing any. It's the oil, or maybe the huckleberry candles."

"It's not a goddamn candle. I smell perfume," Chaz declared. "The exact same stuff my wife used to wear."

A glacial silence, then: "Your wife?"

"Late wife," Chaz amended hastily.

"How come you never mentioned you were married?"

Joey found herself rooting for Medea. *Tell her the truth, you coward.*

"It's a very painful memory," he said.

"When did she pass away, Chaz?"

A different sort of silence followed, as uncomfortable as the first. Joey longed to see his expression.

He said, "I'd rather not get into it. Too depressing."

"Obviously not *that* depressing," Medea remarked caustically. "I see you're still ready for action."

"Yeah, well, he's got a mind of his own."

Medea sounded unamused. "Like I said, I don't wear perfume. Whatever you're smelling is in your imagination."

It's Chanel, Joey almost whispered.

Before leaving the island, she had innocently dabbed a fleck behind each ear. It was significant that Chaz had sniffed out her scent amid the putridly sweet fumes from Medea's traveling head shop.

"Look, I gotta go," Medea said abruptly.

"No, let's try again."

"I'm not liking the vibes here, Chaz."

"Wait a sec. Now hold on. Please?"

The despair in Chaz's tone was genuine. Hearing him get shut out was almost as good as a wedding-ring ambush, which Joey decided to postpone out of sympathy for Medea.

Who was now out of bed, briskly gathering up her candles and oils.

"You can't go. You *can't*," Chaz was saying. "Just look at me!"

"Very impressive. You should get it bronzed."

"You want to take a bath? We could try it in the bath." He blocked her into a corner, his toes nearly touching hers.

"Chaz, I said no."

"Hey, come on. Don't be like this."

Joey heard a guttural exclamation that elongated into a slow pleasureless moan.

"Stop!" Chaz blurted finally.

"You sure don't listen very good," Medea said.

"You're—really—hurting—me!"

"In reflexology school they gave us special exercises to make our hands strong. Can you tell?"

"Oh my God," said Chaz.

"I bet I could snap it like a bread stick."

"I'm sorry I didn't tell you about my wife. I'm sorry for everything."

"Now, don't get all mushy on me," Medea said.

"You gotta stop. Those fingernails . . ."

"They've gotten long, haven't they?"

"I'm begging you. I'm *begging*," Chaz said.

Joey was enjoying herself. She liked the girl's style.

"I'll let go now," Medea was saying, "but if you so much as *wiggle* that thing in my direction before I get out the door, I'll damage you so badly that you'll never have a sexual experience again. Not even with yourself. Understand?"

"Yes. Ouch! Yes!"

They dressed wordlessly. Joey could envision the dazed, whipped-puppy look in her husband's eyes; she had seen it herself, that time she'd decked him for calling her a crude name.

"Well, good-bye," Medea said, poised at the doorway. Joey noticed that she was wearing hemp flip-flops.

"Sorry about tonight. Honestly," Chaz said. "Can I call you again?"

"Are you fucking serious?"

It was then the floor quaked beneath Joey, as if a refrigerator had been dropped from the roof. A wail of inhuman duration swelled up from elsewhere in the house.

"Oh Christ," Chaz said weakly. "What now?"

Medea was already running by the time Chaz found whatever he was fumbling for in the drawer of the nightstand. Joey Perrone waited to hear him jog down the hall before she scooted from beneath the bed and peeked around the corner. The steak knife felt flimsy and ridiculous in her hand, but she didn't dare put it down.

The shades were drawn on all but one of the bedroom windows.

Mick Stranahan looked inside the house and was discouraged by what he saw: a prodigiously heavyset man, stark naked and swilling from a jumbo bottle of Mountain Dew. Initially, Stranahan thought the man was wearing a tatty sweater, but on closer scrutiny it appeared to be an astounding cultivation of upper body hair. The man sat alone, watching country-music videos on television; no sign of Charles Perrone, the frizzy-haired woman or Joey. Stranahan ducked below the window and pondered his bleak options. A confrontation with the mountainous stranger seemed unavoidable if Stranahan intended to search the house.

Joey had left the spare key inserted in the back door, so Stranahan simply turned the knob and walked in. Cautiously he moved through the empty kitchen, heading toward the darkened hallway. He paused to listen by the guest room, then stepped inside.

The ape man squinted up at him in bafflement, runnels of lime-green soda streaming down his jowls.

Stranahan turned off the television. "I need to look around the house," he whispered. "Are you going to give me any trouble?"

"What a dumbass question. You bet I am."

Muffled pounding and a creepy, disharmonious mewl came from the direction of Chaz's bedroom.

"Are you a friend of Mr. Perrone?" Stranahan asked the hairy stranger.

"I'm his bodyguard. And I been waitin' days for this."

The man got up and trailed Stranahan out of the room.

"Where do you think you're goin'?" he demanded. "What the hell're you lookin' for?"

Stranahan turned and said, "Friend of mine. A lady friend."

The man scratched thoughtfully at his crotch.

"Go ahead and knock me on my ass," Stranahan told him. "I'll probably holler like a baby, but at least it'll spook everybody out where I can see who's who."

The man said, "You nuts, or what?"

"It's not much of a plan," Stranahan conceded, "but it was the best I could do on short notice."

The goon seized him by the collar and began moving toward the back door. Stranahan used the man's own momentum to steer him into a corner, then drove an elbow into his Adam's apple. The man didn't pitch over right away, so Stranahan followed with a right hook to the base of the neck, throwing all his weight into the punch. The man toppled, swiping blindly as he fell. The house shuddered to its beams.

Stranahan ducked outside, circled to the front and crouched behind the Hummer in the driveway. Inside, the bodyguard erupted with a hellish howl as he regained respiratory function. The frizzy-haired woman was the first to bolt, her flip-flops spanking on the walkway as she galloped for her car. Stranahan waited two full minutes after she was gone. When no one else emerged, he retraced his path to the kitchen window. There he saw Chaz Perrone, standing naked in a posture of helplessness over the prone, flopping figure of the ape man. In profile a pistol was visible in Chaz's right hand; beneath that, a jutting manifestation of sexual readiness.

Stranahan heard the nearby slam of a heavy door and, moments later, an automotive ignition. His pulse was pounding as he hurdled a hedge of ixoras and ran toward the road. The Suburban was moving away slowly, lights off. Stranahan waved his arms as he ran after it, thinking: Surely she'll be checking the rearview, after what just happened. Any sane person would worry about being chased.

Finally, at the far end of the block, the brake lights flashed and the passenger door swung open. Mick Stranahan jumped inside and motioned for Joey to hit the accelerator.

Ten miles later, when he finished lecturing her about taking crazy chances, she said, "Nice haircut, sport."

"Hey, at least I don't smell like a Dumpster at Woodstock."

Joey smiled mischievously. "That's not what Chaz thought."

Sixteen

Tool was in a more talkative mood since they'd detoured to a convalescent center so he could "pop in" on somebody named Maureen. Obviously she was his hot new drug connection; probably a rogue nurse, Chaz Perrone had surmised while watching Tool configure an array of fresh fentanyl patches on his shaven shoulders.

"Tell me about your wife," Tool said on the long drive west.

Chaz was caught off guard. "What about her?"

"What was she like before she died?" Tool asked.

"Beautiful. Blond. Smart. Funny."

It was a part of Chaz's widower script that required no rehearsal, because it was the truth. Nonetheless, he found it disquieting to speak the words aloud, as if they reminded some weak and sentimental part of him what he'd lost. Disdainfully he appraised the stubborn, useless bulge in his trousers.

"So how come you ain't all sad and blue?" Tool asked.

"Who says I'm not."

Tool gave a salacious laugh. "It's only been—what, a week?—and already you're on pussy patrol."

"If you're talking about that woman who came over last night," Chaz said, "she was a professional masseuse."

"Yeah, and I'm a fuckin' astronaut. Come on, Doc, what happened 'tween you and your old lady?"

"None of your damn business."

"Aw, relax," Tool said.

Chaz was annoyed by Tool's prying, though he realized that interpersonal sensitivity was not a signature trait among crew bosses on vegetable farms. In fact, the question posed by Tool could just as easily have come from any of Chaz's golfing buddies, and the answer—although it could never be uttered—was simple: Joey knew too much. Or if she didn't *know*, she certainly suspected.

What other choice did Chaz have but to kill her? If the Everglades scam was exposed, the media would have crucified him; a bribe-taking biologist would be front-page news even in a sewer of corruption like South Florida. Chaz surely would have been sent to prison or whacked by Red Hammernut, or possibly both.

He found it ironic that, if the truth ever came out, Tool more than anybody would appreciate the *cojones* that it took to throw Joey off the cruise liner.

As they approached the pump station, Chaz stopped on the shoulder of the levee and kept the engine running. The marsh shimmered under azure skies that stretched as far as the horizon, but Chaz would have been infinitely more relaxed in the parking garage of a shopping mall. He dreaded having to forsake the steel embrace of his Humvee for the loathsome, predator-infested wilderness.

Tool said, "Nice'n peaceful out here."

"Yeah. Paradise."

"What, you'd rather be sittin' bumper-to-bumper on I-95? Are you sick in the head?"

Chaz leaned on the horn to frighten off lurking panthers. Ignoring Tool's puzzled scowl, he said, "Okay, let's get it over with."

Then he climbed down from the Hummer and began changing into his wading gear. Tool examined the new red seal on the left front tire and pronounced it airtight—that was how Chaz's morning had begun, with a flat. The steak knife protruding from the tread had come from the set in his own kitchen, and Chaz assumed that the culprit was the same man who'd broken into the house and tangled with Tool.

"Hey, lookit the gator." Tool pointed to a four-footer nosing curiously out of the saw grass.

"Adorable," Chaz said.

"He's a chunky little sumbitch, huh?"

"Sure is." Chaz thinking: It's like I died and woke up on the fucking Discovery Channel.

He was unsheathing the two-iron when he heard gunfire, prompting him to dive beneath the Humvee. Peeking out, he saw Tool sloshing out of the saw grass and up the embankment, dragging the limp alligator by its tail. The butt of Chaz's pawnshop .38 was visible in a front pocket of the goon's overalls.

Perfect, Chaz thought bleakly. He could see the headline: EVER-GLADES BIOLOGIST BUSTED FOR POACHING.

"Ever tried one a these?" Tool was grinning as he presented the dead animal for inspection. "The way to do it, you batter the chunks and fry 'em in peanut oil."

Not so long ago, the egregious stupidity of plugging a gator would have propelled Chaz into a tirade. Now he wearily accepted such incidents as further proof that life was unraveling beyond his control. In an act of laughable futility, he tried to explain to Tool that shooting a federally protected species was a crime punishable by heavy fines and prison time. Tool chuckled and told him not to worry, the evidence would be gone after supper.

As Tool loaded the oozing corpse into the back of the Humvee, Chaz stepped aside without objection. He was well beyond his default thresholds of shock, disgust or even anger. He picked up the two-iron, clipped a sample-collection container to his waders and trudged into the brown water.

"Need a hand?" Tool, calling from the shore.

"No, sir," Chaz said.

His confidence in Tool's bodyguarding skills had been eroded by the man's lackluster performance against last night's intruder, who—by Tool's own bitter account—was eighty pounds lighter and twenty years older than Tool himself. That the prowler had fled unscathed from Chaz's home was less discouraging than the fact that Red's hired goon had been left blubbering and puking on the floor. Tool had spent the rest of the night in loud recuperation, an ice-filled towel wrapped around his throat. His description of the attacker matched no one known to Chaz Perrone, who figured it was a seasoned thug recruited by Detective Rolvaag as part of the blackmail enterprise. When Tool announced his intention to dismember the intruder the next time their paths crossed, Chaz had to restrain himself from sarcasm.

"You want the gun?" Tool yelled from the embankment.

"I'm fine," Chaz snapped irritably.

With the golf club he hacked a path through the cattails, which had grown dense since he'd last visited this particular sampling site. The lush bloom was a bad sign, indicating a copious and harmful influx of agricultural-based phosphorus. The result was what legitimate biologists would call a "loss of characteristic calcareous periphyton mat." In plain English, it meant that Red Hammernut's farms were flushing so much fertilizer into the water that it was choking part of the Everglades to death.

If any of Dr. Charles Perrone's colleagues were to drive up unexpectedly and observe the proliferation of cattails, they would know instantly that Chaz had been faking the phosphorus readings. That was why he ordinarily uprooted the incriminating fuzz-tipped stalks, but today there were so many . . . and he was far too preoccupied to spend hours slashing in the muck.

Chaz groped at his crotch through the thick rubber leggings and thought: If I died now, they'd never get the coffin shut.

Sixteen hours after swallowing the blue pills, he still carried a baton in his pants. There was absolutely no sensation other than bulk, a numb and obstinate stiffness that even the creeping chill of the pond could not deflate. For Chaz it was the cruelest of afflictions, an enduring yet pleasureless woody.

Hurriedly he dipped up the sample and flailed back toward the levee. Droopy-eyed from the drugs, Tool commented that it was the silliest goddamn job he ever heard of, fillin' bottles with swamp water.

"Does it pay good?" he asked. "I want a gig like this."

"Help me out of these waders," Chaz said. The gnats and flies that were tormenting him displayed no appetite for Tool, whose moist carpet of body hair served as a natural pest deterrent.

"Hurry up!" Chaz said, Tool tugging listlessly at the heavy leggings.

Considering his streak of bad luck, Chaz elected not to dump out the water sample at the site, as he sometimes did to avert the risk of leakage on the Hummer's sweet-smelling upholstery. It turned out to be a prescient decision—the capped Algine-brand container was positioned fortuitously on the front seat when they unexpectedly encountered Marta, Chaz's boss. She was driving her State of Florida pickup truck down the dike in the opposite direction, toward the spillway from which Chaz and Tool had departed. Chaz's rampaging paranoia was such that he refused to consider the possibility that Marta's appearance was part of a routine patrol.

"You're already done out here?" she asked.

Chaz nodded and held up the bottle of water.

"Want me to take that? I'm heading back to the office anyway," Marta offered.

"Oh, no. That's all right." Chaz gripped the container with both hands, in case Marta tried to reach in and snatch it. If she or any other scientist at the water district tested the sample for phosphorus, Chaz would be finished. So would Red Hammernut.

Predictably, Marta was taken aback by the sight of Tool in the passenger seat.

"Grad student," Chaz blurted. "He asked to ride along for a day. I didn't see the harm."

Tool might as well have been wearing a strapless evening gown, the way Marta was staring. "Where do you go to school?" she asked.

Tool turned inquiringly to Chaz, who said, "Florida Atlantic."

"Yeah," Tool grunted. "Floor Dilantic."

Marta smiled gamely. "Well, that's a good program. But you're supposed to sign a liability waiver if you're out in the field with district staff. In case of an accident or something."

"My fault. I forgot," Chaz volunteered, thinking: Thank God I covered the dead gator with my waders.

Marta turned her truck around and waved good-bye. As they followed her down the levee toward the highway, Tool said to Chaz, "Lookit you. Your hands are shakin'."

"Have you got any idea what would've happened if she'd seen"—Chaz was jerking his chin toward the backseat—"*that*?"

"Oh, I had a story all ready to go."

"I'm sure," Chaz said.

"Could say we found the poor thing shot on the dike and we was runnin' it to the vet doctor."

Brilliant, Chaz thought. An alligator ambulance service.

"My stomach's killing me," he muttered.

"Plus, they's a leech on your face."

"That's not funny."

"Just a lil'un." Tool pinched it off and flicked it out the window. "Damn, boy, you's white as a sheet. Maybe you oughta find another job. Seriously."

If only it were so simple, Chaz thought. He touched the tender spot on his cheek and wondered disconsolately if leech slime was toxic. The cell phone rang, but he made no move to grab it. Tool checked the caller ID and announced it was a blocked number.

When Chaz picked up, the blackmailer said: "You're right. We should do a meeting."

Again with the Chuck Heston voice, though it was easier on the nerves than the Jerry Lewis.

"Anytime," Chaz said. "Tell me where and when."

"Midnight. The boat docks down at Flamingo."

"I forget where that is."

"Invest in a map," the blackmailer said curtly, "and don't bother to bring the caveman."

Chaz said, "So it *was* you last night at the house."

"Yep. How was your hot date?"

"Very funny."

"Still, I was impressed by how quickly you've gotten past your grief."

"See you at midnight," Chaz Perrone said.

Joey stood alone in front of the bathroom mirror and said, "Girl, now you've gone and done it."

She had tried to be good, tried to stay the course. She'd even started a list:

1. He's too old for me.
2. I'm too young for him.
3. He's got a rotten track record.
4. I've got a rotten track record.
5. He's never heard of Alicia Keyes.
6. I've never heard of Karla Bonoff.
7. He lives on an island and shoots at strangers who mess with his dog.
8. I live—

That was as far as she'd gotten with her "Ten Sensible Reasons Not to Sleep with Mick Stranahan." Surely there were more than seven, but instead of knuckling down to remember them all, Joey had gone ahead and slept with him.

"You've lost your marbles," she told herself in the mirror.

To make matters worse, it had been her idea. Three in the morning, she's lying alone in bed with the windows open and the taste of the ocean breeze on her tongue. Every time she shuts her eyes she hears this weird, steady chirping noise—*screek, screek, screek*—and every time she opens her eyes it stops. So the noise is strictly in her mind, driving her batty, when all of a sudden she figures out what it is: bed springs. The chirping noise inside her skull was the sound made by the mattress springs while Chaz was trying to hump his hippie date and Joey was under the bed.

Recalling that surreal scene—cowering like a trespasser in what was once her own bedroom, eavesdropping on the lustful exclamations of a man who was, until only a week ago, her own husband and partner—Joey had felt degraded and lonely and pathetic. She'd gotten up and quietly made her way to the living room, where Mick Stranahan was asleep on the couch. Gently she had squeezed beside him, telling herself at the time that all she wanted was a sympathy snuggle; somebody strong to hold her for a little while.

But once she had pressed herself against him and fell into the easy rhythm of his breathing, she'd realized that sweet platonic hugging wasn't going to cut it. She needed more.

"I'm so lame," she said, and splashed her face with cold water.

When she went outside, he was sitting on the seawall, talking on the cell phone. After he hung up, he asked her to sit down.

"You look about eighteen years old this morning," he said.

"Nice try, Mick."

"It's true." He whistled for Strom, who was nose-to-nose with a grumpy pelican.

"We should talk about last night," Joey said.

"I was dog-tired. I did my best."

"That's not what I meant. You were wonderful," she said, "but I think we ought to clarify a few things."

He patted her hand. "That's the last thing on earth we ought to do. Trust me."

Joey pulled away. "Don't make fun. I'm being serious."

"Me, too," he said. "I've had more of these morning-after chats than you have, and not one has ever resulted in clarity, inner peace or mutual understanding. Let's go eat some breakfast."

"But I'm afraid it was a grudge fuck," Joey said. "That's what Rose would call it."

"Ah. More worldly wisdom from the book group."

"Well? What if I jumped your bones just because I was furious at Chaz?"

"Then I owe him one," Stranahan said. "Bless his lying, murderous, cheating, burnt cinder of a soul. Aren't you getting hungry?"

"No!"

He pulled her close and held her there, Strom nuzzling the back of her neck. "Last night you were gloating, remember? Telling me how Chaz got stuck in neutral," Stranahan said, "how his cannon had jammed, all because he smelled your perfume. You said it was priceless—that was your word. Priceless, knowing he was crippled by the thought of you."

Jocy had to smile. "It *was* a moment. I heard him tell her that he couldn't feel a thing. He was numb from the waist down."

"Well, there you go," Stranahan said. "That's a hundred times better than a routine grudge fuck, even saucy Rose would agree. Now, if I don't get some black coffee in my veins—"

"Mick, hold on."

"Hush." He held a finger to her lips. "Honestly, I don't want an explanation of what happened last night. Allow me the middle-aged illusion that you were overcome by my stoic, virile charms."

Joey slumped playfully against his shoulder. "Okay, cowboy, I give up."

"That's my girl."

"Was that Chaz you were calling?"

"It was," Stranahan said. "We're on for midnight."

"And what are we demanding, blackmailwise?"

"Good question. I was hoping for one of your famous lists," he said. "Meanwhile, I expect Detective Rolvaag to visit our young widower soon. There's been a surprising development in the investigation of your disappearance."

"Do tell."

"*Shocking* is the word for it," Stranahan said. "Simply shocking."

Karl Rolvaag turned the place upside down.

Two entire pythons, fourteen and a half linear feet of muscle, yet somehow they'd disappeared like fleas inside his puny apartment.

Incredible, Rolvaag thought. Where could they be?

The previous night he'd forgotten to latch the lid of the tank after refilling the water bowl. It had happened twice in the past, but his sluggish pets never noticed. Now it was springtime, when snakes become active, and the prowling pythons had taken advantage of his carelessness.

Rolvaag searched beneath the furniture, above the bookcases, behind and inside the major appliances—nothing. When he got to the bedroom, he experienced a ripple of apprehension, for he saw that he'd left a window open. Had the snakes escaped outdoors? The detective gazed seven stories down at the grid of shuffleboard courts that was the social and geographic hub of the Sawgrass Grove Condominium. Along a line of bedraggled hibiscus bushes, Nellie Shulman was walking her precious Petunia, a foul-tempered cur that appeared to be a cross between a chinchilla and a wolverine. Several of Mrs. Shulman's neighbors were occupied by the same ritual, attached by dancing leashes to manic balls of fluff. From his vantage Rolvaag counted five dogs, all of them edibly sized for a python. The detective understood the urgency of finding his missing pets before they got hungry again.

First, though, he had to nail Charles Perrone.

On the way to work he called his source at the phone company, who without much grousing agreed to help. Time was running out, and Rolvaag needed to catch Perrone in a lie that couldn't be discounted as a misread wristwatch or some other innocent mistake. Rolvaag's man at the phone company promptly called back with numbers and names, only one of which was important to the detective.

Ricca Spillman opened the door as soon as he flashed his badge. She looked as if she'd spent the night in the trunk of a car.

"Are you all right?" Rolvaag asked.

"Soon as I make some coffee."

Rolvaag noticed at least half a dozen empty beer bottles in the trash, and no sign of company. He said, "I'm investigating a missing-person case. I believe you know her—Joey Perrone."

Ricca appeared to wobble. Rolvaag helped her navigate toward an armchair.

"I wasn't even there," she said.

"Where?"

"On that cruise."

"I know you weren't," said Rolvaag, perplexed.

"Why are you here?" She laughed abjectly. "Somebody put my face on a milk carton, or what? Suddenly I'm Miss Popularity."

The detective said that he'd watched Charles Perrone make a call from a pay phone in a Fort Lauderdale hotel. "It was Saturday evening, the day after Mrs. Perrone disappeared. The number that Mr. Perrone called was yours. When I asked him who he was talking to, he gave the name Ricca."

She sagged. "What else did he say? No, wait, I want to call a lawyer."

Rolvaag pulled up another chair. "You don't need a lawyer, Miss Spillman. I just want to ask a few questions about Mr. Perrone's relationship with his wife. Your personal impressions and observations."

"Observations?"

"You know—did they seem happy? Did they argue a lot?"

Ricca eyed him sullenly. "Mr. Perrone and I didn't spend a whole lotta time talking about Mrs. Perrone."

"But did you notice anything . . . any unusual signs of tension when the two of them were together?"

"I was never with the two of them *together*," Ricca said sharply. "I was only with Chaz."

"Joey wasn't ever home when you were there?"

Ricca seemed genuinely insulted. "I don't know what Chaz told you, but I'm not into threesomes, okay? Not my scene."

The detective frowned. "I'm very sorry. I believe Mr. Perrone might've misrepresented the nature of your association."

"You're damn right he did."

"He said you were their cleaning lady."

"Come again?" Ricca sat forward.

"That night in the hotel lobby, he told me he was calling to give you the alarm code so you could get in to do the house."

"The cleaning lady." Ricca's voice was like wet gravel.

Rolvaag flipped through the back pages of his notebook. "Here it is—Mr. Perrone said you were the cleaning lady and I could check it out myself. He said your first name was Ricca, but he couldn't remember your last name."

Ricca swallowed hard, working her jaw.

"So I got it off the toll records from the phone company," the detective said.

Ricca rose, rubbing her eyes with a wrinkled pajama sleeve. "Listen, I gotta get ready for work."

"Is there anything else you can tell me?" Rolvaag asked.

"Yeah. I don't do houses, I do hair," she said. "And Chaz's burglar alarm was broke, so the code didn't matter anyway. You can check it out."

Not exactly a smoking gun, Rolvaag thought, but it's better than nothing.

Back at the office, he rushed to tell Captain Gallo everything that Ricca Spillman had said. Gallo shrugged.

"So, Perrone lied."

"Again," Rolvaag said.

"So, he had a secret squeeze. Doesn't make him a killer," the captain said. "Of course he lied about the phone call. What'd you expect him to say—'Yes, Officer, I was just chatting with my girlfriend. She was all broken up to hear about my wife falling overboard and drowning on our anniversary cruise.' Come on, Karl. Sometimes a lie isn't a clue to anything. It's just a reflex."

On that subject, Rolvaag could not dispute Gallo's insight. The detective pleaded for a few more days to lean on Ricca. "She's highly pissed off at Perrone. She might give us something useful."

Gallo shook his head. "If she's not wearin' a diamond engagement ring from your prime suspect, I ain't interested. We need a motive, Karl. Something more reliable than the word of a sulking bimbo—unless she was in on it, too."

"Not likely," Rolvaag said.

A courier appeared with a plain cardboard envelope zippered in plastic. Gallo automatically reached for it, but the courier said it was addressed to Rolvaag. Surprised, the detective opened the envelope and removed a legal-size document.

Gallo cracked, "What's that, a paternity suit?"

Rolvaag was so engrossed in the contents that he wasn't listening.

"What?" Gallo pressed. "And don't tell me it's another job offer."

The detective continued reading, turning the pages. "I'll be damned," he murmured to himself.

Gallo exhaled impatiently. "Karl, don't make me pull rank. What the hell is it?"

Rolvaag glanced up with bemusement. "The last will and testament of Joey Perrone," he said, "leaving thirteen million dollars to her loving, devoted husband."

Seventeen

A tow truck dragging a rust-pocked Cordoba nearly clipped Karl Rolvaag's unmarked sedan as he turned into West Boca Dunes Phase II. The detective noticed the battered old car on the hook, figuring that kids from across the tracks must have stolen the thing and ditched it in Charles Perrone's neighborhood. Nobody who lived there would be caught dead driving a heap like that.

Rolvaag parked next to Perrone's yellow Humvee, its leering chrome grille speckled with bug splats. Parked crookedly in the swale was a second car, a spotless new Grand Marquis. The bar-code sticker on a side window pegged it as a rental. Rolvaag touched the hood, which was cold. He heard someone hammering behind the house and walked around to the backyard, where a man he recognized as Earl Edward O'Toole was pounding a white wooden cross into the lawn.

The detective set down his briefcase and identified himself. He said, "Were you a friend of Mrs. Perrone's?"

Earl Edward O'Toole seemed thrown by the question. He shook his head negatively and went on hammering.

"Is the cross for her?" Rolvaag asked.

Earl Edward O'Toole mumbled something indecipherable. Rolvaag stepped closer in order to read the hand-lettered inscription on the cross:

Randolph Claude Gunther
Born 2-24-57
Returned to the Forgiving Arms of
Our Lord and Savior Jesus Christ on 8-17-02
Please Don't Drink and Drive!

"Friend of yours?" Rolvaag asked.

"My dog," said Earl Edward O'Toole, avoiding eye contact.

"That's quite a name for a dog. Randolph Claude Gunther."

"We called him 'Rex' for short."

"I never heard of one living forty-five years," the detective remarked. "Parrots can. Tortoises, too. But I'm not so sure about dogs."

Earl Edward O'Toole took another hard swing with the hammer. "Well, he come from good stock."

"What's that on your back?" Rolvaag said. "Those stickers."

Earl Edward O'Toole hesitated. "Medicine," he replied guardedly.

"For what?"

"I get seasick."

The detective counted five patches and whistled.

Earl Edward O'Toole said, "I'm takin' a sea cruise."

"Yeah? Whereabouts?"

Again Earl Edward O'Toole paused. "Haiti," he said after a moment. "Me and my ma."

"That's a fine idea. Take your mind off poor old Randolph." Rolvaag was enjoying himself. Interludes with such entertaining freaks would be rare once he got back to Minnesota.

"Can I ask why you're planting the cross here? I don't see a grave."

" 'Cause he . . . he died in a plane crash," Earl Edward O'Toole said, "and there wasn't nuthin' left to bury."

"But it says 'don't drink and drive.' "

"On account of the pilot was trashed at the time."

"Ah. And these other crosses?" The detective pointed toward three more, stacked flat on the grass. "Who are they for, Earl?"

"Rex's puppies. They was all on the same plane," Earl Edward O'Toole answered peevishly. "How the hell'd you know my name anyway?"

"Nice chatting with you." Rolvaag picked up his briefcase and headed toward the house, where Charles Regis Perrone was waiting cheerlessly at the back door.

The white crosses had been erected along Glades Road, west of the turnpike; four of them in a cluster, memorializing a terrible head-on. With numb resignation Chaz had watched Red Hammernut's goon uprooting the crosses, until a car screeched to a halt on the shoulder of the highway. Two young men identifying themselves as brothers of the late Randolph Claude Gunther had leapt out of the car and angrily confronted Tool about stealing the markers. The men had brought fresh-cut sunflowers to hang on their brother's cross, and a volume of Bible verses from which to read. With Tool ignoring their remonstrations, the men had begun preaching loudly at him, invoking Satan and other Biblical scoundrels. Tool had responded by heaving the two brothers into a roadside canal, shredding their book of verses and eating the flowers. Chaz had looked on with the shivers.

Tool had returned to the Hummer, carrying the four crosses on his shoulders, saying brightly, "I got a whole field of these suckers at home."

"Hmmm," Chaz had managed.

"They look real nice in the ground, plus you don't gotta prune 'em like you do trees and shrubs."

"Excellent point," Chaz had said, making a mental note to call Red Hammernut first thing in the morning to plead for a new bodyguard.

After they'd returned to Chaz's house, Tool had borrowed a hammer and announced that he was planting the traffic crosses temporarily in the backyard. Chaz would have objected more strenuously if he'd known that Karl Rolvaag would be dropping by.

"How do you know Mr. O'Toole?" the detective asked at the door. It was the first time Chaz had heard the thug's actual name.

"He's just a friend of a friend."

"The friend being Samuel Johnson Hammernut?" Rolvaag said.

"Yes, well, actually he was an acquaintance of my wife's. I barely know the guy."

"Mr. O'Toole or Mr. Hammernut?"

"Neither of them," Chaz said innocently.

The detective rubbed his chin. "That's sort of strange."

"What do you mean? 'Strange' how?" asked Chaz, on the verge of a blowup. The cop was toying with him, like a cat batting around a ball of yarn.

"Your Humvee—one of Mr. Hammernut's companies purchased it for you," Rolvaag said, "according to the records at the dealership."

Oh shit, Chaz thought.

"You hardly know the man and he's buying you a sixty-thousand-dollar sport-utility vehicle?" Rolvaag now actually scratching his head, just like that flaky Columbo character on television. Chaz was seething on the inside but he managed to look calm.

"Let me explain," he said to the detective. "The Hummer was a birthday present from Joey. Red knew—Mr. Hammernut—he knew the salesman personally, so he got a really sweet deal. Joey paid him back later."

"With a check, or a wire transfer? Actually, it doesn't matter. Either way, the bank should have a record."

Chaz Perrone shrugged. "I don't know how she handled it. It was her money."

Now they were sitting in the kitchen; Chaz with an untouched beer, the cop with his usual Sprite. During lulls in the conversation, sizzles and pops could be heard from a frying pan on the stove.

Chaz leaned forward and lowered his voice. "Can we please cut all this ridiculous bullshit? Just tell me how much you want."

Rolvaag seemed genuinely baffled.

"Oh, come on," Chaz said. "Save me that god-awful trip to Flamingo."

"You're losing me."

Not wishing to spook the crooked detective, Chaz didn't want to come right out with the word *blackmail*.

Rolvaag said, "You should be aware that I've already spoken to Mr. Hammernut in LaBelle. He described Mr. O'Toole as a former employee, not a friend. Said he hardly remembered him."

Chaz sat back and crossed his arms. "Fine. We'll play it your way."

Like I've got a choice, he thought.

Glossy with perspiration, Tool lumbered into the kitchen to check on the entrée. "Three more minutes," he announced, and walked out.

"He's staying here with you?" Rolvaag asked.

"Yeah. While his double-wide gets fumigated."

"What's with the highway crosses?"

"I'm not sure," Chaz Perrone said, "but it might have something to do with him being a deranged, half-witted sociopath."

"Right."

"He claims to be carrying a bullet slug in the crack of his butt."

"Everybody's got problems," Rolvaag said.

"Is there, like, a particular reason you're here?" Chaz inquired. *Besides the sheer sadistic joy you obviously get from busting my balls.*

"Yes, of course," said the detective.

"Then can we get to it, please? I've got a three-hour drive to the middle of nowhere, thanks to you."

Rolvaag reached for his briefcase, but then Tool reappeared, briskly toweling his sweaty torso. With uncharacteristic buoyancy he asked if anybody was hungry.

"Because I could eat a bus," he said, forking crispy hunks of alligator tail from the frying pan onto a platter.

Apparently, Rolvaag will be staying for supper, Chaz thought, and I'm helpless to stop it. He hoped that Tool had efficiently disposed of the illegal reptile carcass.

"I hope you like chicken," Chaz said to the detective.

Tool let out a cackle. "We're talkin' *major* chicken. Serious fuckin' swamp chicken."

"Smells delicious," Rolvaag said, "but no thanks. I've got a lasagna waiting at home."

"And my stomach is acting up again," Chaz chimed in, with barely masked relief. Gnawing on the deep-fried ass of a prehistoric lizard was not his notion of a gourmet experience. In fact, only imminent starvation could have induced him to consume anything from the sullied waters of Hammernut Farms.

"Then I'll eat the whole fucker m'self," Tool said eagerly.

So barbaric was the gustatory spectacle that Chaz Perrone and Karl Rolvaag retreated to the living room, the detective pausing to admire the re-stocked aquarium.

"Those little blue-striped fellows—are they wrasses?"

"Your guess is as good as mine." Chaz thinking: Do I look like frigging Jacques Cousteau?

"You were about to ask me something," he said, "before we got interrupted by Chef Cro-Magnon."

Rolvaag sat on the sofa and opened the briefcase. Leafing through a file folder, he said, "Yes. I need a sample of your wife's handwriting."

"What the hell for?" Chaz knew it wasn't a well-measured response, but the detective's request had flustered him.

"For comparison purposes," Rolvaag said.

Chaz rolled his eyes and snorted, an unfortunate reflex whenever he felt confronted by authority. It had caused him problems in college, as well.

"I don't need much," Rolvaag said. "A few lines in pen or pencil."

Chaz stood up and said he'd see what he could find, which of course would be nothing. He had thrown away everything Joey had ever written to him—birthday cards, love letters, Post-its. The detective hovered while Chaz pretended to search.

"I put away most of her stuff," he said, pawing through a bureau drawer in the bedroom.

"I remember. Where are those boxes?" Rolvaag asked.

"Storage." Chaz thinking: Under about five thousand tons of raw garbage.

"Even just a signature would be fine," Rolvaag said.

"Hang on. I'm still looking."

"What about her checkbook?"

Chaz shook his head and dug into another drawer. He didn't know where the detective was headed with the handwriting angle, but it couldn't be good.

"Credit card receipts?" Rolvaag said.

"God only knows where she put them."

"How about cooking recipes? Some people jot their favorite ones on index cards."

"Joey was a fantastic girl, but not exactly queen of the kitchen." Chaz trying to sound fondly reminiscent. "We ate out a lot," he added with a forced chuckle.

Rolvaag suggested searching Joey's car. "Maybe there's an old grocery list crumpled on the floor somewhere."

"Good idea," said Chaz, knowing full well the futility of that exercise. Rolvaag poked around the garage while Chaz picked through the Camry, which smelled faintly of his wife's killer perfume. Fearing another untimely erectile episode, Chaz breathed through his mouth in order to minimize his exposure.

Eventually he heard Rolvaag saying, "Well, thanks for taking a look."

The cop was a damn good actor, Chaz had to admit. Not once had he slipped out of character. Chaz had been waiting for some subtle acknowledgment of the situation—a sidelong wink, the wry flicker of an eye. Yet Rolvaag had betrayed no awareness of the blackmail scheme while sustaining his front as a dogged and upright pursuer of clues. A less perceptive criminal might have discarded the theory that Rolvaag was the one shaking him down, but Chaz Perrone wasn't swayed by the detective's performance. The more Chaz thought about it, the more unlikely it seemed that anybody had seen him push Joey off the *Sun Duchess*. Chaz remembered how careful he'd been to wait for the decks to empty first. He remembered standing alone at the rail afterward and hearing nothing but the rumble of the ship's engines; no voices, no footsteps. The blackmailer had to be bluffing. Nobody could have witnessed the murder of Joey Perrone.

And now Karl Rolvaag, who'd plainly never believed Chaz's account of that night, had decided in the absence of evidence to make him pay for the crime in another way.

As they returned to the living room, Chaz coyly asked, "Who's your favorite movie star?"

"Let me think." Rolvaag pressed his lips together. "Frances McDormand."

"Who?"

"She was in *Fargo*."

"No, I meant *guy* movie stars," Chaz said.

"I don't know. Jack Nicholson, I guess."

"Not me. Charlton Heston is my favorite." Chaz watched for the slightest flush of color in the detective's face.

Rolvaag was saying, "Yes, he's good, too. *Ben-Hur* was a classic."

And that was it; not a blink of surprise, not a hint of a smile. Chaz Perrone was so aggravated that he couldn't stop himself from saying, "Anyone ever tell you that sometimes you sound like him?"

The detective seemed amused. "Like Charlton Heston—me? No, that's a new one."

What an iceberg, thought Chaz.

He said, "Sorry I couldn't help with Joey's handwriting. I can't believe there wasn't something of hers lying around the house."

"No sweat. I'll call the bank," Rolvaag said. "They'll have all her canceled checks on film."

"Can I ask what this is about?"

"Sure."

The detective removed a large envelope from his briefcase and handed it to Chaz Perrone, who couldn't stop his fingers from trembling as he opened it. He skimmed the first paragraph and asked, "Where'd you get this?"

"Keep going," Rolvaag advised, and strolled off to the kitchen.

By the time Chaz finished, his heart was hammering, his shirt was damp and his skull was ringing like a pinball machine. Before him lay a photocopy of an astounding document, "The Last Will and Testament of Joey Christina Perrone." For Chaz it was the ultimate good news/bad news joke.

The good news: Your dead wife left you 13 million bucks.

The bad news: The cop who thinks you murdered her finally found a motive.

Chaz placed the papers on his lap and dried his palms on the sofa. He flipped again to the last page and eyed the signature.

"Is it hers?" Rolvaag standing at the doorway, popping another goddamn Sprite.

"I swear I didn't know anything about this," Chaz said. "And you can put me on a polygraph."

"Check out the date it was signed—only a month ago," Rolvaag said.

"Joey never said one word to me about this."

"That's interesting."

"Don't you think I would have told you about it if I'd known? For Chrissakes, I'm not an idiot." Chaz could feel his gears slipping. "Is this the real deal, or is it just part of the setup? And don't act like you don't know what I'm talking about."

The detective said, "I couldn't tell whether it's authentic or not. That's why I'm here, Chaz. That's why I wanted a sample of Mrs. Perrone's handwriting."

"You listen to me—no more games!" Chaz bellowed. "No more bullshit, okay? You're a fucking crook and I know exactly what you're up to. This isn't Joey's will, it's a goddamn fake! You couldn't find a way to prosecute me, so now you're going to frame me, then make me buy my way out. . . ."

Here Chaz contemplated ripping the will into pieces for dramatic effect. However, in the back of his mind a tiny voice reminded him of the slim but sobering possibility that he was mistaken about Rolvaag; that the shocking legal instrument was legitimate. Chaz found himself inadvertently clutching it with both hands, the way Moses (at least as portrayed by Chuck Heston) clung to the holy tablets of the law.

Maddeningly immune to insult, Rolvaag said, "You can keep it, Chaz. I've got copies."

Tool entered the room, his cheeks shiny with gator dribble. He asked what all the hollering was about.

"Mr. Perrone got a little upset with me," the detective explained, "but he's calmed down now."

Chaz said, "Not much."

Tool said, "Doc, you look like shit on a dumpling."

"Thanks for noticing. Can the detective and I have some privacy?"

When the two of them were alone again, Rolvaag said, "I asked you about the signature."

"It looks sort of like Joey's. Close enough anyway," Chaz said. "Whoever you got to forge it did a good job."

Rolvaag's expression remained unchanged. "Let me be sure I understand. You're accusing me of fabricating this will for the purpose of implicating you in your wife's disappearance?"

"Duh."

"But you mentioned blackmail. I don't get it."

"Try the dictionary." Chaz thinking: The fucker wants to see me squirm, forget it.

Rolvaag thought for a moment, then said, "So the plan would be that you pay me off, and I'll make your thirteen-million-dollar motive go away. Mrs. Perrone's will vanishes."

"Exactly. And don't forget your bogus eyewitness."

"What?" The detective cocked his head slightly, as if listening for the faint call of a rare songbird. It was a reaction so nuanced as to be chillingly convincing.

"What eyewitness?" he asked.

Chaz felt his stomach turn. Holy Jesus, either this guy is *really* slick or I've just made the worst mistake of my life.

"What eyewitness?" Rolvaag said again.

Chaz laughed thinly. "I'm kidding, man." It was a conversation for which he had not rehearsed.

"It didn't sound like you were kidding."

"Well, I was," Chaz said. "You Scandinavians, I swear."

Rolvaag quietly closed the briefcase. "I'm not blackmailing you, Mr. Perrone."

"Of course you're not."

"But you should still be careful," the detective said, rising. "More careful than you've been so far."

Eighteen

Joey struggled with the list of blackmail demands, but all she truly wanted from Chaz Perrone were, besides his eternal suffering, the answers to two questions:

(a) Why did you marry me?

(b) Why did you try to kill me?

"Pick a number," said Mick Stranahan. "This is supposed to be a shakedown, remember? How much dough can he scrape together?"

"Beats me." Joey turned to stare out the window.

Flamingo was a fish camp in Everglades National Park, on the southernmost shore of mainland Florida. Only one road led there, a two-lane blacktop that sliced through thirty-eight miles of unbroken scrub, cypress heads and saw-grass prairies. Although they were speeding through absolute darkness, Joey sensed a pulse of unseen life all around them. The post-Miami hush was so soothing, the night so engulfing, she was unable to focus on the details of the blackmail. The deeper they drove into the Everglades, the smaller and more absurd Chaz Perrone seemed.

Stranahan parked the Suburban in a cluster of cabbage palms near the campground, a short jog from the marina. By now it was ten o'clock and most of the campers, besieged by insects, had retreated to their sleeping bags. Mick fiddled with the dashboard stereo but the radio signal was spotty.

Joey said she'd never before been to the park. "Chaz refused to take me. He said it reminded him too much of work. Actually, I think the bugs creep him out."

"The bugs."

"Mosquitoes especially," she said. "Then there's the snake issue—he's terrified of being bitten by a moccasin. At home he used to practice injecting the antivenin serum into grapefruits."

"Boy, is he in the wrong line of work," Stranahan remarked. "You ever wonder why? How the hell he got where he is?"

Joey had always assumed that her husband made a wrong turn in graduate school.

"I meant to ask you," Stranahan said, "who's Samuel J. Hammernut?"

"Some rich redneck pal of Chaz's. I met him at the wedding," said Joey. "Why? What's he got to do with all this?"

"I made a few calls about the Hummer. It was bought for your hubby by Hammernut Farms."

Joey had no idea why Mr. Hammernut would have given Chaz a brand-new SUV. "You're just now telling me this? Who did you call?"

"Friends who do that sort of thing—trace paperwork. Friends in law enforcement," Stranahan said. "Remember I told you this was all about greed. My guess is that Chaz has some sort of dirty arrangement with Hammernut, and that maybe you got in the way."

"But how? What did I do?"

Stranahan told his theory to Joey, who was intrigued but skeptical. "Who ever heard of a crooked biologist?" she asked.

"Who ever heard of one with a bodyguard?" he countered.

Joey conceded the point. She had been surprised, and tickled, to learn from Mick that her husband was now being protected by paid muscle.

"Look, there are cops who take payoffs," Stranahan was saying, "judges who fix cases, doctors who cheat Medicare. Are you telling me Chaz is too pure to sell himself—the man who pushed you into the ocean to die?"

He's right, Joey thought. Obviously the jerk is capable of anything. She scooted closer and put a hand on Mick's knee. He kissed her on the top of the head, but she could tell he was tense. He pointed toward the motel building and said, "Your room's on the second floor. Stay put until you see me signal with the flashlight."

"Three blinks. I remember."

They watched a pair of raccoons shuffle into the campground, emerging moments later with a loaf of bread and a bag of Doritos.

Stranahan said, "Isn't the idea to make him panic?"

"Yeah. Tighten the screws."

"Then what the hell. Let's ask for half a million."

Joey laughed. "Good Lord, Chaz doesn't have that kind of money."

"I bet he knows someone who does."

They took the Grand Marquis, Tool saying that the Hummer practically glowed in the dark. Red had told them to stay cool, no matter what. Listen to what the guy has to say and tell him you'll think about it. Don't be a smartass, Red had warned Chaz. And don't hurt nobody, he'd said to Tool, not just yet. Once we find out what the sumbitch wants, then we'll figure out what to do about him.

The plan was to arrive at Flamingo early and find a spot for Tool to hide, but they got delayed because Tool made another pit stop before they hit the turnpike. Chaz didn't bother to ask. He stayed in the car and practiced whipping the .38 out of his waistband while Tool put on his tent-size lab whites and marched into the Elysian Manor convalescent home.

Maureen was sitting up, watching television. She had brushed her hair and put a touch of makeup on her cheeks.

"Well, look who's here," she said. "Pull up a chair. Larry King is interviewing Julie Andrews. What a doll she is."

"I brung you some supper." Tool placed a covered dish on the bed tray. "It ain't very hot. Do they got a microwave somewheres?"

"Why, thank you, Earl." Maureen lifted the lid and said, "It smells grand. What is it?"

"Uh, chicken. Swamp chicken, they call it."

"Doctor says I'm supposed to steer clear of fried foods, but I can't honestly see the harm. Since I'm dying anyway, right?" She picked up a piece of fried alligator and popped it in her mouth.

"Good, huh?" Tool said.

Maureen nodded eagerly as she chewed. And chewed.

"The food they serve us in here is a horror," she whispered. "Fresh poultry is a real treat."

"Well, I'm glad you like it. Now I better go."

"Already? Please sit and visit."

"I got a 'portant bidness meetin'."

"At night? What kind of business, if I might ask."

"Bodyguardin'," Tool said.

Maureen's blue eyes sparkled. "That's so interesting, Earl. What sorts of people do you guard? Dignitaries? Diplomats? Show business types, I bet."

"Not hardly."

"Oh." She sounded disappointed.

"The job I'm on now, he's a doctor," Tool said, though he considered the title a hype job, as attached to Chaz Perrone.

"A doctor—well, that's something!"

"Only he don't work on people. He's, like, some kinda scientist."

Maureen said, "He must be very important, to need personal protection."

"Don't get me started."

"Is he with you now? I'd enjoy meeting him."

Tool said, "He ain't no charmer, trust me. Thinks the world of his self but, I swear, the nigras and spics used to pick tomatoes for me had more common sense than—"

Maureen's bony fist shot out and nailed Tool in the soft declivity below the sternum. He bent double and heard himself deflate like a tractor tire.

"Earl! Shame on you!" she said. "Don't you *ever* use that kind of hateful language around me."

He hung on to the bed rail, slowly straightening himself.

"What would your mother do," Maureen went on, "if she were alive to hear you talk like that?"

"Sh-sh-she's the one I learnt it from," he wheezed. "Her and my daddy both."

"Then shame on them, too. Here"—she handed him a Dixie cup from the bed tray—"drink up. You'll feel better."

"Damn," Tool said, gulping at the water. The crazy old witch had really thumped him. In his whole life he couldn't remember anybody ever throwing a punch at him and getting clean away with it. Once he'd damn near crippled a couple of sorry beaners just for lookin' at him funny-like in the package store.

Staring now at Maureen, as frail and brittle as a fallen leaf, Tool knew he could have killed her with the back of his hand. Strangely, though, he didn't want to. And it wasn't as if he was holding back the urge, he just plain had no desire to harm the woman, despite what she'd done. He wasn't pissed, either, which was even more confusing. What he felt—and he wasn't sure why—was sorry.

He heard himself say so.

Maureen reached out and plucked at his sleeve. "And I'm sorry, too, Earl, for striking you. It wasn't very Christian of me," she said. "How are you fixed for medicine?"

"Fine, ma'am. The patches you give me this mornin' ought to last for the weekend."

"You know, my husband was a Chicago police officer."

"You tole me, yes'm."

"One time he used the word *nigger*. I heard him let it slip," Maureen said. "He was on the phone to his sergeant or somebody. He said, 'Some nigger robbed a Korean grocery and we chased him into Lake Michigan.' When he hung up, I tapped him on the shoulder—he was a big fella, too—and I said, 'Patrick, if I ever hear you use that hateful word again, I'm taking the kids and moving back to Indianapolis to live with Aunt Sharon.' And you know what?"

"He never done it again."

She smiled. "That's right, Earl. Do you believe God made each of us in His own image?"

Tool said, "I ain't always so sure." He crossed his arms across his belly in case she took another swipe at him.

"To be honest, some days I wonder myself," Maureen said. "They've got one nurse here, Earl, I swear she's on loan from the depths of hell. Talk about the *b* word! But here's what I believe—can I tell you? Then you're free to be on your way."

"Sure," Tool said.

"I believe it's never too late to change. I'm eighty-one years old, but I still think I can be a better person tomorrow than I am today. And that's what I'll believe until I run out of tomorrows," she said. "Oh, one more thing—you promised to go see a surgeon."

"Yeah, I know."

"About the bullet in your you-know-what."

"I been real busy," Tool said.

"Young man, you listen here. Life's too darn short to be dragging around that kind of a personal burden."

"Yes'm."

"Now get a move on, before you miss your meeting," she said. "And be careful tonight."

"Don't worry."

"Whatever it is you're up to." Maureen flashing him a sideways glance. "Go on now, Earl."

She flicked a papery hand toward the door, and returned her attention to the television.

They got all the way to Florida City before Tool spoke, which was fine with Chaz Perrone. He wasn't thinking about the blackmail meeting; he was fantasizing about what it would be like to have $13 million, in the stupefying event that the will bearing Joey's name turned out to be authentic. The irony would be epic, for she wouldn't have left Chaz a nickel if she'd suspected him of forging the Everglades data. Since it was dated only weeks ago, the will could be legitimate only if Joey hadn't figured out Chaz's deal with Red. . . .

Meaning he had murdered her for no reason, or at least the wrong reason.

Contemplating the possibility made him light-headed and queasy. Unless otherwise convinced, he'd stick to the more plausible hypothesis that Karl Rolvaag had fabricated the document to intimidate him.

"I'm hungry," Tool grumbled, wheeling sharply into the parking lot of a Miami Subs shop.

"Bring me a Coke and some fries," said Chaz.

"Git it yourself."

Chaz hid the .38 under the front seat and followed Tool into the restaurant. Chaz had begged and pestered for a new bodyguard, but Red Hammernut had refused, saying Tool was rock-solid.

Rock-headed is more like it, Chaz thought. They sat in a booth, Tool wolfishly attacking a turkey sub the size of a football.

"Where's the gun?" Tool, spraying half-mulched lettuce.

Chaz pointed at the car through the window.

"Ever shot anybody?" Tool asked.

"No."

"Ever shot *anything*?"

"Birds," Chaz said.

As a kid, he'd used a BB rifle to snipe at the sparrows and warblers that woke him in the mornings.

Tool said, "You got no bidness with a gun 'less you practice. I been shot by a joker once already and that's plenty."

"Stop worrying."

At the entrance of Everglades National Park, a ranger inquired about their lack of fishing gear and camping equipment. A notice taped to the kiosk warned against bringing firearms inside the park.

"We're meeting some friends," Chaz said. "The Thornburghs. They're in a brand-new Airstream, Michigan plates. Got an Irish setter named Mickey that rides up front. Did they come through here yet?"

"Couldn't say. I just now came on duty."

"Well, I'm sure we'll find 'em." Chaz, waving pleasantly.

A mile down the road, Tool spoke up. "Where the fuck'd you come up with that one?"

"Pretty good, huh?"

"What's a Airstream?"

Chaz said, "A motor home. You know, like a Winnebago, only not so clunky. He sure went for it, didn't he?"

"And that bullshit about the dog—you just all of a sudden thought that up?"

"Yep." Chaz couldn't tell if Tool was impressed or disgusted.

"I never seen nobody could lie such a way."

"Hey, sometimes you've got to think fast," Chaz said. "That ranger, see, it's none of his business if we've got fishing poles or whatever in the car. But I can't come out and say that to his face, so I cook up a story and off we go."

Tool nodded, both hands on the wheel. "Pretty damn smooth," he said.

The sky was clouded and starless. Ahead of them, speared by the twin beams of the headlights, was a canvas of blackness. At first Chaz thought they were riding through a rain shower, but the splattering sound turned out to be a hail of bugs hitting the windshield. When a marsh rabbit appeared on the center stripe, Tool casually swerved to miss it. Chaz told him to stop the car right away.

"Why, you gotta take a piss?" Tool coasted the sedan off the pavement and braked.

"Turn us around," Chaz said.

"What for?"

"Hurry!"

Tool made a flawless three-pointer and headed slowly back up the road until they came to the rabbit, which hadn't moved. Chaz reached beneath the seat and took out the pistol. Tool blinked at him slowly, like a drugged toad.

Chaz said, "You told me to practice, right?"

"Not on a fuckin' bunny."

"It's just a big overgrown rodent," said Chaz, betraying an ignorance of taxonomy that would have appalled his colleagues but was lost on Tool. "A rat with big ears," he added, stealthily opening the car door.

Tool said, "You shoot that thing, you're gonna eat it for breakfast."

"Yeah, right."

"Doc, I ain't kiddin'. My momma used to tell us, 'Anything that dies, fries.' Ain't right to waste a critter just for sport."

Chaz wondered if the medicine patches were making Tool loopy. Why should he care about a dumb rabbit? Chaz leaned across the hood of the car and took aim at the animal, which remained motionless in the lights. When the .38 went off, the rabbit hopped straight in the air, spun around once, dashed in a circle and then stopped. Its eyes were wide and its nose was quivering.

"Shit, I missed," Chaz muttered, and fired again. This time the animal flattened itself to the pavement and laid back its ears, as if hiding in the scrub.

Tool said, "That's enough, Rambo."

"Just one more." Chaz thinking: It's okay for *him* to plug an alligator.

"You're done," Tool said gruffly.

"Not quite." Chaz shutting one eye and squinting down the barrel.

"I said no."

Tool goosed the accelerator a millisecond before Chaz squeezed the trigger. He felt himself vaulted airborne and, suspended in flight, he witnessed the tawny blur of the rabbit disappearing into the tall grass. He came down hard in the loose gravel and rolled twice. For several moments he lay still, dazedly watching the insects swarm around the headlights of the idling car. Soon he heard the crunch of footfalls and saw the broad silhouette of Tool above him.

"Help me up," Chaz said with an imprudent lack of remorse.

"You're one dumb fuck of a so-called doctor."

Tool picked up the .38 and stalked back toward the Grand Marquis.

"What the hell's wrong with you?" Chaz hollered after him. "Were you trying to kill me?"

He struggled to his feet and brushed the pebbles off his clothes. When he got back into the car, Tool jabbed a finger in his chest and said, "If I was tryin' to kill you, pretty boy, you'd be havin' this conversation with Saint Peter."

Chaz waited another ten miles before asking about the gun.

Tool said, "You're done for the night."

"But what if I need it later? What if this asshole blackmailer decides to play rough?"

Tool seemed to think that was quite funny. "Boy, you won't need a gun," he said. "You got *me*."

Nineteen

Stranahan was already on the water when the Grand Marquis rolled up at the marina. The caveman got out slowly while Chaz Perrone practically ejected himself from the passenger side, slapping frenetically at his face and neck. They walked back and forth along the slips, eventually choosing an unoccupied houseboat and prying the door. The caveman ducked inside while Chaz hopped back on the dock, stumbling over a coiled rope. After a while he began to pace in and out of the shadows, still flailing at the bugs. At midnight Stranahan called out his name and Chaz dropped into a ludicrous semi-crouch that he must have picked up from a Jackie Chan movie.

Stranahan waved. "Over here, numbnuts!"

Chaz approached tentatively, continuing to affect the coiled pose of a kung fu master. He seemed alarmed to see his blackmailer sitting in a small canoe.

"Hop in," Stranahan said as he nosed up to the boat ramp.

"No way."

"This was your idea, Chazzie."

"The meeting, not the place," Chaz said, "and not the damn canoe."

Stranahan laid the paddle across his lap and gave Chaz some time to size him up. Then he said, "If you want to hear the deal, park your ass in the bow."

Chaz glanced uneasily toward the slip where the houseboat was moored.

Stranahan said, "That's another thing. I told you to leave your pal with Dr. Leakey."

"What are you talking about?"

"You're such a dolt. I should *triple* my price."

Chaz stepped gingerly into the canoe. "Where do I sit?"

"You don't sit," Stranahan said. "You kneel."

With long, even strokes he began paddling down the Buttonwood Canal toward Whitewater Bay.

"Can I borrow the bug spray?" Chaz anxiously pointed to a Cutter's squirt bottle in the bottom of the canoe. Stranahan tossed it to him.

"Where we going?" Chaz, spritzing himself.

"There's nothing to be afraid of, as long as you don't tip us over."

"Don't worry, I'm not moving a muscle." Chaz put down the bottle and got a death grip on the sides of the canoe.

"Moccasin Pass. That's where we're headed," Stranahan said. To his knowledge, there was no such place. However, the ominous name produced the desired effect.

"Holy shit," he heard Chaz Perrone murmur.

"Supposedly it's got the biggest water moccasins in the 'glades," Stranahan went on, drawing a defeated groan. In person, Joey's husband was pretty much what Stranahan had expected—soft and whiny under pressure.

"You've also got your crocodiles and sharks, mister," Stranahan said, switching momentarily to his Jerry Lewis voice, "which is why I strongly recommend against flipping the canoe."

Chaz fell silent. When they reached Whitewater, Stranahan stopped paddling and instructed Chaz to turn around, which he did with the utmost care. When Stranahan aimed a flashlight in his face, he flinched and looked away.

Stranahan said, "You're sulking, aren't you? You think I'm having fun at your expense."

To taunt such a pismire was almost unsporting, but it diverted Stranahan from a nagging but barbarous impulse to beat the man into hamburger hash. Perhaps the day for such uncivilized festivities would come, but for now he'd settle for the sight of Charles Perrone's ears turning black with mosquitoes. It had been Joey's fine idea to replace the insect repellent with tap water.

"How'd you get into my house?" Chaz asked.

"Trade secret."

"Are you the one who cut up that picture of my wife and put it under my pillow?"

"No, that would be the picture fairy."

"Who the fuck *are* you? What do you want from me?" Chaz whacking at both sides of his head.

"Money, for starters."

"There's more?" Chaz hacked out a sour laugh.

"Plus I'd like you to answer a few simple questions. That's it."

"What questions? You're shaking me down over something I didn't even do."

"Fine. Then don't pay me a penny," Stranahan said. "We'll let a jury decide—my word against yours. By the way, have you ever been to scenic Raiford, Florida, home of the Union Correctional prison?"

Chaz swore and slapped himself again on the head.

"Nice shot." Stranahan turned off the flashlight. "I guess the only way to prove I'm not bullshitting is to tell you exactly what happened on the *Sun Duchess*. Listen carefully."

"I am," Chaz said with a grunt.

"It was a week ago tonight," Stranahan began. "You and your wife came on deck shortly before eleven and walked toward the stern. Nobody was outside because it was raining. Oh, I almost forgot: You were wearing a dark blue blazer and charcoal slacks. Mrs. Perrone had on a cream-colored skirt, white sandals and, I believe, a gold watch on her wrist."

Joey had also told Stranahan the color of her blouse, but he'd forgotten. He flicked on the flashlight and saw that Chaz looked drained and unsteady.

"You want me to keep going?"

"Suit yourself," Chaz croaked.

"So the two of you were standing alongside the rail, Mrs. Perrone just staring out to sea, when you pulled a really clever move," Stranahan said. "You took something from your pocket and dropped it. A coin, a key, something that made a sharp noise. Then you pretended like you were bending down to pick it up—remember?"

From the bow of the canoe, nothing.

"But instead you grabbed your wife by the legs and flipped her overboard. It happened so fast, she didn't have time to fight back. You still with me?"

When Stranahan zapped Joey's husband again with the flashlight, his eyes were wide and glassy. Stranahan had seen similar expressions in the studio of an amateur taxidermist.

"You look like you're coming down with something," he said. "Did you ever get vaccinated against that icky Nile virus?"

Chaz coughed violently. "There's a vaccine?"

If it had been almost anyone else, Stranahan might have felt sorry for the wretched fool.

"Why'd you do it, Chaz?"

"I didn't."

"You're calling me a liar? Ouch."

Chaz said, "Just tell me how much you want."

"Half a million bucks."

"Man, you're fucking crazy."

"Cash," the blackmailer said. "Hundreds are fine."

A light breeze had sprung up from the southeast, nudging the small canoe farther into the vast black bay. The mild rocking motion that Stranahan found so calming seemed to have the opposite effect on Joey Perrone's husband.

He said, "Where'm I supposed to come up with five hundred grand?"

"Hey, Chaz, I've got an idea." Stranahan thinking: It's like shooting fish in a barrel. "You could ask your pal Hammernut!"

No flashlight was required to gauge Dr. Charles Perrone's reaction. The raucous whoop of his vomiting incited a lusty reply from a male heron wading the shoreline a quarter of a mile away.

Mick and Chaz had been gone only twenty minutes when Joey made up her mind to leave the motel room. She put on a baggy cotton jersey and tucked her hair under her Marlins cap and walked down to the docks. In the parking lot she spotted a big black sedan that looked like the one parked in front of Chaz's house the night before. Leaning against the car was a tall, wide man wearing dark overalls over a fuzzy shirt. When Joey got closer, she saw that the shirt was actually a coat of dense body hair.

The man spotted her and said, "Come here, boy."

Joey positioned herself beneath one of the light stanchions, in the hope he would see that she wasn't a threat.

The man said, "You deaf, or what? I said to come here."

"You're the bodyguard, aren't you?" Joey asked.

He swatted her with the back of his hand and she went down. With a twist of her jersey he yanked her up off the pavement and dropped her on the trunk of the sedan.

"You ain't no damn boy," he said. "You's a girl."

Joey fumbled to pull down her jersey, which had bunched up around her bra. She faintly tasted blood.

"Hey, don't get freaked. I'm here with the blackmailer."

"No shit?" the man said curiously.

"He's my boyfriend."

The man seemed to want to think about that. Joey let him.

Then he grabbed the back of her neck and said, "I could kill ya right now. Feed ya to the goddamn gators and by dawn there wouldn't be nuthin' left, not even bones."

He was squeezing so hard that Joey feared she would pass out. The man was strong enough to pinch off her head with his fingers.

"And killing me," she said, "would accomplish . . . what exactly?"

After a moment's contemplation, he let go. "Yeah. It's your boyfriend is the problem."

Joey rubbed her neck. "I'm not trying to tell you how to do your job, but if anything happens to him, the cops will be getting a package containing all kinds of interesting tidbits about your client."

"Client?"

"The guy you're guarding. Charles Perrone," Joey said. "Can I ask your name?"

"They call me Tool."

"I'm Anastasia." Ever since she was a little girl, she'd wanted to call herself that. It sounded so much more feminine and elegant than Joey.

The man named Tool said, "Your boyfriend, what's he want from the doc?"

Joey said she didn't know. "I'm just the lookout. He handles the business end."

The man turned halfway and looked toward the boat ramp. "Where's that canal go to?"

"Beats me. Whatcha got stuck on your back?"

"Nuthin'."

Joey stepped forward and placed a hand on each arm. She had

never in her life seen so much hair on a human being. "You turn around," she said. "Come on, Mr. Tool."

Pulling him into the pale circle of light, she noticed that irregular swaths had been crudely shaved across his shoulder blades. Several tan patches had been attached in no particular configuration.

"They's medicine stick-ems," Tool explained.

"For what?"

"Killin' pain."

"Uh-oh. You're sick?" Joey asked.

"I got me a bullet in a real bad spot."

A truck pulled into the parking lot; a cab pickup with blue police lights mounted on the cab.

"That's a park ranger," Joey whispered.

They watched the truck make a slow pass through the marina area. When it was gone, Tool said, "Where's that damn canoe? This is takin' way too long."

"Well, the two boys have lots to talk about."

Tool patted the front pockets of his overalls. "Damn," he said. "My cell phone. Be right back."

He stomped down the docks and disappeared inside a dark house-boat. When he returned, he was swearing at the portable phone in his hand.

"I can't get no signal down here," he complained.

"Who're you calling?" Joey asked.

"None a your bidness."

"Who's paying you, anyway? Not Chaz Perrone, I know."

Tool snatched the front of her jersey and yanked her face close to his. "Stop with the goddamn questions, y'hear?"

His breath smelled oniony and a sickly damp heat rose from his skin. "I don't feel right," he said.

"Maybe it's the medicine. How about I grab you a Coke?"

"How 'bout if you shut up?"

"Okeydoke," Joey said.

Tool sat on the fender of the car, which sagged under his heft. For ten minutes he poked angrily at the keypad of his cell phone while Joey leaned against a piling and watched a school of electric-blue baitfish race in and out of the shadows. She thought of the little canoe some-where out in the darkness and wondered if Mick was sticking to the script, or if he'd blown a fuse and done something unforgettable to her husband.

"Fuck it. I give up," Tool said at last, shoving the phone into his pocket.

"May I speak now?" Joey asked archly.

"Sing and dance if you want."

"You ever been married?"

"Yeah. Common-law," said Tool. "Six years. No, seven."

"What happened?"

"She went home to Valdosta for a funeral and never come back. I heard later she run off with the boy from the undertaker's."

Joey said, "Did you know that Mr. Perrone pushed his wife off an ocean liner?"

"I figgered it must be somethin' like that."

"Could you imagine ever doing that to somebody?"

"All depends," Tool said. "I hurt my share a people, but never no women unless they lit after me first. Maybe she started it, his old lady. Maybe the guy was self-defendin' hisself."

"Does he ever talk about her?"

"Not hardly. When I ast him, he said she was pretty and smart and all. But he didn't say what happened, only that she's dead. The rest ain't none a my bidness."

"He didn't tell you why he did it?"

"You don't lissen worth a damn, know that?" Tool hoisted himself off the fender, as if he were going to grab her again.

She took a step backward. *Pretty and smart and all.* That's what Chaz was saying about her now that she was gone. "I wonder if he loved her," she said quietly.

It made Tool laugh. "You say 'love'?"

"The whole thing bothers me, I can't help it." Joey sensed that Tool was telling the truth about how little he knew.

"What I seen," he said, "the man loves hisself more'n anything on this earth. He sure ain't one to cry and mope around and such."

Wait until Chaz hears what Mick Stranahan has to say, Joey thought, then you'll see some moping.

She said, "You think he did it, too. I can tell you do."

"Makes no difference in my pay either way."

"Your line of work, you can probably look once in somebody's eyes and know right off if they're lying. Mr. Perrone didn't fool you for a second, I bet."

Tool seemed immune to female flattery, a rare trait among men, in Joey's experience. She tried a different approach.

"How long have you been a bodyguard?"

"This here's my first crack at it."

"No wonder you're jumpy," Joey said. "Don't worry, Chaz will get back safe and sound, as long as he doesn't do anything stupid."

"He's capable," said Tool. "What I'm trying to figger out is how your boyfriend fits into the program, how he come to—whatchacallit?—*mastermine* the blackmail."

"He was in the right place at the right time. That's all."

"Is he the same one broke into my man's house last night? 'Cause he got some payback due if it is. Middle-aged guy? Real tan? Looked sorta like him in the canoe, but I couldn't see so good from that houseboat. Damn windows all grimed up with salt."

"He's the one," Joey said. Tool would find out anyway as soon as Mick returned with Chaz.

"He's old enough to be your pa, ain't he?"

"Not hardly," she said defensively.

"Well, he's a strong sumbitch, I'll give him that. He hurt me good." Tool probed thoughtfully at his Adam's apple.

"He gets around all right for a geezer," Joey agreed. "Say, what was your wife's name?"

"Jean. Jeannie Suzanne is what we callt her."

"You miss her?" Joey asked.

"Not no more. Time heals is what they say."

"Do you think Mr. Perrone misses his wife?"

Tool said, "You tell me. He took all her pitchers down—every pitcher in the house, gone."

"But he told you she was pretty."

"That's what he said, but she coulda been a hog snapper for all I know." Tool shrugged. "I don't get paid to figger this shit out."

Joey said, "I've got to be going now. Thanks for the chat."

Tool seemed disappointed. "You can't hang around for when they come back?"

She shook her head. "Better not. I've got my orders."

"Me, too," Tool said with weary frustration.

It was by far the worst night of Charles Perrone's life.

"You done?" the blackmailer asked.

Chaz wiped off his lips and spit hard over the side, trying to purge the pukey taste from his mouth. He had no clue how the man had found out about Red Hammernut. It was the second piece of disastrous news that Chaz received in the canoe, the first being that the blackmailer had in fact witnessed Joey's murder.

"You're surprised that I've done my homework," the man said. "So was Ricca."

He knows about Ricca, too? Chaz thought miserably. What a nightmare.

He boxed at his head, trying to vanquish the unbearable chorus of mosquitoes. The damn things seemed to have drilled through his eardrums into the meat of his brain. Other disturbing sounds rose from the darkness of the bay; loud violent splashes, piercing cries of birds.

This is hell, Chaz told himself. That's where I am.

"Your buddy Hammernut owns some serious farmland south of the big lake," the man said. "I'm guessing you fake the water tests to make it look clean. Saves him a fortune, too. How much is he paying you? Besides the new Hummer, I mean."

Chaz turned away, anticipating another blast from the flashlight. "You don't know what you're talking about," he insisted hoarsely.

"Oh, I know exactly what I'm talking about. So do you."

Chaz couldn't make out the blackmailer's expression, but the white crescent of a smile was visible.

"And here's another bulletin for you, Chazzie boy: Karl Rolvaag isn't in on this deal. I've never met the guy in my life, and you'd better pray that I don't."

Chaz fought back a fresh impulse to gag. He lowered his head and waited for the sensation to pass.

"What about the fake will?" he mumbled to his kneecaps.

"What will?" the man said.

"Oh Jesus."

"If you barf in this canoe, you're swimming home."

Chaz said, "I'll be all right. Just give me a minute."

It dawned on him that he wouldn't even know which way to swim. The sky had cleared but the glittering constellations offered no navigational guidance, Dr. Charles Perrone being as ignorant of astronomy as he was of the terrestrial sciences.

"Whose will?" the blackmailer asked again. "Your wife's?"

"Never mind."

So, it *was* real, Chaz thought, the document that Rolvaag had shown him. Thirteen million dollars with my name on it, and all I've got to do is avoid Death Row.

"Let's say I scrape up the money," he said.

"Yes, let's say." The blackmailer laughed. "Bring it in a suitcase. Now for the questions."

"Oh, come on," Chaz said.

"I've only got two. First, why did you marry her?"

Swell, thought Chaz. I'm being shaken down by Montel Williams.

"Because I really liked her," he said impatiently. "She was fun and good-looking and sharp. I thought I was ready to settle down."

Without warning, the blackmailer clobbered him with the paddle, the flat side landing squarely on the crown of Chaz's head. He saw it coming even in the dimness, an arcing downward blur. On impact he let out a moan and pitched forward. The canoe rocked but did not flip.

"All you wanted," the man said, "was a hot girl on your arm, Chazzie. A girl your buddies would notice and talk about—the female equivalent of a new Rolex. You weren't getting married, you were accessorizing."

Chaz slowly pushed himself up from the bottom of the canoe and repositioned on his knees. He touched his scalp and felt a rising knot. Meanwhile the blackmailer had resumed paddling, as if nothing had happened. He looked tan and solidly built, but he was so much older that Chaz had been completely surprised by the sudden blow. It was the sort of thing a young hothead might do.

"And the fact she was rich didn't hurt, did it?" the man said.

"I never asked for a dime," Chaz protested.

"Which leads to my second question: Why'd you throw her into the ocean?"

Chaz swallowed in a way that sounded like a dying bullfrog. He had no intention of admitting the crime.

"I guess you want to spend the night out here," the blackmailer said, "alone."

"Anything happens to me, you don't get paid."

The man's laughter made Chaz shudder. "Try to understand, junior, it's not just the money. I'm pissed."

"But you didn't even know her!"

"Funny, though, I feel like I do." Calmly the man swung the paddle out of the water and batted Chaz in the face; not hard enough to knock him over, but hard enough to crimp his nose.

"Goddamn!" Chaz cried, a warm trickle running down his fingers.

The blackmailer said, "As you can tell, I'm taking this whole thing very personally. Tell me why you did it and I'll row you back to the docks."

"I just can't."

"Chazzie, you know that *I* know exactly what happened. All I'm asking you is why."

The guy had a point. He already knew everything, and Chaz wasn't keen on getting smacked again.

"What if you're wearing a wire?" Chaz was pinching his nostrils, trying to stanch the bleeding. Now he sounded like a cartoon duck.

Again the blackmailer's grin gleamed in the starlight. "You're priceless," he said, peeling off his T-shirt. Then he held the flashlight at arm's length and aimed it back toward his bare chest, which was quickly darkening with mosquitoes.

"See? No hidden microphones," he said to Chaz. "Feel better now?"

"I guess."

"Then answer the question, please."

"I thought Joey had busted me," Chaz heard himself say. "I thought she'd figured out the water scam."

"And for that you heaved her overboard? In the middle of the fucking Gulf Stream?"

"You don't understand," Chaz said. "If she ever blew the whistle on me and Mr. Hammernut . . . you can't possibly understand the implications. The thing is, I was out of options. If only she . . ."

"What, Chaz?"

If only she'd given me a reason *not* to do it, Chaz thought. Like showing me the new will.

"Never mind," he said.

The blackmailer began paddling with more purpose, and Chaz marveled at how briskly they were gliding across the water. Being averse to exercise, he'd never been a fan of canoes; a ski boat powered by a two-hundred-horse Mercury was Chaz's idea of a dream ride.

"How's the shnoz?" the blackmailer asked him.

"It hurts." Chaz's nose had swollen to the size of a bell pepper.

Soon they came to the long canal through which they'd entered the bay, and Chaz was immensely relieved. The blackmailer was taking him back to Flamingo.

Suddenly the man stopped rowing and leaned back. Chaz could see the shine of his sweat and hear the ravenous buzz of insects on his face and chest. "Want some bug spray?" Chaz asked.

The man chuckled. "No thanks." He extended the paddle to Chaz and said, "Your turn, killer."

"What?"

"Yeah, I'm whipped."

Chaz took the paddle and examined it as if it were an intricately engineered device.

"Please don't tell me you've never rowed a canoe," the blackmailer said.

"Of course I have."

Chaz tried to remember the last time—way back in grad school, on some scummy lake in North Carolina. He and another student were helping a professor trace the dissolution of muskrat feces in bottom sediment. Chaz had ended the day with oozing blisters on the palms of both hands. He couldn't swing a golf club for a month.

"Hurry up, Chazzie, we're drifting back to Whitewater."

"Sorry, but I'm not up for this. My head's killing me."

"You'll be fine."

"But I'm still bleeding, for God's sake."

"Did you ever see *Deliverance*?" the blackmailer said. "Remember what happened to the chubby guy?"

Chaz Perrone started paddling.

Twenty

Being labeled a crook was a new experience for Karl Rolvaag, and it kept him awake much of the night. He was more intrigued than indignant, for it was impossible to feel insulted by someone like Charles Perrone. The blackmail accusation was so boggling that the detective viewed it as a critical twist in the case, a clue no less important than the fingernails in that soggy bale of weed.

Rolvaag stood in his ritual cold shower for nearly twenty minutes, replaying in his head the odd conversation with Joey Perrone's husband. He didn't doubt that the man was being extorted, but by whom? And with what sort of information?

Perrone had snidely referred to a "bogus eyewitness," which raised in Rolvaag's mind the tantalizing possibility of a real one. Yet such a scenario would require that the witness be nearly as venal and ice-blooded as Perrone himself; someone capable of watching a woman murdered and not trying to stop it; someone who, instead of rushing to the police, would go directly to the killer with a demand for hush money.

Given the pestilential abundance of lowlifes in South Florida, it was surely possible that Perrone's crime had been randomly observed by someone equally degenerate. Still, Rolvaag thought it more likely that the blackmailer wasn't a fellow cruise passenger but, rather, some enterprising scammer who'd read about Joey Perrone's disappearance in the newspapers. In any event, the detective was not displeased that the threat had driven Perrone into such paranoid agitation that he'd accuse a police detective of masterminding the plot. Criminals in such a ragged state of mind often made reckless mistakes, and it was Rolvaag's hope that the remorseless widower would continue on a path of self-sabotage.

Most tantalizing was the link between Perrone and Samuel Johnson Hammernut. Rolvaag had found nothing to substantiate Perrone's flimsy story that the sixty-thousand-dollar Humvee had been a gift from his wife, with Hammernut acting innocently as a middleman. Rolvaag believed that the farm tycoon had intended the Hummer— and one could only imagine what else—as payola for Chaz. It had been Rolvaag's observation that men like Red Hammernut were not spontaneously generous, and usually demanded something valuable in return.

What would a lazy, unscholarly biologist such as Perrone have to offer? The detective had a hunch.

Then there was the remarkable Last Will and Testament of Joey Perrone, which had excited even the laconic Captain Gallo. If the will proved to be bogus, the forger was most likely the blackmailer. What better way to turn up the heat on Perrone than to chum up the cops with a $13 million motive for murder?

However, if the will was genuine . . .

The detective turned off the water and stood there, dripping and thinking. He wasn't sure if the damn thing was legit or not. One handwriting expert said the signature looked authentic; another thought it was a fake. The trust officers in charge of Joey Perrone's fortune had a signed will in their files, but they had balked at providing a copy in the absence of a death certificate.

Whether or not the document delivered anonymously to Rolvaag proved genuine, he intended to do everything in his power to prevent Mr. Perrone from collecting a nickel from Mrs. Perrone's estate. The surest way to accomplish that, in the detective's view, was to lock Mr. Perrone away for the rest of his natural life. That mission had come to occupy Karl Rolvaag so exclusively that he had temporarily postponed the chore of boxing his belongings for the move to Minnesota.

He toweled off and pulled on a pair of jeans. On his way to the kitchen he noticed that another sheet of paper had been slipped under his door, presumably by Mrs. Shulman or one of her operatives. The repeat intrusion was enough to make the detective consider a blocking measure, such as shag carpeting, but he'd be vacating the apartment soon enough.

Rolvaag picked up the paper. It was a flyer featuring a color photograph of a frail-looking, rheumy-eyed dog:

LOST!!!
Pinchot, 11-year old male Pomeranian (neutered)
Cataracts, diverticulitis, gout
If found, please do not approach or attempt to handle!
Please contact Bert or Addie Miller at Sawgrass Grove 9-L
$250 Reward!!!

Rolvaag was heartsick. Even though the condominium board had warned the Millers about letting their senescent pooch off the leash, the detective felt personally responsible for the fate of little Pinchot— hobbled, half-blind and easy pickings for a prowling python. Rolvaag resolved to spend the remainder of his Saturday searching the property for his escaped pets, one of which doubtlessly would be slowed by a telltale Pomeranian-sized lump. Of course the Millers would be consoled and fully compensated.

First, though, Rolvaag had one bit of leftover police work.

He picked through the loose scraps in his briefcase until he found the number for Corbett Wheeler in New Zealand. The detective was leaving a long message on the answer machine when Joey's brother picked up the phone and said, "Start over, please. I was dead asleep."

Rolvaag apologized and asked, "Did your sister have a will?"

"Yes, but let me guess. A new one has surfaced."

"It seems so. And it leaves everything to her husband."

Corbett Wheeler laughed. "I told you he was a fuckwit, did I not? How can he possibly believe he's going to get away with this?"

"Here's the thing, Mr. Wheeler. I don't think Charles Perrone is the one who forged the will, assuming it *is* forged."

"Joey wouldn't leave that pussbucket enough money for bus fare to—"

A crackle of long-distance static obscured Corbett Wheeler's terse commentary.

"I was hoping you had a copy of the original will," Rolvaag interjected.

"Of course I do. But getting back to Chaz—what makes you so sure he's not the forger?"

"Because the new will would establish him as the prime suspect in your sister's disappearance. It gives him a big reason for killing her, which is one thing our case has been lacking." One of many things, the detective might have added.

"To be honest," Rolvaag went on, "I don't think Chaz is foolish enough—or even greedy enough—to put himself at such risk."

Corbett Wheeler hooted. "And I think that's exactly what he *wants* you to think. Come on, man, who'd go to all the trouble of setting him up?"

"That's what I'm trying to find out." Rolvaag didn't share with Corbett Wheeler the possibility that someone aboard the *Sun Duchess* had witnessed Joey's murder. He was always careful not to raise the hopes of a victim's relatives.

"It would be helpful to see the will that you've got," Rolvaag said.

"No problem." More static. ". . . It's in a lockbox in Auckland."

"Could you FedEx a copy?"

"How about if I deliver it in person," Joey's brother said.

The detective tried not to sound too excited. "That's even better. But I thought you weren't ever coming back to the States."

"Me, neither, Karl. But things have changed, haven't they?"

On the other end, Rolvaag heard what sounded like the soft pop of a bottle being opened. The detective felt a sudden craving for a cold Foster's.

Corbett Wheeler said, "It looks like my late little sister needs someone to see after her interests. And, by the way, the real will doesn't leave me anything, either—in case you're wondering about *my* motive."

The detective assured Joey's brother that he wasn't. "When will you be arriving?" he asked.

"Day after tomorrow. The service is next Thursday."

Again Rolvaag was caught off guard. "What service?"

"The one I'm arranging in memory of Joey," Corbett Wheeler replied with a muffled burp. "Can you recommend a nice church, Karl? Catholic, Lutheran, Methodist—doesn't really matter, as long as there's room for a choir."

As Red Hammernut listened to Chaz Perrone's story, he thought of the many blessings that had come his way, but also of the toil. A big farming operation like his was a challenging enterprise, relying as it did on rampant pollution and the systematic mistreatment of immigrant labor. For Red it was no small feat to keep the feds off his back while at the same time soaking taxpayers for lucrative crop subsidies and dirt-cheap loans that might or might not be repaid this century. He reflected upon the hundreds of thousands of dollars that he'd handed out as campaign donations; the untallied thousands more for straight-up bribes, hookers, private-yacht charters, gambling stakes and other discreet favors; and, finally, the countless hours of ass-kissing he'd been forced to endure with the same knucklehead politicians whose loyalties he had purchased.

This was no easy gig. Red Hammernut got infuriated every time he heard some pissy liberal refer to the federal farm bill as corporate welfare. The term implied contented idleness, and nobody worked harder than Red to keep the money flowing and to stay out of trouble. Now the whole goddamn shebang was in danger of falling apart because of one man.

"Pay him. That's my advice," Chaz Perrone said in cocksure summary. "I know it's a shitload of money, but what else can we do?"

They were sitting in Red Hammernut's office, overlooking the toxic though tranquil pond. Chaz and Tool had driven straight from Flamingo to LaBelle, arriving at four in the morning and nodding off like junkies in the parking lot. Chaz's nostrils were blood-encrusted and his face was pocked extravagantly with crimson insect bites. Red Hammernut couldn't help but stare. The man looked like a photo out of an exotic medical textbook.

"He's got us by the short and curlies," Chaz was saying of the blackmailer. "I don't see where there's any other choice but to pay him."

Red Hammernut said there was never only one choice, regardless of the problem. "But lemme see if I understand the situation, 'cause you tore through it pretty fast. What about the cop? The one you thought was breakin' into your house and talkin' like Moses on the telephone?"

"I was wrong. It's not him," Chaz said shortly. "He's not mixed up in this."

"Which is at least one piece a semi-good news, right?"

"Except he found out from the dealership about you buying me the Hummer."

"Well, hell," Red Hammernut said.

"So I told him you were friends with Joey and you did it as a favor to her—got me the Hummer for my birthday. And then she paid you back."

"That's the best you could do? Sweet Jesus." Red Hammernut turned to look at Tool, whose head was lolling. "You all right?"

"Just real tarred."

"Then go lie down."

"Yessir, that's an idea." Tool kicked the chair away and curled up like a bloated bear on the carpet in front of the desk. Red Hammernut shook his head.

Chaz said, "So if the detective asks you about the Hummer—"

"Don't worry, son, I'll give'm the same story you did," Red Hammernut said. "Now let's talk about this blackmail business. The sumbitch wants half a million bucks, and for some reason you think I'm the one ought to pay."

"Red, I don't have that kind of money."

"My question is, What's he gonna do if you *don't* pay? Worst case? Tell the cops he saw you push poor Joey overboard."

Chaz bleated, "Isn't that enough?"

"First, he's gotta prove he was on board that ship."

"Don't worry. He was."

"Then it's his word against yours." Red Hammernut thinking how the media would go wild once the accusation became public. So far, Chaz had demonstrated no capacity for steadiness under pressure, and Red Hammernut doubted that his composure would improve once he was named a murder suspect. If Chaz had in fact killed his wife, he might come unspooled under tough questioning by the cops. That could prove catastrophic for Hammernut Farms, and even more so for Red personally.

"This asshole knows everything," Chaz was saying.

Red Hammernut clicked his teeth. "Yeah, I heard you the first time."

"Knows about the Hummer, the phosphorus tests—don't ask me how, but he put it all together."

"Bad luck," Red Hammernut said.

It was his own damn fault for buying that H2; he'd done it only because he was sick of hearing Chaz whine about needing a four-wheel drive. The way Red figured it, the blackmailer probably hired a private eye to do a paper check on Chaz, which led him to the Hummer's bill of sale. Once Red's name popped up, it wouldn't take fucking Matlock to make the connection between the farm and the biologist who was testing its waters for pollution.

"It's a tur'ble fix, I give you that," Red Hammernut said to Chaz. "But half a million big ones ain't a very appetizin' option."

"But Joey left me zippo, Red. All I've got is what's in the bank."

Red Hammernut calculated that he'd slipped Chaz twenty to thirty grand in cash over the years, most of which had probably been pissed away on greens fees and lap dances.

"Relax, boys. Let's put on our thinkin' caps."

Reaching into the bottom drawer of his desk, Red pulled out a bottle of Jack Daniel's and poured three glasses. Tool slurped his from a supine position.

"So, how long till he wants an answer?" Red Hammernut asked.

"He said he'd call Monday morning," Chaz said.

"And he ain't alone in this deal, right? You said there's a girlfriend."

Tool spoke up from the floor. "Name of Anna somethin' or other. She don't know much."

"Good," Red Hammernut said, though he had marginal confidence in Tool's assessment. "She wasn't totally scared to pieces of you?"

Tool grunted. "Didn't appear to be."

"Don't you think that's strange?"

"Chief, I give up tryin' to figger out women a long time ago."

"Amen," said Chaz Perrone.

"Well, let's assume the girlfriend knows what the blackmailer knows," Red Hammernut said, "and proceed from there. Who's ready for another belt?"

Tool raised his glass for a refill. "When can I go home, Red?"

"Soon as this mess is over. Won't be long, I promise."

"I miss my yard. All them pretty white crosses."

"Just hang in there, son," Red Hammernut said. "You're doin' a world-class job."

Chaz Perrone cleared his throat. "To be honest, Red, there's room for improvement. No offense, but it needs to be said."

Red Hammernut hoped Chaz would have more sense than to complain about Tool in Tool's presence, but he was wrong.

"Take last night," Chaz pressed on. "I end up all alone with that psycho blackmailer in the middle of the frigging Everglades. *In a canoe.*"

"You're alive, ain't ya?" Tool said.

Red Hammernut couldn't see over the edge of the desk, but it sounded like Tool was scratching himself.

"Yeah, I'm alive. No thanks to you," Chaz snapped. Then, appealing to Red: "The bastard hit me over the head with a paddle. And look what he did to my nose!"

Red Hammernut tried to sound sympathetic. "Guy's got a mean streak, that's for sure."

"I thought the whole point of having a bodyguard," Chaz griped, "was to protect me from shit like this."

Tool raised his head and, by way of rebuttal, said: "Thar weren't 'nough room in that canoe for all three of us."

"Then how about the other night at the house?" Chaz needled. "The man kicked your ass."

"We ain't gonna talk about that," Tool said.

"Water under the bridge," Red Hammernut agreed.

"He's gotta be fifty years old, at least," Chaz went on, "and he damn near killed you!"

Tool's tone hardened. "Now you're just tellin' stories, boy."

Red Hammernut's patience ran out. "Both of you, I swear, just shut the hell up. This ain't no kindygarten."

Chaz fidgeted while Red slowly sipped his drink. Tool dozed off and began to snore.

After a few edgy minutes, Chaz let it rip. "What do you think, Red? About paying the guy."

"I think you got some brass balls, considerin' you're the one got us into this train wreck."

Chaz looked wounded. "Why? What did I do?"

Red thinking: That's the $500,000 question.

"This is serious," Chaz persisted. "Whoever this guy is, he could take us all down."

Of that fact, Red Hammernut was keenly aware. "Wait outside, son. I need to have a word with Mr. O'Toole."

"Good idea." Chaz headed confidently for the door. "Maybe he'll listen to you."

Red Hammernut walked around to the other side of the desk. With the toe of an ostrich-skinned boot he nudged Tool in the rib cage. The big man looked up dolefully and blinked.

"Red, please don't send me back to Boca fuckin' Raton."

"How 'bout I double your pay to a thousand a day?"

Tool sat up. "The doc kilt his wife."

"Yeah. You're probably right," Red Hammernut said.

"He had a woman over, did I tell ya? Ain't been widowed a week and already he's pokin' poon."

"If he were the Pope of Rome," said Red, "I wouldn't need your help."

Tool, still itching, unhooked the straps of his overalls to improve access. "Truth is, chief, I ain't cut out to be no bodyguard."

"Truth is, that ain't your job description. Not anymore."

Samuel Johnson Hammernut winked and slapped an envelope fat with cash on the desk. Tool brightened.

"I'll take another drink," he said.

Red passed the bottle.

Twenty-one

Joey was baking in the sun, stretched out on the seawall, when she saw the glint of an airplane high overhead. It made her think of her parents and she had to smile, picturing that doped-up circus bear in the co-pilot's seat of the doomed Gulfstream. Hank and Lana Wheeler had lived and died with a flair that Joey envied. In that spirit she removed the top of her bikini and tossed it on the dock. It landed on the nose of Mick's Doberman, who awoke with a curious snort.

From out on the water came a rowdy hooray, followed by the sound of clapping. Joey spun around and blushed—two men were motoring slowly past the island in a dark green flats skiff, no more than fifty yards from the shore. The men were in their late twenties or early thirties and wore loose-fitting pastel fishing shirts of the style found in high-end outdoor catalogs. Strom shot to attention, shook free of the bikini top and began to bark. When Joey covered her breasts with her arms, the fishermen booed. She lay down and closed her eyes, hoping they would go away. She had come to cherish the solitude of the island, and to appreciate Mick's antipathy for uninvited visitors.

Strom was clattering up and down the dock in a slobbering rage that would have deterred most sensible persons, but the glimpse of a half-naked woman had obliterated what scant common sense was possessed by the young men in the green skiff. Joey could tell by the engine noise that they were edging closer.

Idiots, she thought.

Even in the middle of Biscayne Bay there was no avoiding this distinctly male brand of bad behavior. A sea breeze delivered their randy chuckles and lewd low-toned commentary, one of the men offering a favorable critique of her legs while the other speculated hopefully on the presence of a tattoo. In vain Joey prayed that their frat-house blather would be drowned out by Strom's manic barking. Yet when she looked up again, the boat was no more than sixty or seventy feet from the seawall.

"Hey, babe," one of the men said. "Let's see those tits again."

Joey could easily imagine Chaz in that skiff, making the same smirking, cloddish approach to a total stranger. Calmly she got up and walked to the shed where Mick stowed his fishing tackle. He'd been teaching her how to cast a spinning rod, and it seemed like a good opportunity to practice her accuracy. Distracted by a second sighting of her breasts, the two fishermen failed to take note as Joey tied the large plastic minnow to the line—a hefty deep-sea plug bristling with multiple sets of treble hooks.

Strom circled deliriously as Joey advanced, weapon in hand, to the end of the dock. The young man in the bow of the skiff was emitting a gargling sound, presumably in appreciation of Joey's physique, as she drew back the spinning rod. His gaze never left her chest, so he didn't see the fishing lure arcing brightly through the noonday sky. Joey wasn't sure if she snagged his shirt or the flesh of his neck, but in any case she jerked hard enough to spill the howling imbecile into the water.

She had reeled him halfway to shore when Strom, surrendering to ancient instincts, sprung off the dock and lustily attached himself to the thrashing angler's thigh. His companion bellowed in alarm but gave no thought to heroics; instead, he jammed the skiff's throttle into reverse and backed smartly away from the island.

The tumult was still in evidence when Mick Stranahan arrived a few minutes later in the Whaler with Rose, Joey's worldly friend from the book group. Strom released his grip on the fisherman and paddled somewhat ineffectively toward Mick, who with Rose's assistance hauled the slippery dog into the boat. Making no move to unhook the swimmer, Stranahan bit through the fishing line and instructed the driver of the skiff to come fetch his dumbass partner. The cucumber-sized lure remained attached like a garish brooch to the floundering man's shirt. Joey also spotted a ragged hole in his cargo shorts—Strom's zestful contribution—as the man clambered over the gunwale of the skiff, which immediately departed at top speed.

The wild scene seemed surreal to Rose, who hopped off the Whaler, hugged Joey ferociously and exclaimed, "You're the hottest-looking dead person I ever saw!"

Joey noticed that Rose had bleached her shoulder-length hair to a hue of blond that would have impressed the Gabor sisters. She wore a pullover, black tights and white high-top sneakers—on her way to the gym, no doubt, when Mick had intercepted her.

He pointed toward the receding speck that was the green skiff, heading for the mainland. "Those jackasses give you a hard time?"

"They tried," Joey said, "but Strom and I taught 'em some manners."

Mick pulled her close, kissed her neck and whispered: "Better put your top on. You're getting fried."

While Rose and Joey caught up, Mick set the picnic table and fixed a lunch of conch chowder, grapefruit salad, sardine sandwiches and sangria. It was a coolish day and they took their time, Rose frequently interrupting Joey's story to rail against Chaz Perrone.

"That sonofabitch," she said for at least the fifth time. "I still can't believe he pushed you overboard!"

Joey said, "And I can't believe I didn't break my neck."

"You still haven't gone to the cops?"

"This way is better. This way I'm getting answers."

"Speaking of which," Rose said, rummaging through her handbag, "I think I found what you wanted at the library."

She produced a folded stack of Xeroxed newspaper clippings. Stranahan grinned as he read the first headline aloud: LOCAL FARM CITED AS GLADES POLLUTER.

"Surprise, surprise," Joey said.

Rose noisily attacked a carrot stick. "So, tell me. Who is this Samuel Hammernut, and what's he got to do with your husband?"

"He owns him," Mick interjected, "or so it appears."

Joey told Rose about the water-testing that Chaz did in the Everglades, and about the new Humvee purchased for him by Hammernut Farms. Rose gave her a consoling hug and said, "No offense, sweetie, but I always knew that man was a whore. So, what's next?"

"My brother's flying into Lauderdale on Monday."

Rose looked intrigued. "The one from Australia, who nobody's ever seen?"

"New Zealand," said Joey. "You and Corbett are the only ones who know I'm still alive. Besides Mick, I mean."

"Who, by the way, wouldn't even tell me how you two met."

Joey gave Mick the "Are you kidding me?" frown. "He saved my life is all," she said to Rose. "He's the one who pulled me out of the ocean."

Rose reached for the pitcher of sangria. "That is *so* incredibly romantic. He actually saved you? Like from drowning?"

"Sharks, too," Mick added dryly. "And giant mutant octopi."

Joey pinched his earlobe. She was glad that he'd cooled off since last night at Flamingo. He had been furious to hear that she'd left the motel room to chat with Chaz's bodyguard.

Rose said, "I assume that your brother's coming here to kick Chaz Perrone's cowardly ass."

"He'd love to, but no," said Joey. "He's arranging a memorial service for me at some church in Boca. There'll be a notice in the papers."

Rose looked at Stranahan and then back at Joey. "You guys are bad."

"Not compared to Chaz," Mick said.

Rose set down her glass and rubbed her hands together. "So, tell me. What can I do to help?"

Joey said, "You can come to the service."

"Of course."

"And hit on my husband."

Rose thought about it for a beat or two. "Do I have to sleep with him?"

"I'd rather you didn't," Joey said.

Charles Regis Perrone had a bounty of experience dealing with aggrieved women, and for Ricca he pulled out all the stops. Twelve dozen long-stemmed roses, Godiva chocolates, a magnum of Dom—all were delivered to her apartment that Saturday afternoon. Still, she wouldn't pick up the telephone. Her adamantine refusal to make contact was exasperating but also arousing; a tough, take-charge side of Ricca that Chaz had never seen. He was confident that once she agreed to meet with him, he could win her back with his dependable arsenal of stage charm, counterfeit sincerity and unforgettable sex. As he rang her doorbell for the third time, Chaz checked his pockets for the potent blue pills that would, if all else failed, endow the ultimate persuasion.

"Go away," Ricca said from the other side of the door.

"Sweetheart, please."

"Fuck you, Chaz."

"Honey, this isn't fair."

When Chaz heard the click of the dead bolt, his spirits soared. The door opened and Ricca said, "What the hell happened to you?"

"Mosquitoes."

"Your ears look like rotten guavas."

"Gee, thanks. Can I come in?"

"You've got five minutes."

Chaz stepped inside. He tried to hold her but she pulled away.

"Where are all the roses?" he asked.

"Dumpster," Ricca said.

Chaz winced, thinking of the bill from the florist.

"The champagne, I poured down the toilet," she added.

"I see. And the chocolates?"

"Oh, those I'm keeping," Ricca said, "except for the nougats. You've got four minutes left."

She was standing against the door, one hand poised on the knob. She wore rumpled sweats and no makeup, and she looked exhausted.

"What's going on? Why won't you see me?" Chaz asked.

"Because you killed your wife."

"Who told you that?"

"A guy who saw the whole thing."

Chaz felt the blood draining out of his skull. He backed against a chair and sat down.

Ricca said, "He saw you push Joey overboard. Told me exactly how you did it."

"And you believe him?" Chaz's voice fluttered like Slim Whitman's.

"How you grabbed her by the ankles and flipped her backward over the side," she said. "God, I haven't slept in two nights."

"The guy's shaking me down is all. He heard about Joey on the news and—"

"This is a first for me, Chaz. Dating a wife-killer."

"Hold on. You're taking the word of some stranger, some dirtbag scammer—"

"You told that detective I was your cleaning lady." There was frost in Ricca's voice. "The *cleaning lady*?"

Chaz cursed to himself. He remembered Rolvaag bracing him about the phone call from the lobby of the Marriott. The cop didn't even have his notebook open at the time, so Chaz hadn't given it a thought. The sneaky bastard must have total recall.

"Rolvaag came to see you?"

Ricca nodded heavily. "Asking all kinds of questions."

Chaz tasted bile and swallowed hard. "Well, what was I supposed to tell him, Ricca—that I was calling my girlfriend? The guy's looking to nail my ass."

"No shit. He went to all the trouble of tracing the call."

"I'm sorry. So sorry," Chaz said. "You've got no idea how bad I feel."

Ricca showed no sign of melting. "Here's my question: How come he doesn't believe you?"

"The cop? Oh, please." Chaz laughed scornfully. "He's just trying to make a reputation for himself, busting a doctor for murder."

Ricca rolled her eyes as if to say: Not that "doctor" thing again.

"Let's go grab a bite to eat."

"I'm not hungry," she said, "and your time's up."

Chaz was stunned to see her open the door and motion for him to go. "Don't do this," he said. "Don't give up on me so easy. I'm begging you, Ricca."

And, by God, he *was* begging.

"It's over," she told him.

"One drink. Give me a chance to change your mind."

"No, Chaz."

"One lousy drink? You won't be sorry."

"All right, but not here. You'll just end up trying to talk me into bed."

Chaz was swept by relief. "Name the spot," he said.

Ricca selected a bar at a nearby bowling alley, for its thunderous lack of intimacy. Saturday was league night and Chaz would have had more success making himself heard over a cruise-missile attack in downtown Baghdad. While Ricca went to the rest room, he fished out the bottle of blue pills and, seeking to avoid a repetition of his painful tryst with Medea, tapped only one into the palm of his hand. He swallowed it dry and checked his watch. The magic mojo potion should start working in an hour, by which time he hoped to have thawed Ricca's heart.

When she returned, Chaz ventured a tender squeeze of her elbow, which she yanked away as if he were infected with some pustular disease. He was flabbergasted by her animosity, which seemed unshakable, and also by her self-discipline. He had plowed through three martinis before she finished half a Miller Lite. Over the symphonic clatter of bowling pins he apologized repeatedly for the "cleaning lady" reference, which he calculated to be more of a sticking point than his wife's murder.

Still, Ricca didn't cave.

"Time to go," she said.

"Not yet. You've gotta let me finish."

Chaz considered himself a master bullshitter, but the cheap vodka seemed to have blunted his improvisational skills. He found himself blurting, "Didn't Rolvaag tell you about Joey's will?"

"Nope," said Ricca. "Anyhow, you said she was giving all her money to the animals. Yaks and pandas, you said."

"Well, that's what she told me. But yesterday that cop shows up at the door with a new will and asks what do I know about it. A will that Joey signed, like, a month ago!"

"Whatever, Chaz."

"Honey, she left *everything* to me."

"Why would she do an idiotic thing like that?"

Chaz leaned forward and dropped his voice. "Thirteen million bucks!"

"That'll buy you lots of cigarettes in prison. You should learn to smoke."

"Ha-ha," Chaz sneered, but he was crestfallen. He could hardly believe that the news of his future fortune hadn't rekindled Ricca's ardor. What had happened to that frisky, free-spirited girl who tinted her pubic hair and shaved him a shamrock?

"Don't you understand what this means?" he persisted. "Think of what we can do with thirteen million dollars—the incredible places we can go, all the cool stuff we can buy."

"Chaz, you snuffed your wife."

"How can you say that?"

"Take me home," Ricca said, "right now."

In the parking lot she remarked upon his oddly stilted gait.

"Twisted my knee," he mumbled.

"Doing what—climbing off the bar stool? Turn around and let me see something."

"Just forget about it."

"Chaz, turn around."

He was too vain to refuse. Even in the face of such impenetrable frigidity, Chaz believed that a glimpse of the thickening bulge in his pants might win Ricca over. Her reaction, however, was empty of delight or anticipation.

All she said was: "Are you serious?"

Chaz dusted off a golden oldie. "I can't help it, honey. See what you do to me?"

"Wow. Would you like me to fix it?"

Chaz incautiously moaned in the affirmative. Ricca kneed him and he moaned again, though this time not from desire.

She said, "I want to go home. Can't you get that through your head?"

He drove in silence, his mind blaring. Ricca was definitely going to be a problem. A humongous problem. While she couldn't implicate him directly in Joey's disappearance, she would be valuable to prosecutors seeking to lay out a seedy scenario for murder—the pretty mistress, to go along with Chaz's windfall inheritance. Judging by her disposition, Ricca would be pleased to do her civic duty and testify against him. With little coaxing she would share with salivating jurors a luridly embroidered account of the affair, as well as her current low opinion of Dr. Charles Perrone as a human being. Her appearance in court would be devastating.

Chaz said, "Tell me honestly. You really think I threw Joey overboard?"

"Yep."

"You'd believe a total stranger, some scumbag drifter who shows up at the salon and gives you a wild story."

Ricca said, "I know when men are telling me the truth. It doesn't happen often, but when it does, I *know*. And, P.S., he didn't exactly look like a scumbag."

"Are you kidding, the guy's a fucking animal! He nearly beat me into a coma with a canoe paddle."

"I'm so sure."

"Check out my nose!" Chaz was amazed that she seemed to be taking the blackmailer's side. Suddenly he remembered Tool's intriguing revelation: *The blackmailer had a girlfriend.*

Oh Jesus, thought Chaz. Now it made sense. The asshole tracks down Ricca, tries to pump her for more dirt. She says no way, not unless you cut me in on the score. Next stop: Flamingo.

Ricca must have been the girl that Tool had seen on the docks. She was in on the scam!

"Just how much did you tell this guy?" Chaz asked warily.

"Which guy, the cop or the blackmailer?"

"The blackmailer."

"Nothing, Chaz. All I did was listen."

"Yeah, right."

Ricca glared. "Screw you."

"And what about Rolvaag? What'd you tell him?"

"I told him I wasn't really your maid. I made a point of clearing up that little misunderstanding."

"Ah," Chaz said. "So now he knows all about us."

"He would've found out anyway."

"I suppose so."

Ricca said, "Hey, you missed my street."

What other choice do I have? Chaz wondered.

"Where are you going? Turn around," Ricca demanded.

Chaz reached under the seat for the Colt .38, which he had reloaded before leaving the house. He pointed it at Ricca and said, "We're not going home."

"What—now you're gonna rape me?"

"Don't flatter yourself."

For twenty minutes he headed west on a road that followed the Hillsboro Canal toward the Loxahatchee National Wildlife Refuge, a sprawling preserve on the eastern apron of the Everglades. Ricca stewed silently while Chaz held the pistol in his left hand, dead level with her heart. He was surprised how composed he felt, how confident and clearheaded. Once, when Ricca began fiddling with the door lock, Chaz raised the .38 to her temple. His arm remained straight and steady. In the glow of the dashboard he could see Ricca staring at him with wide, fresh eyes.

Finally she was scared.

Chaz turned off on a dirt trail that led to a locked metal gate. Whistling to himself, he flicked on the high beams, aimed the Humvee down a steep embankment and rumbled along a shallow ditch until he had bypassed the barricade. Then he gunned it back up the slope onto a narrow rutted levee, where nothing but night-cloaked wilderness lay before them.

"Oh God," Ricca said.

Chaz remained silent. Focus was essential. When he killed Joey, he never lost focus, never strayed from the script, never left the zone.

Ricca said, "Since when did you buy a gun? I thought you hated guns—"

With the tip of the blue-plated barrel, Chaz touched a button on the CD player and the Hummer filled with a blast of George T. and the Delaware Destroyers. That nasty slide guitar obliterated Ricca's yammering, and Chaz slipped gratefully into the buzz of the music, which was better than popping speed.

He drove down the levee for another fifteen minutes before he braked and ordered Ricca out. She stood squinting into the headlights, brushing the insects away from her face and trying not to break down. Chaz felt a subtle, ugly gnawing in his gut. He would have much preferred a silent ambush, as with Joey, but Ricca had left him no such option.

"So it's true about your wife," she said, her voice tight.

"Yeah. I'm afraid so."

"Chaz, how can you do this to me?"

"Same way I did it to her." He sat on the hood of the Hummer and aimed out between the headlights. Later, Tool would help him get rid of Ricca's car and clean out the apartment. Make it look like she skipped town.

"You can't kill me, Chaz. You cannot do it," she declared. "Joey wasn't looking you in the eye the way I am. She didn't know what was coming."

This, Chaz lamented, is exactly the sort of sticky scene that I wanted to avoid.

He said, "What I can't figure out—if you cared so much about my wife, how come you were sleeping with me?"

Ricca seemed to shrink.

"Well?" said Chaz.

"Because I was a fool."

"Keep going."

"And selfish," she added hoarsely.

"Now we're getting somewhere. Tell me about you and the black-mailer," he said. "Is it strictly business, or are you screwing him, too?"

Ricca bristled. "My God. You're cracking up." She cupped a hand over her brow so she could see him better. "Your hand's shaking."

"Like hell it is."

"Take a look, Chaz."

"Just shut up."

"Plus, you still got a boner. What's *that* all about?"

Chaz had been hoping with all his soul that she wouldn't notice. Those fucking pills were unbelievable.

"It's bad enough you're pointing a *gun* at me," Ricca said, "but that, too?"

He estimated that she was no more than thirty feet away; an easy shot. "Turn around," he told her.

"I'll do no such thing."

The marsh beyond was teeming with jumbo alligators. Beyond the headlights Chaz could make out half a dozen pairs of large eyes, glowing like embers. Ricca's corpse would be gone by daybreak. What the gators didn't eat, the turtles and raccoons would.

She said, "I'm not turning around!"

"Then hold still." Chaz sighted down the short barrel, gripping the .38 with both hands the way he'd seen it done a thousand times on television.

Jesus, she's right. I'm shaking like a damn wino.

"Chaz, you don't know what you're doing."

"Hold still, I said."

"This is a major mistake. The fuckup of all fuckups. . . ."

He held his breath and pulled the trigger. Ricca shrieked but did not fall.

"You rotten little cocksucker!" she cried, hopping up and down. "That's not even funny!"

Swell, Chaz thought, she thinks that I missed on purpose. Or maybe that I'm shooting blanks.

He stiffened and again took aim, wondering: How in the name of God did I not hit her? She's a hundred times bigger than that frigging rabbit.

The second shot caught Ricca in the left leg and spun her one full rotation. To Chaz's surprise, she still didn't go down.

"Look what you did!" She clutched at the punctured limb. "Are you fucking crazy?"

Incredible, thought Chaz. I should've brought a buffalo gun.

Another mosquito stung his cheek and he swatted himself so violently that he slid off the hood of the Hummer. Ricca capitalized on the distraction, gimping into the darkness with surprising swiftness. Chaz collected himself and took up the chase, lengthening his stride when he spotted the blur of gray sweat togs ahead of him. He was closing the gap, when suddenly Ricca vectored off the rutted path and, to his profound amazement, dove headlong into the swamp.

Chaz aborted the pursuit instantly, for nothing so terrified him as the prospect of entering the piss-warm water of the Everglades in total darkness—gagging on soggy duckweed, being lashed to ribbons by the serrated saw grass, and finally getting sucked one leech-covered leg at a time into the inky, inescapable muck.

Not me, thought Dr. Charles Perrone. No thanks.

As Ricca tried to swim away, he stood on the embankment, firing his pistol until she rolled over and sank with a gasp. Before long his ears stopped ringing and the water glassed off and the night hummed back to life. Chaz peered at the spot where Ricca had gone down and observed nothing but a fleet of water beetles skating back and forth in the reflected starlight. Something substantial splashed farther away, in a thicket of lily pads. Probably just a coot or a garfish, Chaz thought, but why push my luck? The place is lousy with gators, and I'm out of bullets.

He jogged back to the Hummer, spun a nifty 180 and headed back toward town. His heart was thumping like a baby sparrow's, but he felt lightened and liberated and pleased with himself for turning the hated, haunted swamp into an accomplice.

Twenty-two

Karl Rolvaag said, "You look lovely this morning, Nellie."

"Coming from a degenerate like you, that makes me want to hang myself. You heard about poor Pinchot?"

"I did," the detective said. "They find him yet?"

Mrs. Shulman was bobbing from side to side, trying to see past him into the apartment.

"Poor Pinchot isn't here, Nellie."

"Then you don't mind if I look around?"

"Actually, I do." Rolvaag didn't want her to notice that the snake tank was empty.

She snarled, "I wouldn't put it past you, kidnapping some poor little puppy for your own depraved pleasures. You probably made a video of it. You probably put it out on the Internet!"

Daffy old bat, thought Rolvaag.

"I did not feed Bert Miller's dog to my snakes," he said, almost adding: But accidents happen.

Mrs. Shulman said, "Well, you certainly enjoy hearing those helpless little mice shrieking in agony. Just imagine how much fun a Pomeranian would be!"

"That's a totally irresponsible accusation." The detective choked down a sneeze. Nellie Shulman had drenched herself in a perfume that stunk like rotting gardenias.

"Then why can't I come in? It's Sunday morning, after all."

"Because you called me a degenerate," Rolvaag said.

"Well, you are. Anyone with a thing for snakes is a sick, sick bastard." She tried to sneak past but he lowered a shoulder and blocked her. "The Millers are devastated!" she declared.

Rolvaag already felt terrible. He had searched the grounds of Sawgrass Grove for three hours, but the only snake he'd found was an ornery black racer that bit him on the thumb of his left hand.

"I saw you prowling around outside yesterday," Mrs. Shulman said, "hunting for more tasty little dogs."

"Nellie, have you been mixing your medications again?"

She poked him in the belt buckle. "Just because you're a cop, you think you can get away with anything. Well, you're wrong, mister. We're going to evict your heathen butt just like we evicted Neville— and he was a deacon in his church!"

Gordon Neville, a retired highway engineer, had been forced to leave Sawgrass Grove after a bawdy after-hours shuffleboard match with two women he'd met during outpatient physical therapy at Imperial Point.

"We nailed him, and we'll nail you, too," vowed Mrs. Shulman.

Rolvaag closed the door firmly in her face. He was halfway to the bedroom when he heard a rustle behind him. He hoped it was one of the missing pythons, but it turned out to be Nellie, sliding another flyer into his apartment. The detective picked it up and morosely looked at the photograph.

MISSING!!!
Our beloved darling Pandora
Blue point Siamese kitten, rhinestone collar
Easy to Identify: Seven toes on her right front paw!
Please return her to the Mankiewiczs at Sawgrass Grove 17-G
Reward: Our eternal gratitude!

What else can I do? Rolvaag wondered. Snakes can't be baited and trapped like bears.

His shrub-to-shrub search having failed, all that remained was to wait for the pythons to reveal themselves. The detective had already decided not to take his pets to Minnesota, the climate there being hostile to tropical reptiles. Leaving them at large in Sawgrass Grove, however, would be perilous not only for the domestic fauna but for the snakes themselves. Many of Rolvaag's elderly neighbors shared Mrs.

Shulman's harsh sentiments, and had no interest in seeing the pythons captured alive. A garden rake or the business end of an orthopedic cane would do the job nicely.

Rolvaag ate a light breakfast, showered and packed an overnight bag, including a map of the Everglades Agricultural Area. The map had been provided by Marta, Charles Perrone's supervisor at the water-management district. She had helpfully marked in red ink the dirt roads and levees upon which Dr. Perrone normally traveled to collect his water samples. Although the map didn't provide the names of the deed holders whose property abutted the wetlands, Rolvaag had shaded with a no. 2 pencil the approximate boundary of Hammernut Farms.

The detective wasn't surprised by what the red lines seemed to show, but he needed to see for himself.

Before leaving the apartment he opened the window overlooking the courtyard, on the wildly improbable chance that his snakes might find their way home.

"You've been awfully quiet today," Joey said, "not that you're ever a chatterbox."

Through the bay window they could see Rose flailing in the kayak. Twice already she had flipped it, although she'd gamely declined assistance.

Stranahan said, "I whacked your husband with a paddle last night. I should've told you but I didn't."

"Don't sweat it. He gets on everybody's nerves."

"I even thought about killing him," Stranahan said.

"So? I think about it constantly."

"There's a slight difference."

"I know," Joey said. "I'm only fantasizing. You've actually done it before."

"Right."

"And it messed you up."

"I've finally gotten to where I sleep through the night."

"We're not going to kill Chaz or any such thing. You said so yourself."

Joey kissed Mick on the mouth, leaving him gloriously dizzy. She said, "Thanks for putting up with all this. You deserve a medal."

"It's not too late to bail. Go to the cops and tell them what he did."

"Not yet."

Rose had tipped over again, and Strom had leapt in to help. The gulls and terns were pitching a fit, but Rose was laughing uproariously as she helped the clumsy dog get to shore.

"This whole thing could blow up on us," Stranahan said, half to himself.

Joey squeezed his arm. "Everything's under control."

Stranahan wasn't so sure. The cast of characters—himself included—was undisciplined and, in varying degrees, unstable. Falling for Joey was a prime example: It wasn't part of the plan, but Stranahan was doing it anyway. And the harder he fell, the more powerful was his urge to beat the everlasting shit (and, ideally, a confession) out of Dr. Charles Perrone. Stranahan told himself to get a grip.

Joey said, "You're thinking about us, too. I can tell. The big picture."

"Unfortunately, my résumé speaks for itself."

"Well, it's true I've never been with anyone like you," she said, "but I'll bet you've never been with anyone like *me*, either."

"That's a fact."

Last night he'd challenged her and Rose to write down the names of all the Beatles, a screening protocol for younger women that in past times had saved Stranahan from certain doom. Rose had gotten only three out of four correct, but Joey Perrone had passed with flying colors, crediting a BBC special that she'd watched one night on the History Channel while Chaz was out with his buddies at a titty bar.

Stranahan had to smile, for there was no point in pretending he could walk away now. In Joey's presence he was helpless and driven and probably happy. Someday she would leave, as they all did, and he'd return to his slow-motion existence, revolving peaceably as it did around a dog, a boat and some corroded fishing gear. This was the embedded cycle of his life, as predictable as the tides.

Joey nudged him and said, "Mick, stop already. I can hear the gears grinding."

"Sorry."

"Relax, okay?" She peeled out of her swimsuit and led him toward the bedroom. "And that's an order," she said.

Chaz Perrone dreamed he was being mauled by a fifteen-foot alligator with two hungry heads, one chewing on his left leg and the other chewing on his right—a mad contest to see which gobbling maw would reach his crotch first. He woke up wailing, and saw Tool standing expressionless at the foot of the bed.

"Just a nightmare," Chaz said, trying to compose himself. He was soaked with perspiration, which he hoped was a result of the dream and not the feverish onset of West Nile virus. The night before he had counted thirty-four mosquito bites on his face, and at the moment every one of them itched like poison ivy.

Tool said, "Your mother's on the phone."

"Jesus, what time is it? Tell her I'll call back."

"Tell her yourself, dipshit. It's your ma, for God's sake."

Chaz had detected a menacing chill in Tool's attitude since they'd left LaBelle. In retrospect, he wondered if it had been unwise to badmouth the man in front of Red Hammernut.

As soon as Tool left the room, Chaz picked up the telephone and heard a familiar question from Panama City: "Any news, son?"

"No, Mom."

"How are you holding up?"

"Some days are better than others," Chaz answered sorrowfully. It was still important to appear needful of sympathy.

"Don't give up hope yet."

"Mom, it's been, like, nine days. Nobody can survive that long in the ocean without food or water."

"Think positive thoughts," she said.

"Mom, please."

"Didn't you see *Cast Away*?"

Chaz Perrone sucked his teeth. His relationship with his mother had delaminated during his late teens and early twenties, though not because of her marriage to Roger, the wiggy RAF pilot. Rather, Chaz's mother had come to notice (and comment often upon) the fact that her son was failing to outgrow the more obnoxious traits of his adolescence. Her list included laziness, habitual self-gratification, a deeprooted lack of ambition and a reflex aversion to truthfulness. Chaz refused to address the merits of these charges, instead bitingly informing his mother that it would be folly to take career advice from a senior cashier at Target. Once he'd received his doctorate at Duke, Chaz's mother apologized tearfully for having doubted him. He made a fuss about forgiving her, but in fact her opinion had never mattered enough to either wound him or warm him. He indulged her with a phone call every so often, but it was purely an act of charity. His mother would ramble on about how proud she was; how marvelous that her only son was using his brilliant scientific knowledge to save the Everglades from human destruction. She was such a liberal drip, it was pathetic. She had adored Joey, too, another reason that Chaz wasn't eager to chat.

"Miracles do occur," his mother was saying. "Roger and I have been praying for her every night."

Chaz sighed. "Joey's gone, Mom. They'll never find her."

"Have you thought about seeing a psychic?"

"No. Have you thought about getting a brain scan?" Chaz slammed down the receiver. "Dingbat," he grumbled.

"Ain't no way to talk to your momma." It was Tool again, filling the doorway like a load of bricks.

Chaz foolishly advised him to mind his own damn business, at which point Tool snatched Chaz off his feet and rather effortlessly heaved him against the wall. Chaz was inclined to remain crumpled in a sobbing heap for the remainder of the morning, but Tool seized him by the hair and hoisted him upright.

"You call her back right this minute," he said, slapping the phone into Chaz's limp hand. "Call her back and say you're sorry. Else I'm gonna stomp on your nuts."

As soon as Chaz gathered himself, he phoned his mother and apologized for being so rude. It was difficult, though not nearly as painful as the alternative.

"It's all right, Charles, we understand," his mother assured him. "You're under a great deal of stress right now."

"You've got no idea," he said.

"Have you thought about trying Saint-John's-wort? It seems to be helping Roger level off."

"Good-bye, Mom." Chaz gently set down the phone.

Tool dragged him to the kitchen and placed him in a chair. "Where'd you go last night, Doc?" he asked.

"See a friend."

Chaz was working up the nerve to tell Tool the truth; that he'd gone out and coolly, efficiently committed a homicide. Maybe the dumb gorilla would think twice about knocking him around like a rag doll. On the other hand, Chaz was fairly certain that Red Hammernut wouldn't approve of his unilateral decision to eliminate Ricca Spill-man. Chaz had a feeling that Red didn't trust him with any responsibilities beyond signing his name to the phony water tests.

Tool said, "You took your truck off-road. The tires was covered with mud."

"My friend and I went for a ride," Chaz said.

"You ain't 'posed to go nowheres without me."

"But you were asleep. Snoring like a train."

"Where's that gun?" Tool asked.

"I, uh . . . I don't know."

Tool grabbed his throat. "Where's the fuckin' gun?"

"Backpack," Chaz peeped.

"And where's the fuckin' backpack?"

"Hummer." Chaz jerked a thumb in the general direction of the driveway.

Tool let go of him and headed for the door. Chaz gingerly massaged his neck, congratulating himself for having had the foresight to dispose of the spent shell casings and wipe down the .38. When Tool returned, he displayed no suspicion that the pistol had been recently fired. He placed it on the counter and matter-of-factly inquired, "So, who'd ya shoot?"

Chaz began to stutter.

Tool slapped him. "Spit it out, boy."

Obviously the working dynamic between the two men had changed. "You're not supposed to be slapping me around," Chaz complained. "You're my bodyguard, for Christ's sake!"

Tool shook his head. "Not no more. Now tell me—who was it? I smelled the barrel, Doc. I know what you done."

Here goes, Chaz thought. "Remember that lady with the little blue Ford? The one who came by last week?"

"I 'member. Your grief nurse, you said."

"Yeah, well, she got it in her head to make trouble. It was going to be bad."

"Is that right," Tool said.

"Ricca was her name. I'm pretty sure she hooked up with that asshole who's blackmailing us. I bet she was the one you saw down at Flamingo."

Tool frowned. "She sure didn't look familiar."

"But it was dark. And you said she wore a hat."

"Yeah, but still." He remembered the blue-Ford lady as being sort of short and stacked. The one with the ball cap seemed taller and thinner.

"Listen," Chaz said, "I need you to help me ditch her car and go through the apartment. We should make it look like she ran out on her rent."

Tool eyed him as if he were a tick. "That's two girls you whacked. What's up with you?"

"Come on. Will you help me or not?"

Tool dug a bottle of Mountain Dew out of the refrigerator and took a chug. "I ain't a bodyguard no more," he reiterated. "Now on, I'm your 'baby-sitter' is what Red says. That means I can spank your sorry ass, you don't do zackly what you're tole."

"My baby-sitter," Chaz repeatedly thinly. It was even more degrading than he'd feared. "I'm calling Red right now. We'll get this nonsense straightened out."

Tool shoved his cell phone at Chaz. "He's on the speed dial. Number one."

Red Hammernut was empathetic but unmoved. He said that while he was sensitive to Chaz's feelings, the gravity of the blackmail situation required that Mr. O'Toole take a more proactive role. Chaz was left with the unnerving impression that Red's goon would not be protecting him so much as holding him in custody. He was, more or less, under house arrest.

Cheerfully, Red Hammernut added, "Relax, son. Soon as we're done with this greedy prick who's shakin' us down, everything'll go back to normal in your life."

Chaz doubted that seriously. He said, "You're gonna pay him, aren't you?"

"Oh, he'll be paid. Don't you worry."

After Red said good-bye, Chaz passed the cellular back to Tool, who asked, "How come you didn't tell him 'bout that woman you shot?"

Chaz turned away. "Guess I forgot."

"Don't ever set foot outta this house without me. You hear?"

"Aye, aye," Chaz said, assuming incorrectly that Tool would miss the sarcasm. Tool promptly clouted him in the head and told him to get with the damn program.

Chaz shrank away, shielding himself with his arms. He was sick and tired of getting pummeled, first by the smartass blackmailer and now by this hairy troglodyte. He hadn't suffered so many bruises since the night he got wiped on roofies and fell down the stairs of a sorority house in Durham.

"All right then," said Tool, and went out back to plant a new cross that he'd uprooted off Highway 27 during the drive back from LaBelle.

Chaz fixed himself a cup of black coffee. By nature he was neither thorough nor introspective, but he reviewed with some attention to detail the events of recent days. That his stock had fallen with Red Hammernut was clear, and it caused Chaz to wonder if Red was now reconsidering his past commitments. In exchange for carrying out the Everglades scam, Chaz had been promised a plum position with Hammernut Farms—staff biologist, with a fat salary, big office, slutty blond secretary, whatever he wanted. That was the deal. They had drunk a toast and shaken hands on it.

But now . . . now it seemed to Chaz as if Red was blaming him for the entire unfortunate shitstorm, from the jerkoff detective snooping around to the jerkoff blackmailer demanding half a million bucks. True, none of it would be happening had Chaz not chosen to push his perfectly innocent wife off the cruise liner—but how could he possibly have known that some conniving dirtbag was lurking in the shadows, watching the whole damn thing?

It was unfair of Red Hammernut to lose faith so easily, to tie Chaz on a short leash and put him in the hands of a chowderhead like Tool. With a measure of bitterness Chaz concluded that Red was underestimating him, just as his mother had underestimated him not so many years ago. He believed that Red's tepid assessment of his character might be different had he witnessed Chaz in action the night before at Loxahatchee; the smooth and unflinching way that Chaz had taken care of the Ricca problem. Red surely would have been impressed, he thought. Maybe even amazed.

As he watched Tool plant yet another white cross in the yard, it began to gnaw at Dr. Charles Perrone that Red Hammernut was now treating him like a liability instead of an asset.

And he knew what men like Red Hammernut did with their liabilities.

Twenty-three

Joey and Mick Stranahan were waiting when Corbett Wheeler's chartered Falcon landed at Tamiami. He stepped out wearing a long black drover's coat and, over an explosion of reddish-blond hair, a wide-brimmed leather hat. He sported a lushly ungroomed beard, and he carried a burl walking stick of the sort favored by fast-water trout fishermen. Two inches taller than Stranahan, Corbett Wheeler shook hands in a way that suggested the closure of a sensitive, high-stakes business deal. Then with one ropy arm he twirled his sister until she giggled. On the drive to Dinner Key he insisted on sharing Polaroids of a prize ewe named Celine, a Coopworth–East Friesian hybrid that had survived a nasty bout with foot rot to become Corbett's most fertile breeder.

"Isn't she gorgeous?" he enthused.

Mick and Joey chose to treat the question as rhetorical. To Stranahan, Corbett Wheeler confided: "These are the most peaceable creatures on God's green earth. Strange as it seems, I vastly prefer their company to humans."

Stranahan said he understood completely.

"There's no sort of unnatural attraction, if that's what you're wondering," Corbett added sternly. "Joey will back me up on that."

She said, "It's true. Corbett is partial to women. He's been engaged what—three or four times?"

He nodded remorsefully. "I'm impossible to live with. I crave my solitude."

"Then you'll approve of the island," Stranahan said.

"Yes, but first the ship!"

"What a champ," Joey said.

Corbett Wheeler tipped his hat. "Anything for you, little sister."

Three hours later, after an arduous mission to the Gallería Mall, they were standing on the fantail of the M.V. *Sun Duchess* in Port Everglades, waiting for the sun to set. Joey's brother was looking over the rail, pointing with his walking stick, saying, "Christ Almighty, I can't believe you didn't die in the fall."

"I turned it into a dive," Joey explained. "That's what saved me—four years on the college swim team."

Stranahan noticed her shying away from the side of the ship. When he asked if she felt all right, she said, "It's just a little creepy out here, that's all."

"We don't have to go through with this," he said.

"Like hell we don't."

Still gazing down at the water, Corbett Wheeler whistled. "It was me, I wouldn't have made it."

"If it was you," Joey said, "you wouldn't have married someone who'd push you overboard."

Her brother shrugged. "Relationships are complicated. That's why I'm partial to livestock."

Stranahan watched the meandering procession of tugs and freighters and fishing boats. The roiling cross-wakes would have made for an interesting ride in his skiff.

"You rented this whole ship?" he asked Corbett Wheeler.

"Just for the night."

Joey asked how much it cost, and Corbett told her to mind her own business. "One of the engines is down for servicing, so the cruise line was delighted with my offer. Tomorrow they're leasing out the Commodore Deck for a bar mitzvah!"

Joey had worn a baseball cap and sunglasses so that she wouldn't be recognized by any of the crew. According to the newspapers, Chaz had provided a photograph that was copied and distributed to all hands after she went missing.

She held up a pair of large shopping bags. "Mick, are you ready?"

"How about a cocktail first?" Joey's brother proposed merrily.

"Amen," said Mick Stranahan.

. . .

Tool sat down next to Maureen's bed and whispered, "Hey, there."

Her eyes opened halfway. When she smiled, Tool noticed that her lips were blotchy and dried out. For a moment he wondered if she'd gotten sick from the gator meat that he'd brought the other night.

He said, "What's all this?"

An oxygen tube trailed to her nostrils. A plastic bag filled with fluid hung next to the bed rail on an intravenous rig, dripping into a hole in her right arm.

"I took a turn," she said weakly.

Tool tried to swallow but found he couldn't. He stared down at the aluminum tin on his lap. "I brung a piece a Key lime pie."

"Thank you, Earl. Maybe later."

"What happened?" He was worried and confused.

"Nothing happened. This is just how it goes."

"What? How what goes?"

Maureen said, "Up and down, Earl. Good days, bad days."

She reached over and smoothed the shiny hairs on his hand. He was gripping the bed rail so tightly that his knuckles had gone pale. "How's the bodyguarding business?" she asked. "Tell me about your big meeting the other night."

Tool said, "You just rest. Don't talk no more."

He placed the pie tin on the bed stand and grabbed the TV remote. He clicked through the channels until he found a nature show about white pelicans, which he thought might interest Maureen. He remembered her saying that she had been keen on bird-watching until she'd taken ill. He recalled her telling about the day that she'd spotted a red-cockaded woodpecker, which was sort of like a red*headed* woodpecker except hardly any of them were left on the whole entire planet. So Tool figured he couldn't go wrong with any TV program that had to do with birds.

Sure enough, Maureen right away lifted her head and scooted higher on the pillow. She said, "Did you hear that, Earl? They migrate all the way from Canada to Florida Bay, the white pelicans do."

"Well, I'll be damned," said Tool.

Maureen began coughing, a wet hack that he found alarming. He lifted her upright and whumped her between the shoulder blades, which only made her moan. Gently he set her back on the pillow. A nurse who'd heard Maureen making noises came into the room and demanded to know what Tool was doing.

"It's all right. He's my nephew," Maureen said, slowly catching her breath.

The nurse was a small Hispanic woman who was struggling to reconcile Tool's uncommon physical appearance with his white medical coat.

"He's a doctor," Maureen added.

"Oh, really?" said the nurse.

"From the Netherlands."

When the nurse was gone, Maureen said, "Normally I don't like to fib, but I believe she would have called Security."

Tool asked, "Where's your kin? How come they don't never visit?"

"My daughters live in Coral Gables—it's a long drive, and they've got the kids to worry about. I see them on holidays."

"Ain't that far," Tool said. "It's a hop on the interstate is all. They could come weekends, at least."

"Did you need more medicine?"

With some effort Maureen rolled herself toward the wall. Her gown was open in the back and her skin looked dull and waxy. Tool observed that all the fentanyl patches had been removed.

She said, "Take what you need."

"They's all gone."

"Oh?" She rolled back and faced him. "I'm sorry, Earl. They must've peeled them off when they put me on the morphine." Her eyes flicked to the IV bag. "They gave me a squeeze pump so I don't have to bother the nurses—who, by the way, are just sitting on their flabby duffs doing nothing, complaining about their no-good husbands and reading the *National Enquirer*."

Tool said, "I don't need no more stick-ems. I just come to say hi." The truth was, he'd missed her company. It was the damnedest thing.

"I think there's one left in that drawer," Maureen said. "Go on and take it."

The patch was still in its wrapper. What the hell, thought Tool. He slipped it in his breast pocket.

"Earl?"

"Yeah."

"Something's bothering you. What is it?"

"I'm fine," Tool said.

"You are *not* fine, young man. Talk to me."

Tool stood up. "Go on back to sleep." He decided not to tell her about Perrone shooting that woman, and all the rest. Maureen wouldn't understand, and besides, he didn't want to upset her.

Once more she reached for his hand. "It's never too late for choosing a new direction—what they call a sea change. Promise me you'll keep that in mind."

He said, "You're gonna be okay. Them doctors, they'll getcha some stronger dope. I'll see to it."

Maureen closed her eyes. "Listen to me, Earl. It's yourself you ought to be thinking about. Life goes by so darn fast, every wasted moment is a crime." One blue eye opened and fixed on him. "And every crime is a wasted moment."

Tool assured her that he'd stay out of trouble. "This job'll be done soon, then I can get on home."

"But I've got such a bad feeling," she said.

"Stop it, now. Don't you worry."

He found it jarring to feel sad for this woman, who was practically a stranger. She in no way reminded him of his mother, who had been loud and short-tempered; a world-class blasphemer. Yet as Tool watched Maureen tugging the sheets up to her chin, he felt the same creeping helplessness, the same heavy premonition of loss as when his mother had taken sick.

"You go see the surgeon yet?" Maureen asked.

"No, ma'am. I been real busy."

With skeletal fingers she pinched a clump of his knuckle hair and twisted it until he let out a cry.

"Earl, you can't walk around with a lead slug up your bottom. It's bound to affect your outlook."

Tool jerked his hand away. "I'll get it took care of, I swear."

"It could well be the turning point in your life," she said. "What they call an epiphany. Or at least a catharsis."

He assumed those to be the surgical terms for a bullet removal, and he promised Maureen he would schedule the operation as soon as he got a break in his bodyguarding schedule.

"I'll be back later in the week," he promised.

She looked up at him warmly. "Do you pray, Earl?"

"Not in a while," he admitted. Thirty years at least.

"That's all right."

"Well, I better go now."

"Every time my faith is shaken, I look up into the big blue sky and see God's work practically everywhere. Just imagine a bird that flies all the way from Manitoba to Key West. Every single winter!"

Tool found himself turning toward the TV screen. A large flock of snowy pelicans was taking flight, rising in a flurry from the rippled surface of a marsh. With a little imagination it looked like a long sugar-white beach breaking to pieces and blowing away in the wind.

"I'd like to see that someday," Tool said.

Soon Maureen's hand slipped from his, and Tool knew from the heaviness of her breathing that she'd fallen asleep. He watched the bird program until it was over, then switched off the television. As he was leaving the convalescent center, the Hispanic nurse got in step beside him and asked if he was really Maureen's nephew.

"I don't see much resemblance," the nurse remarked.

"That's 'cause I'm adopted," Tool said.

"Really. And back in the Netherlands you're a physician?"

"No, a *doctor*," he said pointedly.

"Ah."

Sneaky little bitch, Tool thought, squeezing himself into the Grand Marquis. Thought she could trick me!

Fifteen miles away, in the Loxahatchee National Wildlife Refuge, a man with one eye was skinning a dead otter. The man was tall and his hands were large and his skin was as brown as an English saddle. He wore dungarees, military boots, an opaque shower cap and a thread-bare T-shirt with a lewd lapping tongue silk-screened on the front. His beard was a spray of braided silvery tendrils, the tips of which were green and mossy with dried duckweed. The man looked ancient and mildly demented, although he moved with the fluid confidence of an athlete or a soldier, both of which he once was.

The otter had been killed a few hours earlier by a poacher who hadn't realized until too late that he himself was being stalked. The man with one eye had easily disarmed the outlaw, stripped off his clothes, bound his wrists and ankles with saw grass, then staked him on a hemp leash to an alligator nest.

Ricca Spillman had witnessed it all.

She was floating in a state of suspended awareness. Even after two days she wasn't certain if the one-eyed man was real; if he was, however, he had saved her life.

The man informed Ricca that they would eat the dead otter because that was better than leaving it to the buzzards. When she inquired about the fate of the poacher, the one-eyed man said, "If the gator doesn't get him, I suppose I'll cut him loose. All depends on his manners."

"What about me?"

The man made no response, the blade flashing in his hand as he deftly peeled the flesh of the otter away from the damp thick fur. When he was done, he said, "Tell me again about your boyfriend."

Ricca repeated the story of Chaz Perrone while the man prepared a small fire. The otter meat smelled funky, but Ricca was so famished that she forced it down. The man devoured everything else in the fry pan, crunching noisily into the marrow of the animal's bones. Afterward he kicked dirt over the flames, wiped his palms on the seat of his dungarees and lifted Ricca into his arms.

"How's the leg?" he asked, and began trudging through the scrub.

"Much better today. Where are we going, Captain?"

That was how the man in the shower cap had asked to be addressed.

"There's another camp not far." He carried Ricca as lightly as if she were pillow fluff.

She said, "How soon can I go home?"

"You have a pleasing voice. It makes me want to sleep in your arms."

"Will you take me home? Please?"

"Sorry," the man replied, "but I can't go near the highway. Please don't ask—the traffic sets me off."

The next camp was a small clearing in a stand of palmettos. He set Ricca on the ground, lit another fire and heated a pot of coffee. From a canvas duffel marked U.S. POSTAL SERVICE he took out a volume of poetry.

"Oliver Goldsmith," he said.

Ricca raised her eyebrows quizzically. The man opened the book to a dog-eared page and placed it on her lap. "Read that aloud, please."

"The whole thing?"

"Just the first stanza."

Ricca, whose interest in poetry had peaked with "Green Eggs and Ham," read it first to herself:

> *When lovely woman stoops to folly,*
> *And finds too late that men betray,*
> *What charm can soothe her melancholy?*
> *What art can wash her guilt away?*

When she recited it out loud, the man in the shower cap smiled patiently.

"You don't much care for the poem. I can tell," he said.

"What 'guilt' is he talking about? I don't feel guilty, I feel pissed off!"

"Understandable. The sonofabitch shot you."

"And he lied, too. About everything!"

The man took the volume of poetry from her hands and returned it to the duffel.

Ricca said, "I'm dying to get even with the bastard. Will you help me?"

The man popped the glass eye from its socket and cleaned it with the dingy tail of his T-shirt. He had heard the gunshots from half a mile away; slogged through the saw grass and muck and high water, half walking, half swimming. By the time he'd gotten there the shooter was already gone, a pair of red taillights shrinking down the levee. Ricca had desperately submerged herself in a clump of lily pads. The man with one eye had located her by following the intermittent gasps that she made when extending her lips and nose to the surface. Shaking and bleeding from a wound in the leg, she had nonetheless tried to fight him off, reasonably assuming from his appearance that he was some kind of dangerous swamp pervert.

"I'm sorry, but I can't help you. I'm going through a rough personal spell," he told her now.

"What do you mean?"

"For starters, I'm hearing the same weird duet all day and all night in my head—'Midnight Rambler' as performed by Eydie Gorme and Cat Stevens. I'm sure they're perfectly nice folks, but frankly I'm ready to shove a sawed-off down my throat. One blessed hour of silence," the man said wistfully, "would be welcome."

Ricca said nothing. The sight of his hollow eye socket, dank as a cave, was creeping her out.

"On top of that, I'm hallucinating almost constantly," he went on. "I'm assuming, for example, that in reality you bear no resemblance to Lady Bird Johnson."

"Who?" Ricca asked.

"The wife of our thirty-sixth president. He was the fellow who sent me to Vietnam," the man explained. "To me, you look exactly like Mrs. Johnson, which I know must sound preposterous. You're a much younger woman, with cinnamon freckles and curly hair, yet when I look at you, all I see is Lady Bird."

"Know what you need? A doctor."

The one-eyed man grinned, and it struck Ricca that he must have been extraordinarily handsome before he went bonkers. Even now, she felt an unnerving stir of attraction.

He said, "It's entirely possible that I'm dying."

"No way, Captain."

"There were times in my life when I would have jumped at the opportunity," he allowed, "to hunt down your shiftless boyfriend and haul him out here for a private party. I'm not talking mundane revenge, either, but a textbook exercise in predation. Please understand, there's a primordial formula for survival on this planet, and men like your Chad—"

"Chaz," Ricca said.

"—tend to perform poorly without dry socks, dental floss and air conditioning. Even that wretched low-life poacher whom I hog-tied this morning is better equipped for this world than—Chaz, is it?" The man clawed at his ears. "That god-awful singing, it will *not* stop."

"I can't hear a thing."

"Last week it was David Lee Roth and Sophie Tucker. The panfish in these canals must be loaded with mercury." He leaned over and stared hard for several moments into the flames. "You say your beau works out here in the 'glades?"

"That's right. He tests farm water for pollution."

"Too bad we've never crossed paths, he and I." The man chuckled to himself as he worked the glass orb back into its socket. "I can carry you as far as the dike. From there a friend of mine'll drive you into town."

"Then what?" Ricca asked.

"Me, I'm heading west." He handed her a cup of coffee. "The other day I got so damn hungry, I ate a pygmy rattler. Normally I leave reptiles alone, but a mighty powerful urge took hold. Anyhow, I go to grab the little sucker, and suddenly there's the face of Dr. Henry Kissinger staring up at me, flicking that little forked tongue of his! Fucking Kissinger!"

Ricca Spillman had never heard of him, either, but she politely asked, "So what'd you do?"

"I chewed off his head, of course," the man said, "and fried his scaly ass in canola oil. Point is, I'm navigating a rocky patch in my private life—I positively can't be anywhere near the highway, or crowds, or humanity in general. I wish to God I could help you, but I'm taking a pass."

Ricca said, "That's okay. I'll figure something out." She wondered if the rattlesnake story was intended as some sort of mystical lesson.

As if reading her mind, the man said, "Go with your gut, darling. Simple as that."

"I'll work on it."

After dousing the fire, the burly hermit scooped her up and splashed out across the marsh. It was an hour's hike under a blistering sun, yet he wasn't even breathing hard when they reached the levee. A mud-splattered Jeep was parked on the road. Waiting behind the wheel sat a younger man wearing a knit watch cap and dark shades. He looked restless and intense.

The captain kissed Ricca on the forehead and told her to be careful on that bum leg.

She returned the kiss and said, "Thanks for saving my butt."

The man with one eye saluted dashingly. "It was an honor, Mrs. Johnson."

Twenty-four

Dr. Charles Regis Perrone bounced behind the steering wheel of his Hummer, weaving down the levee at a ludicrous speed. Every so often he poked his head out to scan the sky, which was full of helicopters. It was the weirdest spectacle, choppers buzzing over the Everglades like giant candy-colored dragonflies.

Chaz felt like the Ray Liotta character in *GoodFellas*, racing around like a lunatic with a load of hot guns, wondering if the helicopter following him was real or imaginary—except that instead of that Harry Nilsson song from the movie, Papa Thorogood was blasting in Chaz Perrone's ears, asking who did he love.

It was ideal road music, but Chaz couldn't get into the spirit. He was heading out to collect another water sample, and he was highly agitated. Maybe there was an innocent explanation for the helicopters baby blue, green, red, white, baby blue again. . . .

Maybe a hunter or fisherman had gotten lost, Chaz speculated. Except these weren't rescue-type choppers he was seeing—they were private executive-style models, similar to the nifty little Bell 206 leased by Hammernut Farms to ferry Samuel Johnson Hammernut back and forth across his holdings. Red had given him the grand tour soon after Chaz signed on as his mole; Chaz's first and only helicopter ride, swooping low over the checkerboard fields of crops. From the air Chaz had been able to track the precise path of the pollution, the gridwork of shallow brown canals that carried the tainted runoff from the soil of Hammernut Farms to the throat of the Everglades. "God's septic tank," Red had called it, guffawing behind tinted goggles that had made him look like a psychedelic fruit fly. Dr. Charles Perrone had laughed, too, an obsequious reflex though hardly insincere. Chaz gave not a damn about the wetlands below, or what a continual soaking with fertilizer might do to them. . . .

Shit, Chaz thought, here comes another one!

He kept his eyes on the red-striped helicopter for so long that he nearly drove the Hummer off the levee. The jostling awakened Tool, who mumbled, "Slow down, dickbrain."

Urgently, Chaz jabbed a finger upward. "Check it out!"

"A whirlybird. So what?"

"There's a whole bunch of 'em!"

Tool sneezed, then wiped a woolly arm across his nose. "Maybe they's shootin' a movie."

As Chaz scanned the horizon, his head twitched back and forth. It reminded Tool of a lizard scouting for bugs.

Tool said, "You crash this fucker into the water, I'll strangle your ass before ya can drown."

"But what if they're following us?" Chaz asked.

"What if fish had tits?"

"I'm serious. Jesus, see that blue one? Right behind us! Look in the mirror!"

Tool, who was feeling the effects of a fresh fentanyl patch, slammed his eyes shut. "Whirlybirds. I swear to God," he said, and promptly nodded back to sleep.

Chaz parked at the spillway, struggled into his wading gear, grabbed the two-iron and slogged into the brothy water. He counted seven helicopters in the sky, each circling at different heights. That they were surveilling him seemed chillingly obvious, so Chaz was careful to conduct the runoff sampling with diligence and deliberation. He tried his hardest to appear unconcerned, although he peed copiously into his waders when the baby-blue chopper dipped low and slowed to a hover directly above his head.

By the time Tool awoke again, Chaz was racing back, halfway down the levee. The helicopters were gone.

"Gimme the cell," Chaz said.

"Whaffor?"

"I need to call Red."

Tool tossed the phone to Chaz, who was sweaty and flushed with anger. Chaz speed-dialed the office in LaBelle and demanded to speak to Mr. Hammernut.

"He's where? *Fishing?* That's terrific," Chaz snapped at Red's secretary.

Tool smiled drowsily. Fishing sounded like a pretty sweet way to spend the day.

Chaz was fuming. "Then put me through to his voice mail."

"Call him later," Tool advised.

"No, no, this can't wait. Red? Red, this is Chaz. Listen to me real good: We get out to the second spillway this morning and the whole damn sky is full of helicopters—I'm not sure who they are, or where they came from, or what the fuck's going on. But since you're the only one I know that can afford to hire a goddamn fleet of choppers . . . what I'm trying to tell you, Red, is be careful. *Very, very careful.* You don't want anything bad happening to me, you truly don't. You want me to stay happy and calm and cool, which is dead opposite of the way I feel right now—shit, the machine cut me off!"

Chaz was so upset that he was panting. Tool grabbed the phone and said, "Boy, you done lost your marbles."

"That's what you want me to think, isn't it? That's the secret plan, right?"

Chaz poked his head out of the Hummer and looked up anxiously. The sky was bright and clear and empty, except for a solitary vulture rafting high in the thermals.

Joey Perrone had remembered that *GoodFellas* was one of her husband's favorite movies; that's what gave her the idea for helicopters. Corbett was thrilled and said it would be spectacular. He called the charter service himself and put the whole tab, more than twenty-three grand, on his platinum card. Joey didn't like to fly because of what had happened to her parents, but Corbett promised that she'd have a fine time. Choppers are a blast, he said.

And he was right. The baby-blue Bell Ranger picked them up on the island and shot out low across the bay, then up the coast. Corbett took the seat next to the pilot; Joey sat beside Mick Stranahan, both hands latched to his left arm. He pointed out Stiltsville, where he'd once lived; then Key Biscayne, South Beach, the high-rise canyons along Collins Avenue. The helicopter banked and began to pass over dense suburbs gridded by impossibly congested roads. Joey could see that the interstate was locked down in both directions because of an accident; at the vortex of the traffic jam was a twinkling of red and blue emergency lights.

Corbett swiveled in his seat and raised his voice to be heard over the rotors: "No offense, Sis, but I'd stick darning needles in my brain before I'd live in a place like this."

Later, as the pilot angled northward, Joey heard her brother gag in revulsion at the sight of western Broward County, where new subdivisions were erupting like cankers in all directions; thousands upon thousands of cookie-cutter houses, jammed together so tightly that it looked like you could jump from roof to roof for miles on end. Where there were no homes stood office parks, shopping plazas and enormous auto malls—acres and acres of Toyotas and Chryslers, cooking in the sun. Only a slender dirt levee separated the clamorous tide of humanity from the Everglades.

"At least they left a lake or two for the kids," Joey remarked.

Mick shook his head sadly. "Rock pits," he informed her. "Hundreds of feet deep. That's where they dredged up the fill for the roads and houses."

"But what used to be out here? Before all this?"

He pointed toward the other side of the levee. "That," he said. "The widest river in the world."

Corbett let out a sarcastic whoop. "I just saw a tree!" he cried. "I swear to God. A real tree!"

Before long, the sprawl gave way to wet saw grass prairies that undulated like flooded wheat in the brisk spring breeze. Except for an occasional airboat, gnat-sized specks on the tan landscape, there was no evidence of human occupation. Stranahan spotted three small deer bounding for the shelter of a tree island, and it occurred to Joey that—except for the occasional garbage-looting raccoon—these were the first truly wild animals that she'd seen since moving to Florida. She'd always been curious about the Everglades, but Chaz had refused to take her along on field trips, claiming it would violate the water district's rules. That he never spoke of the place, except to gripe about the snakes and the insects, was even more stunning to Joey now that she'd finally seen it for herself. How could Chaz—a biologist, for God's sake—*not* be dazzled?

Obviously, however, he wasn't. He had betrayed the wetlands as nonchalantly as he had betrayed Joey. He had sold out—this greedy swine she'd married—so that megatons of noxious crap could be pumped day and night into the glistening waters below. Maybe for someone as soulless as her husband it wasn't much of a reach, Joey thought, from killing a place to killing a person.

"Look out there," Stranahan said.

The other choppers had arrived, six in all, flying clockwise in concentric circles. It was quite a show. Joey turned to Corbett and said, "You've outdone yourself. This is fantastic!"

Chaz Perrone's yellow Hummer was hard to miss, even without the plume of dust trailing it down the levee. Stranahan handed Joey a pair of binoculars, through which she could see her husband's windblown head protruding from the driver's window and cocked toward the sky.

"He does not look overjoyed," she reported, drawing a gleeful cackle from her brother.

Their pilot was on the radio, double-checking the flight paths and altitudes of the other helicopters. A Cessna from the Palm Beach Sheriff's Office broke in, a Sergeant Robinson inquiring about all the chopper activity. The pilot of the baby-blue Bell replied that they were rehearsing an aerial chase for the new James Bond movie, a glamorous lie that produced the desired effect: The police Cessna banked sharply and drifted away. Authorities in South Florida were famously accommodating to the film industry, and had been known to shut down major freeways so that a teenaged vampire drag-racing scene could be shot and re-shot without artistic compromise.

When Chaz finally parked the Hummer and waded into the water, Joey insisted on buzzing him. It was Corbett, however, who persuaded the pilot to put the aircraft into a hover directly above his brother-in-law's hatless noggin. The helicopter stayed high enough that Chaz couldn't have seen who was aboard, but he didn't even try. It was amusing to watch him fumble with the water bottle while pretending not to notice the shadow of the chopper, or its earsplitting racket.

"That's enough," Joey called out, and the pilot pulled away.

They circled at a greater distance, alternating low sweeps with the other helicopters, until Chaz finished with the sample and sped off in the Humvee.

"What do you suppose he's thinking?" Corbett asked.

"Unhappy thoughts," Joey said.

Mick Stranahan laughed. "Wait until he sees the newspaper."

Later, after returning to the island, they all went fishing in the

Whaler. Stranahan caught several nice yellowtails, which he fried Cuban-style for dinner. Afterward Corbett lit a cigar and Joey modeled the silk Michael Kors skirt that she'd purchased at the Gallería. Mick uncorked a bottle of Australian cabernet. The three of them sat together on the seawall and watched the sun go down, Strom parking his black brick of a head on Joey's lap.

"What should I say about you on Thursday?" Corbett asked. He was drafting his speech for the memorial service.

"You can say I was a kind and loving sister," Joey said.

"Aw, come on. We can do better than that."

Stranahan said, "Say she was a tiger. She never quit fighting."

Corbett beamed. "I like that."

"Say she was full of life and had a big heart."

"No, a *dumb* heart," Joey said.

"Not true." Mick touching her arm.

"I'll say you were idealistic," Corbett said.

Joey frowned. "Which is just another word for *naïve*."

"Then say she had great legs," Stranahan said.

"Well, why not?" Corbett chortled.

Joey covered her ears. "Stop it, both of you."

Corbett hadn't been able to line up a choir on short notice, so he'd settled for a trio of guitarists. "They do the folk Mass at the Catholic church in Lighthouse Point. The priest tells me they're pretty good."

Joey said, "What if Chaz doesn't show up?"

Corbett tipped up his red-blond chin and blew a wreath of smoke. "Oh, he'll be there. He knows how bad it would look if he didn't."

Stranahan agreed. "Right now he's scared to death of making a wrong move. He's got no choice but to play the grieving widower to the bitter end."

"God, I wish *I* could be there," Joey said.

Stranahan shot her a look. "Don't even think about it. You promised."

"But I could make myself up so that he'd never know it was me."

Her brother said, "Joey, this isn't *The Lucy Show*. The man tried to murder you."

She was silent for a while, sipping her wine and stroking Strom's sleek neck. The sun dropped over the horizon and the sky over Biscayne Bay turned from gold to pink to purple. Joey wondered what her husband would wear to the service. Where he would sit. What he might say to her friends. Whether he would notice Rose in the first pew.

Of course he would notice Rose.

"Now, that was a first-class sunset," Corbett said, flicking his cigar into the water. The hiss roused the Doberman. Corbett whistled and the dog clambered to its feet.

Stranahan got up, too. "Let's go take another look at the video."

Corbett remarked that it had turned out surprisingly well, for having been shot in a single take. "You two have a future in television."

"Hey, I just thought of something." Joey rose, smoothing her skirt. "What if Chaz wants to say something at the memorial service? What if the jerk decides he's got to get up and make a speech?"

"Damn right he's making a speech," Corbett said. "I already left a message on his answering machine. Told him he's getting five minutes in the pulpit to make you sound like the saint you were. Told him it better be good."

Captain Gallo pointed at the jelly jars on Karl Rolvaag's desk and said, "Those are the worst-looking urine specimens I ever saw."

Rolvaag faked a chuckle, out of deference to rank. "It's just water."

"After passing through what—a diseased buffalo?"

"Water from the Everglades." The detective had meant to conceal the jars inside his desk, in order to avoid precisely this conversation. Normally, Gallo took a much longer lunch hour, but evidently his bimbo du jour had stood him up.

He peered disgustedly at the hazy contents of the jars. "Christ, there's bugs and crap floatin' around in there."

"You betcha," Rolvaag said.

"Can I ask what the hell it's doing out here?"

Unlike most of the other detectives, Rolvaag never felt comfortable lying to Captain Gallo's face, even when it was the eminently sensible thing to do. This time he gave it a try.

"It's for my snakes. There are too many chemicals in the water coming out of the tap," Rolvaag said. "All that fluoride and chlorine, it's not healthy for them."

"And that shit *is*?" Gallo asked incredulously. "You're a head case, Karl, no offense. Who else do you know has pets that need swamp water and live rats?"

The detective shrugged. Telling Gallo the truth wouldn't have accomplished anything. He would have scoffed at Rolvaag's field trip as a waste of time, which it most definitely was not. Using Marta's map, Rolvaag had located by automobile a sampling site adjacent to Hammernut Farms. There he had waded barefoot into the cattails and filled three mason jars with water the color of root beer, which he'd delivered to a professor friend at Florida Atlantic University. Rolvaag's amateur samples had revealed illegal levels of suspended phosphorus at 317, 327 and 344 parts per billion, respectively. The figures contrasted dramatically with Dr. Charles Perrone's suspiciously consistent findings of only 9 ppb in the runoff from the vegetable fields.

Rolvaag did not share his own test results—or his damning conclusions—with Perrone's co-workers at the water district. While politely deflecting their questions, he'd gotten the distinct impression that none of them would be heartbroken to see Chaz dragged off in handcuffs. The detective had offered no details about his investigation, for it was possible that the scientist's fraudulent water charts were unrelated to the death of his wife. If Joey Perrone's last will and testament was authentic, Chaz might have killed her purely for the money. If the will was a forgery and Joey's inheritance was not an incentive, Chaz might have killed her for any one of a dozen pedestrian reasons that drove spouses to homicide.

Explaining the phosphorus scam would have brought either a blank stare or a skeptical snort from Captain Gallo, who'd have instantly pointed out the difficulty of selling such an arcane motive to a homicide jury. Nonetheless, the fact that Charles Perrone was faking the Everglades data was a valuable piece of information for Karl Rolvaag. It put the strange blackmail scheme into a more ominous context, considering what was at stake for Samuel Johnson Hammernut. Disclosure of his illicit arrangement with the biologist would be devastating, financially and politically. The pollution violations would draw hefty government fines, and bribing a state employee was a felony punishable by a hitch in prison. Even if Red Hammernut managed to escape conviction, the publicity alone would forever stain the reputation of his company. Rolvaag believed that the crusty tycoon would do whatever was necessary to protect himself from the blackmailer and also from Chaz Perrone, whose loyalty would evaporate as soon as the cell door slammed behind him.

When Gallo asked how the case was going, Rolvaag said, "Not so great. I'm getting mixed opinions on Mrs. Perrone's will. Her brother says it's a fake. Unfortunately, so does one of my two handwriting experts."

"Does that mean somebody's trying to set hubby up for a fall?"

"Possibly. Chaz hasn't got many admirers."

Rolvaag sneezed convulsively. It was one of those days when the captain had put on his cologne with a fire hose.

"Too bad about the will," Gallo said. "I thought we had our lucky break."

"Me, too."

"So you're finally ready to bag it?" Gallo asked hopefully.

"Unless something breaks loose, I don't know what else to do," Rolvaag said. In truth he knew exactly what to do: sit back and watch.

"No sense banging my head against the wall," he added.

"You gave it a helluva shot," Gallo said.

"Oh well."

"By the way, Karl, I got your paperwork on the resignation. I tore it up and threw it in the trash."

Rolvaag said, "That's all right. I made copies."

"Would you knock it off already?"

"I'm quitting, Captain. Seriously."

"For Edina, Minnesota? Leaving Florida?"

"Honestly, I can't wait."

Another dog, a toy poodle, had gone missing at Sawgrass Grove. Rolvaag had never heard of binge feeding by pythons, but he couldn't discount the possibility. *Something* seemed to be preying on his neighbors' pets, and his missing snakes were prime suspects. The detective planned to mail an anonymous check for one thousand dollars to each of the grieving couples, an act that would clear not only his conscience but also his bank account.

"You've got a bright future here," Gallo said.

Rolvaag tried not to appear amused.

"The man himself has taken notice of your good work," Gallo added in a confidential tone. The man being the sheriff.

"I thought he was ticked off about me interviewing Hammernut," Rolvaag said.

"Hell, no, Karl. He was just covering his ass is all. He's a big fan, trust me."

The detective did not for a moment suppose that the sheriff was a "fan," and he could barely summon the energy to act flattered.

Gallo said, "For Christ's sake, what have I gotta do to change your mind? And don't say 'Indict Charles Perrone.' "

Rolvaag smiled. "Don't worry."

The detective had accepted the fact that Perrone would never be charged with murdering his wife, even though he had most certainly pushed her off the cruise ship. What had saved Rolvaag from abject discouragement were the jars of cloudy liquid on his desk; swamp water salted with the harshest man-made fertilizers. That Chaz Perrone would betray a place as hallowed as the Everglades for money was proof of his congenital dishonesty, rancid morals and general worthlessness. Yet while the discovery of the biologist's sleazy crime had confirmed Rolvaag's suspicions about the so-called scientist, it was more ironic than revelatory.

Because Charles Regis Perrone was doomed.

The detective had never been more sure of anything. After sifting every wisp of information that he'd gathered, Rolvaag realized that he needn't waste another minute trying to send Chaz Perrone to Death Row.

The man was already a goner. Toast.

He was arrogant and impulsive, and Samuel Johnson Hammernut was going to make him disappear. Even had Rolvaag wished to intercede, he would only be delaying the inevitable.

Chaz Perrone was, as his brother-in-law had observed, a hopeless fuckwit. If for a moment he feared that his fakery of the pollution data would be exposed, Perrone would immediately roll over and rat on Red Hammernut, meanwhile casting himself in the least felonious light. And who would foresee this scenario sooner or more clearly than the man who'd recruited the young biologist precisely for his cravenness and casual mendacity? Red Hammernut could smell a butt fuck coming a mile away, and he'd never stand still for it.

Karl Rolvaag could now leave South Florida with a measure of peace, if not satisfaction. Chaz Perrone would never be prosecuted for killing his wife, but he would be punished.

All that remained to nag at the detective was a solitary loose end, something that had turned up on a routine inquiry to American Express. In the twelve days since Joey Perrone went overboard, somebody had used her credit card to rent a Chevrolet Suburban, and also to purchase women's shoes, makeup, designer sunglasses and numerous articles of fine clothing, including a two-piece Burberry swimsuit. Rolvaag didn't believe that Chaz Perrone was reckless enough (or tasteful enough) to embark on such a shopping spree, though it was possible that one of his female acquaintances had found and pocketed Joey's gold AmEx while visiting Chaz's house.

"I can't believe you're actually boxing up all your shit," Gallo was complaining, his knuckles planted on Rolvaag's desk. "I can't fucking believe you're going through with this."

The detective smiled apologetically. "I miss the snow," he said.

One more visit to West Boca Dunes Phase II. Then he could start loading the U-Haul.

Twenty-five

Charles Perrone said, "I'm not going anywhere."

"Red says different." Tool leaned against the refrigerator, gnawing a stick of beef jerky and sucking at a jumbo Mountain Dew.

"I don't care what Red says!"

Rolled in Chaz's right hand was the *Sun-Sentinel*, which he brandished like a lead pipe. A notice on the obituary page said that Joey's brother was holding a memorial service at St. Conan's on Thursday morning, and that Joey's friends and loved ones were invited to "come share their memories and celebrate her effervescent life spirit."

Spare me, Chaz thought. A photograph, taken when Joey was about eighteen, accompanied the announcement. Now the phone was ringing off the wall and that New Zealand nutcase, Corbett, had left a pushy message telling Chaz to write up a five-minute speech.

"You better damn well care what Red says," Tool warned.

"Oh yeah?"

The deterioration of Chaz's mental state had failed to shake his hope that the last will and testament in Detective Rolvaag's possession was authentic, and that ultimately he'd be inheriting $13 million from Joey's estate—at which point he could say adios to Samuel Johnson Hammernut, and thereafter never set foot in that godforsaken sump known as the Everglades.

"He says it'll look real bad," Tool went on, "you don't show up at your own wife's service."

"I don't care how it looks. I won't go."

Chaz's nerves were still jangled from the helicopter blitz, which in his memory loop now seemed less like the chase scene from *GoodFellas* and more like the flying-monkey scene from *The Wizard of Oz*. Meanwhile, Red Hammernut had offered no response to Chaz's accusatory phone call from the levee, and the uneasy silence only added to a cascade of anxieties. What a psychological pounding Chaz had endured since that night on the *Sun Duchess*—the creepy break-ins at the house; the lurking detective; the witness turned smartass blackmailer; the Ricca crisis; and now mysterious spy choppers!

Chaz's current game plan was not to leave the walled confines of West Boca Dunes Phase II until the rest of the fucking world stopped picking on him.

"I won't go to the service," he repeated with ill-advised defiance.

Tool capped the jug of Mountain Dew, calmly stepped up to Chaz and decked him with it. When he tried to get up, Tool bonked him again. The second blow busted a seam in the plastic bottle, unleashing a stinging green fizz that sprayed Chaz flush in the face. Tool jerked him off the floor and said, "Somebody's ringin' the doorbell. Get rid of 'em."

Chaz thrashed his head violently, collapsed to his knees and scuttled like a wounded crab beneath the kitchen table.

Tool sighed. "Swear to God, I wisht I'd had your sorry ass in one a my tomato crews."

He trudged to the front door and flung it open. The cop was standing there, holding a briefcase. Tool nodded him inside.

"Is Mr. Perrone here?" Karl Rolvaag asked.

"In the kitchen." Tool spun on a booted heel and headed to his bedroom for a snooze.

The detective found Chaz rocking in a fetal position beneath the table. "Bad day?" he asked.

"Stomach problems." Chaz was relieved that his reflex to lie was unimpaired.

Rolvaag joined him on the floor. "I've got a couple of questions that can't wait."

"What else is new." Chaz pawed miserably at his burning eyelids.

"Your wife had an American Express card."

"So do the frigging Muppets."

"Where is Joey's?" the detective asked.

"Like I told you before, I got rid of all her stuff. Everything," Chaz said. "It was too painful having it around the house. The credit card was probably in one of her purses that I threw away."

"Which purse? The one she had on the cruise?"

"How should *I* know? I tossed 'em all."

"Any chance that the card and her driver's license were stolen?" Rolvaag asked.

Chaz uncurled slowly and rose to a sitting position. He thought about the break-ins—wouldn't it be just his luck if the blackmailer had rifled through the boxes in the garage and found Joey's AmEx?

"Reason I ask, the card has been used several times since your wife disappeared," the detective said.

"Not by me!"

"Mostly for ladies' apparel, makeup, that sort of thing."

Chaz was honestly baffled. He hoped that it showed.

"Would any of your wife's friends do something like that? Or any of *your* friends?" Rolvaag asked.

Chaz knew what the detective meant: girls Chaz might be boffing on the side. He said, "How would they get hold of her card? I'd have to be a complete idiot!"

Rolvaag's expression indicated that the possibility had occurred to him.

It had to be the blackmailer, Chaz thought. Or maybe Ricca. Who else had been inside his house and could have swiped Joey's American Express card?

"Hey. What about Mr. O'Toole?" Chaz blurted eagerly.

The detective smiled. "I can't see him in a Burberry bikini, but you never know."

"Well, maybe he's got a girlfriend," Chaz said, thinking: And maybe someday cows will play lacrosse.

"Hey, you know what? I bet Joey's credit card got stolen on the cruise ship," he said excitedly. "Those cabin attendants, they all had master keys to the staterooms."

Rolvaag conceded it was possible. "In any case, you might want to notify American Express and cancel your wife's account."

"Oh, absolutely," Chaz said, although he'd never get around to doing it. In idle moments he would find himself daydreaming about the many slender, dark-skinned beauties who worked aboard the *Sun Duchess*, and wondering which of them was now lounging on a beach in Aruba, sunning herself in a new Burberry two-piece.

.   .   .

When Rolvaag returned to the office, Captain Gallo intercepted him at the door. "Mrs. Perrone's brother is here. He looks like he's auditioning for an Outback commercial."

Corbett Wheeler stood in the waiting area, chatting earnestly with a spindly, gap-toothed woman whose crack-addled offspring had just been caught stealing the air bags out of a marked police cruiser. Wheeler wore a wide-brimmed hat and a long cowboy-style coat, and he carried a wooden staff that looked sturdy enough to pound fence posts. When Rolvaag walked up and introduced himself, Wheeler thrust a large brown envelope at him.

"My sister's will," he said. "The *real* will."

"Let's go back to my desk. You want some coffee?"

Joey's brother idly leafed through a book of mug shots while Rolvaag studied the old will. It divided Joey's fortune among several charities and conservation groups, the largest share going to the World Wildlife Mission. The detective took out the document that had been sent to him and carefully compared the two signatures. Although they were not identical, they weren't so dissimilar as to rule out the newer one as a forgery.

Corbett Wheeler held up the mug-shot album and asked, "Who *are* these people?" His expression was that of an anthropologist who had stumbled upon evidence of a lost tribe.

"Known burglars," Rolvaag replied.

"That's amazing. These are only the *known* ones?"

"Just the ones who work the beaches. We've got four more volumes that cover the rest of the county."

Corbett Wheeler closed the album. "That lady I was talking to earlier—is her son's picture in here?"

"If it's not, it will be."

"Lord. How do you do this every day without going mad?"

"Actually, I'm moving back to Minnesota."

"Good for you. And they've got no crime up there?"

"Sure, but it's seasonal," Rolvaag said. "Breaking and entering is hard work when it's twenty below. The crowbar tends to freeze to your fingers."

He laid the two wills side by side on the desktop, so that Joey's brother could examine the signatures. "I'm no expert," Corbett Wheeler said, "but yours looks like a trace job."

"A pretty good one, if it is."

"Well, Chaz Perrone has had plenty of opportunity to practice."
Corbett Wheeler was well aware that the fake will had been drawn up
by Mick Stranahan's shyster brother-in-law, then signed by Stranahan
with deliberate though subtle imperfections. Corbett had a role to
play, as Stranahan did.

"Joey wouldn't leave a penny to Chaz. Take my word for it."

"I wish I could," the detective said.

"Meaning you haven't got enough to arrest him."

"Correct."

Corbett Wheeler shrugged. "Too bad. But you know something?
I'm a firm believer that what goes around comes around."

Rolvaag thought of Chaz's dicey status with Red Hammernut, but
he said nothing. "Would you mind if I came to the service?"

"Noon tomorrow. Be my guest." Corbett Wheeler leaned closer.
"The bereaved widower will be delivering a eulogy."

"I can hardly wait."

Joey's brother stood up and shook Rolvaag's hand solidly. "Thanks
for trying."

"It's been a tough case, unfortunately."

"What happened on that cruise ship was no accident, believe me.
That low-life yuppie turdhopper shoved my little sister overboard."

Rolvaag said, "That's what I think, too. Proving it is the pisser."

He accompanied Corbett Wheeler to the waiting area, which had
been taken over by a troop of visiting Boy Scouts. Rolvaag himself had
been a Scout when he was a teenager, back in the Twin Cities. His most
enduring memory was of the day he'd nearly sliced off his thumb while
whittling a miniature totem pole.

"They do any sheep farming up in Minnesota?" Corbett Wheeler
asked.

"Yes, I believe they do."

"You should give it a try, Karl, if you ever burn out on police work.
The lamb is a universal symbol of innocence, you know."

With that, Joey Perrone's brother raised his burl walking stick,
pushed open the door and walked out.

After sleeping with Mick Stranahan, Joey concluded that her physical
relationship with Chaz Perrone had not been as exceptional as she'd
thought. While Mick wasn't as robotically durable as her husband, he

was far more attentive, tender and enterprising. For Joey it was something of a revelation. With Mick, there was no furtive peeking at his own clenched buttocks in the mirror, no collegial exhorting of his manhood, no self-congratulatory rodeo yells when he was finished. In Chaz's embrace Joey had often felt like a pornographic accessory, one of those rubber mail-order vaginas. With Mick, she was an actual participant; a lover. The orgasms had been quake-like with Chaz, but then he would immediately demand to hear all about them; he was always more interested in the reviews than in the intimacies. With Mick, the climax was no less intense, but the aftermath was sweeter, because he never broke the mood by asking her to grade his performance. It wasn't only because he was older and less egocentric than Chaz Perrone. No, Mick had manners. He knew how to stay in the moment.

Joey lay her head on his chest. "It sure was nice of Corbett to leave us alone for the afternoon."

"A gentleman and a scholar," Stranahan murmured sleepily.

Corbett Wheeler had taken the Boston Whaler up to Virginia Key. From there a car service was supposed to ferry him to Fort Lauderdale for a meeting with Detective Rolvaag. Joey had offered Corbett the keys to the Suburban, which was parked in Coconut Grove, but he'd said no thanks. He feared that he might maim or murder somebody in a traffic altercation.

As soon as the skiff had slipped out of sight, Joey and Mick jumped into bed and camped there. They remained comfortably entwined even when a squall blew across the bay, banging the warped wooden shutters of the house and whipping rain through the window screens.

"I could live out here forever," she said later, when the sun peeked out, "not that I'm inviting myself."

Stranahan said, "Consider yourself invited. But think about it first."

"You don't want me?"

"More than anything I do. There's just not much to do around here. Some people find they need more than a sea breeze and a Kodak sunset."

"Some women, you mean," Joey said.

"Hell, I don't even have a dish for the TV."

"Then that's it, buddy. We're through!"

Stranahan tugged her close and kissed the bridge of her nose. He said, "Think about it first. Please?"

"Geezer."

"Hey, I meant to tell you. That was a brave thing you did, getting back on that ship the other day."

Joey told him not to change the subject. "But, I admit, you looked damn sexy in the blue blazer."

"An historic moment," he said, "never to be repeated."

"Well, I appreciate the sacrifice."

"You looked pretty hot yourself in that silky little number."

"Dirty old man," Joey said.

Boarding the *Sun Duchess* again had been nerve-racking and eerie. The deck was lower than the one from which Chaz had tossed her, but the view staring down was the same—terrifying. Joey was still amazed that she'd survived her plunge to the sea. She had never been a religious person, but ever since that night the concept of a beneficent and all-seeing God seemed not so implausible.

"Sometimes I can still feel Chaz's hands around my ankles."

"I wish I could make you forget," Stranahan said.

"They were so cold, like he'd held them in a bucket of ice," she said. "Mick, is this brilliant plan of ours really going to work? Because I'm not so sure anymore."

"It's not too late to pull the plug. From what I saw of Chaz in the canoe, he's pretty much off the rails already." Gently, Stranahan rolled Joey over onto her back. He propped himself on one elbow and looked down at her. "We could go see that detective tomorrow morning. Take our chances in court."

She shook her head. "I can't risk it. Chaz is way too slick."

"He could've fooled me."

"Get a couple of women on the jury and watch out," she said. "He's got a way of working on the fairer sex. I'm living proof—*barely* living proof."

Stranahan said, "Okay. Then we go ahead like we planned."

"Right."

But Joey was queasy with doubt. What would her husband do when she surprised him? Try to bullshit his way out of it? Run away? Break down and blubber like a baby? Keel over from cardiac arrest?

Attack her?

Chaz's reaction was impossible to predict, but Joey knew exactly what she intended to say; the questions had been gnawing at her since that long night at sea. She had come to believe that rage was what had

kept her afloat all those hours, kept her clinging to the bale of pot—
furious at Chaz, furious at herself for marrying such a beast.

"Did I tell you about the poem?" she asked Stranahan. "It was
the night he proposed. We were doing dinner at my apartment. He
brought me a love poem that he swore he'd written himself. And me,
the classic airhead blonde, I believed him."

Stranahan said, "Let me guess where he stole it. Shelley? Keats?"

"Get serious, Mick."

"Shakespeare would be so obvious."

"Try Neil Diamond," Joey said.

Stranahan froze in mock horror.

"Oh, Chaz was clever," she said. "He knew I was too young to be a
fan."

Laughing, Stranahan fell back on the pillow. "Which song? No, let
me guess: 'I Am, I Said.' That's pure Chaz."

"No, believe it or not, this one was called 'Deep Inside of You,' "
Joey reported ruefully. " 'Let me be the man who' . . . blah, blah, whatever. God help me, I thought it was sort of sweet at the time. He wrote
out the lines on the back of a wine label that he'd saved from our very
first date. Unbelievable."

She turned on her side and Mick tucked against her.

"A few months later I was talking to the bookkeeper at my parents'
casino," she said, "a great old broad, as they say. She wanted to know
all about my new husband, so I told her how romantic he was, how
he'd written poetry for the night we got engaged. And Inez—that was
her name—says to me, 'Doll baby, I'd love to hear it.' So I took the
wine label out of the drawer where I kept all the mushy stuff Chaz gave
me, and I read the verses aloud over the phone. And naturally Inez
busts out laughing, just like you, and proceeds to give me the scoop on
fabulous Neil, whom she'd seen no less than a dozen times in concert.
Needless to say, she knew every damn song by heart."

"So, what did Chaz say when you busted him?" Stranahan asked.

"I didn't."

"Aw, Joey."

"I couldn't," she said. "The deed was done, we were already married. So I convinced myself that it showed how much he loved me,
going to all the trouble of plagiarizing from some old pop star. I told
myself he probably went through a hundred songs before he found just
the right one. Hey, it's the thought that counts—just because he ripped

off the lyrics doesn't mean he's not sincere. And that's how I rational-ized keeping quiet."

Stranahan said, "You were afraid he'd make up a new lie if you braced him about it."

Joey nodded dismally. "Exactly. I didn't want to give him the chance. I wanted to keep on believing it was a fluke."

"And here you are."

"Yeah, here I am."

Stranahan lightly kissed the back of her neck. "For what it's worth, I can't write poetry, either."

"Mick, why won't you let me go to the memorial?"

"Because you're the dearly departed. You're supposed to be dead."

"But I can wear a disguise," she said. "Come on, I want to hear Chaz's eulogy."

"I'll take along a tape recorder. Maybe this time he'll steal some-thing off *Sgt. Pepper.*"

Joey wriggled out of Mick's embrace and relocated to the edge of the bed.

"That phony lying bastard," she muttered. "He'll have everybody in tears."

"Not me," said Stranahan, reaching out for her again.

Twenty-six

Stranahan drove to Boca in the old Cordoba, which he'd ransomed from the impound lot for three hundred bucks. He parked at a Winn-Dixie a few blocks from the church, so that no one would see him arriving with Joey's brother. Stranahan had planned to wear the muskrat-brown hairpiece that Joey had bought for him at the Gallería, but he changed his mind. He wanted Chaz Perrone to recognize him right away from the canoe trip. He wanted to rattle the sonofabitch.

The Catholic folk-guitar trio was called the Act of Contritionists. They were playing "Michael, Row the Boat Ashore" when Stranahan walked into St. Conan's; he feared it was only a matter of time before they tackled "Kumbaya." The church was three-quarters filled with Joey's friends and neighbors, mostly women. Many had attended Joey's wedding, and some might even have sensed she was marrying an incorrigible louse. They wouldn't have said a word to her about it, of course, and she wouldn't have listened if they had.

Rose looked resplendently wanton in the front pew. She wore a tight knit top over a short black skirt, black fishnet hose and stiletto pumps. Her blinding dye job appeared freshly retouched, an onyx choker accented her long pale neck, and her lips were the color of fire coral. By comparison, the other members of Joey's book group looked like spinster aunts. Near the rear of the church sat a medium-built, fair-skinned man in a dark gray suit that was shiny from wear. He had cop written all over him. Stranahan assumed it was Karl Rolvaag, and he chose a seat a dozen rows up, on the other side of the aisle.

"Kumbaya" came and went, in rounds. Still no sign of Chaz Perrone. Stranahan began to worry.

Joey's brother had shed the drover's coat for a three-piece blue pin-stripe. He'd made a game effort to tame his beard and wild mane, but he still looked like an outlaw biker who'd been dressed by his attorney for a bail hearing. On the altar stood a velvet-cloaked table, upon which Corbett Wheeler had placed a framed eight-by-ten of his sister, who was sitting cross-legged on the grass next to a palm tree. Her hair was mussed by a breeze, and her laughing face was lit by the sun. The mourners would have been startled to learn that the photograph had been taken by Joey's brother less than twenty-four hours earlier on a private island on Biscayne Bay, and that she'd been giggling at the sight of a prematurely retired middle-aged man baring his well-tanned ass, and that the same sinewy fellow now sat among them at St. Conan's, waiting impatiently to deliver blackmail instructions.

The guitar trio commenced an upbeat Calypso version of "Blowin' in the Wind," which Corbett Wheeler terminated with a brusque slashing motion across his neck. He approached the pulpit and intro-duced himself.

"We're here to celebrate the life and times of my magnificent baby sister," he began. "Joey Wheeler."

At Joey's insistence, her brother had agreed not to use her married name at the ceremony.

"She was a fighter, a real tiger, but she also had a generous heart. She was always the idealist in our family, the dreamy romantic," he said, "the one who believed in the innate decency and honesty of everyone she met. Sometimes, unfortunately, she was mistaken. . . ."

Corbett Wheeler owlishly scanned the church as he let the sen-tence hang. Several mourners, evidently aware of Chaz Perrone's serial infidelities, traded knowing glances.

"Still, Joey never lost her belief that most people were basically good and honorable, deep down in their souls."

Her brother went on to tell a couple of stories, which got the crowd sniffling. The first was about their parents' funeral, where four-year-old Joey stood at the grave site and sang "Leavin' on a Jet Plane," revising the lyrics to suit the peculiar circumstances of Hank and Lana Wheeler's demise ("The bear is packed, you're ready to go . . .").

The second anecdote concerned the tragic fate of Joey's first hus-band, whose saintly virtues were enumerated at length by Corbett Wheeler, although he'd never met the man. "Benny was the light of my sister's life," Corbett said, generously overselling Benjamin Middenbock's luminosity. "Before saying her final farewell, she placed in the casket his favorite fly rod and a selection of bass poppers that she'd tied and painted herself. She said she was glad, for the sake of the pallbearers, that Benny's hobby wasn't bowling."

It took a beat or two for the mourners to smile.

"So, yes, Joey faced times of profound sadness in her life," her brother continued, "but she never let herself be defeated by it. She never lost her sense of humor, or her optimism—she was the most positive person I ever knew. The most hopeful. And also the most unselfish. She could have lived like a princess but she chose a simple, ordinary life, because she believed that was the secret to true happiness. That, and fine Italian footwear. . . ."

The line brought a weepy laugh from Joey's fellow shoppers. "She wasn't perfect," her brother went on. "She had weaknesses, as all of us do. Impulsive moments. Blind spots. Lapses in judgment."

Corbett Wheeler stopped just shy of indicting Chaz Perrone by name. And where the hell *was* the would-be widower? Stranahan wondered.

"No, my little sister wasn't a perfect person," her brother said in summation, "but she was a truly good person, and we'll all miss her dearly."

A white-haired priest stepped forward and, in a lugubrious Eastern European accent, recited the Lord's Prayer. The Act of Contritionists followed with a thirteen-minute rendition of "Bridge Over Troubled Water" that left everyone sapped. Next up was Carmen Raguso, the Perrones' most gregarious neighbor and the face-lift queen of West Boca Dunes Phase II. She told of the time that Joey had helped round up the stray cats behind the Kentucky Fried Chicken and then taken them for neutering to a veterinary clinic in Margate. Joey had paid for all the kitty surgeries—more than two thousand dollars total, Mrs. Raguso recalled. Another time Joey had arranged for a private seaplane to transport an ailing bottle-nosed dolphin from a beach on Grand Bahama Island to the Seaquarium in Miami. The mammal, which had been suffering from a bowel obstruction, recovered fully and was returned to the sea.

"Why couldn't that dolphin have been frolicking in the Gulf Stream the night Joey fell off that ship, and come swimming to her rescue?" Mrs. Raguso said. "Why can't life be more like the movies?"

Other friends got up and attested to Joey's quiet charity, love of nature and kindness toward the less fortunate. Rose was the last to speak. As she made her way to the podium, Stranahan noticed that the men in the audience, including Detective Rolvaag, seemed to perk up.

"Joey was the star of our book club, without a doubt!" Rose began. "She was the one who got us hooked on Margaret Atwood and A. S. Byatt and P. D. James," Rose bubbled. "Heck, we would've wasted six whole weeks on Jane Austen if it weren't for Joey. She was a sweetie pie, sure, but she was also a firecracker. Not afraid to kick off her shoes, no ma'am. You should've heard her reading the juicy parts from Jean Auel's latest! Lord, she almost made the walls blush."

Stranahan thought: My Joey?

"Who is that gabby woman?" Chaz Perrone groused.

Tool said nothing. In fact, he hadn't said boo all morning. He thought it unforgivable that Chaz hadn't invited his own mother to the memorial service.

He and Chaz were watching the eulogies from the sacristy, out of sight of the assembly. Having falsely diagnosed himself with the West Nile virus, Chaz was in a shaky frame of mind. The stiffness in his neck was most likely the result of being belted by a two-liter bottle of soda, but in his hypochondriacal funk Chaz suspected it was the first telltale symptom of the bug-borne encephalitis, soon to be followed by fever, convulsions, tremors, stupor and ultimately a coma. At one point during the night he'd pleaded with Tool to take his temperature, but the sadistic bastard had walked in carrying a frozen bratwurst and a jar of petroleum jelly.

How insulting, Chaz thought, to die from a fucking mosquito bite.

Payback from that hellhole of a swamp.

By his own calculation, approximately half of the thirty-four bites on his face were either scabbed or inflamed, the result of relentless scratching. At their first meeting, outside the church, Joey's brother had commented upon Chaz's volcanic complexion and inquired somewhat insensitively if he'd been tested for monkey pox.

Screw that sheep-humping wacko, Chaz thought.

Hoping for a nugget or two he might crib for his own speech, Chaz tried to pay attention to Rose's lively though meandering tribute. He found himself pleasingly diverted by the shortness of her skirt and the

boldness of her stockings. She looked like a gal who knew how to spell
f-u-n.

"You ready, Charles?"

Chaz jumped in surprise, Corbett Wheeler having slipped into the
sacristy through the back door.

"You're the headliner, man. The one they're all waiting to hear."

Chaz peeked out and thought: Who *are* all these people? He was
surprised that his wife could draw such a crowd. Some faces he vaguely
recalled from the wedding reception, but most were strangers. On the
other hand, Chaz had seldom bothered to inquire what Joey did during
the day while he was working, golfing or chasing other women. Nor
had he displayed much curiosity about her past social life, before
they'd met. Chaz's domestic policy was never to ask questions that one
wouldn't care to answer oneself.

"Who's your friend?" Corbett Wheeler asked. Without waiting for
a reply, he greeted Tool heartily and pumped his hand. "I can tell by
your outfit you're a man of the soil."

Tool had come to church wearing his black overalls, which he had
laundered for the occasion. Chaz Perrone had not wanted him to
attend the service, but Red Hammernut was emphatic.

"I used to run crews on a vegetable farm," Tool said.

Joey's brother beamed. "I've got two thousand head of sheep."

Tool seemed impressed. "Yeah? What kind?"

God help me, thought Chaz. The mutants are bonding.

Rose said something that got a good laugh, and suddenly Chaz felt
Corbett Wheeler's meaty hands steering him out of the sacristy and up
a small flight of stairs to the pulpit. Chaz was trembling as he adjusted
the microphone and fished through the pockets of his suit in search of
his notes. He was alarmed to realize that his penmanship, once precise
and consistent, had degenerated to the sort of sinuous, pinprick scrawl
associated with UFO correspondents and future workplace snipers.

He raised his eyes to the gathering and immediately froze, for
there was the blackmailer, three rows from the front, grinning like a
hungry coyote. Chaz Perrone jerked his gaze to the other side of the
church only to spy Karl Rolvaag, his chin impassively propped on his
knuckles, as if watching a hockey game.

Chaz's throat turned to sawdust. When he tried to speak, he
sounded like a busted violin. Joey's brother delivered a glass of water
but Chaz was afraid to drink it, fearing it might be spiked.

Finally he licked his lips and began: "Ladies and gentlemen, allow me to tell you about my wife, Joey, who I loved more than anything else in this world."

At that moment, Joey Perrone was reaching into the bird feeder to retrieve the spare key for the house she had once shared with her husband. She entered through the back door, disabled the alarm, hurried to the bathroom and vomited her breakfast.

Get a grip, she told herself. For heaven's sake, you're not the first woman who ever married the wrong guy.

Just because you happened to pick one of the wrongest guys who ever lived.

The bed was unmade. Joey lay down and took slow, measured breaths. On the pillow she smelled Chaz's shampoo, some mango-scented goop that he'd bought at that Ricca woman's salon. Joey stared at the ceiling and wondered if Chaz had been lying right here when he'd made up his mind to kill her; plotting while she'd dozed beside him, clueless.

She went to the living room and put on a Sheryl Crow CD that both of them had liked. The music made her feel better. She took a seat on the sofa, where Chaz had left his backpack unzipped in typical disarray. Inside, among wads of blank water charts and half-completed mileage vouchers, was a photocopy of the bogus will that Mick had sent to the detective. Chaz had underscored in red ink the paragraph that ostensibly bequeathed his wife's entire fortune to him. In the margin he had drawn three dancing exclamation points. Joey flipped to the last page and eyed the signature, which Mick had traced off one of her credit card receipts. It was good enough to fool her husband, who would be greedily predisposed to embrace its authenticity.

The ass.

Imagining himself so irresistible and smooth, such a studly operator, that Joey—in some impulsive swoon—would have shredded their pre-nuptial agreement and decided to leave him everything. Knowing Chaz, he'd already conjured a theory to explain the stunning turn of events. He probably figured that Joey had planned to surprise him with the good news on that final night of the cruise, but she'd never gotten the chance. Then, after she was gone, Corbett had anonymously slipped the will to Rolvaag in order to stir suspicion about what had happened; to brand Chaz with a clear motive for murdering his sister.

At least that's how Chaz might put it together, Joey thought. The appeal of inheriting $13 million would bring its own sunny plausibility, regardless of the odds.

Joey returned the document to the backpack, then turned off the CD player. When she approached the aquarium, the fish rose up in a manic glitter of anticipation. The man from the pet shop had re-stocked the decimated tank with neon gobies, a rainbow of wrasses, a butterfly fish, a queen angel, two clownfish and a yellow tang. Their life expectancy would be short under Chaz's inattentive guardianship, but for now all the fish were frisky and bright. Joey sprinkled three pinches of flaked food into the water and watched the kaleidoscopic frenzy.

The decorative centerpiece of the aquarium was a ceramic ship-wreck, a schooner keeled bow-first in the gravel. Joey dug into her jeans and took out her platinum wedding band, bouncing it in the palm of one hand. She didn't bother to re-read the engraving on the inner rim, which she knew by heart: "To Joey, the girl of my dreams. Love, CRP." Joey closed her fist around the ring and, with the other hand, lifted the lid off the tank.

"Try nightmares, schmucko," she said. "Girl of your nightmares."

Chaz had settled in comfortably at the pulpit. Miraculously, the stiff-ness in his neck had vanished and the scabs on his face had stopped itching.

"I've gone over this tragedy a thousand times in my mind," he was saying, "and I can't help but thinking it was my fault. If only I'd told Joey to wait for me that night, if only I hadn't taken those few extra minutes in the cabin, we would've walked out on the deck of the ship together. She wouldn't have been standing alone at the rail in that slip-pery rain—I would've been right beside her, and this tragic accident would never have happened."

Chaz knew the risks of recounting such bald fiction before an audi-ence of potential witnesses—any decent defense lawyer would have counseled against it. But Chaz thought it was important to show Rolvaag that he was sticking to his original story. At the same time, he couldn't resist the opportunity to feed speculation that Joey had been battling with inner demons so dreadful, she'd confided in no one, and that she might even have done herself in.

"I've replayed the evening over and over again in my head," Chaz said, "but there are always more questions than answers. How many of you have read a book called *Madame Bovary*?"

As expected, all the members of Joey's book group raised their hands. So did Karl Rolvaag and perhaps a dozen others in the church.

Chaz said, "Joey was reading this novel on our cruise. Afterward I got curious and read it myself." In truth, he'd pulled a two-paragraph synopsis from a Flaubert fan site on the Internet.

"It's about a young Frenchwoman who's bored and unhappy with her life. She marries a man she hopes will bring her excitement and fulfillment . . . a doctor." Chaz made his voice crack, so that even the dimmest bulbs in the audience could make the connection. "But it's sad, because Madame Bovary still isn't satisfied, so she sets off on all these escapades that bring her no lasting happiness. And at the end of the story, this poor confused woman winds up killing herself."

There was an uneasy hush in the church. Chaz pressed forward without pause.

"After finishing the book, I admit I was pretty depressed. I couldn't help wondering whether my Joey was unhappy, too. Whether she identified in some way with the restless wife in the story, and hid those feelings from me." Chaz lowered his head and let his shoulders sag. When he looked up again, he saw that the blackmailer appeared to be dozing. Meanwhile, Rolvaag's expression (or lack thereof) hadn't changed.

"But I've thought about it and thought about it," Chaz went on, "and after speaking to so many of you who knew and loved my wonderful wife"—another outrageous lie; he hadn't returned a single phone call—"I'm more certain than ever that she was a very happy person at heart. A positive person, as her brother said. A firecracker, as her dear friend Rose described her. A fighter and an optimist who loved life. That's the Joey Perrone I knew. That's the Joey Perrone I adored. And that's the Joey Perrone . . ."

At that instant Chaz was distracted from his peroration by a lone figure entering the church somewhat awkwardly on crutches.

"I will mourn for . . ."

A woman, Chaz observed, who was pegging purposefully up the center aisle.

". . . for the rest of my . . ."

Some frizzy-haired klutz with a plaster cast on one leg, interrupting his big tearjerker finale. Who would be rude enough to pull such a stunt?

"... my, uh ... my ..."

Ricca.

No way! Chaz thought. It's not possible.

"... my life," he rasped, clutching the sides of the podium.

The assembly noticed his unsteadiness, and a ripple of concerned murmuring broke out. He forced himself to look away as Ricca sat down beside the blackmailer, who politely took her crutches and stowed them under the pew.

Fuck me.

The breath emptied from Charles Regis Perrone in a stale sibilant rush. He reeled from the pulpit and staggered toward the sacristy, gulping like a doomed tuna. He made it as far as the doorway before his legs turned to noodles, Tool catching him on the way down. Chaz lowered his fluttering eyelids to the mellow harmony of "Where Have All the Flowers Gone?"—a smooth and savvy segue by the Act of Contritionists.

Ricca whispered to Mick Stranahan: "You were right about that dickhead. He did kill his wife. He told me so."

"What happened to you?"

"Long story short—he dragged me out to the boonies and shot me. Can you believe it?"

Stranahan said he could, easily. "What are you doing here?"

"Freaking him out," Ricca said. "It's crazy but I wanted Chaz to see I was still alive. What can he do to me in a church?"

"Did you go to the cops?"

"Not yet, but I will."

"Can I ask a favor? Could you wait a couple of days?"

Ricca smiled. "So you really *are* blackmailing him."

"Oh, it's better than that," Stranahan said. "But in the meantime, you be careful. Chaz will insist on seeing you. He's going to beg and cry and probably offer you a ton of dough to keep quiet."

"And then he'll try to kill me again."

"Of course. But I'm going to give you a phone number. Be sure to call it before you go meet with him."

Stranahan scribbled the information on the back of a prayer card.

Ricca didn't recognize the name or the number, but she slipped the card into her purse. The guitar trio ended its song and the church fell silent. Corbett Wheeler returned to the pulpit.

"This has been a most difficult day for all of us," he said with a sideways glance toward the sacristy. "Speaking for myself, I still can't really believe my sister is gone. It seems like just this morning that she was teasing me about my farmer shoes and my Aboriginal haircut."

Everybody chuckled, but only Stranahan got the inside joke. Joey had needled her brother mercilessly while he was dressing for the memorial.

"Thank you all for coming today, and for sharing your memories. Joey would have been touched," Corbett Wheeler said in conclusion. "I know that many of you wish to express your condolences to her husband, Chaz. He'll be waiting to speak with you on your way out."

"Sweet," said Ricca.

"Easy does it," Stranahan warned.

No one was more stunned than Charles Perrone to hear, upon regaining consciousness, that he would be personally greeting the mourners outside St. Conan's. He complained that he was too weak and distraught, but Joey's brother took him by the arm and told him to buck up. Tool made no effort to intervene on Chaz's behalf, having stopped to look at the photograph of the doctor's dead wife on the altar. It was the first time Tool had seen a picture of Joey Perrone, and she reminded him of somebody.

But who? Tool couldn't recall. That was one of the drawbacks of the narcotic patches—they scrambled up your memory at times.

He went outside and found a shady spot under a banyan tree. Lowering himself to the ground, he propped his head against the trunk. As he watched Chaz shake hands and give hugs on the steps of the church, Tool thought again about the photo of Mrs. Perrone on the altar. He wondered how a pretty, smart-looking girl could hook up with such a shitweasel. There was plainly no damn justice in the world.

Tool was annoyed when a man ambled up and sat next to him.

"Remember me?" the man asked.

"Sure do." It was the guy who'd slugged him in the throat that night at Chaz's house. The blackmailer.

Tool's eyes narrowed. "Lucky we ain't alone."

"I don't blame you for being mad. I belted you pretty good."

"Jest wait'll next time, boy."

"That's what I wanted to talk to you about." The blackmailer lowered his voice. "The money drop."

"The what?"

"For the blackmail payoff."

"Oh. Yeah." Tool shifted uncomfortably. His rump was inopportunely aligned on the knob of a banyan root, which poked against the embedded bullet.

The man said, "I've got a feeling Chaz is going to try something exceptionally stupid. That would be bad for him, and also for Mr. Hammernut."

"Don't worry. He ain't gone try nuthin' long as I'm there."

"Glad to hear you say that." The blackmailer pointed toward the doorway of the church. "You recognize those two people?"

Tool squinted. "The one's a cop."

"Right, that's Detective Rolvaag. How about the dark-haired lady on crutches?"

"Maybe." Tool dug into his overalls to scratch at his crotch.

The blackmailer said the woman's name was Ricca Spillman. "Your boy Chaz tried to kill her the other night."

"No shit?" Tool said, though he knew it was true. He also knew that he should tell Red, because this was serious. The doctor had gone and shot a girl, who, instead of dying quietly, was now chatting it up with a cop. Tool got up and began kneading his buttocks. He could feel the old rifle slug chafing against his tailbone.

The blackmailer stood up, too. He said, "I'd prefer to steer clear of Rolvaag for now, so I'll be on my way."

Tool shrugged. He noticed that the woman on crutches was being approached by Mrs. Perrone's brother, the sheep farmer. More bad news, thought Tool.

The blackmailer said, "For whatever it's worth, I'm sorry about what happened last week at the house."

Tool said, "We ain't done with that yet."

"I figured not."

"Hey, where's your girlfriend? The one that was down at Flamingo?"

"Oh, she's home cleaning the machine guns."

Tool wasn't sure if the guy was joking. Then, out of the blue, it hit him—that's who the picture on the altar looked like: the blackmailer's girlfriend. It had been dark when he'd met her that night on the docks, but what he'd seen of her face strongly resembled the dead woman in the photograph. Hell, maybe they were kin. Maybe the blackmail was a revenge-type deal.

"Mister, can I ast you somethin'?" Tool said.

"Nope," said the blackmailer, and then he was gone.

In a way, Chaz Perrone was relieved to have Corbett Wheeler beside him in the receiving line, sharing the burden of cordiality. It was hard work being polite and commiserative, especially when faking it. Chaz could handle about twelve seconds of heartfelt sympathy from each mourner before passing them down the row like a sandbag. He concluded from their worried expressions that he must have looked like hell, what with the shakes and the damp upper lip and the festering mosquito bites. But all that was good for his act—the grieving husband, falling apart at the seams.

Handshake and hug.

Handshake and hug.

Chaz Perrone struggled to maintain a passable mask of sorrow, but he felt his mouth twist into an ugly scowl when the blackmailer came down the line. The man pressed an envelope into Chaz's hands, leaned close and said in that hokey Charlton Heston voice: "I hear helicopters, Chazzie."

Reflexively Chaz glanced up, but he saw only a small plane trailing a Budweiser banner, heading for the beach.

"See you tomorrow night," the blackmailer said, and strolled away.

Chaz had no time to be flustered, for he'd caught sight of Ricca, conspicuously yakking with Rolvaag about God knows what. The detective appeared cordial and at ease, certainly not acting as if he'd just been informed of an attempted homicide at Loxahatchee. Still, it was all Chaz could do not to bolt like a jackrabbit.

As he was snatched into the moist embrace of Mrs. Raguso, tearful and vaguely redolent of mozzarella, Chaz was dismayed to hear Corbett Wheeler excuse himself from the receiving line. Pinned to Mrs. Raguso's bosom, Chaz watched disconsolately over her shoulder as Joey's brother sauntered over to Ricca and struck up a conversation.

Unbelievable, Chaz thought. *I am so fucked.*

Within moments Ricca began clomping toward him, Corbett Wheeler leading the way. Chaz extricated himself from Mrs. Raguso, though not in time to flee.

"Your housekeeper," said Joey's brother, "would like a private word."

"Sure," Chaz said, thinking: *Housekeeper? Christ, she's never going to let me forget that one.*

Corbett Wheeler assumed the primary consoling duties as Chaz stepped away from the line. Ricca stood off to the side, eyeing him about as warmly as a barracuda. The tripod effect of her crutches made a conciliatory hug unfeasible.

In a half whisper he said, "We need to talk."

"Go blow yourself, Chaz."

"I was crazed that night. Completely out of my mind."

Ricca said, "Save it for the jury, you sorry prick."

"I apologize for cleaning out your apartment, too. And getting rid of your car," Chaz said. "I panicked, honey. What can I say?"

"You look like shit. Are those cankers all over your face?"

"Mosquito bites. I'm coming down with the West Nile."

"Good. I hope your balls rot off," Ricca said.

"Look, you've got a right to be pissed. What I did was a horrible thing."

"Duh, yeah?"

"But it wasn't the real me. I was whacked-out," Chaz insisted. "Seriously. What can I do to make things right?"

"Besides dying a slow, miserable death?"

"Shhhh. Please, honey, not so loud."

"Two hundred and fifty grand," Ricca said flatly. "In cash."

"Really?" Chaz felt washed with relief. He'd always pegged her as a money-grubber. It was the cheeriest possible news.

"Plus a new car. Mustang convertible," she said. "You don't come through, I'll be going to visit my new best friend." She cut her eyes toward Karl Rolvaag, now chatting with the white-haired priest.

"Wait, Ricca, don't! I'll give you my answer now!" Chaz reached out, but she raised a crutch menacingly. "The answer is yes," he told her in a low voice. "Whatever you want."

"Wait for my call," she said curtly, and limped away unassisted.

Chaz returned to the receiving line, which had dwindled to a handful of Joey's friends. Corbett Wheeler leaned over and said, "They sure don't make housekeepers like that Down Under. She's a hottie."

"Yeah, well, I heard she's got the clap."

Joey's brother chuckled. "Nice try."

Chez felt someone squeezing both his hands: Rose, the miniskirted blonde from Joey's book club.

"Can I speak with you privately?" she asked.

"Of course." Chaz caught a whiff of her perfume, the same kind of Chanel that Joey wore. He gulped, hungry for more; the scent had never failed to excite him. What he remembered most vividly in those seconds after dumping his wife off the ship was the smell of her, lingering alluringly in the air.

Rose led Chaz Perrone back through the doors of the church. It was cool and darker inside. He tried not to stare too obviously at her breasts, which looked anything but mournful under the clingy knit top.

"Your eulogy was just in-credible," Rose said with a hushed awe.

"Well, Joey was an incredible woman."

"My God, wasn't she? I still can't believe she's gone, Chaz. I cannot believe it."

He said, "No, it doesn't seem real."

"But your speech today was just . . . you were like a rock, almost until the end. The Rock of Gibraltar."

"I tried to be strong," he said modestly, "for Joey."

"But how are you doin', Chaz, *really*? How are you holding up?" Rose had found his hands again, caressing them in a worldly manner that brought a tingle. It had been days since he'd thought about getting laid, but all of a sudden that seemed like a fine plan. The perfect antidote for all this doom and gloom.

He said, "Tell you the truth, I'm falling to pieces."

"Honestly, you don't look well."

"The house is so empty and lonely without her."

"I can only imagine," Rose said, her face etched with pity.

Chaz was getting high off the fog of perfume. He gazed at her coral-colored lips and resisted the impulse to part them with his tongue. Wait, he told himself, there's a time and a place.

"Tonight's going to be a rough one," he said. "This service was supposed to be my closure, but I don't feel any different."

Rose interlocked her fingers with his. What an intriguing creature, Chaz thought. He wondered why Joey had never brought her by the house for a proper introduction.

"What say you come over to my place tonight? I'll make us some dinner," she said. "We can rent a movie or whatever. Take our minds off this awful, awful business. You like pasta?"

"Great, I'll bring the wine. Tell me where you live."

He stepped into the daylight and with renewed spirit descended the steps of St. Conan's. At the bottom stood Karl Rolvaag, looking out beyond the sidewalk, where the mourners were dispersing. He was smiling in an amused and private way.

On a whim Chaz stopped. "Hey, aren't you ever going to tell me what it was of Joey's that the Coast Guard found?" he asked.

"Sure," Rolvaag said. "Fingernails."

"God. That's all there was?"

"Yep. In a bale of grass." Rolvaag began to laugh.

"You think that's funny?" Chaz shook his head and walked on.

The detective wasn't laughing about Mrs. Perrone's fingernails. He was laughing about the green Chevrolet Suburban that had twice circled the block to cruise by the church. The vehicle was new and clean enough to be the rental that had been charged to Mrs. Perrone's AmEx card. The sunlight cutting through the Suburban's tinted windshield had revealed the driver to be a woman wearing oversized sunglasses and a ball cap; a young woman with a blondish ponytail.

To Karl Rolvaag it was so funny, so perfect, that he thought he might bust a gut.

Twenty-seven

Chaz Perrone swallowed his last blue pill, then rang the bell. Rose called out for him to come in. He found his way to the kitchen and saw her standing at the stove, talking on the phone, stirring marinara sauce while the linguini boiled. She wore tight cutoff jeans and a chartreuse tube top, which infused Chaz with optimism. He placed the bottle of merlot on the counter and rifled the silverware drawer for a corkscrew.

When Rose put down the phone, she said, "I've got a confession to make. I got home from the service and bawled for a solid hour."

"Me, too," Chaz said with a straight face.

He didn't mention the five Michelobs or the supplementary martinis, which seemed necessary to settle his nerves. . . .

Ricca, the witch, was alive.

God only knew what Red Hammernut was up to.

The blackmailer wanted the money tomorrow night.

And topping it all was the videocassette that had been waiting on Charles Perrone's doorstep when he returned home from church. The tape was grainy and underlit, but the images were sufficiently distinct that Chaz instantly realized what he was watching.

"Chaz, no! What are you doing?"

He hadn't remembered her uttering a word, but in his mind the murder had become a silent blur. That it was Joey on the blackmailer's video was indisputable; her face, her voice, her legs.

Same skirt, same shoes, same wristwatch.

The first time Chaz viewed the tape, he was staggered. The second time, he was gripped with perverse fascination.

It began with a flash frame of the legend SUN DUCHESS, painted across the archway of the gangplank. The next scene was on board the ship; the figures of a man and woman standing in low light by the deck railing. Although Chaz had had his back to the hidden camera, he had no trouble recognizing himself in the frame—the neatly trimmed brown hair, the dark blue blazer and charcoal slacks. Interestingly, his shoulders looked broader and his hips seemed not so thick as they often appeared in the bathroom mirror. As chilling as it was to watch the sequence, Chaz had been pleased about how buff he looked.

Seventeen seconds. He'd timed it with the clock on the VCR. Seventeen seconds from start to finish.

"Chaz, no! What are you doing?"

Hearing Joey's startled cry was more than he could handle sober, so he didn't stay that way for long. He now understood why the blackmailer was so cocky—the fucker had him cold. He had it all on tape.

Pure dumb luck, Chaz thought bitterly. Guy's strolling around on deck, taking home movies of the constellations or the coastline or whatever. We walk into the shot, Joey and me, and next thing he knows, he's recording a homicide.

The key drops on the deck and I bend down like I'm picking it up.

But instead I grab her ankles.

"Chaz, no! What are you doing?"

A flutter of motion, legs in the air.

Then she's gone.

So fast, Chaz marveled. Poof!

He was curious to study his demeanor, which he remembered as cool and steady, but the tape ended just as he began to turn away from the rail.

Six times Chaz had watched the crime on the VCR in his bedroom, his needs escalating from beer to the hard stuff. It was a miracle he'd made it all the way to Rose's house without wrapping the Hummer around a utility pole.

The booze was therapeutic but what Chaz really needed, to sweep the mortal clutter from his mind, was sex. It had been what, two weeks? The last really good time had been on the ship with Joey, in the shower of their stateroom. Since then Chaz had been chronically out of rhythm, off his game, stuck in third gear. Ever since he was sixteen he had relied on a heavy schedule of lovemaking, accompanied or alone, to keep himself centered. Without it, he lost his edge. His brain fogged, his reflexes faltered, his hormones congealed, his testicles ached, his prostate began to calcify. . . .

He poured two glasses of wine and handed one to Rose. All things considered, he felt fairly positive about the evening. He'd been able to slip out of his house unmolested after Tool departed on an errand, probably to score more dope. The goon would never find him here.

"Tell me about your job," said Rose, laying out the dinner plates.

"Not much to tell. It's pretty technical, actually."

"Joey said you work on the Everglades project, testing the water for some sort of pollution."

"Basically, yeah," Chaz said. "But it's chemical elements we're checking for, not sewage-type contaminants. Nothing you could smell or even see with the naked eye." He couldn't stop admiring Rose's lovely hands as she spooned out the pasta.

She said, "That's so cool. I'm sure you must've read *River of Grass* about a hundred times."

"You bet."

"Mrs. Douglas is one of my all-time feminist heroes. An amazing woman," she declared. "Talk about a firecracker!"

"One of a kind," agreed Dr. Charles Perrone, who hadn't read a book from cover to cover in a decade. He was plenty drunk enough to wing it, though.

"How about *Silent Spring*?" Rose asked.

"Let me think."

"You know—Rachel Carson?"

"Sure," Chaz said. "Wasn't she married to Johnny?"

Rose laughed. "Joey aways said you were funny."

"She did, huh?" Chaz refilled their wineglasses. Either the blue pill was starting to work or Rose's left foot was in his lap.

"Do you have a boyfriend?" he asked, trying to sound as if it mattered.

"Been a couple of months," Rose said.

"Ah."

"Things start to build up inside. So many pent-up feelings and urges."

Chaz said, "I know what you mean."

"Sometimes a person just needs to cut loose."

"An emotional release."

"Yes, exactly," Rose said. "To get rid of all the stress and tension. Personally, yoga's never done it for me."

"Me, neither." Chaz thinking: What a refreshing outlook this woman has!

"Could you do me a favor? The Parmesan," Rose said, pointing. "It's in the tall cabinet next to the refrigerator."

"Sure." Chaz got up cautiously, holding his napkin over his lap in order to hide the ascendant bulge. He did not wish to surprise his hostess until the moment was ripe.

His back was turned when she crumbled the small round tablet into his wineglass.

"Life is so unfair," she observed. "Why Joey, of all people?"

Chaz returned to the table and passed the shaker of grated cheese. Then he took another slug of merlot.

"Know what's weird?" Rose said. "The whole *Madame Bovary* thing. Joey never mentioned to any of us that she was reading it. The girls in the club, I mean. Why do you suppose not? We talk about everything we read."

"I can only guess." An errant noodle hung from the corner of Chaz's mouth. He slurped it expertly and continued. "Maybe because that particular book was too personal. Like I said in church, there might've been something heavy going on—depression, whatever—and Joey didn't want me or any of her friends to know."

"Chaz, tell me honestly. Do you think she killed herself?"

"No! I can't . . . I d-don't know," he said, affecting an agitated stammer. "I don't want to b-believe that. Like I said, this was a very happy girl most of the time."

Rose emphatically agreed. "She was. She truly was. That was a terrible question for me to ask—I'm so sorry, Chaz. *Of course* she didn't kill herself. Not Joey."

The subject was dropped, and they chatted pleasantly while they dined—music, movies, sports. It turned out that Rose was considering golf lessons.

She said, "I like any exercise where you don't hardly perspire. What's the matter, hon?"

Chaz grabbed the edge of the table. "I don't feel so good."

The room had started pitching and rolling like a carnival ride.

There seemed to be two Roses, each staring quizzically. In stereo they said, "You want to lie down? You should lie down."

"Good idea."

She led Chaz to her bedroom, sat him on the bed and tugged off his shoes.

"Here. Do as I say." She patted a stack of fluffy pillows. Chaz stretched out and closed his eyes. Christ, he thought, I haven't been this smashed in years.

"Be back in a minute," he heard Rose say before she turned out the lights.

Chaz smiled as he fumbled to unbuckle his pants. He beheld a delicious vision of Rose kicking off her jeans, peeling out of her tube top and sliding under the covers beside him. With some effort he scooted over to make more space in the bed.

Problem was, he really did *not* feel so great.

After a while he became aware of a motorized humming noise. Most likely it was the ceiling fan, but Chaz, cracking his eyelids, couldn't see much in the darkness. Amplified by an excess of alcohol, the fan's humming put Chaz in mind of a helicopter rotor, whirling perilously close to his bare head. He felt a cold prickle of dread and burrowed like a dung beetle under Rose's pillows. In his padded refuge he couldn't hear the jangle of her car keys, or the back door closing behind her.

After Rose drove away, Mick Stranahan turned to Joey.

"Ready?"

"It's now or never."

"Remember the rules."

"No punching. No kicking. No sharp instruments. What else?" Joey said.

"No tears."

"Are you kidding?" she said, and together they entered the house. Joey paused outside the bedroom to dab Chanel behind her ears.

Stranahan whispered, "I'll be right here if you need me."

She went inside, quietly closing the door behind her. There was a slight rustling in the dark, then a muffled voice from the bedcovers: "Rose?"

Joey sat on the corner of the bed.

"Rosie, honey. Come here," Chaz said.

Joey lay down rigidly beside her husband. He nosed his way out of the pillows and blindly beached his head on her right shoulder.

"You smell terrific. That perfume you're wearing, it's my favorite."

"Hmmm," Joey said. Chaz reeked of alcohol and garlic. She felt something blunt and familiar nudging her thigh, and thought: This is what they mean by the term *dickbrain*.

Chaz said, "I might be drunk."

Stoned, too, mused Joey. Rose had slipped ten milligrams of diazepam into his wine.

Chaz groped somewhat imprecisely for her breasts, and she brushed his hand away.

"Stop it," she whispered.

"Your heart's going so fast. What does that mean, Rose?"

If you only knew.

He pressed himself harder against her.

"No."

"Please. I miss her so much," Chaz said.

Joey's eyes gradually adjusted to the dimness of the room. Chaz was lethargic and half-asleep, but she remained on guard.

"Please, Rose. Help me make the pain go away," he said. "Just for tonight."

Without warning Joey started to sob. She couldn't believe it. Sobbing like a baby!

Chaz seemed invigorated by her breakdown, which he no doubt perceived as vulnerability.

"Come on, Rose," he implored, reaching down to tug off his pants, "it'll be healthy for both of us."

"For heaven's sake, how?"

"By getting lost in each other."

That's a new one, Joey thought. Wonder where he stole it. She took a slow, deliberate breath, then sniffed away the tears.

"These are very normal feelings at a time like this," Chaz was saying. "Joey loved us both. She'd understand completely."

"No, Chaz, Joey would *not* understand."

She said this aloud in her regular voice. He stopped wriggling and raised up slightly, trying to see her face. She heard a dry swallow.

"I assure you," she said, "that she definitely doesn't understand how you could try to fuck her best friend the night after her funeral service."

Chaz seemed paralyzed with confusion. Joey reached into his boxers and twisted a pinch of his scrotum between her thumbnail and forefinger.

"Let go! Oh God," he wailed. "Oh Christ, oh Jesus, please, Joey, let go!"

At the silent count of ten, she did. "Now don't move, Charles."

She turned on the lamp and saw that he was rolled up like a large pale hedgehog, cupping his groin.

"You're not real." Her husband squinted at her suspiciously. "You *can't* be real." He bared his teeth and gave off a strange, dissonant laugh. "Lemme see your fingernails."

"Exactly how much have you had to drink?" she asked.

"You're dead, Joey. I killed you myself." Chaz continued to grin like a chimp. "It's all on video!"

She said, "You need to buckle down here, mister. I want some answers."

His head began lolling from side to side, as if his neck had gone to rubber. When he blinked, it looked like hard work.

Joey said, "Don't you dare fall asleep."

"I knew it. I got the West Nile." He cackled harshly. "That's why you're here—the disease makes victims hallucinate."

Rose might have gone overboard with the Valium, Joey thought. The creep was fading fast.

"Chaz, are you listening?"

He nodded. "Loud'n clear."

"Why did you try to kill me?"

"Aw, come on," he snorted.

Joey snatched a shock of his hair and yanked his head upright. "Answer me!"

"I guarantee you I wasn't the only guy on that cruise who thought about shovin' his old lady overboard. Wives, they think about that shit, too. Every married person now and then thinks, Oh what the fuck. I did it, is the only difference. Me! I went ahead and did it."

Joey found herself scanning the room for something jagged and, preferably, rusty. Then she recalled Mick's warning: Don't make it a crime scene.

She released Chaz's hair and his chin dropped to his chest.

He said, "I thought you were gonna rat me out for faking the water tests."

"But I didn't even know what you were doing!"

"So maybe I overreacted."

"Excuse me?" Joey said.

Chaz scratched absently at a dime-size scab on his neck. "You don't understand. Red's deadly serious when it comes to business."

"It was our *anniversary*!"

"Oh yeah, I almost forgot." Chaz looked up. "Thanks for the awesome golf-club covers. I found them later in my suitcase."

"You really are a monster," Joey said hoarsely.

"If you were real, I'd tell you I was sorry."

"And I'd tell you to go straight to hell," she said. "Why did you marry me in the first place?"

Chaz seemed truly surprised at the question. "Because you were hot. And we were so fantastic together."

"Because I was *hot*?" Joey eyed the lamp's electrical cord and thought: No jury in the country would convict me.

Chaz said, "I'm getting really sleepy. Can you go back to heaven now? Or wherever you came from?"

"Didn't you ever love me?" Joey switched off the light in case she started crying again. "Ever, Chaz?"

"Sure I did."

"Then what happened?" she demanded. "First the whoring around, which was bad enough—"

A wary grunt from the shadows.

"—then you push me overboard on our anniversary cruise! I don't get it," Joey said. "If you wanted out so badly, all you had to do was ask. See, they've got this new thing called divorce."

Now all she heard was the low scrape of heavy breathing. Five, ten, fifteen seconds went by.

"Chaz?"

Nothing.

She jerked the pillow from beneath his head and said, "Wake up, dammit! I'm not finished."

A perturbed, groggy groan. Then: "You can't hurt me, Joey. You're already dead."

Arduously he gathered himself and lunged for her, missing in the dark. She pounced on his back, pinning him to the mattress.

"Because I was 'hot'? Are you serious?" Her mouth was inches from his ear.

"Hey, it's a compliment," Chaz said. "Now, can you please get off me? My hard-on's gettin' bent."

"What a moving sentiment. Are you stealing from Neil Diamond again?"

The door opened, throwing a wedge of light on the bed.

"It's okay. We're fine," Joey said over her shoulder.

"Who's there?" Chaz asked, squirming.

The door closed.

"Rose?"

Joey said, "Relax, Romeo, you're not getting any tonight."

"Lemme up."

"It's still only me, Chaz. Your dearly departed wife."

"Can't be."

"But I'm not deceased."

"Are, too."

Joey dug an elbow into his back. "Does that feel real?"

"Bad dream," he groaned.

"Wanna bet?"

"Pinch me in the nuts again. Go ahead, see if I care."

Joey said, "What went wrong with you, Chaz?"

His shoulders hitched. "People change, it's nobody's fault," he said. "Lemme sleep, please?"

"No sir, not yet."

"If you were real, Joey, you would've already killed me by now." Then he sighed heavily and went slack beneath her.

She shook him by the collar, then she pressed so close that her lips brushed the fuzz on his earlobes. "Chaz!" she said sharply. "Chaz, you listen. I'm telling the cops *everything*. And it won't just be my word against yours—they'll have the new will, the videotape, all the Everglades stuff. Your friend Red, he's toast, too. Wake up, Romeo, it's over. Attempted murder, fraud, bribery. Even if you beat the rap, you'll be broke and out of work and owing lawyers for the rest of your miserable life. Ruined, Chaz."

From her husband, not a peep. He had passed out.

Joey climbed off and called for Mick. Together they jostled and prodded Chaz, but they were unable to rouse him.

She said, "Now what do we do? The asshole thinks he's hallucinating. He thinks I'm not real."

"You're not," Stranahan said fondly.

"I'm serious, Mick. Obviously he was bombed when he got here, then Rose doped him into oblivion."

"Gosh. I sure hope he doesn't get a boo-boo on the way home. Drive himself into a canal, or fall asleep on the train tracks."

"Oh no you don't."

"Hey, stuff like that happens. You read about it all the time."

Joey stared at the reprehensible heap of snoring, drool-flecked flesh to which she was wed, and she felt only hollowness and exhaustion. How strange that she no longer wanted to punch him or choke him or kill him, or even just scream at him. All her rage and indignation was dried up, leaving only an aftertaste of disgust.

"You all right?" Stranahan asked.

"Peachy. I married a total piece of shit."

"It's not hard to do. You want to whale on the bastard, now's your chance."

Joey shook her head. "Honestly, Mick, I don't care what happens to him anymore."

"Well, I do," Stranahan said, grabbing Charles Regis Perrone by the ankles.

Twenty-eight

Nellie Shulman cornered him in the elevator. Her housecoat smelled of mothballs and tuna fish.

"Why didn't you tell me you're moving out? What's with all the sneaking around?"

Karl Rolvaag said, "I'm taking a job up north."

"And renting your place out to Gypsies, no doubt. Deviates and loners like yourself."

"I'll be selling the condo, Nellie."

She clacked her yellow dentures. "To another snake freak, right? Some psycho with spitting cobras, maybe."

"Whoever can afford to buy it. That's the law."

The elevator door opened and the detective bolted, Nellie scuttling after him.

"Aren't you the smug one?" she said. "Just because they found Rumsfeld, you think you can dance out of here with a clean conscience."

Rumsfeld was the miniature poodle that had gone AWOL, the third pet missing from Sawgrass Grove. The detective was secretly happy to learn that the incontinent little hair ball had not been devoured by one of his wayfaring pythons.

"They found him behind the Albertsons'," Mrs. Shulman reported somberly, "sleeping in a liquor box. Some bum was feeding him soda crackers."

"What about Pinchot and whatsit, that Siamese?" Rolvaag asked. Poised at his front door, he groped through his pockets for the keys. Mrs. Shulman seemed committed to a full-blown confrontation.

She said, "Don't play innocent with me. Her name was Pandora and you know damn well what happened—you sacrificed her to those vicious reptiles of yours! Same with poor old Pinchot. And my precious Petunia is probably next on the menu!"

"Those are serious accusations you're making, Nellie, with no proof whatsoever."

Mrs. Shulman grew defensive. "It's not just me, everybody around here's talking about it. 'Why else would a grown man keep anacondas?' they say. 'What's the matter with him?' "

Rolvaag said, "They're pythons, not anacondas. And they don't eat house cats or Pomeranians." He hoped his lack of conviction wasn't apparent to the acting vice president of the Sawgrass Grove Condominium Association.

"Know what I think, Nellie? I think you're disappointed that you won't get to evict me. I think you're bummed because I'm moving out on my own terms." At last he found his key and speared it into the lock.

Mrs. Shulman's arthritic talons clenched his arm. "Ha! I'm the only reason you're leaving town!"

The detective smiled suggestively. "You're going to miss me, aren't you?"

"Agghh!" Mrs. Shulman stumbled out of her slippers as she backed off.

Rolvaag quickly entered his apartment and shut the door. He logged on to the computer and clicked open the weather page for the Twin Cities. It was sixty-two degrees and brightly sunny in St. Paul; the glory of a midwestern spring. He wondered if his ex-wife had planted a garden, a hobby she'd abandoned in the suffocating heat of South Florida.

The detective took a can of pop from the refrigerator, sat down in the kitchen and emptied his briefcase. On top of the pile was the rental agreement for the green Chevrolet Suburban. Initially the manager of the car-rental agency had refused to fax it to the Sheriff's Office, but he'd changed his mind after Rolvaag offered to drive there personally and jump up on the counter and wave his gold badge for all the customers to see.

According to the contract, the Suburban had been rented on Joey Perrone's credit card three days after she went overboard from the *Sun Duchess*. Rolvaag placed the rental agreement side by side with a Xeroxed sheet of canceled checks provided by Mrs. Perrone's bank. The signature on the car contract and the signature on the old checks appeared strikingly similar. Next, the detective compared the handwriting on the car contract with that on the will delivered by Mrs. Perrone's brother. Rolvaag studied the characteristics of the penmanship for a few minutes, then returned the documents to his briefcase. Telling Chaz Perrone would be a waste of time; the man was a goner, and there was nothing inside the law that Rolvaag could do to change that, even if he'd wanted to.

He phoned the Coast Guard station and tracked down Petty Officer Yancy. "You know that bale of Jamaican weed? The one we took the fingernails from?"

"Yes, sir. It's in the evidence warehouse," Yancy said, "as you requested."

"Tell them to go ahead and burn it. I won't be needing it after all."

"I'll fax you the paperwork, sir." Yancy paused. "Did they ever find that missing woman off the cruise ship?"

"Nope."

"That's too bad."

"Not necessarily," the detective said.

As soon as he hung up, he started packing for Minnesota.

Tool spent the night beside Maureen's bed at the convalescent home. She slept poorly, making small murmurs that could have been caused by bad dreams, or pain. Red Hammernut had called up angrily, ordering Tool to return to Chaz Perrone's house and keep an eye on the conniving little rodent. Tool had pretended the battery on the cell phone was dying and he couldn't make out what Red was saying.

No way was he leaving Maureen until she felt better.

He found the TV station that showed country-music videos, and that's how he passed the time. Some of the songs were depressing, if he listened too closely to the words, and other songs he couldn't relate to one bit. There seemed to be no end of stories about men who wouldn't stay put in one place, and the loving women they left behind. That's one good thing about farming, Tool thought—you've got a home and you know right where it is.

By daybreak his tailbone was so sore from the poacher's bullet that he had to get up and do some walking. When he returned to the room, Maureen was awake. She looked up and gave a limp smile. The sunlight slanting through the blinds made bright stripes across the bed, but Maureen's blue eyes, once star-like, seemed as dull and gray as lead. Tool noticed that she kept pressing the call button, so he asked what was wrong. She pointed at the IV bag, which was empty.

"I need a refill," she whispered.

"Where does it hurt?"

"They haven't given me a bath in three days. It's so annoying."

"Here." He took the call switch and mashed on it repeatedly with his thumb. They waited and waited, but nobody came.

Maureen said, "In the mornings they're short-staffed. Sometimes it takes a while."

"We'll see about that."

"Where are you going?"

Tool snatched the first person he found who was dressed like a nurse and hustled her into Maureen's room. The woman was startled and confused.

"Earl, that's Natacha," Maureen explained. "She works in the kitchen."

Tool did not release Natacha's arm. "Go fetch somebody to bring this lady some pain medicine. I mean right *now*."

"Natacha, I must apologize for my nephew. He worries too much about me," Maureen said.

Natacha nodded tenuously. Tool let go of her and she scooted for the door, Maureen calling after her, "That lentil soup was heavenly last night. I demand your recipe!"

Tool said, "Ain't they any damn doctors in this place?"

Maureen pulled the top sheet snug to her chest. "The woman can't do corned beef to save her life, but she is the grand diva of lentil."

"Lemme go fetch somebody else."

"Oh no you don't." Maureen wagged a finger. "If you make trouble, they'll ask you to leave. Just sit tight and relax. I'm fine for now."

Tool could tell that she wasn't fine. Gently he rolled her on one side and untied the string of her gown.

"Earl, don't," she said.

"Hush up."

He hiked the top of his lab whites, then reached behind his back and peeled off his last remaining patch. Carefully he centered it between Maureen's shoulder blades and pressed down firmly, so that it would stick.

When he turned her over, she said, "That wasn't necessary, but thank you."

"It ain't too fresh, but it's better than nuthin'."

"Earl, I want you to listen." She held out her hand, which felt cool to his touch.

"Some people give up when they come to a place like this," she said. "I see it in their faces—they just run out of fight. And the weaker you get, believe me, it's tempting. . . . The painkillers they've got nowadays, goodness, the days and weeks slide by my window like a big warm river. But don't worry, I'm not ready to call it quits just yet."

"You can't!" Tool blurted. He felt mad, although he wasn't sure why. "When's the last time you seen your daughters?"

"It's hard for them to get away. The children are in school."

"That's a bullshit excuse."

Maureen laughed softly. "I'd slap you, Earl, if I had the strength."

He was at a loss. "You want, I'll try and give you a bath."

"You'll do no such thing!" She pinched his wrist. "Good Lord, I shouldn't have said a word."

Tool's mother had passed away barely a month after the doctors had told her she was sick. It was in the middle of a tomato harvest, and he didn't get back to Jacksonville in time to say good-bye. He heard himself telling the whole story to Maureen, who said, "Don't feel bad. I'm sure she knew how much you loved her."

"Your daughters oughta be here. It ain't that far away." He pressed the call button so hard that it broke apart in his fist. "Shit," he said. "I'm sorry."

"Earl, you need to calm down. I've got no intention of dying today."

At last a nurse came in with a fresh IV bag, two small vials of narcotics and a diaper for grown-ups. Tool stepped away from the bed to give Maureen some privacy. The nurse was a muscular pitch-black woman who spoke quietly to Maureen in an accent that Tool recognized as Jamaican. He thought about all the pickers from Jamaica that he'd yelled at and slapped around and ripped off, and he felt sort of shitty and low. The nurse who was helping Maureen might have been one of their sisters or cousins, or even a daughter. Her smile was as bright as a sunrise, and when she touched a hand to Maureen's forehead, Tool knew right then and there that he was done with crew bossing forever. He'd never be able to look one of them sweaty black boys in the eye and not think about this moment, about how jumbled and sour he felt toward himself. Somewhere in life he'd taken a wrong-headed turn, and most likely it was too late to back up. For sure he'd gotten in awful deep with Red Hammernut, who now wanted him to do something that would send him even further down the highway to hell. A week ago Tool would've said yes to any fool job, no matter how bad, as long as it paid in cash. But then he'd met Maureen.

"She gonna be okay?" he asked the Jamaican nurse.

"Oh, she'll feel better after breakfast."

Maureen said, "Earl, this is Evie. She's one of the good ones."

The nurse laughed. "I'll come back in an hour for your bath."

As soon as they were alone again, Maureen said: "She's a sharp girl. You should let her take a look at that problem with your you-know-what."

"No thanks." Tool wasn't spreading his ass crack to any female stranger, black, white, or purple polka-dotted.

"For heaven's sake, Earl, she's a professional health-care provider."

"How about some TV?"

"Hmmm-hmmm," said Maureen.

Tool noticed that her breathing had slowed and her eyelids were droopy. The drugs that Nurse Evie had brought, combined with the secondhand fentanyl patch, were taking effect. Maybe now Maureen could grab a decent sleep.

He said, "I better go."

"Thank you for the company, Earl."

"Anytime."

"I didn't even think to ask about your bodyguarding," she said drowsily. "How's it going with that big-shot doctor?"

"Same old crap."

When Tool stood to leave, Maureen turned her face to the wall and curled herself into a shape that reminded him of a question mark.

"Don't you dare give up," he said anxiously.

"Not me."

"I'm dead serious now."

"Earl?"

He could barely hear her speak, so he leaned over the bed rail and balanced his huge head close to hers.

"Yes, ma'am. What is it?"

"Earl, I need a favor."

"Anything."

"It's a whopper," Maureen said.

"Just name it."

"Can you get me out of here?"

Tool smiled. "I thought you'd never ask."

Chaz Perrone awoke nude in his yellow Humvee on the shoulder of Interstate 95, somewhere in Palm Beach County.

Friday morning.

Rush hour.

His bladder was the size of Lake Okeechobee and his skull was splitting open like a rotten melon. He opened the passenger door and tried to take a leak, but it felt as if he were pissing broken glass. Crawling behind the steering wheel, he was relieved to spy the keys in the ignition.

He headed home with careful regard for the speed limits, not wishing to be stopped by the cops and forced to explain his appearance. He was grateful for the absurd height of the Hummer, which concealed his chafed and sallow nakedness from other motorists, save for a few coarse truck drivers.

What the hell happened last night? Chaz wondered, squinting into the cruel morning sun.

The last thing he remembered with clarity was Rose, in those incredible short jeans, leading him to her bedroom. That's when he must have flipped out, because somehow Rose had morphed into Joey and right away she'd started unloading an unholy ration of shit.

Joey, in the same skirt and blouse that she'd been wearing on the night he threw her overboard!

By the time Chaz reached the exit for West Boca Dunes Phase II, he had it all figured out. What had triggered his freak-out was watching the video of Joey's murder over and over; that, combined with too much booze. And hadn't Rose been wearing the same perfume as Joey?

Chaz didn't recall running from the bedroom, but apparently that's what he'd done. Dashed out the front door, dove into the Hummer and took off. Rose must have thought he was totally whacked.

He glanced down at his pecker, which he scarcely recognized in its dolorous, chastened droop. He wondered if he'd ever again be able to

initiate a sex act without being taunted by the ambrosial ghost of his
dead wife.

He wheeled into his driveway and parked next to Tool's Grand
Marquis, checking both ways down the street before loping into the
house. The door to the big goon's room was shut, so Chaz furtively
padded to the kitchen, where he gulped four aspirins with a chaser of
Mountain Dew. Then he stepped into the shower and propped himself
against the tiles, massaging his hangover until the hot water ran out.

When he emerged from the bathroom, the phone was ringing.

"Where you been, son?" It was Red Hammernut. "I left, like, a
dozen goddamn messages on your answer machine."

"I spent the night at a friend's," Chaz said.

"Without Mr. O'Toole?"

"It was an emergency, Red."

"You wanna talk about emergencies? Tell you what, I got a major-
league motherfucker of an emergency arrived just yesterday by Federal
Express. It's a videocassette."

"Oh shit."

"Up to your eyeballs, son. You know about this damn thing?"

"Yessir. I got one, too."

"Is that so?" Red Hammernut sounded like he was working up to a
spit. "I thought I seen plenty in my day, Chaz, but never nuthin' like
this. I'd be lyin' if I said I wasn't shook up."

Red's slurred delivery suggested that he'd gotten an early start on
his cocktails.

"Let's not do this on the phone," he said to Chaz.

"You want me to drive over to the office?"

"Hell no. I'm parked right'n front of your goddamn house."

Chaz went to the window and saw the gray Cadillac idling in the
swale. He stepped into a wrinkled pair of trousers and hurried outside.
The passenger door of the big car swung open and Chaz climbed into
the chill. Red Hammernut was dressed like he'd just stepped off a marlin boat, a sunburned gnome in Eddie Bauer khakis. He had a plug of
tobacco in one cheek and smear of zinc oxide on his radish-shaped
nose. From his thick ruddy neck hung a pair of polarized sunglasses. A
bottle of Jack Daniel's stood open on the seat-back tray; no glass.

Chaz said, "I didn't know the guy had a video camera. When I saw
the tape, I was blown away."

"Son, it's bad, *bad* news."

"The worst," Chaz agreed.

"I gotta say, it was a tur'ble thing to watch. I always liked Joey, I really did," Red said. "I won't ask why you done it, because it ain't none of my business."

Chaz was mildly irritated. "But we talked about it, remember? How worried I was? I thought she'd figured out our whole deal."

He was disappointed that Red hadn't commented on the efficiency of the crime itself; the steel balls it took to go through with it.

"We've got to pay the blackmail, Red. Now there's no choice."

"I 'gree."

"The whole five hundred, right?"

"Yup," Red Hammernut said. "The full load."

Chaz Perrone's relief almost instantly gave way to suspicion. He'd been expecting resistance or, at the least, some loony alternate plan. He knew how much Red cherished his money; dropping half a million bucks was enough to send him on a six-month bender.

"The drop is set for tonight," Chaz said, "on a house somewhere in the middle of Biscayne Bay. The guy wrote down a GPS heading."

"Yeah, Tool told me."

"You talked to Tool?"

"That's right. I already gave him the cash to hold." Red Hammernut took a pull from the bottle of bourbon. "Why you look so surprised, son? The man works for me."

"Yeah. So do I," Chaz reminded him.

"And you're in charge of buyin' the suitcase." Red said this with no trace of sarcasm. "I got you guys a boat for the night, a twenty-three-footer, at Bayside Marina. That's downtown Miami, acrosst from the basketball arena. Tool's good with outboards, you let him drive."

"Whatever," said Chaz.

He was thinking about the scene toward the end of *GoodFellas*, when everything's falling apart for the gangsters and the Ray Liotta character meets the Robert De Niro character at a diner. The two of them are sitting there, calmly talking about all the problems and all the heat—just like Red and I are talking, Chaz thought—when the De Niro character nonchalantly asks the Ray Liotta character to go down to Florida and do a job.

And right then, at that instant, the Ray Liotta character knows he's being set up for a hit.

"Son, I don't want no funny business out there on the water," Red Hammernut was saying. "I told Tool the same thing—pay the sumbitch and get the hell outta Dodge, you hear?"

Just like in the movie, Chaz thought. Once I was the partner and now I'm the problem.

He understood that Red Hammernut was looking at the big picture. The blackmailer posed a threat to Red only as long as Chaz was alive. The Hummer was the most traceable connection between them, and Red could always blame that on Chaz. He could say the biologist had hit him up for a new set of wheels. As a matter of fact, Red could say that the whole Everglades scam, faking the pollution charts, had been Chaz's idea; a shakedown from the beginning.

Once Chaz was gone, who could dispute it?

"I want you guys to get it over with, that's the main thing," Red Hammernut was saying. "Be done with it for good."

Amen, thought Chaz. The time has come.

Twenty-nine

Joey and her brother carried the dinner scraps down to the seawall to feed the fish. Stranahan sat at the picnic table, cleaning his rifle. He was relieved to be home, distant from the lunacy of the mainland. Strom lay at his feet and refused to move, even for a flock of rowdy gulls. All afternoon the dog had stayed near his side, sensing that something was in the works. If only humans were that intuitive, Stranahan thought.

With Strom at his heels, he carried the Ruger to the boat. Joey watched him wrap the gun in an oilcloth and stow it in the bow hatch.

"Mick, get this," she said. "My brother has the hots for my husband's girlfriend."

Corbett Wheeler waved an objection. "Hold on—all I said was, she didn't seem like a bimbo."

"That's what happens when you live with cloven beasts. Your standards take a dive," Joey said. "My advice is not to date anybody you meet at a funeral. Ask Chaz, if you don't believe me."

Stranahan sat down beside her on the seawall, the Doberman nosing between them. Joey clasped Stranahan's hand, the sort of knuckle-busting squeeze that takes place at 35,000 feet during heavy turbulence. She was nervous about the blackmail meeting, as any sane person would be.

Corbett asked, "What're the odds of actually collecting the dough?"

"Not too good," Stranahan conceded.

He anticipated that Samuel Johnson Hammernut would provide all or part of the five hundred grand as bait. Chaz's Neanderthal baby-sitter would guard the stash until they arrived at the drop site, where he'd open the suitcase and encourage Stranahan to count the bills. At the first opportunity he would then try to kill Stranahan. Later, probably on the boat trip back to the mainland, he'd do the same to Chaz Perrone.

There were a dozen unappealing variations of that scenario, and Stranahan had fretted through all of them. Initially he'd planned to make the pickup alone, but Joey and Corbett were adamant about joining him. Stranahan understood; for them it was personal. He also appreciated the tactical advantage in numbers—Hammernut's hired gorilla surely would realize that he couldn't take all three of them by surprise, and Stranahan was gambling that he wouldn't try. The man was more brute than sharpshooter.

Joey said, "If they *do* give up the money, we're donating it to one of the Everglades foundations."

"Anonymously, I presume," said her brother.

Stranahan felt like pouring a stiff drink but that was out of the question. There was a better-than-even chance he'd have to shoot somebody later.

Corbett Wheeler said, "I like your island very much, Mick, but it's a bit too near the city lights for me."

"Ssshh. I'm trying to persuade your little sister it's paradise."

"Little sister is already persuaded," Joey said, wiggling her toes in the water.

Corbett made a wistful pitch for New Zealand. "Once you come, you'll never want to leave."

"If tonight goes badly, we might be visiting soon," Stranahan said, "depending on the extradition policy."

Joey jabbed him in the ribs. "Stop. Think positive thoughts."

To the west, a palisade of violet clouds obscured the setting sun. The breeze died in wisps and the bay slicked off. Stranahan hurried to the boathouse and got out three suits of yellow foul-weather gear. Strom's ears pricked at the faraway roll of thunder.

"Never a dull moment," said Corbett.

Joey said, "The good news is, Chaz can't stand the rain."

Stranahan was more interested in the lightning. He could think of safer places to be than in an open skiff on a large body of water during an electrical storm. The sensible move was to call off the drop, but it was too late.

"Let's go," he said, "before the wind kicks up."

Chaz Perrone locked himself in the bathroom with a stack of smutty magazines and the framed photograph of Joey that he'd lifted from the altar of St. Conan's after the service. His habitual remedy for anxiety was to wank at himself with simian zest, but even the youthful picture of his late wife—centered beatifically amid the cheap porn—triggered only a transient tumescence. His fevered and doleful manipulations were interrupted by a heavy rap on the door.

"Where's that fuckin' gun?" Tool demanded.

"I got rid of it," Chaz lied, hastily tucking himself into his boxers.

"Lemme in."

"I'm on the can!"

"No you ain't." Tool kicked the door open and stared with overt disgust at the photos spread across the bathroom floor.

"God-a-mighty," he said.

Chaz snatched up the picture of Joey and wedged it under one arm. Then he dropped to his knees and started scooping up the magazines, saying, "You don't understand, I'm a nervous wreck. I had to do *something.*"

Tool regarded him as if he were some sort of school-yard flasher.

"The gun, boy."

Chaz said, "I told you. I threw it away."

"Red said no funny bidness out on the water."

"I heard him."

"You done here?" Tool motioned snidely at the toilet. " 'Cause it's time we should go."

"Let me get dressed. I'll meet you outside," said Chaz.

The blue-plated .38 was hidden at the bottom of the laundry hamper. He slipped it with his cell phone into a zippered pocket of a Patagonia rain jacket, which he folded neatly and carried to the Hummer. Tool was enthroned behind the steering wheel, chewing a stick of beef jerky and tapping his stained fingers to a country song.

Chaz said, "What're you doing?"

"What's it look like?"

"You are *not* driving my truck."

"Red said so. Hop in, Doc."

Chaz was steamed. "What about the suitcase?"

He'd purchased a gray hard-shell Samsonite with retractable wheels.

Tool had packed the cash by himself, stack after stack of hundred-dollar bills. Although he'd refused to let Chaz anywhere near the money, the mere sight of it had been intoxicating.

Tool motioned with his thumb. "It's in the back."

Chaz climbed in on the passenger side. To remind Tool who owned the vehicle, he reached for the tuner knob on the stereo. Tool caught his hand and slammed it against the top of the dashboard. Chaz's arm went numb.

"That's Patsy Cline," Tool said simply.

"Christ, I think you broke my wrist!"

"Don't ever mess with the radio when Patsy Cline is on."

Goddamn psycho, Chaz thought. He couldn't feel any fractures, but something in his left hand was either sprained, torn or jammed.

Tool maintained a surly silence during the ride to Miami, though he turned out to be a decent driver. Chaz was holding himself together pretty well until he heard the first boom of thunder and eyeballed the blackening line of clouds ahead of them.

"What if they won't rent us the boat in this weather?" he asked.

Tool seemed entertained by the question. "Don't you worry, Red's got it all took care of."

Chaz opened the envelope and read over the blackmailer's instructions again. "You sure you know how to use a GPS?" he asked.

Tool said it was easy. "One season I had some trouble over at Immokalee, so I went down to Ramrod Key and run a crawfish boat for a feller. He had a import bidness on the side, so we spent some time in the islands, off the books. Made the crossing back and forth from Cay Sal in all kinds a storms."

"Worse than this?" Chaz said.

"On occasion, you bet."

The rain was sheeting by the time they parked at the Bayside Marina and found the boat. It was a twenty-three-foot outboard with a Bimini top and a big four-stroke Yamaha. A Garmin GPS had been mounted on the console.

Tool set the heavy suitcase in the stern. Chaz bundled unhappily into his foul-weather jacket, the hammer of the pistol poking his ribs. He pulled up his hood and peered at the leaking leaden sky. His left wrist throbbed painfully.

Tool found a portable spotlight and plugged it into a battery jack. He seemed surprised that the device actually worked. Tool started the engine and cast off the ropes and motored slowly away from the docks. When they reached the open water, he told Chaz to sit his ass down and he threw the throttle forward. Simultaneously there was a clap of thunder that made Chaz duck.

This is insane, he told himself.

What he had planned for tonight would have been difficult in clear, calm conditions; in a squall it could be suicide. He hunkered low, cringing at every glint of lightning. Tool seemed at ease—one hand on the wheel, the other working the spotlight—though his overalls were soaked and sagging. The rain had slicked down the dense black curls on his arms and shoulders, giving him a surreal lustrous sheen in the twilight.

Soon they passed beneath the Rickenbacker Causeway Bridge, which Chaz had crossed often as a grad student on his way to the Rosenstiel School. The sight reminded him of his long-ago ordeal with sea lice, and he speculated that the hungry little bastards were floating all around them in avid anticipation, should Tool manage to capsize the boat. Also looming in Chaz's imagination was the larger, more lethal menace of sharks. Such attacks were virtually unheard of on Biscayne Bay, one of many facts that Chaz had either forgotten or simply failed to register during his idle schooling in the marine sciences. The ravenous two-headed alligator starring in Chaz's recent nightmares could just as easily have been a hammerhead, given his visceral dread—and lazy ignorance—of both species.

Blessedly the thunder quieted and the downpour faded to a drizzle, although they hit a chilly wall of wind, which buffeted them most of the way to Cape Florida. The ride was more than sufficient to reinforce Chaz's loathing of the great outdoors. Clinging with his uninjured hand to the bench seat, he envisioned himself hurled to the deck with such force that the pistol in his jacket would discharge accidentally. If the shot didn't kill him outright, the noise would probably give him a heart attack.

Navigating with the magic of global satellites, Tool located what was left of Stiltsville, an old community of wooden houses constructed on pilings in the shallow grass beds. Hurricane Andrew had practically leveled the place, and the few remaining structures had been taken over by the National Park Service. The empty, unlit homes looked skeletal beneath the hot-blue flickers of lightning.

Tool turned off the engine and let the boat ride the outgoing tide down the channel. He muttered under his breath, his scowl visible in the green glow of the GPS screen.

"What's wrong?" Chaz asked.

"This is right where he told us to meet him," Tool said, "but I don't like it."

As they came abreast of the last stilt house, Tool lumbered to the bow and heaved out an anchor. The rope went taut and the boat stopped dead, the bow dipping slightly under Tool's bulk. He made his way back to the console and sat down with a grimace.

"Now we wait," he said, rubbing his buttocks.

Chaz checked his watch—it was more than an hour until the meeting. He turned on his cell phone, as the blackmailer had instructed. From the mainland came another rumble and, high in the clouds, a jagged burst of bright light.

"That bunch is still a ways off," Tool said. "If a-hole is on time, we'll be long gone 'fore it hits."

At least one of us will, Chaz thought. He was sure that Red Hammernut had ordered Tool to kill him and make it look like a suicide— the grief-stricken widower, unable to cope with the loss of his wife, decides to join her at sea for eternity.

But Chaz Perrone had 13 million reasons to stay alive, and a plan of his own.

"Where's the damn ice chest?" Tool asked. "I'm thirsty."

"Guess I left it in the Hummer."

"Tell me you ain't serious."

"Sorry." With his good hand Chaz took the Colt from his jacket and pointed it at Tool's massive silhouette.

Tool didn't notice the gun until it was illuminated by a flash from the oncoming storm. Chaz couldn't make out the goon's expression, but he plainly heard the warning: "I wouldn't do that, boy."

"Sure you would," Chaz said, and squeezed the trigger twice.

The first shot punched a hole in the canvas Bimini top. The second knocked Tool overboard, causing a splash that was more of a concussion, like a meat freezer being dropped into a swimming pool. Chaz emptied the .38 into the foamy crater and watched to see if the body would float up right away, like they did on TV cop shows. He'd expected Tool's wintry coat of hair to provide extra buoyancy, yet there was no sign of the dead man bobbing to the surface.

As Chaz pocketed the revolver, his cell phone rang.

"What the hell's going on?" The blackmailer sounded serious and alarmed; no Jerry Lewis impressions tonight.

"I was shooting at turtles," Chaz said. "Where are you?"

Chaz had thought he'd have plenty of time, but the guy was early. He'd heard the gunshots and now he was spooked.

"Turtles?" he said.

Chaz laughed casually. "I was bored. Are you close by? Let's get this done before that damn thunderstorm gets here."

"Where's the ape man?"

"Oh, he couldn't make it."

The blackmailer hung up.

"Shit," Chaz said. He groped around the deck until he found the spotlight. He swept the beam slowly back and forth across the water; no other vessel was in sight.

Moments later, the phone rang again.

"Where *are* you?" Chaz demanded.

"Up here!" said a different voice.

A woman's voice; one that made him stiffen.

"Get rid of the gun," she said. "Over the side."

Chaz worked the spotlight up and down the stilt cottage. Sitting on the edge of the roof was none other than his wife, very much alive. She appeared to be aiming a large-caliber rifle at his head.

"Joey, is that really you?" Chaz whispered into the phone.

The muzzle of the rifle flared orange and the windshield of the boat exploded before Chaz's terrified eyes.

"Does that answer your question?" she shouted.

Obediently he took the .38 from his jacket and threw it into the bay.

The first gunshots had caught Mick Stranahan by surprise.

"I believe numbnuts just killed his baby-sitter," he informed Joey Perrone and Corbett Wheeler.

The three of them were flattened against the roof, invisible to Chaz from the boat.

"Now what?" Joey whispered.

"I honestly don't know."

"Let me see the rifle," she said.

309

Stranahan glanced at Corbett, who nodded sympathetically. "She needs to get this out of her system."

"Easy," Stranahan said when she took the Ruger. He had allowed her to try it once before, blasting coconuts out of palm trees on the island. It had a powerful kick, but Joey had handled it capably.

Stranahan phoned Chaz Perrone on his cellular to find out what had happened on the boat. After a short exchange he hung up.

"That's it," he said. "He's flying solo."

Joey groaned. "What a schmuck."

"If he's killed the bodyguard, then he might be planning to kill Hammernut, too," Stranahan surmised.

"And the girlfriend," Corbett added quietly.

"Ricca. It's all right to say her name," Joey said. "Now, what about us, Mick?"

"Once Chaz sees the Ruger, he'll probably fold. Right now he thinks he's Vin Diesel." Stranahan dialed Chaz's cell number and handed her the phone. "Tell him to toss the gun or the deal's off," he said.

"Where are you?" Chaz was demanding on the other end.

"Up here!" Joey answered.

Corbett and Mick climbed down from the roof and sneaked beneath the house, where the Whaler was tied. Stranahan's idea was that the two of them would swim quietly out to the boat and overpower Chaz. They were peeling out of their clothes when the rifle went off, and they heard Joey shout: "Does that answer your question?"

"Don't shoot!" her husband screamed back.

"Give me ten good reasons why not!"

Thattagirl, thought Stranahan.

Corbett tugged his arm. "Mick, I heard something else."

"Where?"

"Close by. Listen."

Stranahan heard it, too. "I'll be damned."

Game over, he thought with a rush of relief. Thanks to Chaz Perrone's fabulous inefficiency as a killer, they were now free to do what Darwin would have done: back off and let Nature take over. Left to his own greedy wits, Joey's husband had no chance whatsoever.

"There it is again," Corbett whispered intently.

Stranahan nodded. "Music to my ears."

A gust of wind caused the old stilt house to creak and murmur above them. The clouds lit up, and through the pilings Stranahan could make out the shape of the boat in the channel and the figure of Charles Perrone, holding the spotlight in the bow.

"Hurry." Stranahan crept down the catwalk toward the source of the moans—a floundering gray mass that in the shallows might easily have been mistaken for a stricken manatee.

"But what about Joey?" Corbett asked.

"Hell, let her have some fun," Stranahan said. "Come on, help me get this poor bastard out of the water."

Joey scooted off the roof and reappeared at the end of the dock, barely a hundred feet from where the boat was anchored. She wore an over-sized yellow rain suit with the hood down, her blond ponytail whipping in the wind. Chaz struggled to steady the spotlight but the boat was rocking and his hand shook, a condition aggravated by the sight of his wife with a loaded rifle.

So, last night was real, he thought numbly.

"What's the matter, darling?" Joey shouted acidly.

He raised his palms in a gesture of defeat.

"What—you can't figure it out?" she said. "It's simple. You pushed me off the ship, only I didn't drown."

"How is that possible?"

"It's called swimming, Chaz. Where's the money?"

He motioned behind him, where the Samsonite lay flat against the transom. From the dock Joey couldn't see it. The wind was rising, and Chaz didn't hear her speak again until there was a lull between the gusts.

She yelled, "I'm waiting for the ten reasons why I shouldn't blow your head off!"

"What?"

A raindrop splatted on Chaz's nose, and morosely he cast his gaze downward. The black dress hanging in the closet, the cut-up photograph hidden beneath his pillow, the fact that the Coast Guard had found nothing but her fingernails—of course Joey was alive. It all added up.

"Chaz?"

"Just a second. I'm trying to think," he shouted back.

The barrel of the rifle flashed again, and the spotlight shattered in Chaz's fist. Shards of glass and plastic tinkled to the deck.

"Okay, I've got it!" he cried frantically. "I'm mentally disturbed!"

"What?"

"Reason number one why you shouldn't shoot me—I'm sick in the head! Honey, I need help!"

"That's the best you can do?" Joey asked.

Unfortunately, it was. Chaz Perrone couldn't come up with a single good reason why his wife shouldn't blast his brains out. Desperately he sought to change the subject.

"Where've you been for the last two weeks?"

"Watching you making a clown of yourself."

"Joey—"

"Hiding under our bed while you tried to screw a size ten with a rose tattooed on her ankle. It was pitiful."

Chaz felt gutted by humiliation. Medea, he recalled abjectly, the humming reflexologist. It made him shrivel to think that Joey had been eavesdropping during one of his sexual malfunctions.

He tried to turn the tables by slinging guilt. "You put all of us through hell. We had a church service and everything!"

"I'm touched," Joey called out. "Start packing for prison, because I'm going to the cops—and I'm taking the videotape."

"Honey, please."

"There's no golfing in prison, Chaz. No slutty hairdressers, either."

The rain slapping down on the waves sounded to Charles Perrone like cruel applause.

"What about that will?" He heard his voice quaver. "Was it real or not?"

"Apparently you *are* sick in the head," his wife said.

So that's that, Chaz thought bleakly. No 13 million bucks after all. The wind dropped suddenly to a cool sigh, the proverbial calm before the storm.

"I don't understand a damn thing anymore," Chaz spluttered. "Where's the guy who set up this meeting? The sonofabitch who dragged me out in that canoe with all those damn mosquitoes?"

"Oh, he's right here, Chaz, waiting for you to try something foolish."

"Then you're in on this, too?"

Joey let out a hoot. "From day one, darling."

"But why? You don't need the fucking money!"

"It's not about the money," she said. "How can you be such a bonehead?"

A fair question, Chaz had to admit. He'd been wrong about almost everything—starting with the direction of the Gulf Stream—and wrong about almost everyone from Rolvaag to Red Hammernut to Ricca. The reappearance of his once-dead wife left Chaz hopelessly stewed in confusion. The only thing that seemed real was the suitcase containing $500,000. Chaz couldn't help thinking about where it could take him, and how long he could make it last.

"You threw my stuff away!" Joey was saying. "All my clothes and my pictures and my books—even my orchid!"

"Not everything. Your jewelry's in a safe box at the bank," Chaz said. "I'll give you the key if you want."

"Asshole!"

"What if I said I was sorry. Because I really am," Chaz pleaded across the water. "I messed up big-time, Joey. Nothing's the same since you've been gone."

"Wasn't that the whole point?"

A lightning bolt struck one of the other stilt houses, the thunderclap so deafening that Chaz shielded his head. When he got the nerve to look up, he saw through a fresh sheet of rain that his wife had been joined on the dock by the blackmailer, who was shirtless. The man had one arm around Joey's waist, and he was whispering in her ear.

"Don't worry, I've got your money!" Chaz hollered anxiously.

"Keep it!" the man called back.

"What?"

"You keep it, Chazzie."

Joey waved a mocking farewell. "You heard him. Now get out of here before I change my mind."

Chaz hurriedly hauled up the anchor. When Joey appeared to raise the rifle to her shoulder, he sensibly dove behind the console. The gunshot coincided with a boom of thunder, the bullet whining harmlessly above the stern. Chaz held his breath but not his bladder, shivering at the sudden flood of warmth down his legs.

"Aren't you even going to say good-bye?" Joey shouted.

A final burst of shots followed, all high. The tide and a tailwind carried the boat steadily away, the bow spinning in the surface currents. The rain began to sting and the lightning strobed and the air

338

crackled like fire. Chaz stayed low, strangely comforted by the knocking of the waves against the hull. He couldn't understand why Joey and the blackmailer had let him go, nor could he shake the vision of the two of them standing on the dock. They'd looked shockingly comfortable together, more like a couple than business partners, and Chaz wondered jealously if it was possible that his wife was now sleeping with a shakedown artist.

The farther the boat floated from the stilt house, the less Chaz Perrone worried about gunfire. When he finally found the courage to grab for the ignition, he managed to break off the key inside the switch. Not knowing how to hand-crank an outboard motor, Chaz abandoned his fantasy of a high-speed escape. By now there was more than an inch of water on deck, and no evidence of a functioning bilge pump. He crabbed to the stern and clammed onto the Samsonite, in case the boat began to sink. He was banking that the suitcase would float, cash and all.

Two hours later he was wheeling it down the Cape Florida beach, calling on his cell phone for a taxi.

"Mick, I swear to God."

"I'm proud of you for not shooting him." Stranahan lifted the Ruger from her hands.

She said, "I couldn't do it. And don't ask why."

"As long as it's not because you still love him. Then I'll have to go drown myself."

"Love! The man is sewer scum," Joey said bitterly. "But I kept remembering what you told me about how it feels to kill somebody, about all the nightmares that come later."

"It's a good way to end up living alone on an island. You did the right thing," Stranahan told her.

"If I was a better shot, I would've winged him, at least."

"You get big points for hitting the spotlight. Here, I want you to meet somebody."

Earl Edward O'Toole sat upright, a glistening lump propped against a rusty propane tank at the far end of the dock. Corbett Wheeler knelt beside him.

"Mr. O'Toole has a bullet slug embedded in his right armpit," he reported, "and he refuses medical attention."

Tool's sopping overalls were frayed and his hairy arms were bloodied from hugging the barnacle-encrusted piling. That's where Corbett and Mick had found him, groaning and barely afloat under the stilt house. It had taken all their might to muscle him out of the water.

He blinked up at Joey. "I know you."

"Anastasia from Flamingo," she said, bowing. "Nice to see you again."

"But in real life you're the dead girl, right?"

"That's me. The dead girl."

"But I don't get it," Tool said. "Red said there was video of the whole thing."

Corbett cut in: "There is indeed. We made it ourselves. Mick put on a brown wig and played the homicidal husband, Joey played herself, and I held the camera." The tricky part had been staging his sister's tumble over the rail. They had chosen the deck where the lifeboats were hung, so she'd have a safe place to land.

Tool looked amused. "What the hell's this all about?"

"A touchy marital situation," Stranahan said.

Joey sighed impatiently. "That's enough. The man needs a doctor."

Tool winced as he rearranged his bulk. "Lady, your husband is a card-carrying shitwad."

"Thanks for the bulletin."

"Where's the suitcase?"

"In the boat," Joey said, "with Chaz."

"And where's he at?"

Stranahan pointed toward the mountain of weather that was sliding out of the bay toward the Atlantic.

"He took the money. Red's money," Tool said thoughtfully.

"That's our boy." Corbett tried to examine the bullet wound, but Tool knocked his hand away.

"Why did he shoot you?" Joey asked.

"Guess 'cause he figgered I was gone shoot him first."

"Were you?"

"Sure, but then I changed my mind. That's what gets me," Tool said sourly. "Here I go and do the decent Christian thing—which is to let the man off the hook—and what happens? He plugs me!"

Stranahan was putting on his clothes and rain suit. Corbett showed him the 9-mm Beretta that he'd taken from a pocket of Tool's overalls.

Stranahan emptied the chamber, popped out the clip and handed the empty gun to Tool, who flung it off the dock.

"Thing's waterlogged," he said. "Hey, you see him out there anywheres?"

Joey shook her head. Her fists were on her hips as she stared hard into the opaque gloom. The lightning had temporarily stopped, making it impossible to spot a small boat in the distance.

She said, "Mick, you'd better be right about this."

"Stop worrying. He's history."

Tool labored to his feet. "You take me back to dry land, we'll call it even for what happened at the doc's house—you sluggin' me in the damn throat'n all."

"It's the least I can do," Stranahan agreed.

He and Corbett helped Earl Edward O'Toole get in the skiff, which heeled precariously under the load. Joey was hesitant to join them, but there was no other way out of Stiltsville.

Corbett handed out life jackets. Tool couldn't fit into his.

"I gotta lay off them Pringles," he said.

Even in the night shadows Joey could see a thin dark stream running from under his arm. When she advised him to go straight to a hospital, he laughed harshly.

The skiff was wallowing so badly that one rogue wave could have swamped it. Nobody moved from their places as Stranahan motored tediously toward the western shoreline of Key Biscayne. The ride was wet and squirrelly, but it smoothed out when they reached the Pines Canal. They dropped Tool off in some millionaire's backyard, walking distance from Crandon Boulevard.

"Go take care of that bullet," Corbett said.

Tool smiled ruefully, as if enjoying some private joke. "I still don't unnerstand what the hell you people wanted," he said, "what you hoped to get from this whole fucked-up deal."

"Ask *them*." Corbett pointed to his sister and her accomplice.

"Accountability," Mick Stranahan said.

"An ending," said Joey. "Maybe some peace of mind."

Tool flapped his dripping arms in exasperation. "But come on! Life don't work like that!"

"Oh, sometimes it does," Stranahan said.

Thirty

Charles Perrone slept in his own bed, spooning the suitcase. He awoke before dawn, chewed up five cherry Maalox tablets, tossed a toothbrush and three pairs of clean underwear into a grocery bag, then sat down to write out a suicide note.

"To all my friends and loved ones," he began without irony.

Life alone is unbearable. I am reminded of my precious Joey with every sunrise. Although I've tried to stay strong, I'm afraid it's impossible. I clung to hope as long as possible, but now it's time to face the awful truth. She is never coming back and it's all my fault—how could I let her out of my sight that rainy night at sea?

I pray that all of you can forgive me. I only wish I could forgive myself. Tonight I shall reunite with my beloved, so that we may embrace each other on our journey to a dear and better place.

Get my swan costume ready!

Yours in sorrow, Dr. Charles Perrone

Chaz foresaw that his integrity would be called into question once Joey surfaced and went to the police. It was his vainglorious hope that a heart-wrenching farewell message might cast enough doubt upon his wife's lurid story to gain him some getaway time. The salient phrases he had, of course, purloined from an Internet site devoted to memorable suicide notes and famous last words. Chaz was especially fond of the final sentence, supposedly uttered in 1931 by ballerina Anna Pavlova as she exited the mortal stage.

After taping the note to the refrigerator, he manually shredded

the paper contents of his backpack. Special attention was given to
the handwritten tables denoting minimal levels of phosphorus in the
waste from Red Hammernut's farms. The dweebs at the water district
would have been vexed to see that Chaz's charts had been completed
and signed well in advance of upcoming sampling dates. Chaz had
considered saving the forged documents in case he ever needed to
blackmail Red, or testify against him. Now, thanks to Chaz's half-
million-dollar windfall, his most promising option was to disappear
without a trace. He would miss his yellow Hummer, but only until he
bought a new one.

Assuming there was a dealership in Costa Rica.

He was waiting on hold with the cab dispatcher when the doorbell
rang. Quietly he hung up the phone and padded to Tool's room, where
he found a rusty revolver in a moldy gym bag. As he hurried back to
the front of the house, the bell rang again. Chaz remained silent until
the pounding started, as if someone was attacking the door with a cro
quet mallet.

"Yo, knock it off! Who's there?"

"The cleaning lady."

"Ricca?" he said incredulously.

"Open up or I'll scream bloody murder."

"Don't do that." Her yowls could shatter crystal, as Chaz well
remembered from their lovemaking.

Ricca said, "What'd you think the cops are gonna do with a guy
who tries to rape a cripple?"

Chaz hastily wedged the handgun into his waistband and let her in.
She glared as she clomped past him. The door was scuffed and dented
where she had bludgeoned it with her cast.

"How's the leg?" Chaz inquired tepidly.

"Fuck you."

"How'd you know I was home?"

"I tried calling all night long, and then it's six in the morning and
your line's busy." Ricca skidding the plaster heel along the tile floor.

"I was on the computer. Have a seat," Chaz said.

With an impatient sigh she lowered herself onto the couch. "I've
been thinking about my new car—forget the Mustang, I want a Thunderbird convertible instead."

"Sweet," said Chaz. The timing of her visit could not have been
worse.

"P.S., where's my money?"

"I'm working on it. Are you thirsty?"

"I don't suppose you've got whole milk," she said.

Chaz retreated to the kitchen and pretended to search the refrigerator, stalling while he improvised a new plan. When he stood up, Ricca was there—how she'd crept up so stealthily with a bum leg, Chaz couldn't imagine, but her expression was one of toxic contempt. While he had been rooting leisurely through the beer and Mountain Dew, she'd been perusing his suicide note.

"Clever boy," she said. "You're making a run for it."

"What if I told you I was actually going to kill myself. I'm serious, honey, I've been super-depressed."

"And you're packing a suitcase for the hereafter?" She pointed at the gray Samsonite, which sat upright in the hallway.

"Oh, that," Chaz said. "I can explain."

She'd left him no choice but to kill her, *really* kill her this time. He pulled out Tool's second gun.

"Not this again," Ricca sighed.

"Have you got a car?"

Chaz had taken a taxi home from Miami, since the Hummer was at the marina and the keys to the Hummer were in Tool's pocket and Tool was at the bottom of Biscayne Bay.

"Where we going this time?" Ricca asked.

Chaz herded her to the living room. He peeked through the shades and saw that she'd arrived in a generic white compact, an Alamo plate on the front bumper. The trunk appeared adequate for the Samsonite and possibly a carry-on, but not in addition to a corpse with one leg in a bulky cast.

No problem, Chaz told himself. I'll do it in the sticks somewhere, dump her body, then take her car to the airport. There was plenty of time—American had a 5:00 p.m. nonstop to San José.

"Your fish are starved." Ricca peered with maternal concern at the aquarium.

"Fuck 'em," Chaz said. Why was she reaching into the damn tank?

"Lookie here." She held up a small platinum wedding band. "It was hanging from the mast of that little pirate ship."

Struggling to remain calm, Chaz ordered her to put the ring back in the water. She recited the inscription aloud: " 'To Joey, the girl of my dreams. Love, CRP.' Aw, that's so romantic."

He indulged Ricca her sarcasm. Perhaps she already knew that his missing wife was alive and well and determined to ruin his life; that the wedding band obviously had been placed in the aquarium to infuriate him. Perhaps they were even co-conspirators in the plot, Ricca and Joey. Why not? Chaz thought. Nothing could shock him anymore.

Ricca was unable to fit the ring on the proper finger, so she slipped it on her pinkie. "What d'ya think?" she cooed theatrically.

Chaz resisted the urge to shoot her on the spot.

"Don't you move," he said, and for good measure swiped away the crutches and tossed them into the foyer.

"Why was your wife's wedding ring in with the fishes?" she asked, wiggling the platinum-adorned pinkie. "There must be a story."

Back in the kitchen, Chaz fitted the revolver into his battered left hand and hoped that Ricca wouldn't try anything nutty this time. He winced at the memory of her ballsy dash for freedom at Loxahatchee.

With his good hand Chaz rolled the Samsonite toward the door, marveling at the cumbersome weight of wet cash. He shoved the crutches at Ricca and snapped, "Come on, get your butt in gear."

"I dyed my pubes green for you, and this is the thanks I get?"

It was unnerving that she could crack jokes; that she wasn't shaking in fear and begging for her life. "Let's go for a ride," he said.

"How dumb do you think I am?"

"We can debate that later."

"I'm not going anyplace with you, thimbledick."

All that prevented him from shooting her was knowing that a woman's bloodstains on his wall would vastly complicate the suicidal-widower scenario that he had so artfully crafted. He'd invested too much effort in his farewell note to discard it.

"Get up, Ricca. *Now.*"

"Nope. You'll have to carry me."

Wouldn't it be a treat, Chaz thought, to have just one goddamn day when nobody fucked with my head?

Outside, a car horn honked three times. Ricca smiled.

"What now?" Chaz groused to himself.

"Listen, I wasn't serious about the Thunderbird," she confessed, "or the two hundred and fifty grand."

"Then I don't understand. . . ."

"Of course you don't," she said.

The door burst open and there loomed Earl Edward O'Toole, his broad chest crosshatched with white tape.

In a voice as dry as ashes, Charles Perrone said, "You have *got* to be shitting me."

First Joey, then Ricca, now the goon. How can it be so hard to kill somebody? Chaz wondered.

With an incensed squawk he leveled the gun, his bruised and misshapen index finger picking impotently at the trigger. Tool casually clocked him with a left hook to the jaw.

Twelve hours later, the Humvee rumbled down the L-39 levee, Faith Hill singing sweetly on the radio, Red Hammernut mouthing an ivory toothpick while meticulously unspooling the videocassette he had removed from Chaz's VCR.

"Here's what I don't get," Red was saying to Tool. "How come that Ricca girl knew to call *me*? I'm damn glad she did and all, but it's strange how she come to have my name and phone number."

Tool, who was driving, said he had no earthly idea. "You ask her?"

"She said some fella wrote it on a prayer card and gave it to her at Joey Perrone's church service. Whether that's true or not, I guess it don't matter now." Red Hammernut pocketed the toothpick and hawked out the window. "This whole deal has been a royal goat fuck from start to finish. I damn near lost track of which way's up and which way's down."

Tool could have enlightened Red about the doctor's botched attempt to murder not only Ricca Spillman but Mrs. Perrone, but he didn't feel much like chatting. Every rut in the levee reminded him of the fresh slug in his armpit. The discomfort was amplified by his sobriety, Tool having given his last fentanyl patch to Maureen.

From the corner of his eye he saw the tangled remains of the *Sun Duchess* videotape fly out of the Hummer, Red saying he couldn't afford to have that nosy damn detective get hold of it. Earlier, at the office, Red had destroyed his own copy.

He said, "I still can't believe that yuppie cocksucker shot you point-blank. We had such a good plan, too."

Not entirely, thought Tool.

Red had ordered him to kill Chaz Perrone before they got to Stiltsville, but Tool had privately scotched the idea. He'd been doing a lot of heavy thinking over what Maureen had said about making changes—that you were never too old to pick a positive new direction for your life. Tool knew that if he whacked the doctor he'd end up blabbing to Maureen, and he couldn't bear the thought of upsetting her when she was feeling so poorly. So he'd decided that instead of murdering Perrone he would simply heave him off the boat and make him swim to shore. Warn him to never again show his skeeter-bitten puss in Florida.

But the fucker shot him first.

As for the blackmail meeting, it had been Tool's intention—and Red's firm instruction—to deliver the money peaceably. When Tool had expressed surprise that Red was willing to kiss off five hundred grand, Red laughed so hard that a string of snot had shot out of his nose. He told Tool about a James Bond–type gizmo that he'd found at "a Cuban spy shop" in Miami; a transmitter, Red had explained, no bigger'n a pack of Winstons. Tool had tucked it into the Samsonite when he was loading the cash. Meantime, Red was lining up some heavyweight shitkickers to track the suitcase back on the mainland, and to take care of the blackmailer, the mystery girlfriend, whoever else was in on the scam.

But Charles Perrone stole the money first.

Afterward, when Chaz ditched the boat and waded to shore, the Samsonite must have sprung a leak and the transmitter shorted out. Tool had listened to Red pitch a conniption about the money going missing but then the phone rang, the woman named Ricca on the other end saying: "Chaz Perrone's back in Boca, if you're interested."

Red, telling her to wait for him to get there, slamming down the phone and saying to Tool: "Let's get a move on. The dumbass went straight home."

Now the suitcase was stowed safely in the back of the Humvee, along with Charles Perrone, who was headed to the Everglades for the very last time.

"See, it's all workin' out," Red Hammernut said.

Except that Tool still didn't have much appetite for killing Perrone, even though the man had shot him and left him for dead in Stiltsville. It was the strangest sensation. All day long Tool had worried about how to get out of the chore, since Red was coming along to make sure it got done right.

"I sure like this Faith Hill gal," Red was saying. "Know who else? That Shania Twain."

"Yeah, me, too."

"I read where she might be related to the writer fella Twain. The one wrote that famous huckleberry book."

"Is that right?"

" 'Bout this smarty-pants white kid and a big nigra feller and they's on a raft together down some river."

"Okay." Tool assumed that Red Hammernut had been drinking.

"Shania, see, she's like Mark Twain's great-great-great-grand-niece. That's what the article said anyhow."

"Maybe she could do her next video on a raft," said Tool, playing along. "Her and the band."

"Son, that girl could do a video in a Jiffy John and make it look like the Taj Mahal." Red turned to peer in the back of the Hummer. "Hey, our friend finally got quiet."

They'd hog-tied the biologist, hauled him back to LaBelle and stashed him in a refrigerator truck with seventeen hundred pounds of fresh-picked cabbage and celery. Tool had driven himself home to get some clean overalls and irrigate the grassy field where his highway crosses were planted, while Red Hammernut had spent the afternoon entertaining two state senators who'd come up with a promising scheme to subvert the NAFTA treaty and fuck over the tomato grow-ers in Mexico.

Later, when everybody else was gone, Tool and Red had come back to remove Chaz Perrone, blue-lipped and shivering, from the frigid truck. Then, utilizing the latest vegetable-packing technology, they had shrink-wrapped him from head to toe. He was expected to expire from asphyxiation before they arrived at the Loxahatchee National Wildlife Refuge. That was where Red had chosen to get rid of the body, a comfortable distance from Hammernut Farms.

"Guess I'll have to find me another so-called scientist who loves money more'n saw grass and mud fish," Red was saying. "Otherwise Uncle Sam's gonna make me dig some goddamn filtration pond to clean up my water. We're talkin' millions of dollars, not countin' the lawyers and politicians I gotta pay. And they wonder how come the American farmer is a dyin' breed!"

Looking at Red's buffed fingernails and bleached teeth, Tool won-dered when was the last time he'd touched a shovel or a hoe. It was a known fact that Red's late daddy had made a killing off natural gas in Arkansas, and that Red had used his inheritance to buy up row-crop operations all over the Sun Belt.

"Hey, there's the truck," Red said.

Tool braked to a halt next to a dusty Dodge pickup. It had been parked on the levee an hour earlier by one of Red's trusted crew bosses, so that Red and Tool would have transportation out of the Loxahatchee preserve. They intended to abandon the Hummer at the edge of the rim canal, Chaz Perrone's suicide message attached to the dashboard. Red said the note was a bonus, though he wasn't sure what to make of the part about the swan getup.

Dragging their captive out of the Hummer, they were surprised to find that he wasn't dead. With the tenacity of a psychotic gopher, Chaz had gnawed a ragged hole in the shrink wrap, through which he now labored to breathe. It sounded like molasses being sucked down a drainpipe.

"Damnation," Red said. He snatched a Remington twelve-gauge off the backseat and ordered Tool to cut the sumbitch loose.

"You sure?"

"Hell yes."

Tool used a pocket knife to skin off the plastic cocoon. Chaz levered himself to a squat, his clothes sopping and his face flushed.

"Thank you," he wheezed.

Red Hammernut said, "What the hell for? We're still gonna wax your thieving ass."

"Red, I'm so truly sorry about the money."

"I don't doubt it."

"I'll do whatever you want. Just tell me."

The doctor cowered there, shrunken and hollow-eyed, a squalid portrait of guilt. While Tool had no sympathy, neither was he in the mood to watch a man's brains get splattered like oatmeal.

Red said, "It was a setup from day one, right? There wasn't no damn blackmail, just you and some greedy asshole pals."

"That's not true!" Chaz protested.

"I always figured you killed your wife. That much I put together from the get-go," Red said. "But for you to video the whole thing, that's some sick shit. Just to squeeze some cash outta me? Son, you are one evil little bastard."

"Listen, Red. I did *not* kill Joey. She's alive!"

Red glanced over at Tool, who shrugged blankly.

"Hey, then, what you're sayin'—she must be in on this, too."

"Exactly!" Chaz exclaimed. "She's the one behind the blackmail."

"Your dead wife."

"Yes! I found out last night."

Red nodded. "Well, son, you just answered my next question."

"What's that?"

"How low can you go?"

"Aw, Red, I'm telling the God's truth."

"Let's get Mr. O'Toole's opinion."

Tool was watching the sun go down, thinking about the hot, throbbing knot under his arm. "Gimme the shotgun," he said.

Red grinned in relief. "That's my boy."

In the distance, a bull alligator grunted. Tool took the Remington and slotted a shell into the chamber. He told Chaz Perrone to stand up and turn around.

Slowly Red Hammernut backed away, saying, "I believe I'll wait in the truck."

Sure, Tool thought. Wouldn't want no blood on your fancy catalog clothes.

"Get in the water," Tool said to Chaz.

"Tell him I'm not lying about Joey. Please."

"You capped me and swiped the money."

"Yes, I made a horrible mistake. Yes," Chaz said breathlessly.

"You sure did. Now, I'm gone count to five."

"Oh God, don't make me go into that water."

"That's what you did to your girlfriend, right? What's to be scared of?"

Another big gator huffed, somewhere off in a slough.

Mating season, Tool surmised.

Chaz began quivering uncontrollably. He slapped his hands on his thighs and said, "Look at me! Just look!"

It was a sorry damn sight, Tool had to admit. The man was wearing an undershirt, plaid boxers and shiny brown socks—that's how they'd hauled him out of his house. The skeeters were feasting on his soft arms and knobby broomstick legs.

"Want some free advice?" Tool said.

"Okay. Sure." The doctor nodded stiffly.

"Run like hell."

"Where? Out there?" He motioned wildly behind him.

"Yep," Tool said. "Here goes. One . . . two . . . three . . ."

Chaz Perrone lurched down the embankment and crashed into the knee-deep swamp, a setting most unfavorable for an Olympic-style sprint. He fled from the levee in an exaggerated, lead-footed swagger, splashing with crazed desperation through the heavy grass.

Tool's first shot went too far left. His second shot was low, kicking up a small geyser that soaked the droopy rump of Chaz's underpants. The third shot was wide right.

Red Hammernut hopped out of the pickup, bellowing angrily. Tool squinted through one eye, pretending to concentrate.

At the fourth shot, Chaz let out a cry and toppled over.

"Finally," Red declared, only to watch the biologist rise up and resume his sloppy escape, pushing a crooked liquid trail through the saw grass prairie.

Red seized the Remington from Tool and feverishly took aim.

"Hurry," Tool said with a hint of a smile, which Red failed to notice.

"You shut up!"

Red's shot—the last shell in the gun—flew so high off the mark that the buckshot sprinkled down in a loose crescent as harmless as pebbles, well behind the departing target.

"Goddamn." Red jumped off the ground in frustration. "Go get him! Go on!"

Tool laconically declined. "My arm hurts, from where that fucker shot me." Reminding Red of his recent sacrifice in the line of duty.

"But, Christ Almighty, he's gettin' away!"

"Then you go after him, chief," Tool suggested. "Lemme bright the headlights so you can see'm better."

One of the lovesick gators grunted, this time closer.

Red Hammernut did not advance even a millimeter toward the still, dark water.

"Well, *goddamn*," he said, studying the shotgun in his hands as if it had malfunctioned supernaturally. "I'm empty."

"Yup," Tool said.

In a taut and flurried silence the two of them watched Charles Regis Perrone, Ph.D., vanish gradually into the rich copper twilight of the swamp.

Thirty-one

Joey Perrone burrowed into the folds of her brother's sheepskin coat.

"Can't you stay a few more days?"

"Romance and adventure beckon," Corbett Wheeler said. "Besides, my ewes are lost without me."

"I hope you know what you're doing. What if she *does* turn out to be a bimbo?"

"There are worse tragedies, little sister."

Joey let out a cry of mock indignation and tugged Corbett's hat over his eyes. Mick Stranahan carried the luggage to the helicopter, which had nearly given Strom a coronary when it touched down on the island. The pilot re-started the engines and Joey backed away from the din, fighting tears.

Corbett blew a kiss and rakishly twirled his walking stick. Before stepping aboard, he stopped to shake Stranahan's hand. Joey could see the two men talking intently, Mick nodding and appearing to ask questions. He trotted back and stood with her as the chopper lifted off, both of them waving broadly as it thumped away toward the mainland.

"Ricca's meeting him at the airport. She had a quick stop in Boca this morning," Stranahan reported.

"What else?" Joey asked.

"That's it."

"Come on, Mick. What were you guys talking about?"

"Nothing, honest," he insisted. "Your brother just wanted to thank me for taking care of you. He said he knew what a pain in the ass you can be."

She chased him all the way to the dock, where they stripped off each other's clothes and dove in. They were making a third lap around the island when a park ranger's boat surprised them. It was a big SeaCraft with twin Mercs, driven by a muscular Cuban officer in his early forties. As he idled up to the swimmers he broke into a grin.

"Some things never change," he said.

"Hey, Luis."

"Hello, Mick. Hello, pretty lady."

Peeking modestly over Mick's shoulder, Joey gave a minisalute.

"Meet the legendary Luis Cordova," Stranahan said, treading water. "We've known each other since the grand old days of Stiltsville, back when he was a rookie with the marine patrol. Now he's a hotshot storm trooper for the Park Service, spying on innocent skinny dippers."

Luis Cordova laughed as he tossed a rope. "I'm here on official business, you horny old deadbeat."

"Aw, please don't tell me Señor Zedillo kicked the bucket," Stranahan said.

Miguel Zedillo was the Mexican novelist who owned the island. Joey remembered the name from a stack of books on a shelf in Mick's bedroom. He had told her that the writer was in fragile health, and that the island would probably be sold after he died. That's when Joey had piped up and said she'd like to buy it, which had so delighted Mick that he'd immediately made love to her under the picnic table.

"Relax, man," said Luis Cordova. "Far as I know, the old man is still alive and kicking in Tampico. I came out here to ask you about an abandoned boat."

Mick grabbed the rope and Joey clung monkey-style to his back. The ranger pulled them to the transom of the SeaCraft, so that they could rest on the dive platform. Joey was pleased to note that Luis Cordova was a gentleman, strenuously averting his gaze from her bare bottom.

"What boat?" Mick asked.

"Twenty-three-foot rental floated up on the rocks at Cape Florida last night, probably when that weather moved through. No dive gear, no tackle, nobody on board. Just a busted spotlight and some blood spots on the gunwale."

"Human?"

Luis Cordova spread his arms. "That's why I'm here."

"Who did the paperwork trace back to?"

"No paper, Mick," the ranger said. "Rental company says the boat was stolen from the marina before the storm, but I've got a hunch they owed somebody a favor."

"Twenty-three-footer, you said?"

"Blue Bimini top. Yamaha four-stroke."

Stranahan said, "Sorry, Luis. I didn't see any boats."

Joey spoke up. "We stayed indoors all night. The weather was horrible."

"That it was," agreed Luis Cordova, gallantly trying to keep his eyes fixed above her neck. "What's your name, ma'am?"

Joey, who had been covering her breasts with her free arm, let go just long enough to jab Mick in the rib cage. He took the cue.

"She's trying to keep a low profile," he confided to the ranger. "Family problems back home. You know what I mean."

"Did I mention there was a bullet hole in the windshield?"

"No, Luis, you didn't."

"Maybe you folks heard something—like a gunshot?"

"Not with all that hellacious thunder," Stranahan said.

Joey added, "We could barely hear ourselves talk."

Luis Cordova was nodding, but Joey sensed that he wasn't entirely sold.

He said, "Well, I figured it couldn't hurt to ask. Every time there's a bloodstained boat, I think of you first, Mick."

"I'm flattered, but these days I'm living a quiet, normal life."

"Yeah, I can see that," Luis Cordova said dryly. "Sorry to interrupt your afternoon. You want a lift back to the dock?"

"Naw, we'll swim." Stranahan pushed away from the stern, Joey riding his shoulders. "Good seeing you again, man," he called to the ranger.

"Same here, amigo."

"Are you looking for a body?" The question popped out of Joey's mouth before she realized it. Stranahan reached down and pinched her on the butt.

"A body?" Luis Cordova said.

Joey, thinking: How could I be such a ditz!

"What I meant," she said, "was that maybe somebody fell off that boat during the storm."

The ranger told her that nobody had been reported missing. "But don't forget it's Miami," he added. "Sometimes people disappear and nobody ever calls the cops. Anyway, it's a big ocean."

Tell me about it, Joey said to herself.

Swimming toward the house, she couldn't stop wondering about her husband. Had a suitcase crammed with half a million dollars been found on the abandoned boat, Luis Cordova likely would have mentioned it.

And if no suitcase or corpse had turned up, Joey reasoned, the odds were better than even that Chaz Perrone had survived and made off with the cash. It was almost unbearable to contemplate.

"You kept telling me not to worry," she shouted to Mick, who trailed her by ten yards in the water. "Now you happy? The worthless creep got away!"

"Why won't you trust me?" Stranahan called back.

"Because you're a man." Joey blew bubbles as she laughed.

"Fine," he said, "then you owe me two weeks' room and board!"

"Gotta catch me first."

She lowered her head and lengthened her strokes, knifing across the foamy crests of the waves. She could barely hear him shouting, "Hey, Joey, slow down! I love you!"

Geezer, she thought.

Happily she kicked toward the seawall where Strom paced, yapping and wagging his silly stump of a tail.

Red Hammernut licked at the corners of his lips. He'd been spitting and swearing so much that his tongue had gone to chalk. For about the sixth time he proclaimed, "That was the worst job a shootin' I ever saw from a man with two good eyes."

Earl Edward O'Toole kept his two good eyes on the levee road and said nothing. Evidently he was done apologizing.

Red was nearly apopletic about Chaz Perrone's escape. Tool had told him to quit worrying; said the guy was a hopeless pussy who'd never get out of the 'glades alive.

Only what if he does? Red thought.

"That boy can flat-out ruin me," he said somberly.

Tool chuckled. "He ain't gone ruin nobody, chief. He's gone run till he drops."

"You know sumpin' I don't?"

"Just that he's got plenty to be a-scared of," Tool said, "he ever comes out."

"And what if somebody else catches him first? Ever thought about that? Boy's lookin' at Death Row, he'd be tickled to rat out yours truly for a plea bargain."

Tool said, "Don't getcha self all worked up."

On the chance that Chaz might backtrack, they had waited a long time in the darkness on the levee—listening, watching for a shadow to move—until Red could no longer endure the bugs. They left Perrone's Hummer but took the keys, in the event that the sonofabitch was waiting in the weeds nearby. His maudlin suicide note lay prominently displayed on the dashboard—"in case he's polite enough to float up dead," Red had explained.

Now, riding next to Tool in the dusty pickup, Red couldn't stop stewing about all that had happened since the screwball biologist had gotten rid of his wife. It was uncanny how things had unraveled, how swiftly order and reason had spun into mayhem. Red Hammernut was not a complicated or ruminative person; he was a pragmatist and a fixer and a kicker of asses. He didn't believe in fate or karma or the fortuitous alignment of the constellations. If a tide of bad shit was rolling his way, it meant that somebody down the line had fucked up.

Normally Red Hammernut had no difficulty identifying the source of the problem and fixing it—a payoff, a beating or a plane ticket usually did the trick—but the Perrone situation was unlike any he'd ever come up against. All of Red's clout and political connections would be useless if Chaz resurfaced and started blabbing about the Everglades scam. Red now regretted destroying the two videotapes of Joey Perrone's murder, which in retrospect would have been useful in turning the tables on Chaz.

That back-stabbing lowlife.

Oh well, Red thought, at least I got my money back.

The Samsonite was sliding noisily around the bed of the pickup as they jounced along the berm, heading out of the Loxahatchee preserve.

"Why you goin' so damn slow?" he griped at Tool.

"Because I gotta keep the headlights off."

"And why exactly do you gotta do that?"

" 'Cause they's park rangers and game wardens out here," Tool explained. "It ain't like back home, Red. This is a federal deal."

"They can kiss my ass, them feds."

"Plus your boy only left us 'bout a quarter tank of gas."

"Well, that figgers."

By choice Red Hammernut hadn't spent much time in what little remained of the original, untouched Everglades. He preferred the parts that had been drained, plowed or paved—such as the vegetable fields he patrolled by Cadillac or helicopter; flat and orderly rectangles, neatly delineated by ditches and shorn of unruly tree cover. Sometimes you might run across a feral pig or a stray coon, but wildlife was generally sparse on the farm.

Red was not afraid of the wilderness but he wasn't truly comfortable there, especially at night; especially with a shotgun that was empty.

"Those fuckin' feds," he said contemptuously, "and the state of Florida, too, they're gonna bust my hump about dumpin' shit in this water. You wait and see, son. A damn travesty is what it is!"

"Yessir," said Tool, with not as much empathy as his boss would have liked.

"Take them bull gators we heard tearin' it up out there tonight," Red went on. "They been around—what, a hundred trillion years? You think a little fertilizer's gonna bother 'em? Fungicides? Pesticides? Hell, those badass fuckers could eat their weight in DDT and not get sick enough to fart. They're *dinosaurs*, for Christ's sake. They don't need the damn U.S. guv'ment to watch out for 'em."

Tool fixed his gaze straight ahead. "But didn't all the other dinosaurs get extincted?"

"What?" Red Hammernut couldn't believe what he was hearing. "Son, whose side are you on? I don't know what the hell happened to the other damn dinosaurs, and who gives two shits anyhow?"

Tool said, "I shot me a li'l gator just the other day. Wasn't but a four-footer, but still."

"Still *what*?"

Red simmered all the way out of Loxahatchee. He started feeling better only when the truck finally hit dry pavement and he could see the sodium lights of Palm Beach County glowing to the east. "We're gonna put a chopper up first thing tomorrow," he announced coolly. "I ain't worried. We'll track down that gutless bastard."

"If the dinosaurs don't get him first," said Tool, stone-faced.

"Son, you tryin' to bust my balls? Because I ain't in the mood, case you didn't notice."

"Yessir."

"Know what *you* could do tomorrow, Mr. O'Toole? You could take that twelve-gauge out to the range for target practice, so that maybe next time you'll be able to hit the side of a motherfuckin' barn."

Tool accepted the insult impassively, a silence that Red Hammernut misread as submission. He failed entirely to perceive the flimsiness of Tool's loyalty, or to sense the anger that had begun to simmer in the man's simple thinking.

"It's all 'cause of you he escaped!" Red fumed. "It's your damn fault and nobody else's!"

Tool gave a half shrug. "Try shootin' a shotgun with a slug in your armpit."

"Goddammit, just drive. Just get me home."

Closing his eyes, Red thought of the steaming Jacuzzi that awaited. He couldn't wait to scrub the sweat and sunscreen and dead bugs off his skin; sit down to a sixteen-ounce T-bone and a bottle of Jack Daniel's. He was jolted from this reverie when Tool braked the pickup to an abrupt halt on the grassy shoulder of the highway.

Red looked around. "Now what? We blow a tire?"

"Sit tight." Tool pushed himself out of the truck.

"Hey! Get back here," Red hollered. He hopped out and chased after him. "Where the hell you think you're goin'? I ain't got time tonight for this nonsense!"

Tool did not alter his pace. Red got up beside him and began calling him every name he could think of.

"You hush," Tool said, raising a brick-size hand. He stooped to study the small white cross, and removed a spray of shriveled lilies.

"Not now, son. You come back some other day and fetch it, but not tonight," Red admonished him. "Not on my time."

"It'll just take a second."

"You gone deaf? Deaf *and* dumb?"

The name on the homemade cross was visible in the wash from the truck's headlights:

Pablo Humberto Duarte
Loving Husband, Father, Son, and Brother
B. Sept. 3, 1959. D. March 21, 2003
Now He Rides with God Almighty
Remember: Seat Belts Save Lives!

"Just some damn beaner," Red Hammernut grumped. "Probably got trashed and drove hisself into the canal."

"You don't know that," said Tool.

"Just lookit the name. Pah-blow Humm-bear-toe—tell me that ain't a beaner name."

Tool sat on his haunches, elbows propped on his knees.

"Well, hurry it up, then," Red said crossly. "Pull the damn thing outta the ground and let's go. I need a drink and a steam."

Tool didn't budge. Red glowered at him.

"What the fuck, son?"

"I just been workin' the 'rithmetic in my head. This old boy was 'bout the same age as me," Tool said, "give or take."

"The beaner?"

"Mr. Doo-arty here. However you say it."

"Mercy." Red thinking: Lord, please don't let this moron go soft on me.

Tool gestured at the wooden cross. "Least he was a 'husband, father, son, brother'—I ain't *none* a those things, Red. I got no wife and no family . . . one lousy cousin, he's up at Starke for robbin' a goddamn laundry-mat."

That was the end of Red Hammernut's patience. In his judgment there was no good reason for a man of his stature to be standing on the side of State Road 441 on a Saturday night while some hairy half-wit with a bullet up his butt cheeks suddenly gets a middle-life crisis, all because some dead Meskin forgot to buckle his damn seat belt.

Without a thought, Red slapped Earl Edward O'Toole across the top of the head. It was a poor decision, conveying what Tool regarded as an intolerable lack of respect.

"Listen here, you doped-up dickhead of a gorilla," Red said. "There's half a million bucks of my money sittin' like a big hot buzzard turd in the back of that pickup, out in the wide-open spaces, where any damn crackhead in basketball shoes can rip it off and be gone in five seconds. Now, I don't honestly know what's got into you, son, but I'm gonna count to ten and you're gonna yank that stupid fuckin' cross outta the ground and we're gonna get the hell outta Dodge. You understand me?"

Tool didn't move, even to wipe Red's spittle off his overalls.

"One . . ." Red huffed, "two . . . three . . . four . . ."

He had no earthly notion of what to do if the sulking fool refused to obey. Slap him again?

To Red's immeasurable relief, Tool rose slowly and said, "You the boss."

He placed his huge hands around the shaft of the white cross and worked it slowly out of the dirt, so as not to split the pine.

Red said, "It's about damn time. Now hurry up, let's go."

"Not you, chief."

"What?" It was amazing, Red mused, how all the nuts and bolts of one's existence could rattle loose with one bump. "What did you say?" he demanded again, somewhat heedlessly.

Earl Edward O'Toole positioned himself between Red and the truck, his broad frame blocking the headlights. Red felt small and, for the first time, fearful. He was chilled by the sound of Tool's breathing, slow and easy compared to his own.

With a desolate curiosity Red peered upward at the towering shadow. "What now, you dumb ape?"

"Hold still," Tool advised.

Samuel Johnson Hammernut could see the huge man raise both arms high, and for a moment he could see the cross of Pablo Duarte silhouetted against the pearly clouds, and after that he couldn't see anything at all.

The murder of the Everglades, as perpetrated by Red Hammernut and others, is insidiously subtle and undramatic. Unlike more telegenic forms of pollution, the fertilizers pouring by the ton from the sugarcane fields and vegetable farms of southern Florida do not produce stinking tides of dead fish or gruesome panoramas of rotting animal corpses. Instead, the phosphates and other agricultural contaminants work invisibly to destroy a mat of algae known as periphyton, the slimy brown muck that underlies the river of grass and is its most essential nutrient. As the periphyton begins to die, the small fish that feed and nest there move away. Next to go are the egrets and herons, the bluegills and largemouth bass, and so on up the food chain. Soon the saw grass prairies wither and starve, replaced by waves of cattails and other aquatic plants that thrive on the torrent of phosphorus, yet provide miserable habitat for native birds and wildlife.

A primary objective of the government's Everglades restoration project was to reduce the steady deluge of man-made fertilizers. Grudging cooperation came from sugar barons and corporate farmers who could no longer rely on favored politicians to keep the EPA and other regulators off their backs. And while filtration marshes designed to strain out some of the pollutants had shown early promise, the Everglades was still dying at the rate of two acres per day when Charles Regis Perrone made his lonely, woeful trek through Loxahatchee.

He cursed the pungent mire that sucked the socks off his feet, the whips of saw grass that shredded his undershirt and boxers, the clots of lilies and leafy bladderwort that impeded his flight. The sprouts of newly blossomed cattails announced the presence of fertilizer in the water, but that wasn't the source of Chaz's trepidation. He knew that phosphorus was not toxic in the nasty bacterial style of, say, fecal sewage. He also understood that the lower levels recorded at Loxahatchee were more hospitable to native life than the felonious amounts found in the waters contiguous to Red Hammernut's fields.

Still, Chaz Perrone crossed the breeze-swept marsh with a puckering fear that he was being stalked—by Red and his shotgun-toting goon; by voracious disease-bearing insects; by needle-fanged cottonmouth moccasins, blood-slurping leeches and deer ticks; by hydrophobic bobcats and inbred panthers; by the gators whose husky mating calls fractured the brittle silence. . . .

Chaz saw no irony in his own plight, having always regarded himself as more of a bystander than a villain in the poisoning of the wilderness. Blaming the demise of the Everglades on science whores such as himself seemed as silly to Chaz as blaming lung cancer on the medical doctors employed by tobacco companies, who for generations had insisted that cigarettes were harmless. The truth was that people were determined to smoke, regardless of what any pinhead researchers had to say. Likewise, cities and farms were bound to dispose of their liquefied crap in the cheapest, most efficient way—flushing it into public waters—regardless of the environmental hazards.

You can't buck human nature, Chaz had reasoned, so you might as well go with the flow, so to speak.

After taking the job as Red Hammernut's undercover biostitute, he had familiarized himself with Everglades ecology only enough to converse with colleagues and not reveal himself as an ignorant fraud. From his crash course he recalled that the ripe muck through which he now trudged was important in some nebulous way to the ecology, and that the other scientists jokingly referred to it as "monkey puke"—a description for which Chaz held newfound appreciation.

He abhorred getting wet even in benign settings, refusing even to tiptoe into country-club shallows to retrieve an errant golf ball. The idea of slogging buck naked and unarmed through a dark bog was so mortifying to Chaz that he couldn't dwell on it without risking a breakdown. The sky had begun to clear, and enough starlight was being cast upon the water that he could finally make shapes out of shadows. He was especially attentive to those that even vaguely resembled alligators, whose abundance was being confirmed by full-throated rumbles near and far. Chaz remembered from basic herpetology that such territorial outbursts were sexual in origin, and he wondered whether he was in greater danger of being devoured, or defiled. He was aware that most snakes had two operative penises—a topic of high mirth in undergraduate biology—but he could not recall if crocodilians were similarly endowed. It wasn't long before his recurring nightmare of being eaten by a two-headed gator had been supplanted by a vision even more harrowing.

In the distance loomed a tree island, an oasis of higher ground in the midst of the watery savanna. Chaz splashed ahead at a savage pace, adrenalized with dread at the prospect of being double-boned by a randy five-hundred-pound lizard. The saw grass sliced him mercilessly as he advanced, but he remained driven and unbowed. It was only when he reached the bushy hump of dry land and sagged against a bay tree that Chaz paused to contemplate the full measure of his misery.

His muscles were cramping from fatigue and dehydration.

His back stung hotly from a freckling of buckshot.

His arms and torso were striped bloody from the grass blades.

His face was covered by a humming shroud of mosquitoes.

His crotch and thighs itched mysteriously.

And that was only the physical torment. Emotional pain assailed Chaz Perrone, as well.

The $13 million inheritance he'd dreamed of receiving had turned out to be a sadistic hoax.

The wife he had tried to kill was still alive, and on her way to the police.

The girlfriend he'd shot with similar intent had survived, and set him up for an abduction.

The man with whom he'd so profitably conspired had turned on him, and ordered him put down like a lame horse.

And now Chaz found himself filthy wet and abjectly naked, lost and defenseless in a place that he loathed more than any other.

Do I deserve this? he wondered. Really?

He ran a forefinger along one of his shins, skimming off the muck like chocolate icing. Holding it to his nose, he detected no noxious or rancid odor. Even if this gunk is loaded with fertilizers, so what? Chaz thought. It's just mud, for God's sake. It's not like I was clubbing baby harp seals.

A sliver of moon spread a pale bluish light across the savanna. Something rustled heavily, out of sight. Chaz Perrone drew his knees to his chest and silently groped for a rock. Another alligator boomed from a nearby pond.

Who . . . do . . . you love?

Yeah, who . . . do . . . you love?

Thirty-two

Maureen smiled fondly when she saw Tool hobble out of the barn. He opened the door of the truck and arranged himself behind the steering wheel.

"Well?" She held out one hand.

He dropped two misshapen kernels of lead into her palm. "The rusty one is what come outta you-know-where," he said. "The shiny one's from under my arm."

After examining the slugs, Maureen said, "I'm proud of you, Earl. That must've stung like the dickens."

He said the pain wasn't so bad. "Guy's a real pro."

"His specialty being . . . cattle?"

"Livestock in general." Tool had explained to Maureen that a medical doctor would be required by law to notify authorities if a patient turned up with a gunshot wound. A veterinarian had no such obligation.

"The important thing is, you're finally free of the burden," Maureen told him. "No more needless suffering."

"Yeah. Now it's your turn."

"I'm doing all right, Earl."

"Tell the truth," he said.

"The truth is, I'm absolutely elated to be outdoors in the fresh air."

"Wait'll we get clear of this pasture."

"No, it's all glorious," said Maureen, "even the cow poop. Thank you, Earl."

"For what?"

"My freedom. Being my Sir Galahad. Rescuing me from Elysian Manor!"

She tugged him closer and bussed his cheek.

"That's enough a that." Tool felt himself redden.

Nobody had uttered a word of objection when he carried Maureen out of the convalescent home. Nobody had dared to get in his way.

She'd already been awake for hours, sitting upright in bed, waiting with her handbag on her lap.

Pulled the intravenous tube from her arm and got herself to the bathroom. Ditched the hospital gown in favor of a light cotton shift, periwinkle blue. Fixed her hair, put on some lipstick, brushed a little color into her face. Dashed off a note to each of her daughters, telling them not to worry.

At breakfast time the nurse from hell had stalked in, eyeing Maureen as if she were a nutcase; humoring her, telling her how cute and pretty she looked, fluffing her pillows, all the time trying to con her into lying still so they could jab her with another needle.

But Maureen had resisted fiercely, forcing the nurse to call for backup. Eventually two lumpish, pimply orderlies had shown up; the lumpier of the two seizing Maureen's arms while the other attempted to pin her legs—the nurse hovering with a gangrenous smirk; uncapping a loaded syringe and lining up her shot.

That's when Tool had appeared, shiny with sweat, a mammoth miasmal presence blocking the doorway. His work boots were crusty and the overalls hung crookedly off his shoulders, exposing a crude mummy wrap of soiled tape. His arms and neck were damply matted, jet-black curls that at a distance could have been mistaken for an ornate body tattoo.

"Git away from her," he'd said without a flicker of emotion.

Instantly the orderlies had released Maureen and stepped away. "It's all right, Polly," she'd told the quaking nurse. "He's my nephew, from the Netherlands. The one I told you about."

Tool had stomped in and gathered Maureen from the bed, carrying her out of the room, down the hall, past the front desk, through the double doors and into the circular driveway, where he had parked the apple-red F-150 supercab pickup, purchased the day before with $33,641 cash.

Leaving, by Tool's arduous calculation, more than $465,000 in the Samsonite.

With plenty of room for the thirty-one fentanyl patches he had burglarized from a discount pharmacy in Boynton Beach—the medicine meant for Maureen, not for himself.

"It's a beauty!" she'd exclaimed upon seeing the new truck. "But I may need a stepladder."

"Naw," Tool had said, and lifted her royally into the passenger seat.

The pickup had leather-trimmed captain's chairs, loads of legroom, a crackerjack air conditioning system and a cargo bed deep enough to accommodate Tool's entire crop of highway crosses, which he had carefully uprooted one at a time from behind his trailer. The task had taken most of the night.

Appalled by the ratty condition of his bandages, Maureen had insisted that Tool seek out a doctor. For miles she'd begged, until he reluctantly had pulled off the turnpike near Kissimmee and made his way to the cattle ranch on the river. His veterinarian pal had agreed, at Maureen's urging, to extract both of the bullets.

"Soon you'll feel like a new man," Maureen proclaimed, dropping the slugs into her handbag. "Did he give you something for pain?"

"Whatever they use on bulls," Tool said. Truth was, he felt pretty darn fine. "So, where you wanna go?"

"Earl, may I ask a personal question?"

"Sure." They were bouncing along a narrow dirt track, heading off the ranch. Tool turned down the radio, some sappy song about loneliness and heartbreak on the road.

"Now, it's none of my business," Maureen said, "but I'm curious how you can afford a chariot like this on a bodyguard's income."

Tool thought about his answer while he took a long draw of lukewarm Mountain Dew. "Well, you gotta unnerstand," he said, "some cases pay better'n others."

"This turned out to be a good one, then?"

"I'd have to say yeah, all things considered," he said. "So, now it's my turn for askin' a question, 'kay?"

"Fair enough."

"What's your all-time fantasy vacation?"

"You mean, if we could go anywhere in the world?"

"That's what I'm tryin' to tell you," Tool said. "We *can* go anywheres. You just name the place."

Maureen gazed out the window. Her hair seemed thinner and grayer in the direct sunlight, though her eyes were as blue and bright as the sea. Tool could easily picture her as a young woman, not from her features so much as from her open, untroubled expression.

She said, "It's still springtime, isn't it?"

"April, yes, ma'am. Goin' on May."

"I was thinking of those pelicans. They'll be heading north, I suppose."

"All the way to Canada is what it said on that TV show."

"Yes, to Canada. I remember," Maureen said. "Isn't that just remarkable?"

"Must be one helluva thing, thousands a huge white birds comin' down from the sky all together. Flyin' home," Tool said. "I'd sure like to see that operation."

"Me, too, Earl."

"It's a mighty long haul. Sure you're up for it?"

She leaned across and boxed him on the ear. "Don't worry about me, buster. You just drive."

"Yes, ma'am." Tool was beaming as he reached for the radio. "How 'bout some music?"

Karl Rolvaag had a dream that he was being strangled very slowly with a pale silken noose. He woke up clutching at his throat and discovered it snugly enwrapped by a sinewy albino tail. After a few interesting moments the detective managed to extricate himself and turn on the lamp. He trailed the departing length of python across the sheets, beneath the bed and into a ragged hole in the box spring. When Rolvaag cut the ticking away, he found not one but both of his absent companions, balled together in platonic contentment. Upon inspection neither of them manifested any doggy- or kitty-size lumps. To the contrary, the snakes appeared taut and hungry.

Rolvaag was relieved, though not entirely surprised, as the pets missing from Sawgrass Grove had earlier turned up unharmed. Pinchot, the geriatric Pomeranian, had been located at the county pound, where it had been quarantined after nipping a slow-footed Jehovah's Witness. Pandora, the lost Siamese, had been ransomed back to the Mankiewicz family by neighborhood hooligans in exchange for a case of malt liquor.

The detective felt vindicated, but one piece of unfinished business remained. He removed the muscular animals from their box-spring hideaway and draped them carefully over his shoulders; a colorful, though hefty, adornment. He crossed the hallway to Mrs. Shulman's apartment and knocked three times. It was a blessing that she was too short for her security peephole, for otherwise she never would have opened the door.

"Nellie, you owe us an apology," Rolvaag said.

Mrs. Shulman shrank away in revulsion. "You degenerate monster! Get away from me with those slimy things!"

"Not until you say you're sorry."

"The only thing I'm sorry about is not getting you into court, you twisted freak. Now go!"

By now the pythons had taken notice of little Petunia, hopping madly at Mrs. Shulman's slippered feet. The reptiles raised their milky heads and feathered their rosy tongues, tasting the air. Rolvaag could feel their coils tightening in expectation.

"Easy, fellas," he whispered.

Nellie Shulman's pinched, mean eyes widened to fearful bulges when she saw the snakes begin to twitch.

"You sick perverted bastard!" she cried, and slammed the door.

When the detective returned to his apartment, the phone was ringing. He let the machine pick up.

"Karl, get your ass in here pronto." It was Captain Gallo. "We're going on a helicopter ride. There's another situation."

"What a surprise," Rolvaag murmured to himself.

In a way he felt sorry for his boss, who was a smart cop but sometimes oblivious to the laws of the jungle. Gallo had been genuinely flabbergasted only the day before, when the sheriff had called to report that the body of Samuel Johnson Hammernut had been discovered along Route 441 in western Palm Beach County.

It was a most unnatural death, Mr. Hammernut having been fatally impaled on a roadside cross bearing the name of Pablo Humberto Duarte, a prominent podiatrist who had died in a car crash at that location. One rainy evening, Duarte's Mini Cooper had been creamed by a hit-and-run driver who was never apprehended. And while the seat-belt reminder stenciled on the memorial marker was a commendable gesture, no mere safety harness would have saved the doctor's life, the Mini Cooper having been reduced on impact to the approximate size of a bagel toaster.

Because of the ritualistic appearance of the Hammernut homicide, Palm Beach detectives were sniffing for a connection between the farm tycoon and the podiatrist. One theory: Duarte's family had somehow identified Hammernut as the fugitive hit-and-run driver, setting the stage for a macabre act of vengeance.

Rolvaag had gotten a chuckle out of that one. Gallo had not. It made him nervous that a wealthy and influential citizen interviewed by one of his detectives had turned up murdered ten days later.

"Look on the bright side," Rolvaag had told him. "It's out of our jurisdiction."

The captain's mood had failed to improve overnight. When Rolvaag arrived at headquarters, Gallo pulled him into his office and shut the door.

"We're flying out to the Everglades," he said momentously.

"Okay."

"You aren't going to ask why?"

"I can probably guess," the detective said.

Looking uncharacteristically harried, Gallo gnawed rather savagely on his lower lip.

He said, "Karl, I need some friendly guidance here."

"What do you want to know?"

"That's my question: What do I want to know?" The captain tried to wink, but it came off as a tic. "If you were me, Karl, in my position, would you really want to dive into this Perrone mess? Give it some thought, okay?"

As they waited to board the helicopter, Gallo asked Rolvaag what he was carrying. It was a large Rubbermaid container with air holes punched in the lid.

"My snakes," Rolvaag said. He had not come to his decision lightly.

Gallo looked appalled. "Are you fucking serious? What if the damn things get loose?"

"Just don't tell the pilot."

Rolvaag enjoyed the flight, which took them over Fort Lauderdale and across the western suburbs, then north along the Sawgrass Expressway into Palm Beach County. It was boggling to realize that an elevated ribbon of dirt was essentially all that separated 5 million raucous, distracted human beings from the prehistoric solitude of the

Everglades. The detective regretted that during his hitch in South Florida he hadn't spent more time on the other side of the levee; the sane and peaceful side.

"The Palm Beach S.O. invited us out of courtesy," Gallo was explaining, still eyeing the box of pythons. "Whatever they feel like sharing is up to them. It's their case."

"Thank goodness," Rolvaag said.

Against the tans and greens of the savanna, Charles Perrone's Humvee appeared first as a metallic twinkle and then as a bright yellow beacon. As the helicopter drew closer, Rolvaag could make out a couple of squad cars parked on the dike, along with a four-wheel drive that he assumed belonged to the feds. A Loxahatchee park ranger had been first on the scene.

As soon as they landed, Rolvaag and Gallo were greeted by a young Palm Beach sheriff's detective named Ogden. He showed them the suicide note that had been found in the Hummer.

" 'Swan costume'?" Gallo flicked at the paper. "What the fuck is *that* all about?"

Ogden shrugged.

"Did you find a body?" Rolvaag asked.

"Not yet. We're still looking," Ogden said.

The search airboat could be heard roaring in zigzags through the tall grass. Rolvaag would not have been surprised if the remains of Joey Perrone's husband were recovered, but he would have been astonished if the death turned out to be a true suicide.

Ogden said, "I understand you interviewed the subject several times after his wife's accident. Did he seem depressed enough to do something like this?"

"Actually, he didn't seem depressed at all," Rolvaag said. "He seemed like an insensitive jerk."

Gallo felt professionally obliged to elaborate. "Karl had some theories about Mr. Perrone's possible involvement in his wife's disappearance. Nothing ever panned out."

"Unfortunately," said Rolvaag, thinking: Try to make a murder case in two lousy weeks with no corpse.

"When's the last time you saw him?" Ogden asked.

"A few days ago, at a church service for Mrs. Perrone."

"Was he upset?"

"Not particularly. He was hitting on his wife's best friend."

"Nice guy," Ogden said.

"A real prince. Good luck," Rolvaag told him.

"What's in the box?"

"You don't want to know."

Rolvaag picked up the heavy Rubbermaid tub and trekked down the levee. Once safely out of view, he angled down the embankment and set the container on the ground. It wasn't an ideal solution, Rolvaag knew. As an imported species the pythons didn't belong in Florida but, unfortunately, their native India did not figure in the detective's immediate travel plans. At least here the snakes would be warm and relatively safe, as they were too large and powerful to be bothered by hawks, raccoons or otters. Rolvaag was more worried about the dangers from pesticides and other chemicals, recalling the grossly deformed baby snake that he'd found at Hammernut Farms. All he could do was pray that the water here in Loxahatchee was cleaner.

He popped the lid off the plastic box and waited for the pythons to stir in the sunlight. First one and then the other tentatively rose and poked a blunt nose over the rim. Rolvaag marveled as he often did at their sinuous grace. They were the purest of predators, alluring yet devoid of emotion; a brain stem with a tail.

"So long, guys. Do your best," Rolvaag said.

Trudging back toward the police cars, he couldn't help but observe that the vivid hue of Chaz Perrone's Hummer matched almost exactly that of the crime-scene tape surrounding it. It was Rolvaag's belief that Red Hammernut had eliminated Perrone out of fear that the biologist might reveal their corrupt covenant. Another possibility was that Chaz foolishly had tried to shake the farmer down for more money. Regarding the grisly fate of Mr. Hammernut himself, Rolvaag surmised that he had succumbed during some sort of disagreement with Earl Edward O'Toole. The hired brute collected highway crosses just like the one upon which the tycoon farmer was kabobed.

Under ordinary circumstances Rolvaag would have shared all he knew and suspected with young Detective Ogden. Not today, though, for Rolvaag was impatient to get home and pack. Anyway, what would be accomplished by bringing the kid up to speed? His boss probably wouldn't give him enough time to put a dent in the case.

Later, as Ogden walked them to the helicopter, he said, "We'll call you when we find the body."

"If he's wearing a swan suit," said Gallo, "I want to see a picture."

On the chopper ride back to Fort Lauderdale, Gallo hunched close and growled, "I need an answer, Karl. Right now."

"All right. Here it is," Rolvaag said. "If I were you, I definitely would *not* want to know what I know."

Gallo looked relieved, then wary. "You're not just saying that because you think I'm too dense to sort it out?"

"Of course not."

"You believe Perrone is dead?"

"You betcha," the detective said.

"But what if you're wrong?"

"Then I'll fly back for the trial."

"What trial, goddammit? The only witness was the victim."

Rolvaag touched a finger to his lips. "You don't want to know. Remember?"

Gallo lowered his voice. "You couldn't have picked a worse fucking time to bail out on me," he said, "or a worse case."

"It's just about over. Trust me on this."

"*Trust* you? Karl, I can't even *follow* you."

When they got back to the office, Rolvaag noticed that the place was as hushed as an art gallery. All the male detectives were pretending to study case files while they ogled Rose Jewell, who was sitting at Rolvaag's desk and reading a book. She wore pearl-colored heels, a sleeveless white top and a navy skirt so short that she could have caught the croup.

When she looked up and saw Rolvaag, she snapped the book shut and said, "I'm not connecting with Emma Bovary. Sorry, but it's just not happening."

Rose's Broadway-blond hair was accented with a pair of black goggle-sized sunglasses that she'd propped at a saucy angle on her head. "Buy me a cup of coffee," she said to Rolvaag.

"You don't drink coffee," he reminded her.

"It's a figure of speech," she said with a chiding laugh. "It means I want to talk with you alone."

Captain Gallo stepped between them and extended a meaty paw. "I don't think we've been introduced," he said.

"And why should we be? You're married, sweetie." Rose pointed helpfully at Gallo's wedding band. Then she turned to Rolvaag and said, "Are you coming?"

He followed her down the hall to a bank of vending machines. There he bought her a diet soda, which she sipped from the can.

"I noticed all the boxes on your desk," she said. "You going somewhere?"

"Yes. I took a job with a police department in Minnesota."

"Minnesota? But what about Joey?"

"The case is more or less over," Rolvaag said.

"Is that the same as closed?" Rose asked skeptically.

"Not exactly. Just over."

He told her about Chaz Perrone's Humvee turning up at Loxahatchee, and about the suicide note. He related only what he knew as facts, and not his strong suspicions.

Rose leaned against the soda machine and said, "Oh God. There's something I've got to confess."

The detective felt a stab of heartburn. "Please don't tell me you killed him. I already rented the U-Haul."

"For God's sake, no, I didn't kill him," she said. "But I did invite him to my place after the memorial . . . and then I doped his drink." She smiled sheepishly. "I was trying to get him to admit he pushed Joey overboard."

"Did he fess up?"

"No comment," said Rose. "Do I need a lawyer?"

"Not unless Mr. Perrone files charges, and I would say that's a long shot."

She handed Rolvaag the half-empty soda pop, which he tossed in the garbage.

"My mom lives in Minnetonka," she said.

"No kidding? The job I'm taking is in Edina."

"Nice town." Rose clucked approvingly. "I saw you at Joey's service, sitting way in the back of the church, but I didn't know whether it was cool to say hi or not."

"You gave a good eulogy," Rolvaag said. "I'm sure Mrs. Perrone would have liked it."

"I haven't given up on that girl, you know. Weirder things have happened."

"I haven't given up, either," said Rolvaag. He wanted to tell her more, but he couldn't.

She said, "I try to go up and see Mom once or twice a year."

"It's nice in the spring," Rolvaag heard himself say.

"Maybe I'll call you next time I'm there," Rose said. "There's not a whole lot happening in Edina, crime-wise. I'll bet you could spare a whole hour for lunch."

"Oh, at least," said the detective.

As she walked out of the office Rose Jewell never once glanced back, which spared Rolvaag the embarrassment of being caught staring. It was one of the most splendid exits he had ever witnessed. After a moment's recovery he returned to his desk and resumed boxing the files. He checked his voice mail but did not find the message he was expecting. It was possible that he was dead wrong about what had happened; possible, he thought, but not likely.

Rolvaag made sure that the rest of the day passed slowly, to give his telephone time to ring. It didn't. Then, shortly before five, he was approached by a well-set middle-aged man with a deep-water tan. The man introduced himself and presented a faded ID from the Dade State Attorney's Office, where many years ago he had worked as an investigator.

"How can I help you, Mr. Stranahan?" Rolvaag asked.

"Let's go eat."

"As you can see, I'm pretty busy. It's my last week on the job."

Stranahan said, "This concerns a man named Charles Perrone."

Rolvaag reached for his coat. "There's a new place on Las Olas. The burgers aren't bad."

"Mind if I bring a friend?"

The detective found one last notebook in the bottom drawer of his desk. "Fine with me," he said.

The green Suburban was parked three blocks away, in the public lot. At the sight of it, Rolvaag suppressed a grin. He got in the backseat and rolled down the window to feel the sun on his face. They ended up ordering takeout and carrying it to a picnic table on the beach.

Mrs. Perrone was even lovelier than in her photographs. Mick Stranahan let her do most of the talking. When she was finished, Rolvaag said, "Tell me again the last thing you remember."

"Falling," she said. "No, diving."

"And before that?"

"My husband throwing me over the rail."

"And afterward?"

"I woke up at Mick's and it was all a blank," Joey Perrone said. "Until yesterday."

"Then it came back to you all at once? Or in bits and pieces?"

Stranahan spoke up. "Pieces. For a while she didn't even know her name."

Rolvaag put down his notebook and went to work on his french fries.

"They found a floating bale of marijuana that had the tips of your fingernails stuck in it," he said to Mrs. Perrone. "I was wondering how long you'd hung on."

Pensively she glanced at her hands and flexed her fingers, as if trying to muscle up the memory.

"She hung on all night," Mick Stranahan said. "That's how I found her."

Although Joey Perrone appeared vigorous and fit, Rolvaag was nonetheless impressed. Few grown men he knew would have survived such a fall, followed by eight hours in the cold chop of the ocean.

"Where's this island exactly?" he asked.

Stranahan told him.

"But you've got a boat, right? Why didn't you take Mrs. Perrone to a hospital after you found her?" the detective said.

"Because she was in no condition to be moved. It's a small skiff, and a nasty ride when it's rough."

"You don't have a phone or a VHF radio on your island?"

"Just a cellular, and the battery was dead."

"No charger?"

"Broken," said Stranahan. "Same with the VHF."

"So, for the last two weeks—"

"Mick's been taking care of me," Joey Perrone said.

With a straw, Rolvaag swirled the ice in his jumbo Sprite. He said, "You've had quite a go of it." That much of their story he believed.

Mrs. Perrone picked distractedly at a Greek salad. "I know it's just my word against his, but I want to prosecute Chaz for attempted murder. I want to take him to trial."

"That may not be possible," Rolvaag said. "Your husband is missing in the Everglades. There was a suicide note in his vehicle."

Joey Perrone seemed more shocked than Mick Stranahan, who asked if the note looked authentic.

"I think there's a strong possibility that Mr. Perrone is gone for good," the detective replied.

Mrs. Perrone put down her fork and turned away, looking toward the ocean. Stranahan moved closer and laid a hand on her back.

"Damn," she said softly.

"You all right?" Rolvaag asked.

She nodded and stood up. "I want to take a walk."

When they were alone, Stranahan asked the detective where he was moving.

"Home to Minnesota," Rolvaag said. "I figure it's best to get out of here now, while I still remember what 'normal' is."

"Good luck," said Stranahan.

"Just yesterday was one of those only-in-Florida moments. They called me out to see some dead guy by the side of the road. You know these white crosses people put up at fatal accident scenes? He had one sticking in the middle of his gut."

Stranahan took a bite of cheeseburger. "Was he a tourist? Because that's when you hear from the governor, when tourists start getting whacked."

"Nope, he owned a big farming outfit up near Lake Okeechobee. Coincidentally, he was an associate of Mrs. Perrone's husband," the detective said. "Samuel Hammernut was his name."

Stranahan displayed no curiosity whatsoever. When a seagull landed on the corner of the table, he tossed a french fry at its feet.

Rolvaag said, "They held a memorial service for Mrs. Perrone last Thursday and, I swear, there was a guy at the church who looked a lot like you."

"No kidding?" Stranahan offered a soggy slice of pickle to the gull, which mangled it greedily. "The island is lousy with these things," he remarked. "Rats with wings."

"All those years working for the state," Rolvaag said, "did you ever get a case that wrapped itself up in a nice neat package, and all you could do was sit back and watch? Where all the bad guys just canceled each other out and saved everybody the hassle of a trial?"

"A rare treat," Stranahan said.

"Well, this is my first." Rolvaag picked up his notebook and sailed it into a litter basket, spooking the bird. "I figure it's a good note to leave Florida on. What do you think, Mr. Stranahan?"

"I think timing is everything, Karl."

The two men stopped talking when they spotted Joey returning along the beach. She had put on her sunglasses and taken off her shoes and pulled the tie from her ponytail. A big striped ball rolled into her path and, without breaking stride, she gently kicked it back to a small blond boy, who skipped away laughing. Every now and then she would stop to watch the waves froth around her legs, or to pick up a seashell.

The burly unkempt stranger who came shouldering out of the saw grass carried no weapon. Chaz Perrone heaved the rock, which splashed in front of the stranger, and screamed, "Stay the fuck away from me, old man!"

The intruder's grin was alarming in its perfection. From his deportment, Chaz initially had pegged him as a homeless wino, but winos typically did not make a priority of dental hygiene.

"Don't get any closer," Chaz warned. He snatched another rock off the ground and cocked his arm.

The grizzled intruder kept coming. When he was ten yards away, Chaz let loose. The man caught the rock bare-handed and threw it back with surprising velocity, over Chaz's head.

"I played some college ball myself," the man said, "about a jillion years ago."

Chaz shielded his shriveling, bug-bitten privates as he backed against the bay tree. He told himself that the situation could be worse; it could be Red and Tool, with the twelve-gauge.

The man said, "I heard the shots last night, but I was a long ways off."

"What do you want?" Chaz asked shakily.

"Thought it might be a deer poacher. Five rounds from a shotgun means somebody's trying to kill *something*."

"Yeah, me." Chaz turned to reveal the pellet marks in his backside.

"Close call," the man said, with no abundance of concern.

If he was a game warden, Chaz thought, he must have been lost in the boonies for decades. He wore a tattered Stones T-shirt, filthy dungarees and moldy boots that had long ago come unstitched at the toes.

A plastic shower cap was stretched over his hair, and one misaligned eyeball stared emptily at the sky. His silver beard, intricately braided, was accented by a necklace made of teeth.

Human teeth, Chaz observed with consternation. He could see the amalgam fillings.

The stranger noticed Chaz gawking and said, "They're real, if that's what you're wondering. I took 'em off a guy who killed a momma otter for no good reason. Where are your clothes, sir?"

"They got torn off in the saw grass."

Chaz was thirsty, famished and nearly unhinged from lack of sleep, having spent the night ribaldly serenaded by alligators.

"And where's the fellow who tried to shoot you?" inquired the man in the shower cap.

Chaz motioned haplessly at the outlying marsh. "Who knows. There was two of 'em, back on the levee."

The stranger nodded. "Before I decide what to do with you, I need some answers. You mind?"

Chaz answered emphatically. "Anything you want. Just get me out of this goddamn hellhole."

"Understand that I'm not a well person. I'm muddling through a rough spell at the moment," the man said. "For instance, I've got a hunch you don't even marginally resemble H. R. Haldeman. Bob, they used to call him at the White House."

Chaz said he didn't know who that was.

"An arrogant, perjuring, justice-obstructing shitweasel who worked for the thirty-seventh president of the United States of America, an amoral maggot in his own right," the stranger related somewhat testily. "Anyway, that's who I'm hallucinating when I look at you—Bob Haldeman. So keep that in mind. Plus, I've got a hideous duet running like a freight train through my skull—'Hey Jude,' as performed by Bobbie Gentry and Placido Domingo. It's a fucking miracle I haven't disemboweled myself."

"What's your name?" Chaz was trying to stay calm, trying to sound amiable and harmless.

"You just call me Captain. But I'm asking the questions here, you understand?"

Chaz signaled cooperatively.

The man said, "Good. Let's start with basic identification."

"All right. My name is Charles Perrone and I have a Ph.D. in wetlands ecology. I'm employed as a field biologist for the South Florida Water Management District."

"Doing what, Mr. Perrone?"

"It's *Dr.* Perrone." Chaz hoped that the substance of his title would counterpoise his forlorn appearance. "I work mostly out here in the Everglades, testing the water for phosphates," he said. "It's part of the big government restoration project."

The stranger did not seem as impressed, or deferential, as Chaz had hoped. He removed his artificial eye and, with a scrofulous pocket-knife, scraped a dried clot of algae off the polished glass.

Then he twisted the orb back into its socket and said, "What's your name again?"

"Perrone." Chaz spelled it.

"No, ace, your first name."

"Charles. But everybody calls me Chaz."

The stranger cocked his head. "Chad?"

"No, *Chaz.* With a z."

That brought an inexplicable laugh. "Small world," said the man in the shower cap.

"How so?" Chaz asked, though he was already dreading the answer.

"I met a lady friend of yours out here the other night," the man told him.

Chaz's stomach pitched and his tongue turned to sandpaper.

"Ricca was her name," the stranger went on. "She had quite a story to tell."

Chaz smiled weakly. "Well, she's got quite an imagination."

"Yeah? You think she imagined that thirty-eight-caliber hole in her leg?" The man fished into his dungarees, first one pocket and then another. He cackled when he located the bullet slug, which he held up for Chaz to inspect in the pink early-morning light.

The man said, "I dug it out with a bent fishhook and a pair of needle-nose. Hurt like hell, but she's a champ, that girl." He flicked the damaged bullet into the water.

Chaz Perrone stood slack and helpless in defeat. What were the stratospheric odds, he wondered, that this half-senile, cockeyed hippie was the same person who'd rescued Ricca?

The stranger said, "Let me address a couple of points, Mr. Perrone. First, I'm not that old a fellow that I can't snap your neck bones with my bare hands. Second, this isn't a hellhole, this is my home and I happen to think it's heaven. Third, if you're a real scientist, then I'm Goldie Hawn."

In a monotone Chaz recited his academic credentials, which caused the man to squint down at him in brutal incredulity.

"Won't you hear my side of the story, Captain? Please?" Chaz scarcely recognized his own voice.

The madman leaned back and frowned at the rising sun. "We need to be moving along. I expect somebody'll come searching for you soon."

"Nobody I'd ever want to find me."

"Then let's go, junior. There's no time for a pity party."

With dull obedience Chaz followed the one-eyed hermit away from the shaded knoll and into the broiling flat savanna. The saw grass sliced Chaz's flesh with every step, but the sensation no longer registered as pain. Not far away, crossing the same stretch of marsh, were two creamy-colored snakes as thick as tugboat cables; they moved with a fluid and fearless tropism, as energized by their wild new surroundings as Charles Regis Perrone was cowed by his.

"I realize I've been an asshole," he called ahead to the stranger, "but people do change if they get the chance."

"Haldeman didn't," the man snapped over his shoulder. "Besides, I don't think of you as a garden-variety asshole, Chaz. I think of you as a nullity."

Chaz wasn't sure what that meant, but given the context, he assumed the worst. Ricca had doubtlessly painted a most unflattering portrait.

As they advanced deeper into the hostile wasteland, the leaden weight of Chaz's predicament settled fully upon him. Christ, he thought, I can't catch a break to save my life.

Literally.

After what seemed like an hour, the derelict in the shower cap stopped marching and held out a dented canteen, for which Chaz lunged unashamedly. As he slugged down the water, it occurred to him that the hoary bushman would probably know precisely how many penises a bull alligator had.

Another question to which there was no soothing answer, Chaz decided upon reflection.

Still another: What happens to me now?

It was as if the crazed wanderer had been reading his thoughts.

"Did you ever study Tennyson? I'm guessing not," the man said. " 'Nature, red in tooth and claw.' That's a very famous line."

To Chaz, it didn't sound promising. "I'm not going back to Boca Raton, am I?"

"No, Dr. Perrone, you are not."

A NOTE ABOUT THE AUTHOR

Carl Hiaasen was born and raised in Florida. He is the author of ten previous novels, including *Sick Puppy, Lucky You, Stormy Weather, Basket Case*, and, for young readers, *Hoot*. He also writes a regular column for the *Miami Herald*.

A NOTE ON THE TYPE

This book was set in Janson, a typeface long thought to have been made by the Dutchman Anton Janson, who was a practicing type-founder in Leipzig during the years 1668–1687. However, it has been conclusively demonstrated that these types are actually the work of Nicholas Kis (1650–1702), a Hungarian, who most proba-bly learned his trade from the master Dutch typefounder Dirk Voskens. The type is an excellent example of the influential and sturdy Dutch types that prevailed in England up to the time Wil-liam Caslon (1692–1766) developed his own incomparable designs from them.

Composed by Creative Graphics,
Allentown, Pennsylvania
Printed and bound by Berryville Graphics,
Berryville, Virginia
Designed by Virginia Tan